BATTLE
FOR
AMERICA

BATTLE
FOR
AMERICA

WINGMAN, BOOK 18

Mack Maloney

OPEN ROAD

INTEGRATED MEDIA

NEW YORK

Copyright © 2017 by Mack Maloney

Cover design by Michel Vrana

ISBN 978-1-5040-3527-9

Published in 2017 by Open Road Integrated Media, Inc.
180 Maiden Lane
New York, NY 10038
www.openroadmedia.com

For Lois Lane

✈

BATTLE
FOR
AMERICA

PART ONE

CHAPTER ONE

April 1

THREE RUSSIAN TROOPSHIPS sailed into New York Harbor a few minutes after midnight.

The huge vessels were mammoth cruise liners the Russian Navy had converted into military transports. Each had twenty thousand soldiers on board along with tons of combat gear and equipment.

Painted in ocean-gray camouflage, the ships looked like three sea monsters slowly swimming toward the island of Manhattan. Their decks were lined with DShK machine guns and Katyusha rocket launchers, with 75-millimeter naval cannons placed stern to bow. Anxious weapons crews peered into the murk through their night-vision goggles, ready for anything.

But from Coney Island, past the Verrazano-Narrows Bridge, up to Bay Ridge and Red Hook, the waterfront was empty. There was no one for the weapons crews to shoot at, and no one shot at them.

The three giant ships arrived off southern Manhattan at 0030 hours, right on time. They dropped anchor and their troops began unloading.

The Russian invasion of New York City had begun.

✪ ✪ ✪

Four divisions of fifteen thousand men went ashore in less than thirty minutes, using walkways that extended from the ships' mid-decks right into Battery Park. Key objectives around the city had to be seized, including power plants, the airports, and all major bridges and tunnels.

Sailing into New York Harbor behind the transport ships and continuing north up the Hudson River was a pair of huge Tapir landing craft named *Oleg* and *Dima*. Each was carrying four squadrons of massive T-72 battle tanks, more than eighty in all. The Tapirs docked at Chelsea Piers and disgorged their cargo. The fierce-looking tanks and their crews would serve as the invasion's shock troops. Moving with a lot of noise and commotion, they raced to dispersal points throughout the city.

Two more Russian ships appeared. One was a large oceangoing barge with two Yak-38 VTOL jet fighters on board. Behind it was the fuel ship *Boleska*, full of aviation gasoline. Both vessels docked at the old South Street Seaport on the East River where the vertical-lift Yaks immediately took off and began flying over Manhattan.

The thousands of troops, the tanks, the combat aircraft, the thunderstorm of diesel fumes and jet exhaust were all very loud, aggressive, and intimidating. But the Russians had little to fear.

A few weeks before, emissaries of the Russian Army had met with the godfathers of the Red Hand, the five Russian-American crime families that currently controlled New York City. After striking a mutually beneficial deal, the crime families had spread word throughout the city that everyone should stay off the streets the night of April 1.

People were heeding that warning.

New York City was not the place it used to be.

Only about a hundred thousand people lived there now. Hardened by the turmoil that had wracked America since the end of the World War III, they weren't shocked by the sight of Russian tanks rumbling up Fifth Avenue. In fact, very little of what happened across the continent shocked anyone these days.

The Big War began on Christmas Eve a little more than fifteen years ago. Russia launched a poison gas attack on Western

Europe, followed by a massive ground invasion. The United States and NATO responded primarily with airpower, and after intense fighting, the Russians were soundly defeated. But then the traitorous US vice president did two things: He arranged to have the president and his Cabinet assassinated and then he turned off America's antiballistic missile systems, enabling the Russians to nuke the heartland of the United States. Twenty million Americans died as a result.

With the quisling vice president in charge, the United States was forced to capitulate to a Russian construct called the New Order. America's military was disarmed, its most modern weapons destroyed, and the country broken up into a mishmash of independent states, economic zones, and free territories. Most of the population fled to either Free Canada or Mexico. For those who'd remained, catastrophes of all sorts suddenly became routine.

Lacking a central government in Washington to keep order, wars big and small flared up between disparate regions. Geographic neighbors suddenly became postwar adversaries. Illinois, Indiana, and most of Michigan were run by Mafia-type families, the Ku Klux Klan ruled much of the South, California was eventually occupied by an Asian mercenary army, and much of the Pacific Northwest fell into the throes of anarchy. The center of the country, which had taken the brunt of the Russian sneak attack, was a nightmarish wasteland of nuclear fallout and long-lasting hallucinogenic gas. Nothing lived there—nothing could. It had been aptly named the Badlands.

Adding to these problems, terrorist groups moved freely across the country and air pirates roamed the skies. Weakened greatly by the war, Russia had not been able to invade the United States right away. Sowing confusion and distrust inside the fractured country turned out to be the next best thing.

Gallant bands of former US military personnel were always trying to put America back together again, though—with varying degrees of success. Much of the Northeast and many regions just west of the Mississippi River had become relatively stable. Nonetheless, fifteen years after the Big War had ended, most of America was still one huge disaster zone.

This didn't go unnoticed by the slowly resurging military government in Moscow, who, at one point, sent in an entire Mongol army to ransack the continent. But that audacious campaign ultimately ended in disaster for the Kremlin. Other attempts had been made since then, many through Russian proxies, but they'd been halfhearted and poorly planned.

This time, Moscow was serious. In the past two years, a renascent Russia had conquered all of Europe, Africa, and the Middle East, plus wide swathes of territory in Southwest Asia. Though technically allies, Moscow's main rival was the Asian Mercenary Cult, a collection of large, highly mobile armies that dominated China, Southeast Asia, and the Indian subcontinent and had colonies in many other places, including California.

But the rest of the globe was up for grabs, and Russia wanted it. That's why the former United States of America was in their sights again.

Moscow had identified every level of power they thought they'd need to occupy New York City for a long time. In addition to its military personnel, a sizable number of engineers, accountants, mechanics, utility and maintenance workers, translators, and even a squad of arborists had made the voyage to America this time.

Past experiences had taught Moscow the best way to conquer fractured America was not the old and unwieldy blunderbuss approach, but by taking one step at a time.

New York was the first step.

CHAPTER TWO

THREE RUSSIAN MILITARY commanders were in charge of the invasion. Known collectively as the Komand Sostva, they were army general Leonid Alexei, navy admiral Makita Kartunov and military operations field marshal Dmitry Popov, whom everyone called Marshal MOP. The three men could have been brothers. All were in their late sixties, stubby in stature, with red faces, white hair, and substantial paunches. They always appeared together, always in uniform, each man wearing several pounds of medals on his jacket and a large cap weighed down by heavy gold braid.

The trio of commanders had chosen Rockefeller Center, a large section of midtown Manhattan, to be their base of operations. Cleared of all civilians, it was rechristened the Voennaya Zona Midtowna, or Midtown Military Zone (MMZ). They had selected three nearly identical skyscrapers on Fifth Avenue between Forty-Eighth and Fifty-First Streets to be their combined headquarters. Across the street, a fourth skyscraper served as their Joint Operations center.

But the tallest building inside the MMZ, a seventy-story skyscraper once known as 30 Rockefeller Plaza, which towered almost twenty stories above everything else inside the enclave, had been claimed by the NKVD, the newly revived, much-feared Russian secret police. They were a nine-thousand-man brigade comprised of thuggish plainclothes officers, known as the Militsiya, and uniformed policemen, called the Chekskis, nearly all of whom had been recruited from the Zealot Brotherhood of God, a fanatical religious cult native to Russia's southwest. The NKVD command staff had installed an enormous illuminated red star on the roof of "30 Rock." One hundred feet tall, it was so bright that, at night, it cast a crimson glow over everything in Midtown. But the giant icon's purpose went beyond ornamentation: Tons of NKVD communications gear was stuffed inside the star, including one piece that allowed the secret police to listen in on everything being said by the invasion's three military arms, from the commanders on down, twenty-four hours a day.

At 0800 hours, on April 30, more than four weeks into the *Okupatsi*, the three officers arrived on the fiftieth floor of the Joint Ops Building, the old Simon & Schuster Building. They were here for their first monthly situation report.

Two dozen staff officers were waiting inside the opulent top-floor meeting room to greet the high commanders. Mineral water, morning wine, and baskets of oranges decorated the room's huge conference table. A table nearby held kasha, *Butterbrod*, fried eggs, and *tvorog*. All the makings for a sumptuous Russian breakfast. The combined aroma reminded them all of home.

The officer in charge of the joint ops meeting room was Colonel Sergei Gagarin. A lean, sharp-looking man of forty whose family came from East Germany, he'd been wounded leading his troops during fighting in Egypt, losing his right eye, and had sported a pirate-style patch ever since. His talent now was as a professional ringmaster, regularly briefing senior Russian military officers on the progress of the *Okupatsi* without burdening them with too many facts. Gagarin read everything that came into the Joint Ops Building, including all NKVD communiqués. He also sent a nightly report to Moscow.

"If God does indeed love a trinity," Gagarin said to the trio of commanders, referring to a well-known Russian phrase, "then three is our lucky number today."

The superior officers smiled at the show of wit. "Four is always too many," General Alexei responded with a toothy grin. "And two is never enough."

Gagarin indicated the three TV cameras set up in the conference room. "We will film this historic occasion for our friends back in Moscow," he said. He pointed to the microphones hanging from the ceiling. "And they will hear it, too." With a nod from Gagarin, the cameras were turned on. The morning sun suddenly poured into the room, heightening the excitement in the air.

Flanked by their security squads, brass buttons gleaming from recent polishing, the three commanders settled into three identical chairs at one end of the conference table. Their smiles did not subside. Their troops had performed extremely well so far, which was easy to do when no one was shooting at you. But that was the mission. With no enemy to fight, their job was literally to occupy the city. Secure the gains by any means possible and don't let them slip away like in the old days.

Colonel Gagarin introduced the army CO, General Alexei, to the cameras. The commanding officer's report came first.

"The city is secure," he boomed. "Street violence has disappeared, thanks to our troops regularly patrolling all five boroughs. The Militsiya have helped clear the streets of potential troublemakers, and I understand the Chekskis are dealing with the homeless problem. The rackets are up and working again, and business improves every day. Our drug operation located at Chelsea Piers is thriving. Boats come in for pickup, boats go out for delivery, and the money is flowing in. Our Red Hand partners are happy. Even with paying us eleven percent of their profits, they're making more now than ever."

"Good for them," Admiral Kartunov murmured off camera.

"It gets even better," General Alexei went on. "Those people living outside New York City, out in the suburbs? There were several million of them before. But many have now cleared out of the area, obviously as a result of the *Okupatsi*. From eastern New Jersey to western Long Island, the roads have been clogged day and night as they move away from us. That means lots of empty houses for our own citizens to occupy someday. Plus, it means fewer hooligans we'll have to deal with in the future."

Gagarin then introduced Admiral Kartunov.

"Our reinforcement vessels are arriving from the Motherland every day," the naval czar began. "Both military and supply ships. I can report that eighty-five percent of our force's material needs for one year have been delivered to us already. The remainder is en route. Only one ship had difficulties making the crossing, and we are still looking for it. But that's a very small percentage considering the numbers in our fleet. Plus the weather is expected to improve in the North Atlantic soon. That will allow our maritime supply line to move even faster."

Marshal MOP went last.

"All of the city's critical utilities are running again," he began. "Only Russian flags fly over the city. All the signage in Manhattan has been changed from English to Russian. Although the subway system hasn't worked since the Big War, our mechanics have got dozens of transit buses and yellow taxis running again. The garbage trucks and street sweepers have been repaired and are back in operation, so the streets are clean. And we hope to get both airports running within three months.

"We are finally doing the things we should have done years ago. The time, the effort we spent to bring the Mongols here, flying their horses across the Pacific? And moving all that hay and feed? That was a bad dream, thinking those savages could do our dirty work for us. We were wrong to put stock in them and all those other pretenders. Finally, we are doing it on our own, and it is working. If we can put up with the loss of just one navy ship among many, then all is well."

Gagarin's staff was so impressed, they broke out in applause. The commanding officers graciously applauded back. They'd done it. New York City was theirs.

The cameras were turned off and several bottles of vodka were brought into the room. The invasion was an unqualified success—and that called for a victory parade. With one quick vote, the Komand Sostva gave the official go-ahead to throw a

citywide party. It would be held the following day, May 1, appro-
priately enough—May Day, Communism's major holiday.

But one more thing had to be done first.

Just before midnight, five NKVD armored personnel carriers
made their way to Brighton Beach, Brooklyn. The godfathers of
the Red Hand waited for them outside one of the few restaurants
still open in New York City. The five gangsters had been invited
to the round of pre–May Day victory parade parties in Manhattan. The personnel carriers would serve as their limousines.

The NKVD policemen helped the godfathers into the
armored cars along with their assorted capos, *consiglieri*, and
brodyagi, and left Brighton Beach to the cheers of drunken friends
who'd spilled out of the restaurant and onto the streets.

But instead of heading back to Manhattan, the NKVD drove
their guests to the Staten Island landfill, where they shot them all.

CHAPTER THREE

New Jersey

CAPTAIN JOHN "BULL" Dozer blew on his hands, trying to keep them warm. The night air was chilling him to the bone.

Dead man's hands, he thought. *Cold as a corpse. . . .*

It was twenty minutes past midnight. Dozer was huddled inside a small hut atop a rickety sixty-foot tower in the middle of some very thick woods in New Jersey's largely uninhabited Pine Barrens. While most of his men were at their new forward base one mile south, two of his troopers were with him, sitting on old metal folding chairs that squeaked on the hut's uneven floor. A 50-caliber machine gun was mounted nearby. Its barrel was sticking out the hut's only window, which was covered in loose plastic and duct tape to block the gusting wind.

One of the troopers checked the hut's coffeepot, which had been brewing for a while.

"It's ready," he said. The trooper collected three mugs and filled each halfway. Then Dozer took an unlabeled bottle of whiskey from his heavy wool coat and added a generous splash to each steaming cup.

"You know I don't encourage drinking on the job, boys," he said with a straight face, "but sometimes, you've just got to get the blood pumping. . . ."

He toasted the two men. "*Semper Fi. . . .*"

"Grog, grub, and glory," one trooper responded, raising his mug.

"For our brothers," the other added.

Then Dozer took the first gulp.

"Oh, mother of Jesus," he gasped, coughing and cringing at the same time. The spiked coffee tasted vile. He took another huge swig, though—and then another. Suddenly, the warmth of life was flowing through him again.

"Really good stuff," he said between more coughs. Really . . ."

The two troopers tasted theirs.

"Primo," one declared, though almost gagging.

"You mean high octane," said the other with a cough.

One wall of the hut held an ancient video monitor. Its tiny four-color screen was filled with ghostly images at the moment, its tinny speaker spitting out white noise. Every time the tower swayed, the speaker would crackle with static.

Still drinking his coffee, Dozer slid over to the video console.

"Another clear night," he said, adjusting the monitor's contrast knob. "I wonder what Ivan's up to. . . ."

The old video monitor was connected to a similarly elderly video camera, which was attached to a tethered helium balloon flying nine hundred feet above the tower. A primitive gyro built of marbles and rubber bands packed inside a soup can kept the camera steady and aiming fifty-three degrees northeast. Right at Russian-occupied New York City.

Every night, Dozer and his men launched the crude surveillance balloon from the tower and recorded footage of Red Gotham, glowing like a perverse Oz just forty miles to the north. The camera had a rudimentary infrared capability and a telescopic lens. On nights like this, they could make out Russian aircraft, ship traffic, and even troops and people moving around the city.

Usually, what they saw made them feel worse than the night before. Tonight was no different.

By raising or lowering the height of the balloon, the camera could zoom in on a half dozen key spots in Manhattan. Tonight, there was lots of truck traffic, lots of banners being hung across major streets, lots of red lights popping on inside Midtown skyscrapers. Some kind of citywide celebration was in the offing.

"May Day," Dozer grumbled now, refilling their cups with the whiskey-coffee mixture. "Like these Commies need another excuse to get drunk."

A hulk of a man, right down to the buzz cut, chiseled jaw, and scary forearm tats, Dozer was the commanding officer of a patriotic group known as the Seventh Cavalry.

It was a notoriously inaccurate name: None of its members had ever served in the US Army; they were all ex-marines. Nor were they a cavalry. They were actually a ground attack outfit. Boot leather and truck tires carried them into battle.

The hundred-man unit was the remnants of Dozer's last official US military command. Hard-nosed survivors of the ground battles of World War III, he'd led them out of devastated Europe and back to America, where they'd stuck together in the chaotic years since. Many anti-American enemies dedicated to keeping the United States fractured and unstable had risen up in that time, including the Mid-Aks, a ruthless treasonous army from the Middle Atlantic States; the Circle, a collection of the worst criminals and terrorists on the continent; and the Fourth Reich— a name that said it all. Religious nuts, gun freaks, drug lords, drug cults, and the Reds themselves, the 7CAV had fought them all, and many others, for one simple reason: They wanted to put the United States back together again. . . . or die trying.

Just about all of these campaigns to keep America splintered were the work of the Russian superspy Viktor Robotov. Forever lurking in the shadows, Viktor was the anti-Christ for anyone still living in the United States, no matter their religions. In another universe, his name would have been Keyser Söze. Or Dr. Moriarty. Or simply Lucifer. He was in the habit of laying low for months, or even years, spreading rumors of his own demise, only to return to bring a little more misery to an already miserable place before vanishing again. He was the bogeyman for broken America.

The superspy hadn't been heard from in some time, though. And from the looks of things through the 7CAV's camera, the Russians had managed to take over New York City without any help from him—thank God.

As bad as things were, at least this new Russian operation didn't have Robotov's bloody fingerprints all over it.

When a spy plane belonging to one of the 7CAV's allies in northern Maine spotted the Russian invasion fleet off the New England coast, heading south, four weeks ago Dozer knew New York City was the obvious destination. It was no secret the Big Apple was being run by Russian gangsters, so why not the Russian Army?

At the time, Dozer thought, *Here we go again*.

The 7CAV's main headquarters was in Saratoga, Free State of New York, about two hundred miles north of Manhattan. When some quick aerial intelligence found positive elements about the Pine Barrens, Dozer mobilized his men, his equipment, and twenty civilian technicians.

They had deployed in less than a day.

Since arriving in the Pine Barrens, Dozer had spent most of his nights crammed atop the shaky spy tower.

While his men monitored the aerial camera, he usually sat in the opposite corner, hunched over his ancient radio set. A self-taught electronics whiz, he'd sent out a steady stream of coded messages in the past twenty-eight days, announcing his presence to friends and allies and declaring the 7CAV ready to take on the Russian invaders.

Yet he'd received nothing in reply. His radio set was old, but it wasn't broken; he had no problem listening to the Russian military's intercity radio broadcasts coming from forty miles away. But for some reason, no one was answering his calls.

This puzzled him greatly. He'd expected 7CAV would be just one of many fighting units revving up to take on the uninvited Reds. In the past, these combat groups, many run by close friends of his, always flew right to the action, managed to find one another on the radio and then rode into battle together.

But he'd sent out hundreds of messages so far and had not received a peep back.

Russian flags were flying over New York, for Christ's sake.

Where the hell was everybody?

CHAPTER FOUR

THE MAY DAY Victory parade kicked off at eight o'clock the next morning.

Forty columns of *Okupatsi* troops marched past the Fifth Avenue reviewing stand. They looked impressive in their crisp lime-green uniforms. Eyes right, weapons held tight against their chests, their helmets and bayonets gleamed in the early sun.

Follow-on troops carried banners bearing socialist slogans. They were followed by more soldiers carrying huge portraits of Stalin, Lenin, and Marx. All the while, the pair of noisy Yak-38 VTOL fighters circled continuously overhead, red-dye contrails spewing from their exhausts.

Thanks to the joint ops cadre, a bounty of vodka had arrived from Russia earlier that week, twenty-six thousand gallons of it. Carried in huge metal kegs, a substantial portion reached Midtown at the parade's conclusion. This was when the real celebration began. Thousands of soldiers took advantage of the free alcohol. They drank and sang and danced in the streets. Music blasted from everywhere. Fireworks were lit off.

Out on Eighth Avenue, a handful of T-72 tank crews drunkenly fired their massive 122-millimeter guns into the Hudson River, killing thousands of fish. At high noon, the three dozen Russian ships anchored off Battery Park began blasting their horns and would not stop. The Yak fighter jets returned over

Midtown every half hour or so to perform wildly reckless—some said drunken—maneuvers, one trying to outdo the other, to the delight of the boozy crowds below.

This raucous citywide party would last through the night and into the following day.

The Russian success was also celebrated on the top floor of 30 Rock.

Enveloped in security gear, guarded by nearly a hundred Militsiya police, and off-limits even to the three commanders of the Sostva, it was the *kvartira v nebe*, the apartment in the sky, the lavish penthouse that Commissar Vladimir Zmeya Mikhailovich, chief of NKVD operations in America, called home.

With fifteen rooms, six fireplaces, six bars, and two Jacuzzis, the space included a vast kitchen and dining area and an even larger function room. Lots of polished brass, lots of red oak walls. It was wrapped in floor-to-ceiling windows and had a view that seemed to go all the way to California.

By midnight, the penthouse's ballroom was crowded with senior NKVD officers: one hundred and six of them, all in black dress jackets, Cossack pants, and knee-high Kirza boots.

This was a very exclusive group, the top of the NKVD's chain of command in America. Still, every officer had to pass three extensive security checks just to get to the front door, including surrendering all firearms.

There were a similar number of high-priced prostitutes in the room. Some had been dragooned into being waitresses and barmaids; others mingled with the crowd. All were blond; all were wearing short tuxedo-like negligee dresses and black heels. They, too, had had to pass rigorous security measures for entry into the penthouse, including spending a week in isolation, under twenty-four-hour NKVD surveillance.

The penthouse itself was guarded by ninety-two Militsiya special-operations police. They were assisted by two dozen Milashki—or Cuties—an all-female NKVD unit who processed IDs, checked fingerprints, and operated body scanners. All had pledged their lives to keep Zmeya safe.

As for the Chekskis, none had ever gotten within twenty floors of this place. The Militsiya considered their NKVD cousins foul and unstable, a view shared by the commissar himself.

A stage had been set up at one end of the big function room. A curtain behind it hid a massive, well-stocked horseshoe bar and, beyond that, windows to the outside world.

While the city went crazy below, no alcohol had been served up here yet, putting everyone on edge, especially the NKVD officers. Although this was the first reception held in Zmeya's new American apartment in the sky, they'd attended similar functions he'd organized overseas in the last couple of years. They knew how terrifying they could be.

The problem was the boss himself. Zmeya was a masterful tactician, a whiz at intelligence gathering, and as cold and calculating and vicious as they came. He got things done, which is why he was here in New York. The Kremlin adored him.

But Zmeya had issues, one of them being EDS, emotional disregulation syndrome. Antisocial behavior, compulsiveness, hostility, lack of restraint, sexual deviation, he'd displayed all of these symptoms in public at various times. He had medication but took it sparingly.

The commissar also had a second, even more disturbing, condition: He was a bad drunk.

Anything could happen with him after a few cocktails, especially if he hadn't taken his meds. The horror stories were well known. During one gathering in newly occupied France a year ago, Zmeya drunkenly ordered the hats of two latecomers nailed into their skulls because they didn't take them off quick enough in his presence.

Zmeya demanded that his lovers beat him before the act, enjoying bloodletting as foreplay. Videotaping his assignations was routine; three-camera shoots were de rigueur. He also loved to watch other people have sex. As part of his massive luggage train, he carried a giant glass terrarium. Twenty feet by twenty, it contained a king-size bed and nothing else. Toward the end of almost every drunken gathering, Zmeya would select a couple of

guests—not always of the opposite sex—and force them inside
the huge glass room.

They would be ordered to have intercourse or else, while
the commissar and selected attendees sat outside and watched.
If Zmeya liked the performance, the participants would be
rewarded with their lives. If not, and depending on how drunk
Zmeya was, a more unpleasant outcome awaited them.

Attending the commissar's bacchanals was mandatory; it's just
that guests didn't know if they'd live to see the party end. A single
wrong word, or if Zmeya didn't like the look of you—or your
female companion—and you might never see the sun rise again.

The function room's lights dimmed and Zmeya himself finally
stepped out from behind the curtain. There was no applause.
The one hundred officers saluted him, and he saluted back. Then
the room fell silent. Half the crowd was in awe, the rest were trying hard to look that way.

Zmeya was dressed in black as always. A fitted NKVD uniform, a tailored leather trench coat, and Kirza boots. His face was
partially hidden by an oversize black fedora, pulled down low,
and dark glasses.

He was handsome, though, or at least what could be seen of
him. His narrow jawline appeared chiseled from the same granite as the penthouse's kitchen counters, but the rest of his face
was soft and almost feminine. He had blond hair and cobalt-blue
eyes. Standing six feet one and obviously muscular, he was so
good-looking, in the past, people had mistaken him for being
German.

Zmeya reminded some of a younger version of another
ghastly Russian hero, Viktor Robotov, the superspy. Positively
Luciferish in looks, no one ever mistook Viktor for being anything but Russian. Still there was an eerie resemblance.

Zmeya had appeared out of nowhere two years before, joining the reconstituted NKVD as an interrogation officer in Len-
ingrad. In just a few weeks, he'd eliminated all his rivals, quickly
moving up the ranks. Twenty months later, he'd taken over the
coveted top spot, commander of the NKVD's Foreign Opera-

tions Bureau. This was where he and others had planned how to take over the world.

From a nobody to running the most feared police organization in the world in less than two years? Gossip said Zmeya had had substantial inside help during his rocket-like ascent, assists from someone even higher up the very secretive Moscow food chain.

Zmeya stepped up to the microphone. He covertly retrieved a handful of index cards from his pocket and palmed them in his left hand. This would be his victory speech. But he was not a good public speaker and had displayed anxiety when addressing large groups in the past.

"We are here to make the vision of our leaders back in Moscow a reality," he began. "And we have taken a big step in that regard as our forces have successfully occupied the grandest city in the world."

A murmur immediately went through the crowd. Something was not right here. Zmeya usually communicated in a low, surly voice, hunched over the microphone, at times barely audible. He also tended to phrase everything breathlessly, as if every other word contained breaking news.

But now he was standing straight, head up and projecting his voice in an even manner. He was speaking clearly, enunciating every word with its proper emphasis. What's more, his straggly hair appeared to be combed under his hat and he was wearing a sexy two-day growth of beard.

None of this was normal.

"Our goal is to finally put an end to America and replace it with a new country," he continued. "Our new country. One large colony of Russia. A Communist paradise. A paradise we can all live in together."

He paused again, almost laughing at those last few words. He seemed to be happy and nervous at the same time—and completely sober. Again, not normal.

He smiled, briefly, but long enough to elicit another gasp from the crowd. Few people had ever seen him smile. He realized immediately what he'd done, and his face flushed.

He returned to his index cards. "But to get there, a lot of work still needs to be done, and more battles need to be fought. I'll be blunt with you: This continent needs to be cleansed—and we are here to do it."

More murmurs from the crowd, then an uncomfortable silence. A signal from offstage made him put down his notes. This would be a new experience for him. Zmeya unscripted.

"But let's not dwell on such gloomy matters," he said brightly. "Before coming out here, I received a message from Moscow. They are so pleased with the results of this past month, they've asked me to declare this city renamed. It is no longer New York City, my friends. From this moment on, it will be known as Russkiy-NYC."

Now there was applause. A lot of it. It became boisterous and stayed that way until Zmeya signaled for calm. This brought everyone's attention back to him. Again, the people standing before him wondered about his odd behavior. Nothing had changed in his job performance. Just an hour earlier, he'd signed an executive order allowing the Chekskis to execute and dispose of two hundred "homeless hooligans" they'd picked up, including children. As head of the secret police, he'd okayed orders like this every night this week and many during the previous month. No trials. No explanations. Just cleansing.

So why this change?

After the applause died down completely, Zmeya stood in silence for a few seconds. His eyes darted left, and some in the crowd caught the shadow of a woman standing just offstage. She was wearing a long, dark cloak with its hood up, showing only her face, most of which was in shadow. Still, that was enough for people to see that she was stunning.

There had been rumors of a new girl in the commissar's life and reports that she was different. These were hard to give credence to, though, because there were so many Zmeya stories floating around and so many women in the past couple years.

But, at that moment, it seemed like an angel was standing just twenty feet away from him, directing him, encouraging him, making him seem more . . . human.

Finally, Zmeya tossed away the index cards, wished everyone

a good evening, and left the stage with a big wave. Thirty seconds later, he and his companion were seen walking through the shadows backstage, hand-in-hand. Then they were gone, off into the night.

The guests were stunned. *Nothing* like this had ever happened before. Zmeya leaving his own party? It was unthinkable.

But then the guests' surprise turned to giddiness, then giggling, and finally to outright laughter of pure relief.

Maybe they'd see the sunrise after all.

CHAPTER FIVE

May 3

COLONEL IVAN SAMSONOV pushed his way through the revolving door at the Army Building's main entrance on Fifth Avenue and walked into the crowded lobby.

It still reeked of spilled vodka and cigarette smoke from the May Day celebration, forty-eight hours ago. He sprinted to the nearest elevator and hit the button for the forty-fourth floor. Only when the doors had closed did he finally exhale.

Thirty-five years old, tall and sturdy, with a shock of blond Slavic hair, Samsonov was the chief security officer for the army headquarters. He held a senior position, which was good for his career, but his stress level was off the charts. His duty sheet ran the length of three pages, but his primary job was to keep the newly acquired skyscraper protected at all times. This meant around-the-clock guards at every door and every stairway. Machine gun posts on Fifth Avenue covered the front entrances; more protected the back. No one came in without proper papers. Surveillance cameras were everywhere.

The doors to the elevator opened and Samsonov walked to his spacious corner office. It was flooded with morning sun, its massive windows providing a spectacular view of Manhattan. This was certainly not Petrograd Oblast. But he couldn't appreciate the moment because his eyes were instantly drawn to the red-striped courier pouch on his desk.

"Why does God hate me so much?" he moaned.

Actually, Samsonov had two jobs these days. In addition to being the HQ's security czar, he was also the army's liaison officer to the NKVD. He'd had no say in taking on this extra duty; it had simply been handed to him by his superiors, who had made it clear they wanted no trouble with the dreadful secret police and would blame him if they did.

This liaison duty took up about an hour a day. Mostly, it called for him to go through the NKVD overnight field reports and send the ones he deemed relevant upstairs to Army Central Command. But as the NKVD blacked out nearly everything from their own overnights before they ever got to him, the reports were always short and routine. It was just more paperwork for him, but he dealt with it.

His biggest problem with this extra duty was dealing with the Committee of the Revolution for the Protection of the People (CRPP), though their name meant nothing. In reality, they were Zmeya's henchmen, his highly paid executioners. Always dressed in black trench coats and wearing matching black fedoras, just like their boss, they were all murderers, and two were actually *mass* murderers. If one person, or a few people, or hundreds, or even thousands, had to be liquidated for the Motherland, the CRPP would come up with a strategy and then execute it, many times personally.

The committee members had quickly developed a taste for New York City's high life. In the first week alone, they'd ordered Samsonov to get them Cadillacs, yachts, motorcycles, jet skis, CD players, big-screen TVs, gold jewelry, and even boom boxes. He'd had no choice but to fulfill their demands.

But most of all, the CRPP members wanted mistresses, and trying to find the right kind of companions for them had become Samsonov's nightmare. It was a poorly kept secret that Commissar Zmeya had met a woman immediately after arriving in New York City three days into the invasion. Her identity was still unknown to most people, even after more than a month. But those who'd seen her said she was nothing less than the most beautiful woman in America.

She was nothing less than a giant pain in the ass for Samsonov, at least he'd thought so at first. This was because the five CRPP members didn't just want gorgeous mistresses of their own, they wanted ones who looked *exactly* like the commissar's new girlfriend.

Samsonov thought it odd at first that the CRPPs wanted only what their commander had. But then, early in his liaison duty, he'd been given a top-secret photograph of the commissar's latest mistress. Then he'd understood.

The photo wasn't some hasty snapshot. It was a crisp and clear portrait that showed Zmeya's new girlfriend sitting in a plush armchair, leaning forward a little, blond hair cascading down around her soft shoulders. Her enormous blue eyes caressed the lens; her soft red lips were set in an enigmatic half smile. She was wearing a tight black tuxedo jacket with no skirt, just black seamless nylons held up by garters and a pair of black high heels. Her frilly silk blouse was very low cut, almost completely exposing her breasts.

Samsonov had studied the photo many, many times.

To help him in his quest, he'd reached out to unsavory procurement agents working for the rackets. These were men who found beautiful female escorts in other parts of America and brought them to New York City to ply their trade. Every day since, a bright red-striped top-secret pouch would land on his desk with a thud. Inside were hundreds of photos of women in various stages of undress sent to him by these agents.

Samsonov's first duty every morning was to go through the steamy photographs to see if any of the subjects measured up to what the CRPP wanted. It sounded like fun, but he'd come to hate it. Not just because none of the women ever came close to matching the commissar's piece of sex candy, but because it also required Samsonov to interact with the NKVD sublieutenant, Boris Borski, a bottom feeder from the secret police's gene pool.

The man was simply grotesque. Mid-thirties, but looking much older, Borski had a facial scar from badly sewn stitches, the result of a murder attempt gone awry. It stretched across his mouth from one ear to the other and looked like a hideous crooked smile. Borski also walked with a limp and was slightly hunchbacked due to other beatings he'd taken along the way. His hair was too long and always dirty—in defiance of regulations—and he was frequently wearing bits of his last meal somewhere on his chin.

Though officially in the Militsiya, Borski commanded one of the most brutal death squads in the Chekskis. The radical NKVD uniformed cops were cleaning up the city's homeless problem by picking up dozens of people every night and making them disappear. Officially, the vagrants were being deported to New Jersey. Unofficially, none were making it that far across the Hudson River. Borski liked cutting their throats, something psychological there, and his men wanted to impress him. So every night, they made a bloody mess down on the Red Hook docks, where, for other Chekski execution squads, a bullet in the head and a shove in the water would do.

Graffiti showing a hastily drawn bloody smiley face had begun showing up on the streets of Lower Manhattan, always at the site of the latest homeless clearing actions. Serial killers and mass murderers liked to leave their marks. Borski was no different.

But like Samsonov, Borski had two jobs. He was also a willing errand boy for the CRPP. So, every morning he showed up in Samsonov's office and waited for him to go through the new batch of photos and earmark a few possibilities for consideration. Then the human troll would lurch out of the office with the red-striped pouch in hand and head for 30 Rock.

These departures were never quick enough for Samsonov.

It took Samsonov the usual half hour to go through the day's photographs.

Sublieutenant Borski walked in ten minutes into the process. Like every other day, Samsonov found nothing special in the bunch. But by indicating there might be a few possibilities, he knew Borski would leave his office that much quicker.

Samsonov put a paper clip on six photos and then threw everything back inside the red striped pouch. Borski grabbed it, spit in Samsonov's office plant, then bounded down the hallway and to the elevators.

At least that was over.

Now Samsonov had to read the NKVD overnights and decide which ones to kick upstairs. Only then could he finally get to his more important duties.

He opened the blue envelope containing the NKVD reports that had arrived with the red-striped pouch. Last night, the Militsiya had conducted raids on the Upper West Side aimed at thwarting subversive activity. Twelve people were arrested. In the same time frame, Chekski sweeps in the West Village resulted in the roundup of forty-six homeless people who had been "processed." That was it. Nothing new or interesting.

But Samsonov didn't care. He stamped it approved and put it all back in the blue envelope. Then he called his orderly and told him to kick it upstairs.

On this transfer, the orderly handed him a memo from the MOP Building, two skyscrapers over. The message had been typed on pink paper, indicating the lowest possible security level. It was addressed to both Samsonov and his counterpart in the navy HQ next door.

It related in one paragraph that two orderlies working on the top floor of the MOP Building reported seeing a tiny airplane circling buildings inside MMZ around two that morning. The plane was brightly colored and had a strange engine noise. It had orbited the three military buildings on Fifth Avenue, flying level with their top floors and, at times, slowing to a hover. The aircraft's landing gear consisted of two huge fat tires that were nearly as big as the plane itself. The orderlies said that the little plane seemed to be looking for something.

Samsonov lit his one and only cigarette of the day and blew the smoke toward his ceiling. A tiny airplane buzzing the MMZ?

What was this about?

He called his counterpart in the Navy Building and asked if he'd received the memo.

The navy man just laughed at him. "It was a prank, Samsonov," he said.

"How so?"

"Your drunken soldiers broke into the old Macy's department store building last night," he explained. "They were still wanting to celebrate Victory Day, so they found some very large balloons—the Americans call them holiday floats. Your heroes filled one up with helium and let it go and it turned out to look like a beagle flying a doghouse. *That's* what your eyewitnesses saw."

Samsonov spent the next fifteen hours doing his rounds inside the army skyscraper.

It was close to midnight when he finally returned to his office on the forty-fourth floor. A tray on his desk containing a cup of borsht and a chunk of beef was stacked atop another tray holding a cup of goulash and a slice of *Butterbrod*. His dinner sitting on top of his lunch, all of it cold. Almost too tired to eat, but too hungry not to, he sat behind his desk and stuffed the napkin under his chin.

One bite into the goulash, his office lights blinked. He looked up and saw something flash by outside.

He walked over to the window searching for anything unusual in the night. But he found only the darkness cut by the crimson light coming from the NKVD's big red star directly above him.

Then . . . the lights blinked again and there was another flash!

Samsonov saw it clearly this time. A streak of bright flames went right by his enormous east-facing window, leaving a long trail of sparks behind.

"Fireworks," he groaned.

The victory celebration was revving up again on the streets below.

Samsonov wasn't too surprised. Night comes, soldiers go off duty, get drunk, look for mischief, and find it. And why not? The city was theirs.

He started packing his briefcase. If it was going to be crazy inside the MMZ again, then he wanted to get to his billet on Sixth Avenue while he still could.

He was going to pick up his uniform jacket when there was another flash.

When he looked up, he saw a tiny airplane hovering outside his window.

A tiny airplane . . . with enormous front wheels.

Samsonov was staggered by the strangeness of this thing. It was painted in bright, swirling circus colors, and its nose was pointing almost straight up. Defying all laws of gravity, it was holding perfectly still in the air, fire pouring out from behind its propeller. And those tires—they were huge, bald, fat, and permanently set in the down position.

It looked like a gigantic flying toy—and was *so* close to the window Samsonov could see its shadowy pilot looking back at him.

Suddenly, the plane's engine let out an ear-piercing screech. Its nose went down, and in another flash, it was gone.

Samsonov ran back to the window and pressed himself up against the giant pane. The weird little airplane was now flying around the top of the Navy Building next door. Its fiery exhaust made it impossible to miss.

Clearly, the MOP cleaning crew hadn't seen a holiday float the night before.

They'd seen this thing.

Samsonov grabbed the phone and hastily dialed the navy's air barge on the East River. A sleepy officer answered.

Samsonov identified himself and then asked, "Are your planes operational?"

The man replied that they were.

"Get both into the air now!" Samsonov ordered. "There's an unknown aircraft over the MMZ. We must intercept it."

"Why are you bothering me? I don't take orders from the army."

Samsonov was furious. "But as an army staff officer I can recommend your transfer to Kamchatka," he yelled back. "Now do it."

He slammed down the phone and quickly returned to the window. The plane was still in sight, but now it was flying around the top floor of the MOP Building. Samsonov watched in amazement as it went into its fantastic hovering maneuver again, stopping outside the skyscraper's penthouse for a few seconds before rocketing away.

Nearly a hundred of his building guards were on duty on the plaza below. All of them were looking up at the strange little plane. Hundreds more soldiers stuck with overnight paperwork duty were at the windows of other MMZ buildings. Like Samsonov, they were all following the circus plane's every move.

Where were the Yaks? Samsonov was fuming. They were supposed to be ready for takeoff at a moment's notice. But there was no sign of them.

Suddenly, the little plane's flight pattern changed. As if the pilot sensed something, the plane stopped in mid-orbit around the top of the MOP Building, pointed its nose west and left the area at high speed.

The Yaks arrived thirty seconds later. They went over the MMZ at seven hundred miles per hour, making lots of noise but doing little else. Once they'd departed, Samsonov strained to find the little plane in the night again, but it was no use. It was gone.

Its image was seared onto his retinas, though. The astonishing maneuvers, the speed, the hang and hover before darting away again?

It reminded him of a huge flying insect, or even a hummingbird, flitting here and there.

Looking for something.

CHAPTER SIX

May 4

WITH THE VICTORY celebrations complete, Phase Two of the Russian invasion of New York City was scheduled to begin. But, in fact, its changes were already being seen.

During the first month of the *Okupatsi*, the military had deployed its units in urban combat alignments. Heavily armed patrols, manning lots of weapons positions and guard posts, rain or shine, sleeping outdoors and eating meals on the curbstone.

Now more permanent installations were being established around the city. Unit command centers, security checkpoints, guardhouses, outposts on the periphery of nearly every structure with a roof over its head. Large apartment buildings all over New York were being transformed into barracks; smaller ones were being turned into mess halls.

The job of the Russian forces now was to become entrenched in Russkiy-NYC and get ready for the next phase when ordered to do so by Moscow.

Because Phase Two was more hands-on, the Sostva's staff had instituted daily morning briefings in the joint ops suite at the top of the old Simon & Schuster Building. The meetings would be run by Colonel Gagarin, the one-eyed man who knew it all.

The first one commenced at 0800 hours, three days after May Day. The Sostva commanders walked in, right on time, Alexei, Kartunov, and Marshal MOP, along with their security details. The three officers looked hung-over and sleep-deprived, hardly a surprise. They'd celebrated May Day as vigorously as their troops and were still paying the price.

The commanders took their seats and listened impassively as Colonel Gagarin first explained why these morning briefings were necessary. Then he rattled off eight pages of numbers Moscow deemed important for Phase Two. Total kilowatts cranked out by the restarted Astoria Power Station so far. How many supply ships were expected to arrive from Russia in the next twenty-four hours. How many meals would be served to the troops in the field over the same time period. On and on. All the numbers were positive; every one of them proof that the *Okupatsi* continued moving along smoothly.

But the three commanders were only interested in one number: the latest payout from the rackets. Now that the Red Hand godfathers were out of the way, that number should represent an enormous increase in profits for Moscow. And this would be good for the Sostva, because in the eyes of the Kremlin, the higher number, the better the job they were doing here in New York.

As it turned out, Gagarin had saved the best for last.

As of that morning, he revealed, the magic number had reached the equivalent of a million dollars a day in pure profit flowing into Russian coffers.

Awake now and feeling a lot better, the Sostva commanders gave themselves a round of applause, so pleased by what they'd heard. The staff officers joined in. Meeting over, the commanders got up to leave.

But after a stern nod from Gagarin, the navy's chief staff officer, who was in charge of the city's air defenses, timidly raised his hand and told the high commanders that, a couple of hundred people reported seeing a tiny aircraft flying around the MMZ the night before. Nothing serious, just something that looked like it was from a circus. The Yaks had been scrambled but the little plane had flown away before they arrived.

The still-jovial Sostva officers just laughed. They hadn't been aware of this incident or the earlier MOP sighting. Nor had they heard the Yaks roaring overhead around midnight. A vodka sleep was a deep sleep.

"A circus plane?" Alexei finally asked, the three commanders sitting back down. "Are you sure?"

"Many people reported it as such," the navy officer said.

"The army HQ's security chief among them," Gagarin added, slightly adjusting his eye patch. "This craft was universally described as being the size of a compact car but able to fly very fast. It was definitely not a military airplane. It was painted in carnival colors, had enormous front wheels and a very noisy engine. It flew around our three military HQ buildings for a few minutes and then just vanished—like a ghost, many said."

The high commanders were more puzzled than concerned. But it was paramount to them that Moscow not hear of anything that might blemish their success—not even a tale of some weird little *samolyot-nevidimka*, or ghost plane, flying within the supposedly secure airspace above their conquered city. The Gagarin story of the ghost plane had be discredited and quashed.

But how?

A few days into the invasion, MOP had revived one of the city's old AM radio stations.

Red Radio, which now ran twenty-four hours a day, played endless propaganda pieces in both Russian and English, bragging about how well the *Okupatsi* was going. Every three or four hours, an announcer would break in and read the list of rules and regulations for both soldiers and New York's civilians, followed by some innocuous around-the-town stories. Then it would go back to the propaganda.

With this in mind, Colonel Gagarin suggested a broadcast be made on Red Radio retelling the beagle-flying-a-doghouse holiday balloon story that had been floating around, adding that the wayward inflatable had been tracked down, recovered, and destroyed. End of the ghost plane.

The Sostva commanders liked the plan.

They ordered Gagarin to put it into action.

❂ ❂ ❂

But at the stroke of midnight, the ghost plane appeared again.

More than a thousand people saw the toy-like aircraft arrive over Rockefeller Plaza this time. Thanks to the Red Radio broadcast earlier, the ghost plane had been the talk of the MMZ all day, making many soldiers curious. But there were hundreds of civilians, too, who'd either listened to Red Radio or had gotten the word from others. They'd climbed up to the roofs of a number of skyscrapers just outside the MMZ with the hope that the little craft would return.

As before, the tiny plane circled the three main MMZ military buildings one at a time, three trips around each before starting back again. It was noisy but could move very fast. Despite its cartoonish landing gear, it was capable of amazing maneuvers, frequently coming within inches of smashing into a building's sharp corner on wings-up turns. The trail of exhaust left in its wake created gigantic smoke rings around the skyscrapers, three on each so far. This was a big hit with those watching below.

About two minutes into the display, the plane's engine let out a terrific screech. Suddenly, it went up on its tail, and stopped in midair outside the Navy Building's penthouse window. At that moment, a MOP electrical crew working on the roof next door turned on one of their searchlights. It captured the colorful little plane in its beam for a few seconds, and illuminated a small crowd of people looking out at it from inside the navy penthouse.

Then, just as quickly, the plane's nose came down, and with a great burst of flame and power, it vanished back into the night.

CHAPTER SEVEN

May 5

THE NEXT MORNING, the joint ops staff officers were astonished to see the Sostva commanders coming out of the elevators
at 7:00 a.m., an hour early for their 0800 hours daily briefing.

No announcement, no prior warning, they were suddenly just
there.

Colonel Gagarin was informed of the development. He hurried from his office to the lobby to discover the Sostva's early
appearance was not the only unpleasant surprise of the morning.
Pushing his way through the military's security detachments was
an imposing man dressed in a black leather trench coat, huge
fedora, and sunglasses. Tall, dark, handsome—and terrifying.

Commissar Zmeya . . .

He had a dozen of his special policemen with him. Piling out
of the next elevator, Zmeya's men towered over the other security entourages. Black combat uniforms, heavily armed, helmets
with visors that hid their eyes, they instilled fear in everyone.

But for Zmeya himself to be here—in public, in the daytime,
for a routine briefing—was *very* disconcerting. Something must
be seriously wrong.

The principals marched into the conference room. Gagarin
snapped his fingers, and a fourth chair was hastily put in place

at the conference table. But Zmeya had no intention of staying long. He made it clear he had no interest in hearing pages of statistics.

He wanted to talk about only one thing: the ghost plane.

"This aircraft is real," he said, pointing his finger back and forth at the Sostva commanders for emphasis. "It is not a balloon or an illusion. It is an actual airplane, and it poses a real threat to the *Oku-patsi*. It was obviously circling your buildings to collect intelligence of some kind—and as such, you must shoot it down when it returns. And it *will* return. From this moment on, *that* will be your highest priority. Check with Moscow if you doubt my words."

From behind his dark glasses, he scanned the faces of everyone in the room, as if taking a mental video of them.

"The NKVD will be watching, gentlemen," he said darkly. "And waiting . . . for quick results."

With that, Zmeya brusquely left the room, his security detail clicking sharp on his heels. The Sostva commanders scrambled to follow, creating a traffic jam at the conference room door.

Left behind, Gagarin and his joint ops officers were stunned. What the Sostva commanders had deemed nonexistent the day before was now the highest priority for the NKVD and the *Oku-patsi*? Granted, the ghost plane was strange, but it was almost amusing. A drunken circus pilot flying in from somewhere.

As the two uneasy entourages headed for the elevators, Gagarin reached into the hall and managed to grab one of the security men who was last in line. He was an army sergeant attached to General Alexei's protection staff.

"Comrade, explain all this," Gagarin ordered him.

The bodyguard shook his head no, but Gagarin, an army colonel, insisted. "Kamchatka isn't too pleasant this time of year," he said.

The man relented. "You know about the commissar's new *kompanon*?" he asked, in a lowered voice.

"You mean the most beautiful girl in the world?" Gagarin replied.

"That's her," the sergeant said. "She was with the commisar in the navy penthouse last night. There was a reading of famous military poetry for the higher-ups. She organized it, and Zmeya ordered everyone to go. In the middle of it, that flying toy started buzzing around the building. When it stopped by the penthouse's main window, she saw it up close, and it was like she'd seen a ghost. She became dizzy, gasping for breath, and almost passed out. Needed some sniffing salts. The commissar became extremely angry as a result."

The sergeant made a cutting action with his finger across his throat. "It's been unpleasant ever since."

But the joint ops officers were even more confused now.

"Why would that snake get upset over his girl's being frightened by the thing?" Gagarin asked him. "I'm sure it scares *some* people, like clowns do, but the rest of us are laughing at it."

The sergeant lowered his voice even further. He had to hurry or he'd be missed.

"It wasn't the plane that upset her," he said to Gagarin in a near whisper. "It was the pilot. He stood that clown plane on its rear end long enough to look in at her. And she saw him somehow, and that's when everything went to shit. That's why Zmeya is so pissed. And *that's* why he wants the clown shot down."

The man started to leave a second time when Gagarin grabbed his sleeve for one more question.

"And how do you know all this, Comrade Sergeant?" he asked. "All these details and minutiae—it seems too much for an enlisted man to remember."

The sergeant just shrugged.

"Because I was there, good colonel," he replied. "I saw it all myself."

CHAPTER EIGHT

RUSSKIY-NYC WAS PUT on high alert an hour later.

All leaves were canceled. All warships in the harbor went to battle stations. Security around key installations was doubled. Back on Phase One combat footing after just one day, the number of troops in the streets tripled.

And at the stroke of midnight, the weird little airplane appeared over the MMZ once again.

It was now the talk of the entire city. *Thousands*, soldiers and civilians, had taken to roofs all over Midtown, hoping to catch a glimpse of the mysterious little plane.

As before, it seemed to come out of nowhere. One moment, all was quiet, the next, the little plane was over Rockefeller Plaza again, making lots of noise and zooming around the top of the Army Building.

But this time, the two Yak-38 jet fighters were waiting for it.

Circling out over the Hudson River, the Yak pilots had only one order: to destroy the ghost plane. Figuring out who, or what, it was would come later.

Alerted that the aerial intruder had returned, the Yaks banked toward Midtown, weapons ready to fire. Each was carrying two powerful Aphid-6s, an air-to-air missile designed to shoot down other jet fighters. The strange little circus plane was so small that just one Aphid would blow it to pieces. Four missile hits would vaporize it.

But it wouldn't be that simple. The Yak-38 was an unusual bird itself. A supersonic jet fighter that could take off and land vertically, it was built to protect ships at sea, not fight above an urban environment. If its speed fell below a hundred knots in level flight, it would stall and simply fall out of the sky. But because the ghost plane was so diminutive, the Yaks would have to fly uncomfortably close to stall velocity in order to shoot it down.

The jet fighters arrived above the MMZ doing three hundred knots and flying at fifty-five hundred feet. Their look-down radars picked up the ghost plane about a mile below, still circling the Army Building. The YAK pilots hatched a plan. They reduced their speed to one hundred and fifty knots and went down to five hundred feet. Then, just a half mile south of the MMZ, they came in behind the small plane and locked their radars onto it.

But just as they were about to launch their missiles, the weird little aircraft suddenly stopped in midair, its pilot pulling his nose straight up, taking himself out of the Aphids' radar lock. The maneuver fouled the Yaks' firing solution and automatically halted their launch.

The jet fighters roared by the little plane an instant later, their weapons' computers blinking furiously after so abruptly losing their target. Forced to throttle up and make a wide, noisy turn out over the Hudson, it would take nearly a minute for the VTOL jets to get back into firing position. In that time, the ghost plane's pilot calmly pushed his nose back down, and resumed orbiting the top of the Army Building.

The Yaks reappeared a minute later. As their first missed pass was due to high speed, they'd slowed to a seat-puckering one hundred and five knots for another try. Mimicking their initial maneuvering, they reacquired the tiny intruder on their radars and prepared to fire their missiles a second time.

But again, the little plane turned the tables on them. It suddenly tripled its speed, reaching nearly three hundred knots in just a few seconds, and disappeared around the corner of the

Army Building. Once more, the Yaks' weapons computers were thrown off, cancelling another missile launch.

Now both Yaks were forced to kick in their afterburners, lest they stall and crash. In doing so, they created a sonic boom so intense it shattered thousands of windows all over Midtown, causing tons of broken glass to rain down on the streets below.

After yet another wide bank out over the Hudson, the jet fighters returned over midtown for a third time and found the little plane acting strangely once again. Its pilot had put the tiny aircraft into another near hover, but this time, he was about fifty feet *above* the army's penthouse roof.

Just hanging there.

The perfect target.

The Yak pilots immediately fired their Aphids. From only twelve hundred feet away, the quartet of missiles was suddenly heading right for the little plane, four enormous streaks of fire tearing through the night.

But then more magic. The tiny airplane vanished. One moment it was there, the next it wasn't. The Aphid missiles streaked over the Army Building and hit the top floor of the old Honeywell Building three blocks away. Home to the largest counting room for the rackets, the equivalent of three million dollars in Moscow's daily profits was blown sky high in a flash of fire and smoke.

The ghost plane's disappearing act was accomplished by plunging straight down into the narrow space separating the Army and the Navy Buildings, allowing it to avoid the missiles with ease. Pulling up just fifty feet above a large captivated crowd watching on the corner of West Forty-Eighth Street and Fifth Avenue, the little plane climbed again and simply resumed circling the army skyscraper.

But the night was not over.

Early in the invasion, MOP units had resurrected three dozen of the city's old municipal tow trucks. By taking off their towing equipment and installing 12.7 millimeter heavy machine guns, they'd converted them into *bronegruzivikis*, or gun trucks,

a name quickly shortened to Brozis. They were then given to the
NKVD's Chekskis.

The Brozis were waiting in force tonight, per the order of
Commissar Zmeya. They were armed with special ammunition
called ITZP, or instantaneous incendiary rounds, tracers that lit
up bright green on leaving the barrel and stayed lit until they hit
a target. Powerful and accurate, they would make short work of
the ghost plane.

Once the now-unarmed Yaks were forced to leave the area,
the Brozis roared into position all around the MMZ. A dozen
powerful searchlights down on the plaza were switched on. They
quickly caught the ghost plane in their beams.

Suddenly, the sky above Midtown Manhattan was awash in
the violent glow of ITZP fire, thirty-six distinct streams of emerald light rising into the night, heading right for the little aircraft.
No way could it survive such an intense fusillade.

Yet, the pilot didn't try a desperate maneuver like banking
left or right, or diving away. Instead, he expertly weaved his way
through the garish barrages. Twisting, climbing, turning, adding
power, then reducing it, he avoided all of it. Then, incredibly,
the plane resumed making circuits around the top of the Army
Building as if nothing had happened.

The Brozi gunners started firing again, this time leading
the tiny plane with the help of their night-vision goggles.
Another massive wave of tracers filled the sky, heading toward
the top of the Army Building. But this time, at the very last
moment, the little plane went into its hover mode again and
simply let the flood of green streaks go by. It seemed easier
that way.

This barrage didn't disappear into the night like the first one.
Instead, thousands of the green tracer rounds smashed into the
top of the Army Building, blowing half the roof off, while the
rest slammed into the top ten floors of the Navy Building's facing
side. Hundreds on the plaza below fled as the twin hits pelted the
MMZ with a second storm of broken glass.

The gun trucks were immediately ordered to cease firing.

Meanwhile, the little plane had switched to circling the Navy

Building, and after two quick orbits, it jumped over to the MOP Building.

But then . . . something strange happened.

Breaking from its bizarre pattern of flying madly around the tops of the three side-by-side military HQ buildings, the funny little plane started climbing.

And climbing.

And climbing.

And to the astonishment of the thousands below, for the first time, the ghost plane began circling the top floor of 30 Rock, the headquarters of the NKVD secret police.

Earlier in the day, a newly arrived battalion of SA-4 SAM mobile launchers had been dispersed throughout the city.

Their crews had been briefed on what would be expected of them as part of the *Okupatsi* force. But they were also given an unofficial briefing about the ghost plane and what had been happening around New York in the days before their arrival. Their battalion commander strongly emphasized to his crews that they would have nothing to do with the ongoing ghost plane mystery. SA-4s were designed to shoot down bomber formations from hundreds of miles away. They were here to protect Russkiy-NYC against a massive airborne attack, not some flying circus toy with giant wheels.

The SA-4 launch crews were all veterans of the recent African campaign and wouldn't have to be told twice. They knew firing one of the massive SA-4s at such a tiny target, at such close range, inside such a congested area, would be insanity.

The load of fuel carried by just one of their missiles held enough explosive power to devastate four city blocks.

The SA-4 SAM launcher parked near the corner of West Forty-Eighth Street and Fifth Avenue was one of the closest to Rockefeller Center.

Located just a hundred feet outside the MMZ's barbed-wire barrier, its six-man crew had a clear view of all the buildings within the Russian enclave.

Their launcher looked like a tank, a big bulky armored vehicle on two tracks with a large antenna spinning on the top and two gigantic missiles on launch railings hanging off either side. Its commander sat in a small open turret near the front; the rest of the crew tended the missiles from the control hatch in the back.

The crewmembers watched in amazement as the bizarre ghost plane drama unfolded in the night skies above the old Rockefeller Center. Their attention was drawn back down to earth when a large Cadillac roared up to their position and four men in trench coats and fedoras jumped out.

No introductions were needed. The missile crew knew the men were NKVD Militsiya. Not to be trifled with under any circumstances.

The enlisted men were made to stand against a wall nearby while one policeman climbed atop the launcher and accosted the SAM commander. He pointed at the little plane whipping around the top of 30 Rock and barked, "Fire at that mosquito immediately. Sight it, lock it, and destroy it. Now."

The SAM commander just shook his head.

"I am under orders not to shoot these missiles unless the city is in danger of a massive bombing attack."

"This order comes directly from the commissar's office," the NKVD man growled. "Now, fire on it."

The SAM officer tried to reason with the man. "This missile is an SA-4," he said. "It's designed to hit targets twenty miles high and two hundred miles out. Firing it from here, in this crowd of buildings and at such a small close-proximity target, will be inviting disaster."

But the NKVD man angrily waved his protests away. "You are under orders—"

"And what if we hit the building itself?" the missile commander shot back at him, growing alarmed now.

"Then you'll face a firing squad in the morning," the NKVD man spit at him in reply. "You're the experts. Do your job."

But the missile commander did not move. He did not say a thing. He stayed defiant.

Then another screech of tires. Two Brozi trucks had rushed

up from the direction of Forty-Second Street, manned by a dozen fearsome Chekskis and one Militsiya officer.

This officer was hideous. A ragged uneven scar traveled from one ear to another, and he walked with an odd limp. His eyes were red and bloodshot. His nose was running.

"Sublieutenant Boris Borski," he said, flashing his ID card at the other Militsiya. "Is there a disagreement here? Is it about launching a missile at that flying bug?"

No one said anything; they didn't have to.

Borski walked up to the five-man missile crew still standing against the building wall. He addressed the first man in line, a young recruit.

"How many men does it take to safely launch one of these missiles?" he asked him.

"In an emergency situation, only four are needed, plus a firing officer, sir," the young soldier recited crisply.

Borski calmly took out his pistol and shot the man in the temple. He crumpled to the sidewalk, blood gushing from his wound. Then Borski turned to the launcher's commander and said, "This is now an emergency situation."

The SAM officer gave up. One of his men was dead for no reason, and he was sure these psychopaths would just love to kill them all. He gave his bewildered crew their orders, and they immediately began preparing to launch one of their massive antiaircraft missiles at the miniature circus plane.

Their radar switched to active search, they quickly managed to get the plane's tiny blip on their targeting screen.

Seconds after that, they launched their gigantic missile.

All those thousands of people who'd turned out to see the ghost plane watched the SA-4 rise up from the clutter of Midtown.

It looked like a gigantic Roman candle, powerful and ear-splittingly loud. The immense roar of its engine reverberated up and down Manhattan and shattered even more windows. Its tail flame lit up the night for miles around.

Because, as a safety issue, SA-4s were designed not to detonate during the first few seconds of flight, the mystery plane simply banked to the right the instant the giant missile left its launcher and moved out of its way.

Streaking skyward now, with no discernible target in sight, the SA-4's onboard computer essentially canceled its own launch. Its guidance system froze three seconds later, when the missile had reached a thousand feet in altitude. It rolled over hard, its engine still firing, but now unguided.

The thousands of spectators gasped and screamed, running in all directions.

With nowhere to go but down, the SA-4 slammed into Chelsea Piers a few seconds later, obliterating all of the rackets' moneymaking drug labs.

It was a peculiar time for Colonel Ivan Samsonov to discover he was afraid of heights.

Flying had never bothered him; mountain climbing was the sport of his youth. Looking down from his forty-fourth-floor office was never an issue, either. Even his ascent to the top of the Eiffel Tower had been a great experience.

But outside, in the elements, at night, seventy stories up?

He was scared to death.

Yet, here he was, on the roof of 30 Rock, shaking uncontrollably, and not just from the cold. He was holding on tight to a cement post that helped secure the shallow brass railing that ran along the top of the building's outer edge. He was sure if he let go, he'd be blown away.

He'd been up here since late afternoon, having used his Army-NKVD liaison credentials to get by all the security checkpoints cleanly. None of the female Cutie guards had frisked him, which was a good thing, because earlier in the day, he'd disassembled a rocket-propelled grenade launcher—the ubiquitous RPG—and sewed it and two projectiles inside the inner layer of his heavy uniform coat. The reassembled weapon lay just within his reach. He'd spent a lot of time up here praying that if the moment came, he would find the courage to pick it up and actually do something with it.

Acrophobia aside, he'd had one of the best views of what had just transpired over the MMZ. But after the SAM crashed, and while everybody was distracted by the disaster on the waterfront, only Samsonov seemed to notice that the ghost plane went back to orbiting the top of 30 Rock again.

It was the perfect scenario for him. When the plane first roared by him, it was barely twenty feet away.

He managed to load the RPG launcher with one hand while still holding on to the cement post with the other. He leaned out over the brass railing; the plaza below him looked as if it were a hundred miles away, straight down. Trying to keep his sense of balance, when the mystery plane went by him again, he somehow convinced his trembling fingers to pull the trigger.

The RPG rocketed away in a burst of smoke and fire, but it immediately began to corkscrew and quickly disappeared below, a complete miss. Samsonov was sure no one had seen his errant shot, not even the ghost plane's pilot.

He'd done all this for nothing?

A few seconds later, the small aircraft came back around to his side of the building again. But suddenly, it went into its hovering routine . . . right below him.

Samsonov couldn't believe his luck. He grabbed the second grenade, loaded it into the launcher and fired again. This rocket went haywire, too. It twisted its way down two hundred feet and wound up hitting the northwest corner of the already shattered Navy Building. But at that same moment, the mystery plane nosed down and began zooming away from the MMZ—only to find, hanging in the air right in front of it, the cloud of the debris from the second RPG hit.

The pilot only had two ways to go: He could fly so low over the top of the Navy Building that he'd hit at least a few of the people gathered there either with his propeller or his big wheels, or he could fly through the debris.

The pilot picked the second option, blazing right into the haze of concrete and metal, which ripped the plane's fuselage to shreds and made it stagger in flight.

Samsonov was astonished. It wasn't a direct hit, but he was the first member of the Russian military to inflict damage on the ghost plane. And while the tiny aircraft was still airborne somehow, it was on fire and smoking heavily as it wobbled away from the MMZ. When Samsonov last saw it, the small plane was out over the Hudson River, its smoky trail heading toward New Jersey.

Suddenly, he didn't need to hold on so tight to the cement post anymore. He reached into his pocket and pulled out the photo of Commissar Zmeya's gorgeous girlfriend. The most beautiful woman in America. He'd looked at the photo many, *many* times by now—and he'd simply fallen in love with her.

He gently kissed the picture.

Maybe now she'd at least know who he was.

CHAPTER NINE

CAPTAIN "BULL" DOZER was once again huddled in the hut atop his wooden tower, his two troopers close by.

The balloon was up; the picture was shaky. The radio was silent and the coffee was cold. As Dozer had written earlier in the hut's hourly log: "Nothing new." He'd listened to dead air on his radio for hours, hoping, to no avail, to hear from his buddies just as he did every evening, a dismal mission for sure.

At least he and the 7CAV had been lucky to come across the small military base in the Pine Barrens where they could drill and stay battle-ready. Built sometime in the prewar days, the tiny base consisted of a single Quonset hut, a narrow runway meant for helicopters and small airplanes, and a vast refrigerated underground bunker. Although the base was surrounded by nearly impenetrable forest with little more than a dirt path leading in or out of it, its mysterious builders had also installed a large camouflage net that could move back and forth like the roof of a sports stadium. It hid the base from prying eyes in the sky, yet allowed aircraft to come and go.

Theories about the base's origins abounded among the 7CAV troopers. Maybe the bunkers were secret storage sites for WMD. Nuclear warheads, biological weapons, poison gas. That would explain the camo net, but why would such weapons need to be refrigerated? The most radical theory was that the US military had conducted secret interdimensional tests there before the war—experiments that needed low temperatures to work and had to be kept from the public eye.

Tired of the silence, Dozer thought about tuning in to the only channel he could hear on his old rig but decided against it. Red Radio was typically Russian, crude and bizarre. It would run the same propaganda pieces over and over, in Russian and English, trumpeting the disheartening news of how well the *Okupatsi* was going and that the city was back to its old postwar abnormal self.

This canned hoopla would be followed by a tape of a grim-voiced announcer listing the penalties for soldiers caught stealing gasoline, carrying illegal weapons, possessing pro-American literature, or venturing into the Pine Barrens. That always brought a smile to Dozer's face. Even before the Big War, few people had known the Barrens existed, and those who had been aware of it had kept away. Now the Russians were doing the same—for one reason: They must have come across information that the Pine Barrens was haunted.

All kinds of paranormal activity had been reported inside the Barrens over the years. Headless sailors, crying ghosts, phantom horses, strange aerial lights, something called the New Jersey Devil, and on and on. Dozer had met Russians on the battlefield in Europe and had been fighting them in American ever since. He knew that superstition was deeply entwined in their DNA. That's why the Pine Barrens was strictly off-limits to its soldiers. And that's why Dozer had built his tower here.

Occasionally, other voices would break into the occupation forces' broadcasts, reciting badly translated unscripted reports about peculiar things happening around the city. A few days before, Dozer had heard a military spokesman tell the troops: "Don't drink too much on parade day," "Avoid fondling women you don't know," and "Do not vomit in the street while on duty." One had even said, "Stories about an aircraft spotted above the city at midnight doing wonderfully strange flying things are not true. It was a parade balloon depicting a dog."

Whenever Dozer heard these odd reports, he thought, *Boozed-up Russians*. But drunk or not, it was obvious the invaders had not only taken over the city while barely firing a shot, but that they were planning to stay awhile.

Dozer unfolded his portable planning board to work on the second problem he was facing: trying to figure out what the 7CAV could do operations-wise against the Russians. He had mulled over a number of ways they could at least make the Russians' occupation a little less painless. Maybe a series of quick raids around the edges of the city, attacking their fuel lines, convoys, and outlying patrols. Hit and run—all at night. The 7CAV was good at that type of thing. They were also adept at sabotage, and Dozer had considered attacking the Astoria power plant in Queens, now operating under Russian control, or maybe blowing up a section of one of the major bridges. But these would just be pinpricks against the huge Russian army.

While Dozer's men were well trained and well armed, there were only a hundred of them. Just from rough calculations based on what they'd seen from the balloon cam, there were at least sixty thousand Russian troops in New York City at the time of the invasion, and by now, more like sixty-five thousand. Dozer liked to gamble, but not against those kinds of odds.

How the hell were they going to dislodge an army like that? And haunted forest or not, Dozer knew the Russians would eventually figure out where the 7CAV was operating from and seek to destroy them, probably with massive long-range artillery barrages of a type that could level the entire Pine Barrens in just a few hours. Was pissing off the invaders worth all that?

He'd asked himself these questions for nearly a month and hadn't yet come up with an answer. But he knew he had to do something big, even if it *was* one last act of defiance in the name of his long-lost country.

If only he had a little help.

Dozer's hut served another critical function apart from surveillance. It was the 7CAV's air traffic control tower. From here, he and his men helped the unit's cargo planes fly in and out of the hidden base.

The stout, boxy Sherpas could haul a substantial load. This was important, because due to its isolated location, the 7CAV's supply had to come entirely by air. While Dozer was fairly certain that the Reds would not come out to the Pine Barrens unprovoked, the 7CAV still had to be careful operating aircraft so close to occupied New York City. Staying at treetop level, just below the Russian long-range radar net, was essential to the resupply effort. Plus, it all had to be done at night.

A few hours earlier, just after the sun had gone down and the balloon had gone up, the base's camouflage net had been pulled back. The 7CAV's four homely, unarmed Sherpas took off and flew up to Albany, in the Free State of New York, to pick up eight thousand gallons of gasoline in one hundred and sixty barrels. Now, half past midnight, the four planes were expected back at any moment, anxious as always to land and get under the net once more.

Around twenty five minutes past midnight, the tower's spy camera picked up a brief but substantial infrared heat spike coming from New York City; on the video monitor, it looked like a quick, bright flash of light somewhere in Lower Manhattan near the water. This was not the first time the 7CAV had seen such a thing. The past few nights, the IR-equipped camera had detected dozens of spikes that Dozer's techs had identified as fireworks, further proof that the Russians were enjoying their stay in the occupied city.

But while these heat spikes had become routine by now, Dozer told his two troopers to stick to the video monitor just in case anything else unusual happened. He would serve as the Sherpas' air traffic controller tonight.

At exactly 12:35 a.m., he grabbed his night-vision binoculars and leaned out the hut's window, pushing both the 50-caliber and the plastic aside. After a brief scan of the dark skies, he spotted the first Sherpa about five miles out, approaching from the north. It was coming in low and slow over the pines, a tiny strobe light blinking on its nose. Dozer knew the other three cargo planes were right on its tail, flying with no lights at all. He clicked the hut's prewar radiophone twice, sending a coded message back to the hidden base. The Sherpas were home; the camo net should be pulled back.

The four cargo planes roared past the spy tower a minute later, one by one, in a very close line. Their pilots were equipped with night-vision goggles as well. Each put the nose of his aircraft right on the center of the runway that had suddenly opened up a mile away. Bare and blinking LCD lights gave it a vague outline but not much more. Landing this way was not for the faint of heart, especially with a shitload of gasoline on board.

Still, all was proceeding smoothly—until Dozer happened to catch a glint of light coming from behind the last Sherpa.

"What the hell?" he exclaimed as the fourth cargo plane thundered past him.

Incredibly, a *fifth* aircraft was flying right on the Sherpa's tail. Dozer could barely make it out in the dark, but he could tell the plane was much smaller than the cargo humpers and had a very unusual shape. It was also smoking heavily and trailing wisps of flame.

"Jesus Christ!" he bellowed into his radiophone, all thoughts of coded messages long gone. "There's five of them heading your way!"

Telling his two troopers to stay put, Dozer was out of the hut in a second, furiously descending the ladder and falling the last ten feet to the ground. A low but unmistakable klaxon rose up among the pines, signaling the base's security troops to immediately begin countermeasures against the intruder.

The 7CAV had actually drilled for something like this—except the opponent was always incoming helicopters. No one had ever imagined an enemy airplane getting under the dome.

Dozer dove into his jeep, shouting back up to the pair of troopers to keep their eyes open for any other aerial activity. Then he took off along the sand path that led back to the base.

Wheeling in and out of the short scrub and tumbling roots, he could still see the intruder through breaks in the pines. It was flying so close to the last cargo plane's tail, it was being battered mercilessly by the Sherpa's prop wash.

Dozer was hardly an aviation expert, but it seemed impossible that the intruder's heavily damaged airplane was even airborne.

He swore into the wind, "Who the hell flies like that?"

He skidded wildly onto the far end of the runway and floored the jeep's accelerator. Now driving on asphalt and topping eighty miles an hour, he saw the last Sherpa bounce in for a landing, its crew realizing what was going on and quickly veering off the runway. The intruding aircraft pancaked in just a few seconds later. It bounced twice and then began a long, screeching skid down the landing strip, sending clouds of sparks into the night.

Dozer arrived just as the little plane came to a stop at the far end of the runway. Two jeeps of 7CAV soldiers were already waiting for it.

The troops quickly surrounded the damaged aircraft. A gust of wind blew the smoke away and the canopy on the little craft popped open. The pilot raised his hands high over his head. One 7CAV trooper used the muzzle of his M-16 to signal the man to stand up and take off his helmet. To everyone's surprise, he was bald and pudgy, wearing an old, worn-out business suit, without a tat to be seen. He looked like an accountant from the prewar days, a bean counter with bad taste in threads—and certainly not some kind of fantastically gifted pilot.

"Jesus, don't shoot!" he pleaded. "I'm not armed."

"Who the hell are you?" the security team's leader barked at him.

"I'm a numbers runner out of Montreal," the man replied, nervously looking over his shoulder. "I'm a nobody. The lowest guy on the totem pole."

In the parlance of America's vast gambling underground, this man was a worm. Someone who picked up bets here and flew them there.

He was an outlaw, but not a very big one. And he appeared close to wetting his pants.

The team leader looked over at Dozer, who just shrugged. The security man raised his hand and gave a thumbs-up, the signal to the nearby runway crews to close the camo dome. Then he turned back to the intruder.

"What are you doing here?"

"Some asshole shot at me over Poughkeepsie," the pilot replied hurriedly. "I sprang a fuel leak. I was running out of gas and saw these planes, so I followed them down."

But Dozer didn't believe him. Any pilot with such amazing flying skill these days would hardly be running numbers. He'd be leading a freelance air merc squadron or flying for the air pirates.

Dozer walked up to the front of the crashed airplane. "Pretty ballsy flying, Worm," he said to the trembling pilot.

"But I didn't know what I was doing," the man insisted, once again nervously looking over his shoulder. "I was scared to death."

"Scared of what?" Dozer asked him. "Scared of landing here?"

The man turned and pointed up toward the rapidly closing camo dome.

"Shit no, man!" he cried. "Scared of him! That nut behind me."

Dozer and his men looked skyward and were astonished to see yet *another* airplane coming down at them. It was moving very fast, but sideways, just barely squeezing through the small opening that remained in the rapidly closing camo cover. Its wing was on fire, its tail section was falling away, and its very noisy engine was belching black smoke. It was painted in garish circus colors—swirling yellows, greens, and blues—and for some reason, it had gigantic wheels for landing gear.

Everyone scattered—Dozer, the security men, the numbers runner—all runing for their lives. The burning plane went over them a second later, just inches above their heads, dropping a trail of fiery debris in its wake. Dozer couldn't believe what he was seeing. This thing was flying way too fast to land. He was sure it was going to bounce off the end of the runway and crash into the woods beyond.

But then, incredibly, the little plane went straight up, did an impossibly tight 360-degree loop *under* the completely closed camo cover and then nosed down again, all in three seconds. With some speed drained off, the burning plane hit about fifty feet farther up the runway and, with a screech of scorched metal, skidded to a violent halt right next to the numbers runner's plane.

Dozer and his men quickly recovered and ran toward the second plane, weapons raised again. The pilot had already lifted the canopy and, surrounded by smoke and steam, was taking off his scratched and dented crash helmet. He finally stood up.

He was tall and handsome with rock-star looks. His long brown hair almost touching his shoulders, he was wearing an old-style black USAF flight suit. His helmet had images of two lightning bolts on it.

Dozer couldn't believe it.

It was his old friend Hawk Hunter.

The Wingman.

But there was just one problem. . . .

Hawk Hunter was dead.

CHAPTER TEN

MANY PEOPLE BELIEVED the Wingman had died ten years ago.

He'd been killed deploying a string of nuclear munitions in space in hopes of deflecting a comet heading for Earth. The plan had worked, Earth was spared, and a grateful planet mourned the loss of a true American hero.

But in the past few weeks, rumors had been circulating that maybe Hunter wasn't dead after all. He'd been spotted in Football City, supposedly after crash landing the space shuttle nearby. He'd helped take down some Mafia thugs who'd been running Detroit, then he'd busted up an Asian Mercenary Cult genocide program out in Nevada. All this, the rumormongers said, happened in a matter of days.

But it was almost too much to believe, especially for Bull Dozer.

He and Hunter went way back. After the end of the Big War, Hunter had traveled home from devastated Europe on the aircraft carrier *JFK*, the same ship carrying Dozer and the 7CAV. In the years that followed, Hunter had fought with them, got drunk with them, and joined them in their efforts to fulfill the dream of rebuilding America, or at least keeping it from disappearing forever.

They were brothers-in-arms, and when the 7CAV heard Hunter had died, it had taken the whole unit a long time to recover.

But now, apparently, here he was.

The hair, the helmet, the rock-star pilot himself.

A crash team made up of the base's civilian techs quickly extinguished the fire on the little plane with the big wheels. They also doused the numbers runner's plane.

Two flatbed trucks roared onto the runway, and the techs picked up what was left of both planes and loaded them into their bays. The camo net was finally closed and secured; the runway's lights were turned off. While the Worm was sped to the infirmary under heavy guard, Dozer hustled the second pilot into the 7CAV's Quonset hut ops center.

Dozer locked the door behind them and then studied the man. The pilot stared blankly back at him. He was sweaty, unshaven, and rough around the edges, whoever he was.

"You certainly look like you," Dozer said finally. "But I still feel like I'm looking at a ghost."

"So do I," the man said. "Maybe . . . that means we're both ghosts?"

The look in the man's eyes told Dozer he hadn't used those words lightly. There was an awkward silence between them. Finally, Dozer said, "Hey, there's a lot of crazy shit going on out there these days. How can we really know who's who?"

The pilot reached into his breast pocket and took out a small American flag. "Remember Saul Wackerman?" he asked.

The marine officer nodded. When the carrier *JFK* dumped the Seventh Cavalry, Hunter, and thousands of other defeated US soldiers onto the streets of postwar New York City, a brutal turf battle between rival National Guard units had just been fought, leaving entire neighborhoods in ruins. It was their first glimpse of how much America had changed since the end of global hostilities. While walking through the city, they'd witnessed the shooting of an elderly man by a sniper for doing nothing more than waving a small American flag. That man was Saul Wackerman.

"I think about him almost every day," Dozer replied.

"Then you'll recognize this," the pilot said, handing him the flag. "You've seen it before. And you know it's been with me ever since that day."

Dozer studied the flag. Frayed and worn, it had a few blood-stains around the edges, yet its colors were still surprisingly bright. He wiped his eyes. The man was right. Dozer *had* seen this little flag many times. No one could fake this hallowed piece of cloth.

Dozer stuck out his hand; they shook.

But the pilot still looked uncertain.

"Now *you* don't believe *me*?" Dozer asked incredulously. "You don't think I'm real? That's an insult."

Dozer led him to the unit's canteen, twenty steps away. A huge pot was simmering on the stove. The marine officer scooped a little of its contents out with a spoon and gave it to him.

"Taste this," he said.

The pilot did as asked, taking just a bit on the tip of his tongue. He started nodding, and then finally, he smiled. "Freaking whiskey stew, Bull," he said. "Even worse than your coffee."

They embraced, a massive bro-hug between very old friends.

"Have we convinced each other we're not ghosts?" Dozer asked him once the backslapping was over.

"Well, ghosts don't drink, do they?" his friend replied.

Dozer just shook his head and lit a cigar. "They can't," he said between puffs. "Unless they bring a mop."

They sat at Dozer's ops desk, where the 7CAV commander produced a bottle of nasty-looking whiskey and two glasses. He filled both to the brim.

Hunter downed his in two gulps. It was awful, but he'd never tasted anything so good. He felt warm for the first time in a long time.

"Jesus—that's great stuff," he said, coughing harshly.

"Why not the best?" Dozer replied, downing his as well.

He refilled their glasses, clinked his with Hunter's, and said, "Okay—tell me everything."

✪ ✪ ✪

It was the same story Hunter had been telling people since he'd returned from space a few weeks ago.

He remembered blasting off in the shuttle and carrying out the mission to divert the comet but nothing after that. While he knew that some time had passed, the next thing he recalled clearly was being pulled from the wreck of the space shuttle just outside Football City. His saviors were two mutual friends and fellow pilots, JT Toomey and Ben Wa. They took Hunter to Football City, capital of the Free Missouri Territory, which had once been his home. A little later, they helped him clean up some mob business in Detroit. After that, they'd all gone out west, to the old Groom Lake secret base to break up an Asian Mercenary Cult human extermination program.

So, basically, the rumors were all true.

While at Area 51, Hunter had somewhat miraculously found his old airplane, the F-16XL Cranked Arrow.

"Seriously, after a few days with the Football City guys, it was like I'd never left," Hunter told Dozer. "But there's a big piece of my memory that's just blank."

"You don't mean 'missing time'?" Dozer asked him. "Like what some of those UFO abductees claim?"

Hunter shrugged. "Who knows? One astrophysics egghead I talked to thinks I might have crossed over to 'another place,' somewhere else."

Dozer's brow furrowed. The old marine was trying to understand. "What does that mean?"

Hunter sipped his drink. "Another universe, maybe? Another reality?"

Dozer laughed. "That 'expert'—liked to smoke weed, I'm guessing?"

Hunter nodded. "But that doesn't mean he's wrong. The theory is that there are an infinite number of universes and they all butt up against one another. This universe we're in right now might be exactly like the one I originally came from, except maybe there's one more grain of sand in a desert here, or one less drop of water in the ocean, but everything else is the same. Or almost the same. And somehow I passed from one place to another."

"If your intention is to creep me out," Dozer said, "mission accomplished."

"Something happened to me, Bull," Hunter said, draining the second glass of whiskey. "I went somewhere. I just have no idea where."

Dozer refilled their glasses. At that moment, the truck carrying Hunter's little wrecked airplane rumbled by the ops building's front window. The two big tires took up nearly half the truck's cargo bed.

They watched it go by, glowing weirdly in the subdued light of the halogen lamps that dotted the secret base.

Dozer thought a moment, then leaned back in his chair and relit his cigar.

"Well, this is amazing," he said with a laugh. "Because I just realized what you've been doing in that plane. . . ."

Hunter nearly spit out his drink. "I have no idea what you're talking about," he said.

Feet up on his desk, Dozer took a massive puff from his cigar and let it out slowly. The smoke went to the ceiling of the Quonset hut.

"I just figured it out," he said proudly. "That bizarre-ass airplane. A report I heard on Red Radio, them denying that something weird was cruising around up there. Circling their buildings? 'Doing wonderfully strange flying things' is how they translated it."

Hunter really didn't want to talk about this.

But Dozer persisted. "Were you trying to screw with the Commies or something, Hawk? Fuck with their heads with the strangest airplane ever built? Your way of striking a blow for the old USA?"

Hunter stared at the floor. Doing wonderfully strange flying things? *That's* what the Reds thought he'd been doing?

Zooming around those buildings, dodging machine gun fire, missiles and Yaks—some of it could be described as strange. But wonderful?

"It's a really long story, Bull," he finally said.

Dozer held up the bottle of whiskey. It was still three quarters full.

Hunter groaned. "Okay—I was looking for someone. . . ."

Dozer was again relighting his cigar but stopped in mid-puff. "By flying *over* New York City?" he asked, surprised.

"Yes," Hunter admitted.

Dozer finally got his stogie relit. "Well, there are easier ways," he said, again leaning back in his chair. "This someone must be very special."

Hunter looked up at him. "You know who it is. . . ."

Dozer thought a moment and then asked, "The blonde?"

Hunter downed the rest of his drink and nodded, eyes glued to the floor again. "Yeah," he said. "The blonde."

It would be impossible to keep this a secret forever, Hunter knew—and Dozer *was* an old friend. "Okay, pour us another," he said finally. "I'll start at the beginning. . . ."

CHAPTER ELEVEN

"I WAS FLYING back from our raid on Groom Lake," Hunter began. "I was heading east—to Vermont, maybe later to Cape Cod. I wasn't even sure.

"About an hour east of Football City, I realize I'm running out of gas. I'd flown all the way from Nevada to the other side of the Mississippi on a single tank. The XL is fuel-efficient, but it doesn't fly on pixie dust.

"I was looking for someplace to land when the reserve tank went dry. So I started gliding and found a runway in far west Pennsylvania, about twenty miles from Kecksburg, a place they call Mudtown. It was all lit up and their radio landing frequency had a loop recording about stopping for 'gas, grub, and girls. . . .'

"I knew it was a honeypot. Looks like Vegas from the air, but some unsuspecting pilot lands, gets robbed at the rigged poker games or by hookers. The pigeon always gets separated from his billfold in those places.

"But I had no choice. I was descending from 65-Angels and coming down fast. The closer I got, the more the place looked like Dodge City. Wooden buildings, lots of smoke, people in the streets. I could hear the noise coming up from below even as I was gliding in, including lots of gunfire. A real nice place.

"Anyway, I landed with zero guidance from the airport tower. I could see people up there, but they weren't paying attention to who was flying in. The fuel pumps were right next to the terminal and all lit up with neon signs and I was able to roll over to them. But that's when it dawned on me I didn't have any money. I couldn't even remember the last time I'd carried money. It didn't matter, though, because no one was at the pumps. They were all padlocked. So I parked and climbed out.

"The airport was funky. Lots of weird airplanes: old fighters, shit-box bombers, homemade stuff. Stuff that looked like it couldn't get airborne on a bet. All fixed wing, too, no choppers. And a lot of this stuff looked abandoned.

"I could hear yelling and cursing; there was a commotion nearby. I walked into the terminal, which was actually one huge casino, and there was a major brawl going on. Dozens of people throwing punches, breaking bottles, hitting each other with chairs. I could see at least five different kinds of uniforms involved and realized it was a handful of merc groups beating on each other. A five-sided gang fight.

"Lots of people were on the sidelines watching and cheering them on. Hookies, druggies, the usual. I asked one of the girls what was going on. She said, 'The rescue mission isn't going anywhere, but these idiots still want to get paid.'

"Turns out a private-hire copter had been shot down over Mudtown the night before. It had just taken off from the airport when a Stinger or something caught it. It crashed next to an old hotel in a rough part of town about two miles away. One of the passengers was carrying two suitcases full of pure silver. He wound up inside this broken-down hotel with a dozen private goons he'd hired as protection for the ride.

"Meanwhile, word gets around this guy is carrying silver worth three or four million at least. So a couple hundred of Mudtown's meth heads get together and decide to relieve Moneybags of his luggage. You know how industrious those people can be, right? They surround the hotel and start blasting away with automatic weapons. And the only thing protecting this guy was his hired heat and that was becoming a little shaky.

"Moneybags started radioing for help—but just about then, all the radios in the town began crapping out, including those at the airport. He *was* able to get word out on a walkie-talkie that any mercenary group who could mount a rescue mission to the hotel would get a half million pure.

"Within an hour, local merc teams flooded Mudtown. No one big, just ten- to twelve-guy outfits. Freelancers. But by now the situation was very screwed up. No one's radio worked, so these guys just went in helter-skelter, with no communications, no nothing. Most of them got chewed up after just a couple blocks, mainly because they were shooting at each other and didn't know it.

"Finally, they agreed to draw lots and take turns going in. As soon as one group became pinned down after a few blocks, another would advance, relieve the first group, and go another few blocks before getting stopped, with another team moving forward to take their place. The leapfrog approach to war. Not that it made a difference. The fistfight in the terminal was about how the half million should be split when someone finally reached Moneybags. Just about everyone had spilled some blood already, so everyone wanted a piece.

"Meanwhile, no one can figure out a way to actually get to the money guy and haul him out. It was chaos. No one was in charge. No one was sober.

"The bar girl told me the local cops were trying to run the show. They were up in the airport's control tower—that's why they weren't paying attention to flight ops. So, I went up there to see if I could angle a little gas from them and get the hell out of there. I find these five guys standing around a planning table, arguing.

"They barely looked up when I walked in. But then one of them did a double take and, you know, looked like he'd seen a ghost. He asked me, 'Are you Hawk Hunter?'

"Turns out he was at Football City with one of the militias during the little war that followed the Big War. He was out there fighting the Reds just like we were. He'd watched the hundred-plane raid from the ground. A real brother, but he couldn't believe I was among the living.

"Before I could say anything, he asked me if I had a plan to get Moneybags out. He just assumed that's what I was there for.

He showed me a map of Mudtown and where the guy's chopper
got shot down and how he was surrounded by hundreds of meth
freaks in this old prewar Holiday Inn.

"The guy said any rescue team would have to act quickly. The
tower still had a walkie-talkie line open to Moneybags, and he'd
told them the twelve hired goons who'd crashed with him had a
contract that was due to run out at dawn the next morning. These
guys weren't especially hard core—more like gofers with guns—
and this was definitely not their scene. They weren't planning to
renew. So, Moneybags was going to be high and dry if someone
didn't get him out toot sweet. I looked at the map and thought—"

Dozer interrupted him. "Don't tell me you took the gig."

Hunter nodded. "Yeah, I did."

Dozer couldn't believe it. "That's more than just a little nuts,
Hawk."

"Some people would think so," he replied with a shrug. "But I
didn't have any money. I didn't have a job. I didn't have anything.
Just because I fell back to Earth doesn't mean my pockets were
filled with gold when I hit. If I wanted to fly, I needed gas, and to
get gas, I needed some cash.

"So I checked out the map and Moneybags's location, then
I told them I'd fly in alone and pull him out. They said, 'Wait a
minute—you can't *fly* in there—it's urban. It's crowded. No place
to land. And we don't have any choppers here.' But I knew it
wouldn't be that much of a problem if I had the right airplane."

"And that airplane was?" Dozer asked.

"Like I said, when I first bounced in, I saw dozens of rigs
parked on the tarmac. All shapes, all sizes. No copters, but there
was one plane that caught my eye. A little bird with big tires."

"You mean that wind-up toy you just landed in?" Dozer asked
from behind a cloud of cigar smoke. "I'm surprised you're not
wearing the big clown shoes that go with it."

Hunter nodded. "Yeah, thanks for that. It turns out it had
been abandoned there by some merc who'd bought the farm
early in the fighting. The tower guys had no idea what kind of
plane it was. But I did. It was a half-size STOL Highlander. Ever
hear of them?"

Dozer shook his head no.

"They can land on a dime," Hunter said. "And I mean, almost literally. High lift wing. Tiny frame, but big control surfaces. A powerful engine—and really freaking loud. They used them up in Alaska before the Big War to get hunters and sports fishermen into inaccessible areas, but I'm guessing by the circus colors, this one performed at air shows, because it also has a kind of improvised short-term hovering ability using oversize wing slats. Whatever the case, if the pilot knew what he was doing, he could land it in about five feet.

"I told them to tell Moneybags to be ready to move the moment his bodyguards quit. The Mudtown freaks gave the goons a free pass to get out in the morning—less trouble for them to deal with when they went in and rolled this guy.

"I took off in this weird little airplane and flew over Mudtown; it was about five minutes before sunrise, so we were cutting it real close. There were meth heads all over the streets going crazy, firing on this hotel and really tearing up the place. But to their credit, Moneybags's goons were still firing back, and they had some big guns. Thirty calibers. A couple big fifties. Maybe even a flamethrower. It was insane. And no one was looking up, and they sure couldn't hear anything, so I doubt if anyone spotted me. Still, there was a thunderstorm blowing in from the west, so I flew into it, to hide in the clouds for a little while, someplace I was sure nobody could see me.

"The sun came up, and Moneybags's private goon squad punched the clock. I could see them running out of the hotel and climbing aboard two trucks the mooks must have given them to get them out of the way. Anyway, that was the signal for Moneybags to head for the roof."

"The roof?" Dozer said, nearly spitting out a gulp of whiskey.

"I couldn't land in the street," Hunter said with another shrug. "Too much rubble, too many dirt nappers, too much lead flying around. Besides, that little plane really *can* land on a dime. The secret is those big tires. You need something to absorb that initial shock of setting down. If something can eat up that energy, you won't need to roll more than a few feet. The bigger the tires, the shorter the landing.

"So that's what I did. Just as the Mudtown mooks started their attack for real, I landed on the hotel's roof. Came down in one bounce—the plane worked as advertised. In that split second, you know what those clown wheels are all about.

"That's when the storm arrived, and it started raining like crazy. Thunder, lightning, and so much firing going on; the mooks were just pulverizing the bottom floor of the hotel. It was so loud and confusing, I started wondering if anyone even knew I'd landed.

"So, I start looking around for Moneybags. Tracers were going over my head; all kinds of ordnance flying around. The thunder was tremendous, and there were lightning strikes like, just a few feet away. But that's when it really got weird. . . ."

Dozer almost did another spit take. "Really? It's going to get weird now?"

Hunter plowed on. "Moneybags finally shows up, carrying his luggage and running like a madman toward me from the other end of the roof. But right behind him are three more people, wrapped in blankets, and they're running my way, too. I'm thinking, what the hell is this? No one said anything about him having friends. Besides, I'm flying a very small airplane.

"Anyway, they're all soaking wet from the deluge, and I can hardly see them for the rain. I grab Moneybags, pull him in, and stuff him in the back, then I fit the other three in the front somehow. Meanwhile, the meth heads have finally figured out what's going on, and now they're firing mortar rounds up at us. I manage to turn the plane around, hit the throttle, and get out of there."

Dozer held up his hand. "I guess I can understand how these toy airplanes can land short—but taking off?"

"It's a little more complicated," Hunter admitted. "What you do is gun the engine and fly off the side of the building. You go straight down—but only for a few seconds, until you get some air under the wing. Then you pull up into a stall, lower those big wing slats, and the plane stands on its tail almost like you're hovering. The big tires help that, too, because it takes a couple of moments for the momentum to stop and the weight to transfer. Then you hit throttles again, and off you go, straight up."

Dozer rubbed his temples. "I'm nauseous just thinking about it."

"So was Moneybags," Hunter went on. "He was hanging out the open window barfing the whole way back to the airport. He was a mess. Very embarrassing—especially in front of his girls."

"'Girls?'" Dozer asked.

Hunter nodded again. "The three unexpected friends were three gorgeous blondes. One hotter than the next. I couldn't believe it when I was peeling them out of the airplane back at the airport and their blankets finally fell off."

Dozer filled their whiskey glasses again. "Just how 'gorgeous,' may I ask?"

"I can show you exactly," Hunter said. "But this is where everything *really* starts to go south."

He retrieved a photo from the same pocket where he kept the tiny American flag and handed it to Dozer. The marine took one look and nearly fell off his chair. The picture was of an absolutely striking blonde, wearing a tuxedo jacket, nylons, and very little else. Sitting in a chair, low-cut blouse, staring right out at the camera. And those eyes . . .

Incredibly, Dozer knew her. It was Dominique, Hunter's longtime girlfriend. And he'd seen this picture before. Thousands had been passed around the country during what people called the Circle War, a brutal conflict fought not long after the Big War ended and caused by the Russians creating an alliance of the worst anti-America gangs in the country. With superspy Viktor Robotov pulling the strings, the Circle went to war with the United Americans, a newly created alliance of patriotic groups battling to resurrect the United States, including Hunter and the 7CAV. This was when the Russians brought the Mongol hordes all the way over from Siberia to ransack America, only to find out horse cavalry was a painfully easy target for airpower, especially when Hawk Hunter was leading the attack. The Circle was eventually destroyed, causing Robotov to disappear for a while.

But early in the hostilities, this same photo of Dominique had been distributed by the Circle as a form of propaganda, a kind R-rated recruiting poster that appealed to every scumbag in the country. Not only was it of pinup quality—and back then, people hung them up *everywhere*—the underlying big lie was enticing: "Even Hunter's girlfriend has joined us. She is our queen. Fight for her."

It was crazy, it shouldn't have worked, but it did. Dominique's beauty brought thousands into the opposition army. A very weird episode in postwar America.

"Dominique. . . ." Dozer whispered, still studying the photo. "I haven't heard her name come up in a very long time. She's been off the radar at least since you went up in the shuttle."

He handed the photo back to Hunter. "But what was Moneybags doing with a copy of this? I'm surprised any of them are left unstained."

"Turns out Moneybags is a talent agent," Hunter replied. "He informed me of this after he finally stopped blowing lunch. He's also the one who told me the Reds had taken over New York City, and then he admitted he was working for some big-shot Russian Army officer up there. This officer had sent him across the country looking for a very particular kind of girl that some higher-up Russian officers in New York were demanding. We're talking expensive prostitutes. That's why he had all that money."

"I'm not sure I follow," Dozer said, puzzled.

Hunter held up the photo of Dominique again.

"He was looking for women who look like Dominique," he said with weary emphasis. "And this is the photo he was given to find women who were the closest matches. As strange as it sounds, it's a status symbol among the high Red officers in New York to have a girlfriend who looks like Dominique."

Dozer was almost speechless. "That's very screwy, even for the Russians."

"It gets screwier," Hunter said. "Moneybags knew who I was right away, so he knew of my connection to Dominique. He paid me the silver reward, and then he actually apologized for what he was doing—said it was just a job, bringing high-priced call girls who just happen to look like my girlfriend to New York City. But he promised me on the spot that he'd give up the gig, let the three beauties go and leave the area."

"Sounds like a wise decision on his part," Dozer agreed.

"Yes—but he still felt he owed me a favor," Hunter went on. "So before he left . . . he told me where Dominique is living."

"No kidding?"

Hunter just nodded and swigged his drink.

"Hey, nice work," Dozer told him, knocking the ashes from his shrinking cigar. "And you didn't have to beat it out of him. Points for that. So . . . where is she?"

Hunter dejectedly glanced over his shoulder toward New York City.

"Up there?" Dozer asked. "With the Reds?"

"Right in the middle of the Big Red Apple," Hunter confirmed darkly. "Living in Midtown at a very secure location. Word on the street says she's the mistress of one of the very top Russians. *That's* why all the underling officers want girls who look like her. It's one way to kiss the boss's ass."

"Wow," was all Dozer could say. This *was* crazy.

"I've been going nuts ever since he told me," Hunter went on. "I keep asking myself the same questions, over and over. Why would Dominique be involved with the Russians? Is she a prisoner waiting to be rescued, or . . . is she a high-priced escort, discovered by some other talent scout? I mean if she's on the arm of some big shot up there, and all his flunkies want call girls who look exactly like her, doesn't it stand to reason that she's a . . ."

He stopped right there. It was no mere dalliance he'd had with Dominique. They had a long history together. He'd met her in the darkest days following World War III. Moving alone through the devastated French countryside after the fighting had stopped, he'd needed shelter one night, and she'd given it to him. They'd fallen in love within minutes. Not only was she gorgeous, she was smart and funny and had a good heart. And Hunter had made her laugh—and sometimes that's all that was needed. They'd parted painfully soon afterward, but then Dominique had surprised him a few months later when she'd made it over from France to be with him in what had once been the United States.

Because of the battles that followed, though, they'd been forced apart so many times even Hunter didn't know the exact

number. He was always being pulled in two directions. He wanted
to be with Dominique, but he wanted to fight for his country as
well. It was an ongoing struggle. Eventually, they'd withdrawn
to a hay farm named Skyfire, on the elbow of Cape Cod. They'd
wanted to lie low for a while and just be with each other. But
before long, the times turned chaotic again, and because of the
ever-present danger to America, there were wars Hunter had just
had to go fight—and their time apart grew longer. If he remembered correctly, though, he'd been planning to quit the fight for
good after that one last shuttle mission so he could be with her.

But he never got that chance.

"That's why I've been flying around up there," he told Dozer.
"I had to do *something*, so I started looking for her—from the
air. Sounds crazy now, but at the time, it made sense. I found
a straight road near Trenton next to an old gas tank, and that's
been my base and my runway. I've been camping out there for
about a week, flying at night, trying to sleep during the day."

Their glasses were filled again.

Hunter lowered his voice a notch. He was almost wistful.
"When I flew over the city the first time, Bull, the most bizarre
sensation went through me. You know how I have this sort of
extrasensory thing . . ."

Dozer nodded. One of the elements that made Hunter such a
great pilot was a kind of internal radar he had, a type of ESP that
clicked on whenever enemy aircraft were approaching, warning
him in advance to get ready for a fight. He didn't talk much about
this mysterious talent, but all his friends had seen it in action.

"Well, in the same way, I could *feel* a presence when I was
up there flying around," Hunter went on. "It was very freaking
strong. And I'm thinking it *must* be Dominique. So I couldn't
help myself. I kept going back—and I kept feeling it. Buzzing
around in that circus plane, looking into the penthouses of these
three identical skyscrapers on Fifth Avenue—that's where Moneybags said she'd be, most likely. I'll tell you, it seemed like a
party was going on every time I cruised by one of those places.
I could tell: lots of booze, lots of sex. I used to wonder if I was
going to look into a bedroom window one night and see her in

there, between the sheets, doing you know what. But that didn't stop me. I became obsessed.

"Then two nights ago, I caused a ruckus on the top floor of one of those buildings. People right up against the penthouse windows saw me do the hovering act, and I think it really scared a few of them inside. I couldn't see all their faces, but I did see her. Or someone who looked a lot like her. It was only for a second, just a glimpse, before I started flying horizontal again. But it was enough to make me go back.

"So, the next time I showed up, which was last night, they started shooting at me. A couple of Yaks tried to grease me, and then they had gun trucks firing from everywhere. They even lit off a huge SA-2 SAM. But I was able to dodge it all until I ran into some debris caused by something going off, an RPG maybe, and I found my way here."

He let his voice trail off for a moment and took a long drink of whiskey.

"I *know* she's somewhere in New York City, Bull," he said. "And after tonight, I think I know *exactly* which building she's in. Moneybags told me she was in one of the three cookie-cutter skyscrapers along Fifth, but I think he was one building off for some reason. Before I got shot tonight, I had this incredible wave of intuition, and it was telling me that she might be inside the taller building next door, the one with the big red star on top of it. I didn't see anything inside when I went around it, but the vibes I felt once I came close were overwhelming."

Another swig of whiskey.

"If she's anywhere, it's there," he said again. "I just know it. But again, is she a prisoner or a princess? That's what I *don't* know. And that's why I've just got to get back up there and find out for sure."

Dozer shook his head gravely. "I would caution against that, my friend. That would be extremely dangerous, especially if the Russians are so pissed now they're willing to shoot big-ass SAMs at you. Plus, what happens if you do find her? A one-man rescue mission?"

"I've done it before," Hunter told him. "I rescued her from New York City years ago. From another high-rise, in fact."

"But the city wasn't crawling with sixty thousand Russians back then," Dozer reminded him. "And all this heavy weaponry. It's a way different place today."

Hunter leaned back in his chair and studied Dominique's photo again.

"But I still need to do it, Bull," he said finally. "I mean, look at me. I don't even know what fucking universe I'm in. After everything that's happened to me, I'm still very concerned about this Russian thing, but I just want to find her first. Talk to her. See what's what."

Dozer took his feet off the desk and pulled his chair closer to Hunter's.

"Look, Hawk," he said, "I appreciate that you love her. Everyone does. But time goes by fast these days. What we were all doing six months ago is already history, and what we were doing fifteen years ago is already ancient history. You know what I'm saying?"

Hunter nodded solemnly. "You think she might not want to be . . . rescued?"

Dozer winced at the pain he heard in his friend's voice. But that was exactly what he meant.

"You have to at least consider the possibility," he said. "I mean, this high-level Russian officer she's with must know who she is, and must know how tight you two were. And women like her need protecting these days. And she's attracted to powerful men—like you."

"But would she really switch sides, Bull?" Hunter asked him sincerely. "Or is it maybe I'm actually in *another* universe where things like that don't matter as much? Don't people who've found each other generally stick together here?"

Dozer held up five fingers. "Don't you remember?" he said with a grin. "I've been divorced five times. So you're asking the wrong person."

Hunter paused for a moment, then said, "Well, maybe I *am* in the wrong universe. And maybe in this one Dominique is different and not the same girl I loved. Or maybe I'm in the *right* place and she's just changed.

"But either way . . . I've got to know."

CHAPTER TWELVE

IT HAD ALREADY been a crazy night for the two troopers up in the 7CAV spy tower. But it was about to get stranger.

The excitement of the Wingman's arrival an hour ago had finally settled down. The balloon cam was holding steady in moderate winds. The sky was clear of any other airplanes, friend or foe. The troopers even managed to drink another pot of coffee, flavoring it with some no-name whiskey Dozer left behind.

But at exactly 0130 hours, one of the troopers made an alarming discovery. Using his night-vision goggles to routinely scan the glorified dirt trail that led to the secret base, he saw a large heat source about a half mile to the south.

His partner saw it, too. The heat source was moving, and now they could hear engine noise as well. Some sort of vehicle was coming up the hill and heading right toward the 7CAV base.

Because it was passing through such thick woods, the troopers couldn't make out its exact profile; in the eerie emerald world of night vision, it looked like nothing more than a hot, greenish blob. But this blob was substantial in size and mowing down small trees and bushes as it approached. The troopers grimly surmised that a tank, a mobile gun, or some other kind of tracked weapon was coming their way.

Maybe the first of many.

★ ★ ★

Back at the secret base, Hunter quietly greeted the 7CAV troopers as they came into the Quonset hut for chow.

The Seventh Cavalry ate breakfast at one thirty in the morning these days. Because they were so close to so many enemy troops, the unit was on a night-ops schedule; very active between sunset and sunrise and mostly lying low during the day. These troopers were all astonished to see the hero fighter pilot in flesh and bone, upright and breathing, talking to them as if nothing had happened. It was a little spooky.

Once the buzz died down, Hunter sat with Dozer at a dining table away from the rest of 7CAV. The menu this morning was Dozer's whiskey stew, again. It was the staple of the unit. But while Hunter couldn't remember the last time he'd had a real meal, he passed on taking a bowl for himself. He was too restless to eat.

As Dozer drained three enormous bowls of his own creation, Hunter provided more details about his recent activities.

He'd taken the half million in silver from the talent scout and used some of it to buy the plane with the big wheels from the people who owned Mudtown's airport casino, along with some gas. He'd deconstructed the little aircraft, packed it into a pair of massive emptied-out under-wing fuel tanks, attached them to his F-16XL, and then flew to his secret base in Vermont Territory's Green Mountains. He put the clown plane back together again and commenced his bizarre scouting mission of New York City the following day.

But after the clown plane got hit over the city, he let his instinct take over, and it led him to the Pine Barrens. A good thing, too, because he would have never made it back to the highway in Trenton.

On hearing that, Dozer nodded to the next table over, where the bandaged-up numbers-running Worm was working on his third bowl of stew.

"Cosmic sensory perception in your case," Dozer told Hunter. "Dumbass luck in his."

The conversation came back to the present and what would happen next.

Dozer knew Hunter wanted to return to New York as soon as his clown plane was fixed. But he told the Wingman of his own dilemma of how and where to counterattack the Russians. And of having to go it alone.

Hunter was mystified by Dozer's inability to communicate with their old warrior friends, people who should have been here in a heartbeat after the Russians invaded New York City.

"Nothing on your radio," Hunter said. "Just like nothing was happening on Mudtown's radios either. Very strange."

They got down to the crux of the matter. They had similar goals. Dozer wanted to do something in New York City to hurt the Russians and send a signal to Moscow that this wasn't going to be a free ride. And so did Hunter. But the Wingman also wanted to go back to find Dominique.

"How about we plan something together," Hunter suggested. "I'll help you guys do your thing, then I can go do mine—and find her for real this time."

Dozer didn't argue with him. While he couldn't condone the idea of his friend's crazy one-man rescue mission, he knew that in addition to being the greatest pilot who'd ever lived, Hunter was also an expert war strategist and extremely adept at coming up with ideas out of left field that always seemed to work. That's what the 7CAV needed right now.

Dozer gave him a fist bump.

"You got a deal, Hawk," he said. "But only if you promise not to get killed when you go out solo."

"It will be a piece of cake," Hunter deadpanned. "Either that or a walk in the park."

But Hunter knew none of it was going to be easy. Intelligence collected by the spy tower had allowed 7CAV to piece together the Russians' order of battle—their strengths, their weapons, troop deployments, and resupply. And for the first time in Russia's military history, everything appeared to be moving along smoothly.

Conversely, they knew very little about Russian weaknesses, if they even had any. If a small force like the 7CAV was going to take a swing at such a giant, it would be good to know if the giant had an Achilles' heel.

"That's what really scares me," Dozer told him now. "From what we've seen on the balloon cam, and what we've heard them bragging about on Red Radio, and by keeping tabs on how many of their supply ships have arrived already, they don't seem to lack anything. I think the Reds really thought of everything this time."

"There's always a weakness somewhere," Hunter replied quietly. "The trouble is, sometimes it takes so long to find it, it's too late to do you any good."

Now it was Hunter who motioned toward the Worm, who was still feeding his face.

"We need what he already has," Hunter said. "A big bowl of dumb luck."

The base's intruder-alert alarms went off a moment later.

The next thing Hunter knew, he was behind the wheel of Dozer's jeep, driving like a madman through the night.

Around trees, over gigantic roots, through sand pits and small ravines. There were no roads, no signs—and the jeep didn't have any headlights. Hunter couldn't remember the last time he'd driven anything other than an airplane. Making it worse, he was beyond exhausted and really drunk.

He was at the head of the 7CAV's twenty-four-man Quick Reaction Force as it was speeding toward the one and only way leading into the base. Three 7CAV troop trucks full of heavily armed soldiers followed behind him. The trucks were right on his tail, weaving as he was weaving. It was almost as hairy as flying around the Manhattan skyline.

The only reason Hunter was driving was because Dozer was on the radiophone with the two spy-tower soldiers. They'd spotted a large vehicle of some kind approaching the base—and it was at least the size of a tank. The troopers had called it in, climbed down from the tower, and set up their 50-caliber machine gun at a bend in the dirt trail.

Through it all, Dozer remained unflustered. Cigar clenched between his teeth, bouncing around as if the jeep had no shock absorbers, he was getting a running commentary from the two troopers on what was happening and where the heat blob was.

And at the moment, it was just around the bend from them, seconds from revealing itself. But the quick reaction troops were still a half mile away. No matter how fast Hunter drove, they would not reach the men in time.

Whatever it was, the two troopers would have to take it on alone.

Dozer told them to stay calm and to keep talking to him on the radiophone. When he heard their gasps as the heat blob came around the corner a few moments later, he expected the worst.

The troopers said they were ready to fire and then . . . nothing but silence.

A few long seconds passed.

Still nothing. . . .

Finally, Dozer heard one of the troopers say off the radio: "You've got to be kidding me."

Then the other trooper said directly to Dozer, "Captain . . . you're not going to believe this."

The 7CAV arrived a minute later and found something that was indeed unbelievable.

The two troopers were still in position at the side of the trail, still hunched over their machine gun, but in obvious relief.

Twenty feet in front of them was not a Russian T-72 tank or a Brozi gun truck or any other kind of fierce mobile weapon.

It was a New York City garbage truck.

And only one person had been aboard—the driver, who'd been ordered out of the truck by the two troopers and told to lie face down on the muddy unpaved path, hands spread out in front of him.

The Quick Reaction troops off the first truck sprinted over to him and searched him for weapons. He had none. They pulled him up to a sitting position, while the rest of the team spread out and established a defense perimeter.

The driver was a short, round man with a scraggly gray beard and long matted hair. He was shabbily dressed, and although it was difficult to tell his age, late-thirties would have been a good guess. While his eyes looked wild, he was holding a small American flag in his right hand and was waving it vigorously, making sure everyone could see it.

Carrying an American flag in New York was a punishable offense. Dozer knew whoever this character was, he was taking a huge risk just by having the flag on him.

"I'm a friend!" he was crying, his somewhat distinguished voice not matching his ragged appearance at all. "I'm an American!"

Hunter and Dozer climbed out of the jeep, both carrying M-16s, and walked up to the little man. When he saw Hunter, he almost fainted.

"I knew it! I knew you were still alive."

Hunter looked at Dozer and just shrugged.

"What are you doing out here?" Dozer demanded.

The guy just shook his head and began his strange story.

"I'm a weapons buyer out of the old DC," he said. "I was in New York for a big deal when all of a sudden the Russians are getting off their boats. I mean, I'd heard the mob warnings to stay off the streets the night before, but I didn't think the whole fucking Red Army was coming. They sealed off the city that night.

"I was holding a lot of money and trying to figure out how I could get out of the city without some Russian ripping me off. The weeks went by, and I couldn't find anyone to help me. I was living in an abandoned apartment building down near the Staten Island ferry, and there was a nest of Reds down there, which made walking around in the daytime a scary proposition. Plus, they have those crazy Chekski religious nuts riding around at night, and they're even worse.

"I had a shortwave radio with me, but the freaking thing died just as soon as the Reds came to town. I thought I'd be safer if I changed my appearance to make it look like I didn't have a penny. My hair was pretty radical to begin with, so I let my beard grow and didn't wash my clothes, and in a week, I looked like a typical homeless guy. That allowed me to at least go out and move around, or so I thought.

"Then, this afternoon, I saw the Chekskis execute a bunch of homeless people on Houston Street. Right in the *middle* of the day, probably one hundred and fifty in all. A Russian officer was making some of these poor bastards kneel on the street and beg for their lives. He'd pretend to listen while one of his goons would sneak up in back of the person, slit his throat, then cut his head right off. It gave this officer his jollies. Meanwhile, he looks like a monster himself. He has a scar that runs from ear to ear and makes it look like he is smiling. Sick fucker.

"But there I was looking like a homeless person, and obviously there's some cleansing going on. I realized it was just a matter of time before they got me, too.

"So I prayed that the ghost plane would come again tonight, because when that crazy shit started happening over Rockefeller Plaza, a lot of the Russian soldiers weren't paying attention to anything else, and . . ."

He stopped for a moment and looked up at Dozer and Hunter. "You know what I mean by the 'ghost plane,' don't you? Some weird ass airplane—"

Dozer raised his hand and interrupted him. "Yes—we've heard all about it."

The man went on, "Well, once the crazy airplane showed up, I snuck down to the Staten Island Ferry parking lot—that's where they keep all the buses and the garbage trucks. When everyone climbed up on the roofs to see the ghost plane, I jumped into this rig and just started driving. I left my money behind, my clothes, my gun. I didn't want to get caught carrying any of it, but also I didn't care about any of it, either. I just wanted to get out of there.

"I was waved through the only two checkpoints I came to. The guards didn't even look up at me as I drove by; they were too interested in what was happening over Midtown with the little plane. That's the beauty of stealing a garbage truck. It's not a Cadillac. No one noticed me.

"I thought if I could make it to the Barrens, the Reds probably wouldn't follow me in. They're always on the radio telling their guys to avoid this part of New Jersey, so I figured it would be a good place to hide out.

The man took a deep breath. "And that's my story," he concluded.

Dozer lit his cigar. Suddenly, the 7CAV was in possession of two strangers. Not prisoners exactly, but the men definitely presented complications. Just another little problem to add to 7CAV's list.

Dozer looked over at Hunter and murmured, "Another mouth to feed."

But the Wingman wasn't paying attention; he was studying the garbage truck itself. Then he turned back to the little round man. "Where did you say you stole this from?"

"The ferry parking lot, down by Battery Park, near the commie canteen," he replied.

"And is the back empty or full of garbage?"

"Oh, it's full," the guy said in near-disgust. "I could barely get it to do over thirty-five miles an hour, it's so full."

That's when Hunter's eyes lit up. He turned back to Dozer and said, "Bull, old friend—we might have just gotten 'Worm lucky.'"

Thirty minutes later, the garbage truck was parked at the north end of the 7CAV's runway, where the unit's civilian engineers managed to dump its contents onto the tarmac.

Ten of the civvies volunteered to join Hunter sort through the thirty-foot mound of trash. He was operating on the old theory that going through your enemy's garbage was one of the best ways to get intelligence on him. They all donned yellow hazmat suits, helmets, and gloves, and using bayonets as probes, they waded into the mountain of rubbish, looking for anything useful.

There was a lot of the usual. Discarded food products, general litter, empty alcohol bottles. But also the unusual, including lots of discarded Kremlin propaganda leaflets. Written in both Russian and English, many of the leaflets appeared to have been used as dinner napkins by the Red troops. Hunter found it interesting that the troops didn't pay attention to the Russian high command's spin on things.

Twenty minutes in, he and two civilians stumbled across a large cardboard box, something a washing machine would come in. Oddly, it was wrapped tight with plastic tape. Why would anyone wrap a box they were throwing away? Hunter cut off the tape, and like a suddenly sprung jack in the box, a stream of paper flew out. Discarded computer printouts, thousands of pages, all on serrated, hole-punched paper.

Hunter read the first page and tapped his fist twice on his chest. They'd found a potential treasure chest.

He and the two civilians carried the box over to the Quonset hut and set it down next to Dozer's desk. The civvies then departed with Hunter's thanks. Dozer was sitting in his usual position, feet up on his desk, watching over his two new visitors, the Worm and the weapons dealer, who everyone had begun calling the Trashman.

"Any chance there's a couple of cases of vodka in there?" Dozer asked Hunter, studying the box.

"Maybe better," the Wingman replied.

He moved Dozer's feet and dumped the printouts onto his desk.

"These are the daily food-ration orders for every Russian in New York City," Hunter told him.

"No kidding?" Dozer replied, half seriously.

"Not only do they tell us what they eat and how much," Hunter went on, "they also tell us which unit gets what, and they refer to each unit by name. It covers their entire canteen operation for a few days of last week."

Now Dozer recognized the value of the find. At the very least, they'd get an accurate idea of how many Russian soldiers were inside the city and what kind of units they were in, whether they be combat, support, or engineering. But they also might be able to find some hidden weakness, a much sought-after Achilles' heel they could exploit to make the Russians bleed a little.

Sitting at a table nearby, the Trashman was gulping down hot coffee, while across the table from him, the Worm was eating more stew.

Dozer called over to the ragged little arms dealer. "You risked a lot to come out here. And you brought us something we might be able to use. So we owe you."

"How about getting my ass out of here, then?" the little man replied. "I don't care if it ain't DC. I'll go anywhere. Just as long as it's not New York. Those Russians freak me out, man."

Dozer looked at Hunter, who just shrugged.

"We'll see what we can do," Dozer said.

They spread the printouts across the barracks floor and then started reading them, crawling from one pile to the next, drinking coffee mixed with whiskey.

The pages showing food tallies listed large quantities of potatoes, bread, preserved meats, plus the makings for all kinds of soup. Because the Russians had either hired or forced some unlucky New Yorkers to do kitchen work, the lists were printed in both Russian and English.

Many of the army pages specified which units were to be fed, at what time, and how much food they would need per man, per unit, per certain day. So the specialty of each unit was mentioned many times over: infantry, armor, engineers, transportation.

The navy lists were the same, only simpler: warships and supply ships. The Russians didn't sail anything else, so you were either on one or the other and *that* was your specialty when it came to food distribution.

But what amazed Hunter and Dozer was the number of specialist units in the third branch of the *Okupatsi*, the one known as Military Operations Personnel. Paint squads, sign squads, and traffic squads were routinely cited on the meal lists. Carpenters, plumbers, pipe fitters, metal workers, diesel mechanics, computer techs—even soldiers assigned to trim the foliage and cut the grass in Central Park.

It was dawn by the time they reached the end of the computer printouts.

Now they had a much clearer picture of how many Russians were in the occupation force—64,500 or so by Dozer's count—and the amount of combat equipment they had in the city and floating offshore, which was a lot.

But as far as finding any weaknesses in the Reds' order of battle, they'd come up empty. The Kremlin had apparently addressed every last detail of the *Okupatsi*, so they had no weak spots. In other words, for Hunter and Dozer, no Holy Grail.

Exhausted, they finished yet another pot of coffee and sat on the floor.

"They'll be building a fucking dome over the city next," Dozer said wearily. "Because they probably brought a bunch of fucking dome engineers with them."

For some reason, at that moment, Hunter recalled someone once describing Jazz to him as the music found between the notes. What was not there was just as important as what was.

He suddenly sat up. Could the real value of the printouts come from what they *didn't* tell them?

He began scanning the lists again; one page he'd seen had stuck in his mind. Because all the food for the occupation forces came out of the enormous Russian canteen near Battery Park, it was easy to follow how much went to what ground unit and when. It was the same for every ship in the harbor; which ship got what and how much. While the Russian ground units never complained about the amount of food they received, the Russian sailors were constantly asking for more. No matter how much they were already getting, every ship wanted more meat, more potatoes, more ice cream.

Except for one . . . a cargo vessel called the *Bruynyzi*. The ship's name was on the list of vessels requiring canteen service once the invasion began. But that was nearly five weeks ago, and the ship had yet to complain about its daily complement of chow. Why would this crew have manners when none of the others did?

Hunter went back to a graph showing the amount of food sent to navy ships in the past five weeks and discovered the *Bruynyzi* hadn't received any at all, never mind asking for seconds. Could all this mean the ship hadn't made it to New York City?

He began tossing the printouts aside; he was looking for just one page now: a certain sheet that broke down every supply ship's crew and passengers by name and rank. This told you what unit was traveling aboard what ship and what they did in the order of battle.

He finally found the sheet for the *Bruynyzi*—and with it, the Holy Grail.

The *Bruynyzi* was actually an oceangoing car ferry, another civilian ship the Russians had converted for military use. It was carrying yet another MOP unit and all their equipment. But it was the unit's specialty that held the key.

Hunter crawled across the floor to where Dozer had passed out and shook his old friend awake.

"I think the Reds *are* missing something critical," he told the sleepy officer. "Not because they forgot it, but because it hasn't arrived yet."

Dozer replied with a yawn, "Please . . . tell me."

Suddenly, Hunter couldn't stop smiling. The Russians had engineers, plumbers, electricians, and painters. Mechanics and computer techs, doctors and nurses, sanitation experts and bus drivers, even arborists. The list went on and on.

But . . .

"This ship was supposed to arrive the first night of the invasion," Hunter told Dozer. "Maybe it broke down or got lost or sank or something. But I think one thing's for sure, it never made it here."

"So?" Dozer asked with another yawn.

"Look at what it was carrying," Hunter urged him.

Dozer read the sheet and then sat straight up.

The *Bruynyzi* was carrying five one hundred–man companies of the First Moscow Fire Brigade, plus five squadrons of fire trucks, one hundred and twenty five vehicles in all.

"Holy crap," Dozer exclaimed softly. "They don't have a fire department."

CHAPTER THIRTEEN

May 6

IT WAS COMPLETELY dark. No moon. No clouds. No wind. No noise.

Until 2330 hours exactly. That's when the camouflage netting over 7CAV's hidden base slowly opened up.

Then came the growl of airplane engines. Nine in all, coughing to life, the smallest much louder than the rest. Their combined roar washed through the Pine Barrens, shaking the trees and scaring the ghosts.

Inside of a minute, the 7CAV's four Sherpa airplanes were lined up on the runway, awaiting the order to take off.

It had been a long, intense day for Hunter, Dozer, and the men of the 7CAV.

They'd spent most of it on the quartet of homely Sherpa cargo planes. The freight humpers had undergone a startling transformation in the past twelve hours. Each plane now had six machine-gun positions: one in the nose, two on each side, and one in the back next to the access ramp, doubling the crew on each. The planes' old gray dispersion paint scheme had been replaced with jet-black camouflage, nose to tail. An enormous American flag had been painted on both sides of their fuselages just behind the wing.

But the biggest alteration to the Sherpas had taken place inside their cargo bays. All nonessential equipment had been stripped out and large improvised bomb racks had been put in. Then each plane was loaded with a dozen extremely unusual bombs.

By sunset, the venerable Seventh Cavalry had been turned on its head. It still consisted of the same men under the same commander and possessed the same patriotic thirst to hit back against the Russian invaders . . . but technically the 7CAV was no longer a ground attack unit. It was now in the air-assault business.

At 2335 hours, the Sherpas got the go-code to launch.

One after another, they took off, their propellers aided by homemade JATO bottles under their wings. These temporary rocket boosters provided the extra lift needed for the overloaded planes to rise into the night.

Only the noisy fifth plane was left on the runway. Hunter's clown car with wings. Taped and glued and wired back together, it looked stranger than ever.

Dozer was having a shouted conversation with Hunter while the Wingman was doing one last check of his control surfaces. The marine wasn't exactly in a good place, though. He was trying to reason with Hunter.

"You've taken people up in this thing before," he was shouting in Hunter's ear. "There must be room in there for me. I'll be able to help you."

But Hunter wasn't having any of it.

"I'm not taking you," he said, loading some rope and a hastily made three-prong grappling hook into his cockpit. They'd been through it all day. "Like I said, if we both buy the farm, who's going to run your outfit? Too many people count on you—and when that happens, then you truly *are* the commanding officer. And that's when the book says you don't go on combat missions."

Dozer had reached his frustration level. "So how about the people who count on *you*?" he retorted sharply.

Hunter just shrugged. "I was already dead, remember? People stopped counting on me a long time ago."

Dozer threw his cigar on the ground and started to walk away. Hunter felt terrible, but he just had to do this mission alone. Still, there was something he'd wanted to tell his old friend since coming here—and now might be the last time he'd be able to do it.

"Hey, Bull," Hunter yelled.

Dozer walked the few steps back over to the cockpit.

"Listen," Hunter began, "I'm pretty sure I'm not in the exact same place I'd been when I left in the shuttle. It's real close, but a few things are different."

Hunter looked at his old friend now. He'd been trying to hone his memory, and he was certain now that before he'd gone on that last shuttle mission, Dozer had been killed fighting Viceroy Dick's army in the Battle of Indianapolis. That's why, the night before, he'd had such a hard time believing he was really seeing and talking to his old friend. He was going to tell Dozer this because he felt it was something the marine officer should know.

But at the last instant, he stopped himself. Why mention it at all? Bull was here, alive. Other things—and other people—might be different, but in this case, it was actually like a small miracle. Who gets to meet a good friend, living and breathing again, after that friend has passed on?

At that moment, Hunter knew for sure all bets were off. If Dozer was here in this place, but was dead in the time and place Hunter had been in before, then there was a chance that Dominique was not the same woman he'd once loved. Or maybe, even worse, she had simply changed and traded in her beautiful heart for a dark one. He had to find out. That's why this mission was so important.

Switching gears smoothly, he hoped, he said to his old friend, "I just wanted to say you haven't changed a bit, buddy. And take it from me, you're a good guy in at least two universes."

Dozer put a new cigar between his teeth and lit it. Then he grinned widely.

"Good to know," he said.

Then he tapped Hunter twice on the shoulder and was gone.

Hunter did one last check of his flight panel, closed his canopy, and pulled away. The little aircraft rolled down the runway for barely five feet before its engine let out a scream and its nose lifted dramatically.

At full throttle, its wings slotted back, the clown plane ascended straight up, through the hole in the roof, and into the night.

All this activity was a result of the deal Hunter and Dozer had made earlier.

Their objective was to bring the fight to the Russians, giving the 7CAV a chance to make them hurt somewhere while providing Hunter with the cover he needed to carry out his second, more personal mission.

While nothing they did this night could adequately address the mammoth problem of dislodging sixty-five thousand enemy troops from New York City, at least it would give the invaders and their masters in Moscow something to think about.

This is why no one had worked harder that day than Hunter himself. He knew the men aboard the newly lethal Sherpas would be risking their lives, not just to make a statement to the world about the Russian occupation of New York City, but also to allow him to do his thing. He had to make sure that before they left the ground, he had given them every possible advantage to survive the mission.

In addition to designing and helping install the planes' new gun stations, he'd written a complete flight plan for the Sherpas to follow. Not only did it include an exact release point for the "barrel bombs," which would allow them to hit most effectively, he also built in a huge safety factor for the plane crews.

They immediately dubbed it the Goldilocks Zone. It was a combat altitude of exactly three thousand feet that would give them the best chance to get to the target unscathed and escape the same way. Why three thousand? Because Hunter knew the truck-borne machine guns that had fired at him earlier could only reach two thousand feet with any effectiveness. And a giant SA-4 SAM couldn't hit anything below four thousand feet without blowing up first. If the Sherpa pilots stayed at three thousand feet while over the city, then two of the Russians' most deadly weapons couldn't touch them.

Not too hot, not too cold. Just right—the Goldilocks Zone.

Once airborne, the four Sherpas quickly formed a chevron over the base. Taking up position at the nose of the V was the little plane with the big wheels.

Then the five planes turned northeast.

Just beyond the horizon, the crews could already see the crimson glow of Russkiy-NYC.

CHAPTER FOURTEEN

DOMINIQUE WAS NAKED.

Lying in a huge, white oval bathtub in the penthouse at 30 Rock, suds covering half her body, she was methodically washing herself, scrubbing every bit of her skin over and over again. She'd done this at least twice a day for the past four weeks.

Commissar Zmeya could see her from the bed. He'd told her to keep the door ajar while she bathed, and she'd obeyed. He'd been watching her for about thirty minutes, and there had not been a word between them. Yet he'd become intensely aroused by the view.

He still hadn't been able to figure her out; that's what made her so fascinating. Sizing up people was his business. Strong or weak. Brave or cowardly. Sexy or not. He'd met only one kind of woman during his dramatic rise to the top of the NKVD: the Americans called them starfuckers. Women who wanted to be with him because he was powerful. Unpleasantries such as the sight of a little blood before lovemaking or rougher antics during the act had not dissuaded any of them. Hours or even days of carnal romping usually followed, until it was time for them to go.

But Dominique?

She was different.

She'd been waiting for him when he first arrived at Battery Park. It was the third night of the *Okupatsi*, and his own personal cruiser, the *Zosef*, had just endured two weeks on the rough Atlantic. While he did not get seasick during the voyage, he was glad to get back on land.

Because his ETA had been kept a secret, when the *Zosef* pulled up to the dock just before midnight, few were there to notice except the cooks working in the huge canteen nearby. The landing area had been previously swept and secured by naval marines. They'd been quickly replaced by Zmeya's own personal bodyguards.

It had rained all day and was raining still when the ship tied up. Fog mixed with the smoke and steam coming from the giant outdoor kitchen made the visibility almost zero. Zmeya recalled thinking, *Is New York always this dreary?*

With his arrival, the Kremlin's propaganda ministry planned to distribute millions of flyers around the world saying, "Law and Order has reached America" in the form of the famous Commissar Zmeya. When informed he was being branded as the toughest man in the world, Zmeya couldn't say no.

But a photo of him stepping off his ship would be required. He and his security people had been told to expect a MOP photographer and an assistant at the dock. But when they came down the ship's gangway, there was only one person waiting for them.

It was Dominique.

Their eyes met, and Zmeya felt a surge of electricity go through him. He knew who she was immediately, while the security people around him—dumb peasants, all of them—had no idea. In this apocalyptic video-game world of global conquest and heroes and villains, she was a celebrity. And so was he. It was as if they knew each other already.

But what was she doing here?

She was holding a camera with a flash attached. It could have been a gun in disguise, Zmeya had supposed, or a bomb. But in that instant, he couldn't imagine the famous Hawk Hunter's equally famous girlfriend performing a suicide mission. If this was an assassination attempt, the Wingman would have done it himself. And if he was dead as everyone thought, certainly one of his band of merry American patriots would have stepped in.

No, this was something different. This was a woman being bold.

He'd not realized until then how hauntingly beautiful she was. Blond hair, porcelain skin, enormous blue eyes. A face that could launch a thousand ships. She was dressed in an all-black formal MOP uniform, but with alterations. The blouse was form fitting with three top buttons undone. The uniform skirt was very short. She was wearing dark stockings and knee-high boots. Hair tied back, a hint of eye shadow.

Zmeya remembered saying to himself, *I must have this.*

His bodyguards quickly surrounded her, but she'd seemed unaffected by them. She explained in perfect Russian that her commander at MOP had been detained, unable to come, possibly a security issue.

Then she simply asked Zmeya, "So? Can *I* take your picture?"

He'd nodded eagerly, and she snapped off two rolls of film. Then he shooed his security men away so he could talk to her alone.

Of all people, why would the girlfriend of the famous, if departed, Hawk Hunter be welcoming him to New York City? He was completely stumped, not the natural state of affairs for him.

Once out of earshot, he asked her incredulously, "Why are you here? Why would you do such a thing?"

Her answer stunned him.

"I wanted to meet you," she said simply. "I'm attracted to powerful men."

They began living together immediately, mostly in the apartment in the sky.

While he spent his day approving things like a pilot genocide program on the city's homeless, trial runs for hugely expanded NKVD operations in the near future, or a law that would tax all of New York's civilians for essentials like food and water, she'd passed the time dressing up in slinky outfits and wandering about the penthouse, poking into things here and there, reading anything interesting left lying about.

Many times at night, though, if he could skip out on his official duties, they'd stay at a suite he'd arranged for her at the old Ritz-Carlton on Central Park South, where it was much more peaceful. Plus, the place gave him plausible deniability should the Kremlin deem it unfit for the toughest guy in the world to be living with a girl he'd just met. Dominique was funny and smart and hip and sexy. They would stay up nights on end just talking or watching some of his homemade porn. She teased him unmercifully—and faithfully reminded him to take his meds.

It was a strange romance, though. As monstrous as ever in his day job, he had calmed down in his personal life. He hadn't thrown any of his drunken, murderous parties in New York, at least not so far. And although his terrarium had been set up, it had not been used yet. He'd told his top people, including the members of CRPP, that he would not tolerate any acts of sexual brutality anywhere—until further notice.

His personal appearance had also improved. Now his hair was always combed, his posture had straightened up overnight, and he shaved just once every three days. This was all Dominique's doing. She was helping him turn it up a notch, and he liked it. It made him feel even more powerful.

Soon after that fateful night at the docks, he told one of his former mistresses, a member of the Cutie squad, that by getting Dominique, he felt that the last piece of a very big puzzle had finally fallen into place.

Then came the navy penthouse incident two nights before. Three medical officers had been on hand, and they had diagnosed her sudden lightheadedness and dizziness as a result of a lack of sleep or a potassium deficiency.

But he knew it was neither of these things. In reality, she had swooned because she'd experienced both an emotional and physical fright in the instant she saw the plane's pilot.

Literally, as if she'd seen a ghost.

Last night, they'd watched the battle with the ghost plane from their bedroom window atop 30 Rock. Or at least Zmeya had.

His security people wanted to evacuate them at the beginning of the craziness, either by helicopter or ground transport,
but Zmeya had refused to leave. He'd also refused to let anyone
else leave the building. He'd wanted to see it all up close, and so
should they.

He'd shouted encouragement first to the Yaks, then the
Brozis, and finally, for a few seconds, to the SA-2 SAM missile.
But when it obliterated Chelsea Piers, the worst luck possible for
the *Okupatsi*, he began to boil, throwing things and cursing.

Dominique had covered her eyes during the whole thing.
Even when he demanded that she watch the ghost plane's pilot
get what was coming to him, she'd refused. And when he'd asked
her why she acted so odd when the bug plane was flying around
and was it because her old paramour was behind the controls,
she'd shot back that her old boyfriend had died long ago and
he was cruel to bring it up. But he didn't believe her, and at that
moment, it had made him even more furious. The instant he'd
seen Chelsea Piers blow up, he'd grabbed her by the arm and
locked her and himself inside the penthouse's windowless, heavily armored safe room. He'd raged for two hours until she'd
finally convinced him to take his medication.

Up to that point, this had been the most enjoyable month of
Zmeya's life.

Now, he poured himself a glass of mineral water from the nightstand.

He could hear a party starting up with the members of CRPP
and their Dominique look-alikes one floor below. Despite the
disaster the night before, there were small bashes going on all
across the city, military officers celebrating the demise of the
ghost plane.

Though the army people were proudly trumpeting that one
of their own had shot down the aerial pest, Zmeya was too smart
to believe it. He always insisted on seeing the corpse before
declaring an adversary dead.

No, the ghost plane was still out there. He could feel it. And
he no longer had any doubt who was at the controls. The god-

damn Wingman. He was sure of it after the other night. The way the bug was flying, its amazing aerial stunts, and especially Dominique's reaction said it all. And while enemies were useful because failures could always be blamed on them, Zmeya wished with all his dark heart that Hawk Hunter would just stay dead.

He looked down on the city and sighed. *His* city, as he liked to think of it. Heavily damaged the night before but solely by self-inflicted wounds. The question was: Where would they go from here?

When he turned back again, Dominique was sitting on the edge of the bed, staring at him.

She was wrapped only in a towel, and a small one at that. Her skin was still glistening from her bath. The edges of her hair were wet and curling, a hairdo he'd never seen on her before. It reignited his lust.

"You're amazingly quiet," he told her. "You'd make a good spy."

"How many women have met their end on a bed like this with you?" she asked in her lightly French-accented voice.

He shrugged. "Seven?"

"Is that all?" she said, drying her hair with a second towel. "I expected more."

He reached out and tried to grab her, but she inched just far enough away to be out of his reach.

"Have sex with me," he said in a faux-stern tone. Another odd facet of their relationship was that they'd yet to engage in full relations.

"Why?" she asked. "So I can be number eight?"

"But isn't that alone enough to excite you? The ecstasy of it? Not knowing . . ."

"If I'll ever see the sunrise?" she finished his sentence for him. "Maybe if I were a vampire."

"You didn't know what was going to happen that night down at the dock," he told her.

She drew closer and ran her fingers gently down his chest, stopping just above his crotch.

"Of course I did," she cooed.

Zmeya knew he was incapable of loving another human being—he'd been diagnosed as such. But the closest he'd come so far was with this woman.

"You said you liked powerful men," he insisted. "And I'm a powerful man. . . . And I'm a hero to some, too. I *know* you like that. . . ."

That was another thing. Trust her or not, on a carnal level, Dominique's once having been the Wingman's girlfriend was the pinnacle of excitement for him.

"Tell me now," he asked her, not for the first time. "How do you think I'd compare to your famous Wingman?"

She coyly deflected the question with a question of her own. "Why? Do you wish I were someone else?"

Her being coquettish about it was another turn-on. But the fact that the CRPP members had sent out a picture of the real Dominique in order to get girlfriends who were clones of her spoke volumes.

"Have sex with me," he said, trying again. "Please . . ."

"Not yet," she said with a laugh, throwing her hair towel at him.

Those damn two words. He hated them.

"Why make me wait another moment?" he beseeched her.

"So you'll enjoy it more when it comes," she said. "I plan to teach you the tantric way of doing things. The more time you take, the better it is."

She put on a long T-shirt and nothing more.

Zmeya sat up on the bed, narrowing his eyes. "I could make you do it. Right here, right now."

She just laughed at him again. "If you need something right here, right now, then you'd better do it yourself."

He flopped back down on the pillows, foiled again.

A moment later, 30 Rock began shaking.

The tremors were so powerful that Zmeya fell clear off the bed. Dominique immediately went to her knees and crawled into the corner. At the same moment, an incredibly bright flash of light lit up all of southern Manhattan. Then came an earsplitting roar. Dominique braced herself, blocking her ears. It was like the building was about to topple over.

"Do you have nukes with you?" she called across the room to him. It was a strange question.

Then, just as quickly, the shaking stopped.

Zmeya got to his feet and ran to the window. He saw a massive tongue of flame shooting up from the South Street Seaport area. Not a nuke, but a very large conventional explosion.

"The fuel ship," he called to her over his shoulder. "The *Boleska*—it just blew up."

There was a large red suitcase at the foot of their bed; something inside began beeping. Zmeya hurried over to it, undid the locks, and opened it. Inside was a special NKVD radiophone; it could talk only to other NKVD radiophones and was designed to be eavesdrop-proof.

Zmeya picked up the handset and extended the antenna. A readout on the radio's dial told him someone was calling him from his security room, where the party had just started downstairs.

"What have those navy fools done now?" he shouted into the phone.

For the Russian sailors serving aboard the air barge docked near the South Street Seaport, it was supposed to have been a quiet night.

Red Radio had promised as much. Just before evening chow was delivered, an army spokesman had made a special broadcast, speaking first in Russian and then in English.

While the entirety of Chelsea Piers had been destroyed by the crash of the wayward SA-4 SAM missile, the good news was that the ghost plane, the cause of it all, had been shot down by an army colonel named Samsonov.

The weird little aircraft was gone for good; peace had been restored.

The first indication that it *wasn't* going to be a peaceful night for the sailors came just before midnight.

The sun had set long ago, but the East River's waterfront was lit up, as was most of the Manhattan skyline. The Yak barge crew was relaxing out on their floating tarmac, their two VTOL fighter planes tied down nearby, when they suddenly heard a combination of unmistakable sounds.

The loud raspy engine, the whining propeller, an eerie whistling on the wind . . .

It was the ghost plane. True to its name, it was back from the dead.

The plane was flying very fast and very low across the East River, coming right at them from over Brooklyn. Before they realized what was happening, the little circus plane had gone over their heads, giant wheels and all.

They heard its engine screech; its nose went nearly straight up—and suddenly the plane was hovering in midair. Not over the Yaks' air barge, but over the vessel docked next to it, the fuel ship, *Boleska*. . . .

They saw the cockpit window get pulled back and the pilot drop a small package down the *Boleska*'s smoke stack. Then the strange little plane dropped back down to level flight and shot away like a bullet.

The air barge crew were all veterans of the recent war in Europe. They all knew what was going to happen next. They immediately jumped off the barge into the chilly waters of the East River.

The *Boleska* blew up two seconds later.

By dropping an explosive device down the fuel ship's stack, the ghost pilot had ignited forty thousand gallons of highly volatile aviation gasoline below. The resulting blast was tremendous. Those barge crew members in the river found themselves being forced back down into the water by the explosion.

When the survivors finally struggled to the surface, all they saw was fire and billowing smoke. The *Boleska* was gone—blown to bits—and their barge was gone, too, along with the two Yaks and about half of the old South Street Seaport.

Just like that, the *Okupatsi* had no more air force.

The name of the East Village club was Buckskins, and the Sostva's security detail came busting through its door ten minutes before the *Boleska* blew up.

As these security troops took up positions at every exit, cutting off all means of escape, an army lieutenant walked past the startled customers and the club's small stage and approached the bartender.

"Is there a show here tonight?" the officer asked. "You are making cabaret?"

"First act is on in five minutes," the bartender replied, "if that's what you mean. . . ."

"Make this place empty," the officer told him.

The bartender began to protest, but looked at the thirty or so armed soldiers standing about and thought better of it.

"We're closing early!" he yelled to a couple dozen customers. "We just got booked for a private party."

No one protested, and the place quickly cleared out.

The army officer then gave a signal to a sergeant at the front door, who in turn signaled someone out in the street. A dozen more soldiers trooped in, and behind them, the three commanders of the Sostva.

Alexei, Kartunov, and Marshal MOP scanned the place and declared it suitable. All but a dozen of the security troops quickly left the club, taking up secondary positions out on the street. The high commanders took the first three seats in front of the small stage and began clapping their hands. Their personal aides rushed to get several bottles of vodka from behind the bar, ordering the bartender not to interfere.

Drinks in hand, the commanders commenced stomping their feet. The bartender flicked a switch, the stage curtain opened, and four scantily clad, heavily made-up dancers appeared. They all had red hair and were wearing high heels. A cassette tape started playing and the dancers broke into a Roaring Twenties Charleston.

The Sostva officers were immediately entranced, draining their drinks and stomping their feet as the dancers twisted and twirled even closer to them. The first performance took only three minutes, and at its end, the commanders all jumped to their feet, applauding madly.

The roar of the huge explosion came a moment later.

The floor of the club partially collapsed. Bottles and glasses broke behind the bar. Ceiling tiles rained down on everyone inside. Smoke began filling the place.

The twelve security men rushed to the three commanders and literally carried them out to the street.

Something was desperately wrong; the whole eastern sky was lit up. But in the narrow confines of the East Village, it was hard for anyone to determine exactly what had happened. The security troops had their radios crackling, shouting questions into them as other troops formed a phalanx around the Sostva officers, who were still retreating under the club's marquee.

That's when air raid sirens started up all over Lower Manhattan. Everyone's eyes naturally turned skyward to see a formation of five aircraft go overhead, flying very low. Four of the planes looked large and bulky; the fifth was about one tenth their size.

"Four flying elephants and a flea?" Admiral Kartunov said, trying to make some sense of it. "Those aren't ours, are they?"

Air-raid alarms were soon blaring all over the city.

They were attached to the Russian SAM launch systems. All the SAM batteries had air-defense radars as part of their control suites. When these radars picked up four blips flying in from the direction of New Jersey, their automated systems first checked to see if the incoming aircraft were sending out a Russian IFF identification signal, indicating friend or foe. When the SAM stations received no signal at all, their sirens went off automatically, causing immediate confusion in the streets of Russkiy-NYC.

The four Sherpas had flown up the East River from the direction of Governors Island, skirting Lower Manhattan. After Hunter put the clown plane into a screaming climb and joined them to provide cover, the formation banked west over the old United Nations Building and reduced speed. Many people on the East Side and in Midtown could see them clearly now. Even though it was dark, they were flying so low and slow that they were hard to miss.

This was especially true for people doing night duty inside the skyscrapers at the MMZ, which was in the process of coming back to life after the previous night's chaos. All two dozen skyscrapers inside the Russian Zone had their power back on, and small armies of MOP crews were just finishing cleaning up broken glass and patching windows with huge sheets of plywood.

Meanwhile, 30 Rock had been only slightly damaged during the confusing battle. The big red star atop it was still blazing away at full power.

This was good—because it served as a perfect beacon for the oncoming 7CAV aircraft.

The Sherpas broke out of their V formation over Third Avenue and East Forty-Seventh Street, re-forming into a straight line heading directly toward the MMZ. Holding at exactly three thousand feet, the lead airplane reached a point precisely ten seconds away from passing over the Russian Army's cookie-cutter headquarters, and barrels came tumbling out of its open rear-bay door. Gravity and forward motion did the rest. The barrels slammed against the skyscraper's north side like a vertical string of eggs.

Each one exploded with a burst of blue and yellow flame. In the next instant, those flames were literally splashing all over the top floors of the building, a tremendous boom coming with each impact.

The next plane in line mimicked the first plane's actions, just on a slightly different time line. Its string of barrel bombs hit the navy headquarters' broadside. There was another series of blue-yellow explosions, another tremendous wave of fire splashing against the side of the building, another cannonade of deafening booms!

Seconds after that, the third plane dropped its deadly barrels onto the MOP Building. Then the fourth plane, flying slightly off the staggered bomb line, unloaded on the Joints Ops Building across Fifth Avenue.

All the while, the gunners inside the Sherpas were firing down into the MMZ. Their ammo wasn't typical 50-caliber rounds but highly flammable tracer bullets called XCPs. Concocted from a recipe Dozer had come up with years before, they were at least twice as explosive as the ITZP ammunition the Brozis had used against the ghost plane the night before. If just one or two shells, which were filled with palmitic fluorescent acid, hit something even mildly combustible, it would burst into flames.

As the streaks of yellow tracer fire poured out of all four of the slow-moving attack planes, giving them the appearance of huge, fire-breathing dragons, their rain of phosphorous shells exacerbated the chaos inside the Russian enclave.

Where the XCPs were Dozer's contribution, the fire bombs had been Hunter's brainstorm. Their contents came from another old recipe—gasoline, sugar, and propylene glycol, the basic ingredient in antifreeze. Some people called them sugar bombs. The gasoline barrel exploded on impact, the fire ignited due to a small battery-operated fuse, the sugar made the flames sticky, and the propylene made them very hard to put out.

So, the Sherpas were not dropping typical aerial bombs.

They were dropping homemade napalm.

Dominique ran to the window in time to see the first string of fire bombs slam into the Army Building.

"Oh my God," she gasped, more to herself than Zmeya. "*This* could be a problem."

Zmeya had been talking nonstop to his security people one floor below when the Army Building was hit. The explosions shook Midtown for the second time that night.

When the next string of bombs hit the Navy HQ just a couple seconds later, debris from one corner of the building flew off as result of the impact. It sailed through the air and slammed into 30 Rock between the fiftieth and fity-first floor, causing an immediate secondary explosion. The seventy-story building was shaking again.

Zmeya knew instantly that leaving the 30 Rock penthouse by elevator or stairs was no longer an option. He yelled into the phone, "Get all essential people and files and every suitcase radio up to the roof for extraction. Get my helicopter up there immediately."

Zmeya's personal Mi-26 Halo helicopter, one of only a few rotary craft in Russkiy-NYC, was always parked in a lot on Sixth

Avenue. It was a large aircraft, able to carry twenty people comfortably but powerful enough to lift sixty. The crew was always on standby and could scramble in less than thirty seconds.

Still on the phone, Zmeya saw the MOP and Joint Ops buildings get hit. Then the small bomber fleet turned southwest, back toward New Jersey. But just because they didn't bomb 30 Rock directly this time didn't mean they weren't coming back. Plus, the fires down near the fiftieth floor were growing fast.

"Tell those fools in the helicopter to move it," he yelled into the mouthpiece, even as he hastily packed some of his personal items after ordering Dominique to do the same. "We're taking forty people out with us, maximum, and that's only after the radios and the files have been loaded on."

The security officer on the other end asked, "What about the people caught in the higher floors of this building? There's at least a couple dozen administrative workers trapped on fifty-seven."

"Then they should all immediately start fighting the fire on fifty," Zmeya snapped.

There was a long pause, and then the security officer said, "And the people on the roofs of the military buildings? Should we attempt to pick them up?"

Zmeya looked twenty stories down and saw people escaping to the roofs of the three identical military skyscrapers.

"They, too, will be trapped by the fire," his security man said. "And they will have no way to fight the flames."

"Don't worry about them," Zmeya retorted.

The security man tried one more time. "Will we be sending the helicopter back to aid in rescue efforts?"

Zmeya just laughed. "Comrade, it will be much too late by that time."

But suddenly, Dominique was at his side. She grabbed his arm and dug her fingernails into his skin.

"You're leaving people to burn?" she asked incredulously.

At that moment, the helicopter rose up right in front of them, heading for the roof one level above. "There will be no room," he told her dismissively.

She pointed to the people on the roofs of the military buildings; they were already waving desperately at the Mi-26.

"But aren't some of those people down there the heart of the *Okupatsi*?" she asked. "The best that the military has?"

Zmeya finally hung up the security phone, grabbed his red suitcase, and led her by the arm to the elevator that would take them to the roof.

"In a little while," he told her darkly, "those people and whatever the hell they do won't matter."

CHAPTER FIFTEEN

FIFTEEN SECONDS.

That's all it took. Forty-eight bombs dropped; forty-eight bombs hit their targets. But the ramifications of what the 7CAV had done over the MMZ this night would last a long time.

Ten months out of the year, Manhattan's prevailing winds blew north to south, running parallel to the Hudson right down to the harbor. The proliferation of high-rise buildings actually cut down the wind speed dramatically for most of the year. But during April and May, with the change of season, the wind tended to shift and come out of the west, blowing across Manhattan, with fewer skyscrapers blocking its path.

Those were the conditions tonight. The westerly wind was gusting up to fifty miles per hour at a thousand feet, spinning the flames from the four burning skyscrapers into a single massive swirl of fire. With temperatures rising above eighteen hundred degrees, the winds started to blow from every point on the compass. The 7CAV had wanted to start a fire, but they wound up creating a firestorm, a tornado of flame, smoke, and debris so powerful it could generate wind of its own.

This monster began engulfing the MMZ not a minute after the fire bombing. Immediately spreading to a dozen buildings, it began moving east, and out of the MMZ, filling the Manhattan night sky with clouds of superheated air.

That was why Hunter's clown plane was melting.

He first noticed the problem as he trailed the fourth Sherpa in on its bombing run.

Staying close behind and down to three thousand feet exactly, he'd watched as the string of bombs hit the Russian's Joint Ops Building. Suddenly, his foot-controlled rudders became hard to move. Then the bottoms of his two enormous tires began to smolder and trail smoke. The strands of duct tape that were holding much of his cockpit together started to shrivel from the heat. Some looked about to snap.

"Hang in there, Bozo," Hunter whispered aloud to his plane, trying to stay level in the suddenly hot, high-speed winds. "Just a little longer. . . ."

Their bomb loads expended, Hunter escorted the raiders back toward the East River, welcoming the cooler air over the water. While he was not flying the best plane for fighter protection, he did have his M-16 and his .357 Magnum on hand. And the clown plane's side windows opened fairly wide. It wouldn't be pretty, but he was prepared to go at it with anyone in the air over New York if they'd threatened the retreating 7CAV Sherpas.

They overflew the old United Nations Building again then took a wide turn back toward New Jersey. Hunter circled over the East River until he'd lost sight of them. Not only would they have a clear shot home from there, but if he'd planned his next move correctly, he wouldn't be that far behind them.

Finally, he turned back toward Manhattan.

Now came the hard part.

He put the clown plane into a sharp bank and was soon back inside the fiery wind. Thick black smoke had blanketed most of Midtown by now, but his objective stood out like a beacon in the blazing fog. Illuminated by the huge, glowing red star.

Still at three thousand feet, he pointed his nose right at 30 Rock and leaned on the throttles. What he was about to do could take no more than five minutes. In and out and on your way, because he knew from experience that as bad as things were below him at the moment, the initial shock of something like the firebombing would wear off quickly—and then the Russians would start reacting to everything. After that, he wouldn't be able to count on pure chaos to help him with his plan.

Approaching from the south, he flipped down his night-vision goggles at two thousand feet out and zeroed in on the NKVD headquarters. Out of focus and beyond ideal range, the goggles nevertheless detected activity on the roof. Bright lights, blinking on and off, large flashes of static electricity, people running about. Meanwhile, a fire was raging out of control down near the fiftieth floor.

It was hard to say what was going on inside the green blur of artificial light. By the time he could fine-tune his night-vision goggles, the activity on the roof had ceased. All that was left was a cloud of gray smoke swirling above the building that had nothing to do with the fire below.

That was the only clue he needed. The gray smoke was actually engine exhaust. A helicopter had just taken off from the top of the building and disappeared into the night. He began a hasty visual search for it, even as he continued to charge head-on toward his target. The Russians had very few helicopters in theater of operations; the garbage truck's food lists indicated a handful at best. Not many copters worked well in crowded urban environments, plus they were all a pain to transport over the sea, being particularly vulnerable to corrosive salt air. Shooting one down would give the Reds one less of what was already a rarity.

Suddenly, his electronic field of vision was overtaken by the silhouette of an enormous Russian Mi-26 Halo helicopter coming right at him. Two things happened next. He banked hard left, his engine screaming in protest, and avoided a midair collision by seconds. At the same time, he pulled out his massive Magnum handgun and clicked the safety off.

The hard bank became a 360-degree roll, and a moment later, he was flying parallel to the chopper. It was as big as a midsize airliner and twice as noisy. Painted all black, except for a wide, almost-fluorescent red stripe running diagonally along its fuse-lage. Hunter pulled back his tiny side window, stuck out his giant pistol, and started blasting away.

His night-vision goggles allowed him to track his rounds as they spirited across the sky—but none of them came anywhere near the big copter. It had climbed so suddenly, it was like it disappeared. It was great piloting for such a big machine.

He briefly considered pursuing it; a half dozen well-placed shots from his M-16 might do the trick. But, though tempting, he knew it was always wiser to follow the original mission plan. There were fewer unknowns that way.

So he banked hard right, pointed himself back at the big red star, and buried his throttle. At a thousand feet out, he put the small plane into a heart-stopping dive. He dropped almost a quarter mile, straight down, in just a few seconds before finally pulling back on the controls.

The big red star was right in front of him now, shining though the smoke coming from the fiftieth floor. But with one more twist of the stick, he was circling the top of 30 Rock.

His body began vibrating instantly. The feeling . . . It had always been more intense in his head than his heart. But this time, it was helmet to toe, and absolutely pounding through his chest. He didn't remember its being so powerful. Or so thrilling. His intuition had never failed him; he always trusted it to lead him in the right direction.

I got this, he thought as he banked around the west side of 30 Rock.

But suddenly, the feeling became so extreme, he could barely keep his shaking hands on the controls. And then, a voice inside told him, *Stop here*. He yanked back on the controls and went to full throttles. Raising his nose dramatically, he put the clown plane into its magical hovering mode.

He was right outside one of the penthouse's enormous east-facing windows; it actually covered the top two floors of the building. To his immediate left was an enormous bedroom.

That's when he saw her.

Lying on a huge bed, her long blond hair bathed in the crimson light of the fires below. She was wearing the exact same outfit as in the infamous Circle War recruitment photo, but she was also positioned in a very unusual way. Legs and arms wide apart, almost as if she was . . . handcuffed to the bed. Even odder, a figure dressed all in black was lying at her feet. And were those bloodstains on the sheets?

She suddenly turned toward him. Then she screamed one word: "Help!"

An instant after that, the clown plane's nose slammed back down, and he had no choice but to rocket away.

CHAPTER SIXTEEN

IT HAD ALL happened too quickly.

Two seconds, maybe three—that's all the time Hunter had had to absorb the strange scene inside the 30 Rock penthouse bedroom.

A blonde on the bed, a guy in the room, blood on the sheets, a fire raging twenty stories below—it didn't add up to a pretty picture. But *the feeling* was telling him he'd hit pay dirt. In fact, the vibes shaking his body at the moment were stronger than he'd ever felt. She was in handcuffs, very close by—just like last time. And she was crying for help.

That was more than enough for him.

He was going in.

He broke out of his orbit, pushed his throttles to 150 knots, and swung the clown plane five hundred feet out from the top of the smoky building. The superheated air above Midtown was more turbulent than ever. Millions of burning embers were blowing around like little high-speed galaxies, crazily filling the sky. Beautiful, yet terrifying.

He did a quick loop and lined up his nose with 30 Rock's roof, this time coming in from the north. At two hundred feet out, he yanked the throttles back to one third power and went to three-quarter flaps. It was like slamming on the brakes in a race car. The whiplash jerked him forward, then threw him back against his tiny seat. It was painful, but he could tell he'd lost at least seventy knots of airspeed in just a few seconds. Still more to go, though.

The 30 Rock roof loomed right in front of him now, bleeding off the edges of his night-vision displays. But this close, the artificial image was saturated by the big red star's harsh glow, mixed with waves of billowing smoke from the fire on the fiftieth floor, distorting everything. A perfect storm of vertigo-inducing electronics.

At a hundred feet out, he began counting down from five. When he reached zero, he cut the engine completely, went to full flaps, and held on.

He hit the roof an instant later. There was a huge bang and he was thrown around the tiny cockpit once again. But the big clown tires saved his life. This wasn't like landing on the roof of the Mudtown Holiday Inn. This small patch of concrete and rubber was nearly nine hundred feet in the air with fifty-miles-per-hour crosswinds blowing around atop a burning building and, oh yes, a huge firestorm was raging close by. His landing was so violent that his crash helmet broke through the top of the plane's tiny canopy.

But he'd made it.

The plane rolled for a couple of feet then shook to a halt. Hunter scrambled out, taking his M-16 and ammo bandoliers with him. He reloaded his .357 Magnum and made sure his Bowie knife was sheathed in his boot.

He hit the zoom function on his night-vision goggles and took a quick look down on Midtown. The four Russian military skyscrapers were practically engulfed in flames now; poor souls vainly waited for rescue on the roof of each. Hundreds of Russian troops were running around on the streets below. Tanks barreled down Sixth Avenue, and a convoy of Brozis hurryied in the opposite direction, both trying to escape the firestorm. Every street within a half mile of the MMZ was mobbed with people, all moving away from the inferno as fast as they could, any way they could. An enormous traffic jam was in the making. And trying to make its way up very crowded Fifth Avenue from somewhere in

Lower Manhattan was a line of extremely dilapidated fire trucks: a dozen former-FDNY pumpers and ladder trucks that someone had scraped together on the quick. Each had its red light flashing; Hunter could even hear their sirens above the din. They were on fool's errand. Only a large, well-coordinated effort by dozens of fire companies could have made a dent in this hellish scene.

He and Dozer and the 7CAV had certainly found the Russians' weakness. Their plan had worked.

It might have even worked too well. Looking straight down the side of the 30 Rock, Hunter could see close-up the fire that had erupted near the fiftieth floor and was spreading up the southeast side of the building.

In other words, just to make it more interesting, the building from which he had to perform his one-man rescue now had a major blaze of its own.

Very fucked-up times, Major Hunter, he said to himself looking out on it all. *From Mudtown to Midtown. Things are really looking up. . . .*

He retrieved his rope from the plane, measured out twenty feet twice, and cut it with his Bowie knife. He attached the three-prong grappling hook to one end and then kicked out a twenty-foot section of the brass fence that ringed the outside edge of the building's roof. It fell into the flames and smoke below.

Sticking his head through the hole he'd created, he looked over the side of the building, sizing up the penthouse from this new perspective. But all he could see was glass covering the top two floors reflecting the growing fire below. Suddenly, it all looked the same.

He thought for a moment, guesstimating the distance between where he'd landed to where he'd seen the bedroom window. He moved ten feet to his right and took in a deep smoky breath.

This was it. The bedroom where he'd seen her was directly below him; he was certain of it.

He used the grappling hook to secure his rope to one of the fence's concrete posts, making sure it was tight. Then he stood on the edge of the building's roof, turned the safety off on his M-16, and flipped back his night-vision goggles.

"Easy as hell," he said aloud, wrapping the other end of the rope around his hands. "Skyscraper. Handcuffs. Middle of the night. Just like last time—except the fire."

He jumped into the abyss. Three seconds later, his rope went taut. Head down, arms in, boots up, he crashed through the thick plate-glass window.

The noise of the breaking glass alone was deafening. He hit the floor, rolled twice, then bounced up and assumed a classic shooting stance, all in one fluid motion. His M-16 was ready to fire at anything.

But the grand entrance had been for naught.

Not only was the room empty, when he flipped his night-vision goggles back down, he realized he wasn't even in a bedroom, but rather what was obviously an enormous bar. With no lights on anywhere, a few overturned martini glasses, and some sputtering candles, this place dominated the entire southeast corner of the penthouse. And because the fires were burning so fiercely outside, the place was aglow with bizarre, shifting shadows.

He slumped to one knee. That vision of Dominique's being held here as a prisoner or a sex slave, helpless to defend herself until he came crashing through the window to free her and to slay her captors? That all went *poof*!

To have her rush into his arms. To make a grand escape. Same city, different skyscraper?

Not to be. Not in this room, at least.

It was the goddamn rope. He'd measured it twice, twenty and twenty, when he'd meant to do ten and ten. But had he gone too far out and come in too low? Did he crash into the wrong floor? Or was he just a few rooms off? Or both?

One thing was sure, though, she was still close by. He knew because his insides were still shaking.

And the vibes were never wrong.

He began running from shadow to shadow, weapon up, looking for a way out of the vast bar.

It wasn't until he reached the far end of the horseshoe-shaped counter that he found a fire exit. It led to a hallway where it was a completely different scene. It was just as dark, but windows had been smashed at both ends of the corridor and the hot wind and smoke were blowing through at full gale. Swirls of dust and debris were colliding with walls, the ceiling, one another. The noise was incredible.

He turned up the juice on his night-vision goggles, only then seeing the bodies scattered along the hallway. Russian junior officers and administrative people, all of them were wearing NKVD uniforms, some still clutching suitcases and travel bags. It appeared they'd been machine-gunned to death while heading to the roof. With the fire raging down around the fiftieth floor, Hunter could easily see people trying to climb their way to safety. He could also envision a potential panic on the roof with the sole helicopter trying to lift off, leaving many behind.

So someone solved the problem like this.

"Should have brought more choppers, too," he said under his breath.

He moved down the hallway quickly, jumping over the bodies and staying close to the wall. He could just barely see his hands in front of him through the storm of blowing smoke. Suddenly, it was pouring out of the air vents.

A clock is definitely ticking here, he thought. And he'd already been inside at least a minute.

Get going. . . .

He reached a door and found it unlocked. Hoping it was either a stairway or a bedroom, he opened it to find a closet full of short black dresses, and, tellingly, highly stylized ladies tuxedo jackets. He leaned in, took one of the dresses in his hands, and brought it to his face. Electricity alone would have told him if it belonged to Dominique. But there were no sparks.

He hurried to the next door, twenty feet away, pressed against the wall, night vision on full power, M-16 ready. This second door was already open, just slightly. Hunter peeked inside. It was not a fire exit, but it *was* a bedroom. An enormous one. With a huge bed in one corner and several large movie cameras poking out from the three others.

Where porn is made? he wondered.

He moved on. The third door down led to another bedroom with something even more bizarre. It was an enormous aquarium, sitting in the middle of the room, without any water inside. Instead, it contained only a bed. A few dozen chairs were in place around it, like chairs around a boxing ring.

He had no interest in trying to figure out what this was.

He scrambled to the next door, concerned he was taking too much time and moving in the wrong direction. But the instant his gloved hand touched the knob, he was hit with a massive wave of *the feeling*. The new one. The same sensation he'd been experiencing since he started flying around these buildings. But this time it was so strong it staggered him. Coming from somewhere from under his chest, pouring out of his heart, he'd never felt the odd kid of ESP this strongly.

He took a breath and opened the door slowly. His M-16 was out in front of him, its muzzle trembling a bit with excitement. Even above the windstorm in the hallway, he could hear noises coming from the room.

But . . . they were strange noises. . . .

Grunts. Groans. Heavy breathing.

Somebody struggling?

Or having sex?

Or both?

He leaned his head around the corner and cranked his night vision to full power.

And there she was.

About fifteen feet away, bathed in the surreal night-vision glow, she was lying on the bed, wearing a low-cut tuxedo jacket, nylon stockings, and nothing else. She had handcuffs on her left wrist and both ankles, but she was struggling mightily against them with her free hand. That's where the disturbing noises were coming from.

Even though he was looking at her through the waviness of night vision, Hunter could tell she was beautiful. Long blond hair, perfect shape, gorgeous face, huge eyes.

Stunning, yes.

But it was not Dominique.

She couldn't see him. It was too dark in the room. Plus, she was completely distracted with trying to get out of her restraints. He studied the unmoving figure at the foot of the bed. Black coat, black fedora, black shades—and a briefcase cuffed to his left hand. Hunter did a slow zoom-in. The man also had a bullet hole in his right temple and was quite dead.

Hunter crept closer until he was standing next to the bed. The blonde was crying softly as she struggled. He looked down at his M-16 for a moment, silently clicking the safety on.

When he looked up at her again, he was staring down the barrel of a very large hand gun.

Very smooth, he thought. The struggling and the crying were an act.

"No need for violence," he said calmly. "I'm here to help you."

"Shut mouth, drop gun," she hissed back at him.

He did as told, but at the same moment, with his other hand, softly batted the pistol out of hers. Both weapons were soon in his custody.

She didn't show any fear, though, or anger, or even surprise. Instead, when she took a closer look at him, her eyes went so wide they seemed to light up.

The rock-star looks, the old-school pilot suit, the lightning-bolt helmet.

She began to say: "Are you . . . ?"

But he quickly put his finger to his lips, the universal sign to shut up.

"I'm just a friend," he whispered. "Okay?"

She nodded, and he believed she understood. He put both weapons aside. Then things began making sense.

He'd crashed onto the right floor after all, two from the top—just a few doors down from where he'd intended. This girl, who looked so much like Dominique, was obviously a doppelgänger brought here by the rackets procurement agents, maybe even his old friend, Moneybags. He could understand why any of the Russian bigwigs would want her. Even in the ghostly glare of the night-vision goggles, she looked utterly gorgeous.

But who was the dead guy?

"He was a disgusting human being," she whispered, answering before he asked. "I've been his toy for the past few days, but they've been moving me around for at least two weeks, ever since they kidnapped me and brought me here."

"You mean you weren't paid to come to New York?"

She looked up at him suddenly, her huge eyes welling up, her bottom lip quivering. "Why?" she cried softly. "Do you think I look like a hooker?"

Her words hit him like a cannon barrage. He'd just insulted her terribly—unless she was acting again.

"I'm very sorry," he said. "Poor choice of words."

"I forgive you," she replied quickly. The tears disappeared.

He looked around the room again. Booze bottles were strewn everywhere. The smell of pot hung in the air. Razor blades and white powder lay on the nightstand.

"Can you give me the short version of what happened here?" he asked.

"Sure," she said. "Whatever the hell happened out there just now threw everyone here into a panic. And I mean, some of these people were having kittens they were so scared. But only one copter was coming in, and my friend here made it clear that he was leaving me behind.

"He was one of the CRAP guys, that's what we call the really high-up dudes. He had to bring his secret papers with him; they're in that briefcase. His orders were to handcuff himself to the briefcase containing the papers if he ever left the building—and he and the others were certainly doing that ten minutes ago. But he'd used all his cuffs putting me here for a little party he'd planned. He needed one back.

"When he took the cuff off my right hand, I grabbed his gun and shot him in the head. But then he fell so far away from me I couldn't reach his keys. The copter took off thirty seconds later—without him."

Hard to believe, but Hunter was not paying full attention to her, not really. He was trying to listen to the story, but at the same time trying to get a good look at her through night vision.

He was wondering, *Could she really be* that *beautiful? Or is the artificial light playing tricks on me?*

He shook these thoughts away and took the photo of Dominique out of his pocket. He held it up close. "Do you know her?"

Her eyes went wide again.

"She was *just here*," she whispered back urgently. "Her . . . ah, gentleman friend lives one floor up. That's who was evacuating the top of the building. That's who just left in the helicopter. And she was with him."

Hunter nearly fell over. "My God," he gasped. Dominique had been on board the copter he'd just tried to shoot down?

He took a breath and recovered.

"Who is this friend of hers?" he asked—he had to.

"He's only the head of their secret police," she told him, hushing even further when she said "secret." "The top guy, Zmeya. A real nutcase. He looks like a male model, but he has a lot of issues with the ladies."

"Are they . . . They're boyfriend and girlfriend? That type of thing?"

She looked at him through the green world of night vision and smiled, but in a softly exasperated way. "'Boyfriend and girlfriend'? How about I tell you after algebra class?" she teased.

Clearly, she wanted out of the restraints. He located the keys to the handcuffs in the dead man's coat pocket and began the process of freeing her. But he found himself fumbling around. Needing to get very close to her now, he had a problem putting the key into the lock. It was almost embarrassing.

"Are you the person who's been flying around in that crazy airplane?" she asked, almost amused as his struggles continued.

"Why would you ask that?" He finally snapped the handcuffs off her left hand.

"Because you just flew by this window," she said, enunciating each word carefully for his benefit. "That is, if you were the guy flying that circus plane."

"How about we just say all that's top secret?"

She paused a moment. "Okay . . ."

He began working on her leg cuffs. "Any idea where that copter would fly to?"

She shook her head. "All I know is that they don't use it very much, but when they do, you can hear it coming from miles away." Her restraints finally undone, she was as last able to sit up.

Hunter needed to regroup.

Dominique was gone—he'd missed her by seconds and had almost shot her down along the way. Outside, the catastrophic firestorm continued to grow, as did the fire coming up from the fiftieth floor. The noise alone was becoming painful. Smoke and debris were blowing everywhere, somehow even making it into this bedroom. And off in the distance, maybe a couple of floors down, he could hear voices and movement coming closer.

Conclusion: There was no reason to stick around here.

As for the girl . . .

Suddenly, one section of the bedroom wall slid to one side, revealing a hidden elevator. The doors opened and Hunter found himself looking at two dozen Russians squeezed into a lift made for half that many. They were ragged. Their uniforms were ripped and burned, their faces covered with soot. They looked like zombies. Some were carrying automatic weapons, others kitchen utensils, long knives and even forks. No puzzle there. This mob had either heard or seen an aircraft land on the roof of 30 Rock and was here looking for a way out.

Time to go.

Hunter fired a long volley at the Russians with his M-16. It came out of the pitch-darkness at them, hitting some, causing the rest to fall to the deck. Then he grabbed the girl and the attaché case and ran out of the bedroom the same way he'd come in.

Now they were out in the hallway, and the hurricane force winds had not subsided. He looked at her through the night-vision goggles and shrugged. Which way to the roof?

She came up very close to him, her face filling his green world with those huge eyes and the long swirling hair. She said something, but he could not hear her; he was having trouble paying attention again. So she just yanked him back toward the huge bar and they started running.

Over the bodies, through the side door, and around the bar, she gracefully tiptoed through the sea of broken glass he'd caused coming in and led him to the opposite end of the large room. It was a direction he hadn't gone in his initial search. There was a spiral staircase here that led up to the top floor, and the top floor would lead to the roof.

They scrambled up the stairway, Hunter trying his best to listen for any pursuers. He somehow was able to check his watch, too. He'd been inside the building four minutes exactly. Only one to go.

"Tempus fugit," she called to him over her shoulder for no reason. "Especially when you're having fun."

He didn't have time to ask her why she'd said that. They'd climbed the winding stairs up to a bedroom not unlike the one where he'd found her. Just bigger and more grand.

But it was a strange scene here, too.

Lots of bath towels thrown around. Lots of clues the place had emptied out in haste.

Sudsy water in the bathtub. Bedroom sheets still warm. Drinks with ice cubes still in them.

Hunter lifted one of the bathroom towels to his face. At last, he felt a little jolt of static electricity, though it faded quickly. Still, he knew Dominique had been here recently.

He walked out of the bathroom, hoping his freed damsel in distress was pointing the way to another escape route, one that would get them up to the roof.

Instead, she was disrobing. With her back to him, she climbed out of the constricting tuxedo ensemble and into a long T-shirt she'd found on the bed. T-shirt and silk panties—that was it.

But to his surprise, she'd also taken off a wig. At that moment, some sort of last-ditch emergency generator must have kicked in, because all the electric lights in the room popped back on.

Now, for the first time, Hunter saw what this girl really looked like, in real light—and not the emerald world of night vision. He was stunned all over again. Her real hair was blond, but with a shorter, sexier cut. Her eyes were indeed gigantic, but deep brown, not blue. And her looks. Hunter had always thought of Dominique as being regal. This girl looked more like a war-rior. An unbelievably gorgeous warrior from some prewar video game.

He felt another deep pounding in his chest. It was his heart again. Incredibly, the chaos of the outside world had disappeared for a moment. It was just her looking at him, from about four feet away, in real light, tilting her head to the side and asking, "Are you all right?"

That's when they heard the Russian mob arrive downstairs. Some were already coming up the spiral staircase.

He fired off another half dozen rounds, grabbed her hand, and started running again.

They found a door to a small veranda already covered with soot and flaming embers. Hunter took a quick look over the side. The furious firestorm was still blowing east, toward the river, engulfing buildings, vehicles, everything in its path.

Flames were shooting out of 30 Rock big-time now; the fire had reached the fifty-fourth floor. Incredibly, though, some brave MOP soldiers had managed to pull one of the old crappy FDNY fire trucks close to the building and were valiantly trying to fight the fire more than fifty stories above them. *That's guts*, Hunter thought.

The woman began pulling him along again; she'd found a lad-der. He boosted her up to the roof, his hands unintentionally going full panties during the assist. He quickly climbed up after her.

Out on the roof, the superheated winds were blowing in all directions. Flames and smoke were now rising high above their heads. The entire sky filled with millions of burning embers.

"This must be hell looks like," she yelled to him.

He hurried over to the plane and started the engine. It was clear his new friend wanted to get as far away from 30 Rock as possible. But now, as she got her first real glimpse of the escape vehicle, she paused for a moment. Then she just shrugged good-naturedly and said, "If getting out of here means going off the seventy-first floor in a toy airplane, then so be it."

She helped him turn the little plane around and then boosted herself up on one of the big tires and climbed in.

As she looked around the duct-taped interior she asked, "Is *this* thing top secret?"

He'd flipped his night-vision goggles back down and immediately identified a problem. There was so much smoke and debris in the air now, the glare from the big red star made it look like a thick green soup. With or without the night-vision goggles, Hunter would not be able see the other end of the roof, which was crucial for takeoff.

He had to fix this. After making sure his passenger was strapped securely inside the plane and the canopy was closed, he brought his M-16 up to his hip and emptied a clip into the big red star.

He thought he'd just knock out its lightbulbs. Instead, the huge ornament exploded into thousands of pieces. The blast was so intense it knocked Hunter off his feet.

When he looked up again, the red star was gone, leaving only the remains of a lot of mysterious-looking communications equipment that had been packed inside.

Hunter got back on his feet and jumped into the plane.

Revving the engine, he asked the blonde, "Want to close your eyes?"

"I won't if you won't," she shouted back over the noise of the engine.

Just then, the mob of zombie-like Russians burst onto the roof. Hunter pushed his throttles to max, popped the brakes, and the little plane shot away. They were past the mob and up and over the side of the roof in two seconds. A moment after that, the plane was heading straight down.

Hunter quickly began the harrowing process of recovery. He backed off the throttle, counted to three, then rejammed it to full power. He pulled back mightily on the controls at precisely the same moment and let the little plane's odd design do its thing.

It took a few more seconds than it should have. Superheated winds were gusting all around them, slowing down the physics of it all. But finally the air caught under the high-angle wings. The plunge slowed, then they came to a complete halt as the plane turned 180 degrees on its lateral axis. Now pointing upward,

Hunter stayed off the gas for three more seconds, then jammed the throttle forward again—and off they went.

Straight up to the stars.

They reached five thousand feet in seconds, and Hunter turned them over to level flight. While he could still feel the buffeting of the firestorm even at a mile high—it was like driving down an extremely bumpy road—with every second they moved away from it, their flight got less and less turbulent.

Through it all, the mysterious woman had not made a peep, not spoken a word. She'd held on tight as he'd instructed her to do, but she went through the worst of it like a combat veteran.

He turned the steering controls to the left and pointed his nose toward New Jersey. He checked his watch again—he'd been inside 30 Rock for just under six minutes, not much more than he'd planned. This also meant he wasn't too far behind the lumbering Sherpas. He maxxed his throttles, intent on catching up to them.

It was very cramped inside the clown plane's cockpit. He and the blonde were shoulder to shoulder, knee to knee; the NKVD attaché case wound up on her lap. He studied its trio of time locks, then he ran his gloved finger over each of them. He counted to three and then tapped the handle.

The case sprang open in a snap.

"That's impressive," she said sweetly, just loud enough to be heard over the clown plane's rambunctious engine.

Inside the case was a bright-red striped pouch. But it did not contain photos of blondes in slinky outfits. Instead, it held a plain-looking document, a couple dozen pages, written in both Russian and English. Its title: Convoy 56 Deployment Schedule.

"Those CRAP guys used to walk around with these briefcases cuffed to them all the time, like they were pocketbooks," she told Hunter. "Even if they weren't leaving the building. It was their way of showing off to each other. Briefcase envy. But I always thought they were carrying around the secret of warp drive or maps that show where all the nukes are or something. That title makes it seem like a ferry timetable. Unless . . ."

Hunter couldn't resist. "Unless what?"

"Unless it's intentionally . . . bland," she said, finding just the right word.

She wasn't wrong. Misleading headings were a key part of spy craft. Besides, why would the top NKVD guys be walking around with plain old cargo ship information locked to their wrists?

He asked her to read the first paragraph to him.

It took her only a few seconds to do so, despite the dim light emanating from the mini-instrument panel. But even before she was half done, Hunter knew everything was going to change. Just a handful of her words brought his dream of rescuing Dominique to a screeching halt.

His passenger, too, was stunned by what she'd read.

She found his arm and squeezed it.

"If this is true," she said worriedly, "in just a few months, America won't even exist."

CHAPTER SEVENTEEN

ONE MILE BELOW, the firestorm had already moved on from the Fifth Avenue and Forty-Eigth Street area, where the four main military buildings of the *Okupatsi* had stood less than twenty minutes before.

There were piles of smoldering debris ten feet high and lots of smoke overhead. The 30 Rock skyscraper was still on fire, the flames slowly making their way to the top, as were many smaller buildings around it. But what had been the dead center of the MMZ was now four hot, smoky patches in the ground.

The industrious MOP crew who'd managed to position one of the old, broken-down fire trucks up against the NKVD head-quarters was finally forced to surrender to the inevitable and get away from the seventy-story skyscraper before it collapsed. They'd gotten the fire truck's engine turned on and just as slowly as they'd appeared, they began making their way back down Fifth Avenue, dirty, wet, and beaten.

But suddenly, one of the erstwhile firemen saw something moving in the rubble on the corner of East Forty-Ninth and Fifth, what had once been the old Simon & Schuster Building, and more recently, the Russian Military's Joint Ops Building.

The fireman yelled for the driver to halt, and several of the MOP soldiers jumped off the truck and waded into the still-sizzling debris.

Incredibly, there was a man in the middle of it all, digging himself out. He was about halfway to freedom when the firemen reached him. They pulled him out the rest of the way.

He was covered with white ash and powder, but somehow he'd survived the firebombing and the collapse of the building. Even with a few burns and some cuts here and there, he was in surprisingly good shape—and this included his eyepatch.

"Thank you, my friends," he said to his rescuers. "Though I believe I would have made it out in another day or two. . . ."

It was Colonel Sergei Gagarin, the man who ran the joint operations daily briefings.

The man who knew everything.

CHAPTER EIGHTEEN

BULL DOZER THOUGHT his ears were bleeding.

They were ringing so loudly they hurt.

But he didn't care. He was in exceptionally high spirits—and not because of really bad whiskey.

He was alone in the spy tower. So many of his men were involved in the New York City bombing raid, the pair of troopers who usually manned the lookout post were filling in back at the base. So, tonight, way out here in the thick woods, it was just Dozer and the ghosts.

And after a while, hearing the screeches and yelps echoing through the forest became routine.

Almost. . . .

No matter, the night noise in the Pine Barrens had become the background music for one of the happiest moments of his life.

He'd watched the firebombing via the balloon cam. As soon as the napalm-filled barrels began falling, he saw their explosions on the aerial camera's infrared lens, each one creating a blip of light on the video monitor. Dozer counted forty-eight bombs, forty-eight distinct blips.

Each bomb hit its mark. Not bad for a rookie air-assault team.

But about twenty minutes into the raid, something happened that had *not* been part of the firebombing plan. It had been more

than a month since Dozer started sending out radio messages to
the other patriot groups that usually banded together to battle
America's latest enemy. After weeks of no replies, and countless
theories why haunting his dreams, including the most troubling
one—that no one cared anymore—he'd just about given up on
ever hearing from anybody ever again.

But after climbing up to the tower that night, he'd switched
on the old radio anyway, not surprised to hear only static spill-
ing out of the battered, tinny speaker.

After watching the fire raid and praying all his planes
would return safely, Dozer's thoughts went to Hunter, knowing his mission was just starting and wondering if his friend
would live through the night. Jumping into the cauldron of
flame, into a firestorm, into Hell itself, just to find the woman
he loved.

Though no expert on relationships, Dozer still wondered,
was Hunter crazy in love, or was he just plain crazy?

And it was at that moment—that exact instant—that something wonderful happened.

His radio receiver finally came to life.

His back was to it at the time, but it came on so loud, so suddenly, he thought it was an explosion. That one of the creaky
communications devices that made up the tower's console had
short circuited and blown up.

It took him a few seconds to realize the racket was coming
out of the radio's speaker.

Voices.

Calling him. . . .

Voices that he recognized.

All of them yelling, "Come in, Bull," or "Calling 7CAV. . . ."

It was an explosion, all right.

All of the people he'd been trying to contact—his friends,
his colleagues, his fellow warriors—were calling *him*. And by
the timbre of their voices, it sounded like they'd been trying
for some time. So many on so many channels, coming through
all at once—that's when his ears began to hurt, but in the best
way possible.

What had happened? It was as if someone had flipped a switch, or better yet, opened a floodgate, and a tidal wave of radio messages waiting to be sent were suddenly washing all over the cosmos—or at least this part of northeast America.

But whatever the cause, it was good to know that after all this time, he wasn't alone out here.

For the next ten minutes, Dozer replied to as many of the radio calls as he could.

He spoke to a couple dozen old friends—Louie St. Louis, Lieutenant Ben Wa, Captain J. T. Toomey, Colonel Rene Frost, Captain Crunch, the Cobra Brothers, and many more.

And they all said variations of the same two things: "Where have you been?" and "When do we go to war against the Reds?"

It was such an onslaught, Dozer nearly missed the coded signal that came through at exactly 0030 hours.

Just a couple of beeps on the radiophone.

The Sherpas were returning.

He shut off his radio receiver—doing so with a quick apology and a promise to be back in touch soon—and then strapped on his night-vision goggles and stuck his head out the shack's window next to the reinstalled 50-caliber machine gun.

He saw a faint light blinking to the north. The strobe attached to the nose of Sherpa 1.

Dozer crossed his fingers. The Sherpas that survived the raid would be right behind the lead plane, but they would still be flying dark. He wouldn't know who was still alive until they flew by him.

He hastily radioed the base, telling them to open the camo net. Then he turned back to the north and watched as the planes approached.

The first Sherpa roared in, followed by the other three—and trailing slightly behind them, the little plane with the big wheels.

Dozer felt another wave of relief wash over him.

He called back to base, "Five ball in the corner pocket!"

He exited the spy tower quickly, falling halfway down the tree again, and was soon in his jeep speeding toward the base, watching through the trees as each plane landed safely.

There were no wild celebrations on the tarmac.

No high-fiving, no whooping it up.

The crews of the four Sherpas just piled out of their airplanes, exhausted, sweaty, glad to be alive. A few of the men exchanged firm handshakes and slaps on the back; more than a few of the fliers kissed the ground. They'd made it. That's all that mattered at the moment.

Dozer congratulated them all. When he asked, "How did it go?" the overwhelming reply was: "We got them good."

Their airplanes were a mess, though.

All four Sherpas had sustained heavy fire damage under their wings and fuselages. In some cases, the planes' metal exteriors had become so overheated they had crumpled and shrunk. That's how hot it had been in those few seconds above Midtown.

It was a miracle none of the planes had blown up considering their fuel tanks had been exposed to the hellish temperatures. But Dozer knew it would be a long time before any of them flew again, if ever.

Hunter came in on the tail of the Sherpas, flying at max throttle, he'd caught up with the four raiders about thirty seconds before they went into their landing profile. His plane also had a lot of fire damage. He pulled up to where the returning 7CAV crews had congregated, and he killed his engine, his left wing still smoldering. Dozer helped lift his canopy and saw a blonde in the passenger seat.

Hunter climbed out, covered head to foot in soot.

Dozer shook his hand. "Well, was it 'a walk in the park' or 'a piece of cake'?" he asked.

"Both and a Coke," Hunter replied. Then he reached into the side seat of the tiny airplane and helped out the rescued blonde.

An unexpected gasp went up from the 7CAV troopers and civilian techs nearby. Dozer, too, was shocked. This woman wasn't Dominique—but she was just as beautiful, if that was possible. Plus she was scantily dressed.

"This is why I've been divorced five times," Dozer sighed, scanning her up and down.

She was looking around the base in awe. The movable cover overhead, just starting to close. The Quonset hut and the other structures, all perfectly hidden among the trees. The 7CAV troops themselves, in their camo uniforms, almost blended into the shadowy nighttime background.

"Now this . . ." she said. "*This* is top secret."

Hunter helped her to the ground and then retrieved the attaché case from the cockpit. Dozer gave her his oversize winter uniform jacket. It reached her knees and would take a long time to button up.

He took the moment to pull Hunter aside. "I don't want to be out of line here, Hawk," he said in a low voice. "But did you trade up for another model? Or were they just having a sale on angels?"

"She's one of the girls that guys like Moneybags brought to town," Hunter hastily replied, his voice also low. "She was right in with the Reds. Right on top of 30 Rock. But she's no fan of Ivan. She'll be able to tell us a lot about them. But can you have the guys look after her for now?"

Dozer gave him two thumbs-up. She was still buttoning up his loaner coat.

"It's safe to go with these soldiers," Hunter told her, fastening the top couple of buttons for her. "They'll have a medic look you over and find a place for you to spend the night. We'll talk in the morning, okay?"

"If I can go to sleep somewhere, sure," she said agreeably. She turned to go with a few soldiers, but then looked back at Hunter and said, "Thanks for saving me."

Then she was gone, disappearing into the darkness.

Hunter held up the attaché case and said to Dozer. "You've got to see this."

CHAPTER NINETEEN

A MINUTE LATER they were in the Quonset hut, sitting at Dozer's desk.

The only other people inside, the Worm and the Trashman, were at a table at the opposite end of the large barracks. As usual, both were working on bowls of whiskey stew.

Hunter opened the briefcase and took out the NKVD document. There were twenty pages of text and four pages of maps and diagrams. Every page was written in both Russian and English and all of it was marked SOVERSHENNO SEKRETNO. TOP SECRET.

"This didn't come from someone's garbage," Dozer observed.

The documents comprised a report detailing the contents of a group of Russian ships, called Convoy 56, that were presently on their way to New York. This in itself was unusual. Since the first night of the invasion, ships had arrived from Russia on a regular basis, but always in ones and two, never more than that. This document stated nine ships were on their way, sailing as a unit and expected to arrive in New York at the same time. There was even a note attached to the first page saying space had to be made in the harbor to accommodate the new arrivals.

While the types of ships were not mentioned, one was referred to throughout as "VLV"—which Hunter took to mean "very large vessel."

Dozer started reading the document from the beginning and found the first entry alone to be frightening. It stated that a huge amount of weapons of mass destruction were aboard this VLV. It listed fifty-three nuclear warheads, three hundred and two biological warheads, and an astonishing eight hundred and sixty chemical warheads, including canisters full of hal-lou gas, the powdery hallucinogenic mist the Russians had fired at the American Badlands as part of their devastating sneak attack. And it got worse. The VLV was also carrying six dozen mobile guns, six dozen advanced T-72 tanks, some ultralong-range artillery pieces, and many multiple rocket launchers. Also on board were three squadrons of deadly Kamov attack helicopters; each squadron containing eighteen copters.

But even worse, the report cited what were described as antipersonnel bombs on board. *Twenty thousand* of them. To Dozer, antipersonnel bombs meant IEDs—improvised explosive devices, to be used as car bombs, roadside bombs, or even strapped to suicide bombers.

The report *also* had an entry that simply read: "Three full reinforced squadrons, operational," which could have meant just about anything.

The document referenced another ship sailing in the convoy only as "LTV," which most likely meant a "large troop vessel." This entry was just as alarming as the first, because this vessel, obviously huge, was carrying not Russian soldiers or engineers or sailors—but Chekskis.

Thirty thousand of them.

And they were bringing with them thousands of axes, swords, and long knives. Medieval weapons that were of little use on a modern battlefield . . . but perfect for beheadings.

The rest of Convoy 56 consisted of five picket destroyers and two battle cruisers.

Dozer felt his heart drop to his feet. He looked up at Hunter, who was wearing the same pained expression.

"This isn't any 'convoy,'" Hunter told him. "This is a battle fleet, full of nothing but weapons and firepower, with something big and nasty called a VLV out in front."

Dozer used his sleeve to wearily wipe the grime from his forehead.

"And this isn't about just taking over New York City anymore," Hunter went on. "This is about Moscow taking over the entire country—and using New York as their jumping-off point. They've got their cavemen and their battle axes, plus they're bringing nukes. They're going to unleash these fanatics on us; they're going to gas us again. And if we don't roll over for them, they might drop nukes."

Dozer nodded grimly. He indicated a line in the plans about eliminating the "surplus" population of New York City and beyond.

"They're going to do it through terrorism," he said bitterly. "That's how they think they can finally conquer us. Organized, calculated terrorism, from suicide bombers to bioweapon artillery to nukes. And it doesn't even mention the Russian military. Nothing about the army or MOP; none of the ships in the convoy has any reference to the navy. All of this is addressed to the NKVD. In fact, the Red military might not even be aware of what's about to happen."

All the documents were signed at the bottom by Commissar Zmeya, head of the NKVD in America—and Dominique's gentleman friend.

Dozer only recognized the name, though. "He's the mystery-man commissar you hear them praising all the time on Red Radio. Do you know who I mean?"

Hunter laughed darkly.

"I know all about him—now," he replied. "But that's for another day. The priority here is stopping the ships in this convoy from getting here. Or as many as we can. If we don't, then we might as well just shut off the lights. Because if they land and all that stuff is taken off and spread around—as well as thirty thousand more Chekskis?—we'll never get rid of them."

Dozer nodded gravely. "But how do we stop them? This isn't like dropping barrel bombs on Midtown. There's at least one very large vessel carrying all these weapons from hell, and while we don't know what kind of warship it is, you can be sure it's armed to the hilt. And there's another with all those freaks on it.

And then the battle cruisers and other warships? Jeez, man, this is really climbing the mountain."

Hunter ran his hand over his tired face.

"I know," he said wearily.

At this point, Dozer told him about his radio's suddenly coming alive with messages from all their friends—and how they were all eager to fight.

"Did something happen during the bombing runs?" Dozer asked. "Or did you bust up anything in your travels? Anything that might have been serving as a jamming device?"

"Only one very big red star at the top of 30 Rock," Hunter replied. "Lots of gizmos stuffed inside. Might have been a very happy accident."

"Well, at least now we can talk to people and organize some help," Dozer went on. "But you know the usual players—and even altogether, we'll be lucky if we can get a couple thousand guys on short notice. Even that won't be enough with all those religious nuts heading our way, never mind the regular Red troops already here."

Dozer was dead right. How were a couple thousand American patriots going to overwhelm these two massive troop concentrations?

Hunter thought a few moments more, then said, "Okay—first things first. We've got to find these ships and get a look at them. At least then we'll see what we're up against."

The document indicated the ships' last known position. Hunter did some quick calculations and determined they were less than thirty-six hours away from New York Harbor.

"We can't look for them in the Sherpas," Dozer told him. "I'm not sure any of them will ever fly again. From the looks of them, I don't think we have enough duct tape to fix them. And even if we did get them airborne, they won't be able to stay up long enough for a sea search. Those Russian ships are probably still too far out in the Atlantic for us to find them and make it back again. And that includes your clown plane. What we need is something that's really fast. But we don't have any really fast planes here."

"There's only one other option then," Hunter said. "My XL back in Vermont. It's the only plane we can get our hands on that can fly far enough and fast enough to ID those ships and still have time to dream up some way to stop them. But how am I going to get up there with all of our planes so banged up?"

A voice from behind them said, "I'll fly you there."

Hunter and Dozer turned to find the Worm standing right behind them, the Trashman at his side. They wondered how long they'd been there and how much they'd heard.

"In what?" Dozer snapped, upset that the 7CAV's two guests had been eavesdropping.

"In my plane," the numbers runner replied. "I can fix it in a couple hours with the Wingman's help. Then I'll fly him up to Vermont . . . as long as I can keep on going to Canada afterward."

He indicated the Trashman beside him. "I can take him with me—he wants to get out of here, too, right?"

The little arms dealer nodded enthusiastically. "And we can take that blonde you just rode in with, too," he added eagerly. "I'm sure she'll want out, too."

Dozer dismissed them with a wave of his hand. "You've both been eating too much of my stew. You know the alcohol in it doesn't cook away like in other dishes. That's the secret to the recipe."

But Hunter pulled on his chin thoughtfully for a moment, taking off a thin layer of soot with his fingers.

"You know, just because they're looped doesn't mean it's a crazy idea," he said to Dozer.

The marine was mildly shocked. "You're actually considering this? I mean 'crazy' rarely works."

"I know," Hunter said with a shrug. "But it will get me to Vermont, and it takes three problems off your hands. And you talked to Frostie right?"

Colonel Rene Frost was a commander for the Free Canadian Air Force, but he was also a close ally of the patriotic Americans. He'd helped them many times in their quest to put their country back together again.

Dozer nodded. "He was one of the first voices to come through."

"We can ask him to send down a couple fighters to escort the Worm's plane to Canada after they drop me off," Hunter said. "That will make sure there's no funny business once I'm out. Plus, he can look after the girl."

Dozer thought about it then looked at the two men, their mouths and chins stained with stew. "Well, at the very least, it will cut down on our food bill."

CHAPTER TWENTY

NEW YORK'S TWIN Towers were never included in the Russian military's invasion plans.

The 110-story skyscrapers had been deemed too big, too unwieldy, too expensive for the military triad to operate. Plus, Moscow wanted the MMZ to be right in the middle of Manhattan, the heart of the city, not down on the southern tip of the island.

The NKVD, however, had had their eye on the World Trade Center buildings. Luxurious as it was, 30 Rock was never meant to be their permanent home. The WTC's Twin Towers were intended to be the secret police's eventual *world* headquarters, bigger than their present facility back in Moscow. It was from here that NKVD intended to rule the planet.

So MOP had gone through the twin buildings and turned on the essentials. But by far, most of the work had been done on Tower Two, getting the 110th floor penthouse ready for Commissar Zmeya.

It was still a work in progress, but its new resident had to move in a little early.

Zmeya and Dominique had said little to each other since they'd evacuated 30 Rock.

She had not been allowed to gather her things at the Ritz, her off-MMZ hideaway; she'd not been allowed out of his sight.

Their new penthouse in Tower Two still smelled of recent plastering and the floors were mostly unadorned concrete. It was spacious, and somewhat well appointed, but practically empty.

Zmeya had been on his shortwave radio or his radiophone almost every second since they'd arrived. Even Dominique's dressing up in the babydoll lingerie he'd told her to put on did nothing to break the ice.

The fire was still raging across Midtown. It was easy to see from Tower Two. The wind continued to blow it eastward at a slow but steady rate, and there was nothing anyone could do to stop it. The hope was that it would simply burn out when it finally reached the East River. But with any kind of shift in the wind, the catastrophe would probably be prolonged.

To say the Russian military was in disarray was an understatement. Army units could be seen and heard speeding through the streets, but none of them seemed to have any kind of destination. They sure weren't fighting the fires. Some of the navy ships in the harbor had actually pulled anchor and moved to positions closer to New Jersey, just in case all of Manhattan went up in flames.

But most troubling for Zmeya was the loss of his vast eavesdropping and electronic-interference suite formerly housed inside the big red star. Assuming the secret equipment had melted in the tremendous heat of the firebombing, Zmeya couldn't listen in on anybody anymore.

The multitude of different voices usually bouncing around his head was down to one. His own. And that was enough to drive him mad.

He finally spoke to her.

He was at his desk looking out the 110th story window at the glowing, burning city beyond. The smoke alone was incredible.

She was lying on the bed in the next room, staring at the ceiling. Sometimes, when the wind would gust, she could feel the great building sway.

"This is all your boyfriend's fault," he growled loud enough for her to hear. "From the clown plane all the way to trying to burn down this city. He's had a hand in all of this."

"He's supposed to be dead," she called back.

Zmeya laughed at her. "We know you don't believe that anymore, don't we?"

She swore softly under her breath and then said, "We're going to start talking about what each of us believes now?"

He was out of his seat, into the bedroom, and up against her in an instant, a switchblade at her throat.

"He was spotted by many people in Football City not long ago," he hissed at her. "And he was seen flying over Detroit. And at just about the same time, our Asian friends in Nevada swear he was out there in their own backyard, making their lives miserable."

He pressed the knife just a little harder against her skin.

"So you see, my dear, this is why I can't trust you completely," he sneered. "I think you're hoping he's still out there. You might even be in cahoots with him—or more. And *that's* why you won't make love with me. Do I finally have it right?"

Dominique said nothing. She remained cool, which made him even more furious.

He held her even tighter, the knife even closer to slicing her throat.

"Is that the truth?" he demanded. "Is that how it is?"

But suddenly, Zmeya felt something sticking into his groin. He looked down to see Dominique holding a dagger the size of a hunting knife. It was three times bigger than his stiletto and the sharp point was just touching his sensitive area. Yet his first thought was: *Where the hell has she been hiding* that *thing?*

He looked up into her eyes, momentarily speechless. She *was* unpredictable.

"I think it's time for your meds," she whispered.

Her words came with utter contempt, something he didn't totally dislike.

"I think you might be right."

A knock came on their door. It was 0200 hours, but time had lost all meaning in Russkiy-NYC. A crisis was afoot.

Weapons back to their hiding places, Zmeya yelled, "Enter!"

Two Militsiya gunmen walked in followed by the three members of the Sostva.

Summoned here by Zmeya, the trio of bull-doggish officers were in awe of his new, if unfinished, apartment in the sky, especially the view. Their medals clinked as they looked around the place.

There were no greetings. No salutes. Zmeya got right to the point.

"Do you have any idea who bombed us a few hours ago?" he asked them.

The frumpy officers all shook their heads. "We were hoping you'd tell us," Alexei said weakly.

"It was some American patriot gang," Zmeya said, eyeing Dominique, who was back in the bedroom. "We have intelligence that one of their premier leaders is alive and well and operating in the area."

Zmeya led the three high commanders to his desk where a map of New York and New Jersey was spread out.

"Did you happen to see the type of planes that bombed us a few hours ago?" Zmeya asked.

"We did," Admiral Kartunov replied in a smug tone. It wasn't a lie; they'd briefly seen the raiders flying over the East Village. "Odd-looking things. I can't imagine any officer wanting them for an air fleet."

"That's because they weren't military planes, Admiral," Zmeya told him. "They were small civilian cargo planes, adapted to drop bombs. That tells me they didn't fly in from very far away."

Zmeya had circled all the known airfields big and small within a two-hundred-mile radius of New York City. But satellite photos he'd obtained from Moscow showed all of them were in some kind of postwar disrepair and unusable.

"And the bombs they dropped weren't military-issue, either," Zmeya went on. "They were barrels full of napalm with impact fuses. That tells me they didn't have access to an arsenal or stores. They had to improvise."

He studied the map again.

"So we're looking for a hidden base," Zmeya said. "Big enough to support a hundred or so insurgents, along with a short landing strip, maybe fifteen hundred feet. Small enough to keep hidden, but relatively nearby. A place they would never expect us to look."

The officers scanned the map, looking for someplace that would match the criteria. Surprisingly, it was the sleepy Marshal MOP who saw it first.

He put his finger down on a point about forty miles south-west of the city.

The Pine Barrens.

"Haunted place," he said. "We'd punish our troops if they were caught in there. In fact, we broadcast the penalties against it daily on intercity radio."

Zmeya studied the spot on the map for a long time. It was obviously a heavily wooded area, but that didn't mean there wasn't a road or a small field from which aircraft could operate under camouflage.

Finally, he asked Alexei, "How far can your rocket artillery units fire a typical volley?"

"We have BM-30s," Alexei replied proudly. "They have a range of fifty-five miles."

Zmeya tapped his fist softly on the map.

"Gentlemen," he began, "For reasons I can't discuss, this situation has to be settled within the next thirty-six hours. Therefore, I strongly recommend the army gear up its rocket artillery units and deploy them to the most advantageous spot in the city to shoot at this Pine Barrens place. I'll get back to you on the timing."

General Alexei looked puzzled. "Do you have specific target coordinates in mind?"

Zmeya started folding up the map. "If I can get an infrared satellite image from Moscow in time, then yes," he replied coldly. "If not, we'll just keep firing until the whole place is flattened."

That was it. End of meeting. The Sostva officers saluted and left. Ten seconds later, Militsiya Sublieutenant Boris Borski walked into the room.

Zmeya could barely look at him; both the scar and the man were repulsive. He chose to turn away when talking to the freak-ish officer.

"I'm going to give you two assignments, Sublieutenant," he told him. "Both equally important. First, you are to round up two thousand New Yorkers and transport them to Yankee Stadium. Homeless, troublemakers, dissidents, ethnics, the nonproductive types. No one who works for the rackets, but everyone else is fair game.

"On my command, you will execute these people. I don't have to know how you do it; just don't waste a lot of ammunition in the process. And make them dig their own graves first, so we don't squander our manpower. Film it, three-camera shoot, and send the rushes to me."

Borski was grinning from ear to ear, which just made his scar look even more revolting. Mass executions. This was a dream assignment for him.

Zmeya then handed him a short note he'd just jotted down.

"Your second assignment is contained in here," Zmeya said. "It is highly classified. Don't let anyone else see it."

Borski became so excited he left the room without a salute or an order that he was dismissed. Punishable infractions in normal times.

"Idiot," Zmeya said under his breath as he watched him go.

Dominique was soon beside him. She was horrified.

"You can't start exterminating people," she told him.

Only now was he able to take his medication. He grabbed two pills from his desk drawer and gulped them down with a quick swig of water.

"Did you hear me?" she said. "You can't just start killing hundreds of people for no reason."

Close to exasperation, Zmeya finally just looked up at her wearily. "Why not?"

"Because it's not right," she replied emphatically. "It's a crime against humanity."

He just waved her away. "Everything I do is a crime against humanity. That's my fucking job description."

He was a mess. Between what had happened in Russkiy-NYC and his troubles with her, he hadn't been able to sleep in three nights.

"You truly are a horrible person," Dominique hissed at him.

"I thought that's what you wanted," he fired back at her.

"There's a big difference between horrible and powerful," she said, her voice dripping with derision.

"Then I suggest you get that knife of yours out again," he replied, gulping down two more pills, "and use it to stab me in the back, right now. Because Moscow cannot and will not ever make a distinction between those two terms. Not until the planet is theirs. That's why I'm here. I'm the one who can make it happen."

CHAPTER TWENTY-ONE

May 7

THE TWO FREE Canadian F-101 Voodoo fighters arrived over Smuggler's Notch, Vermont, at 0400 hours. Right on time.

Seconds later, their long-range radars picked up a blip coming from the south.

Both pilots lowered their night-vision goggles and immediately sighted the faint but growing orb of green light heading in their direction.

"Worm with Wings, contact," the lead pilot reported back to his base in Montreal.

The two fighters continued circling a spot right over the isolated mountain.

They would wait here and let the small plane come to them.

Hunter saw the flare from the Voodoos' engines right away.

"Time to go," he said. He checked that he had everything he needed: M-16, .357 Magnum, Bowie knife, two-way radio, night-vision goggles.

"About one minute," the Worm said, reading his crude terrain-guidance radar screen. "Better get packing."

It turned out that the numbers runner had been right: His four-seat aircraft—it was a rare DK-ZAG—was battered. But with Hunter's help and using spare parts crafted by the base's civilian techs, it had been made airworthy again in just two hours. The quick flight up from New Jersey to Vermont had been uneventful.

Hunter was determined to keep it that way.

"You know those are my friends in those jets," he told the Worm. "One wrong move, and they will make life very difficult for you. They won't have to shoot you down to make you pay. It'll be more like a cat playing with a mouse. Get what I'm saying?"

The Worm gulped. "That's the last thing I need."

"Don't worry, Mister Wingman," the Trashman said from the backseat. "I'll keep an eye on him for you. I'll even fly the plane myself if I have to."

Hunter rolled his eyes. He turned to the third passenger—the beautiful girl he'd rescued from 30 Rock.

He'd never gotten a chance to talk to her after landing at the secret base. Too many things had had to be done, and as it was, they'd had to wake her from a deep sleep to make this journey. Plus, the old ZAG plane was so loud, conversation had been nearly impossible during the flight.

Seeing her now in the very dim light of the plane's interior, he realized, in some ways, she really did resemble Dominique. The face, the body, a certain kind of aura—these were similarities. But in other ways, this girl was totally different. Younger, but also worldlier, as if she had street smarts, if that was possible these days. The adventure they'd shared in 30 Rock's penthouse just a few hours ago had not been for the faint of heart, yet she'd never wavered. Even though many strange things had happened in those six minutes, she'd rolled like a trained special-ops soldier, seemingly knowing what had to be done, which way to go, all the precisely right things to do.

He found that interesting.

She was smiling now, lighting up the plane.

"Can I trust you to keep these two in line?" he asked her.

She nodded. "No problems there."

"And remember," Hunter told her. "When you land, make sure they take you to Colonel Frost right away. He'll look after you."

"Thank you," she whispered and touched his hand for a moment.

"Thirty seconds," the Worm said. "Six thousand and descending. . . ."

Hunter did one more check of his equipment. All was okay.

"Twenty seconds and you'll be close enough," the Worm said. "Fifty-five hundred feet."

Hunter began to open his side door.

"Don't forget to flap your wings," the Trashman told him.

Hunter fist-bumped the Worm as a way of thanking him, then did the same with the weapons dealer. He wished them both good luck.

"Fifteen seconds," the Worm said. "We're at five-Angels. . . ."

Hunter went to shake hands with the girl, when suddenly she was between the seats, pulling his face toward hers. She kissed him hard, her tongue going halfway down his throat.

It seemed to last forever, and suddenly he felt like he was on fire.

Then the Worm said, "Five seconds. . . ."

Hunter gently broke away from her and caught his breath. He saw her smile one more time.

Then he thought to ask her, "By the way, what's your name?"

She smiled even wider. "That's top secret. . . ."

With that, the Worm gently pushed him out the open door.

Hunter did indeed started flapping his arms, but only as a way to get upright for an instant, long enough to pull the ripcord on his parachute.

The Worm's plane flew on. Hunter watched it disappear into the night as his chute was opening, the two fighter jets slowing to their lowest possible speed and going into a lazy eight pattern in order to escort the plane back to Canada, 110 miles to the north.

But for a moment, Hunter also thought he saw the blonde looking back and waving to him, her hand a green blur in the world of night vision.

That was one amazing smooch, he thought as he slowly drifted down to his hidden base.

❂   ❂   ❂

There was nothing like Hunter's F-16XL.

It was a super-variation of the famous F-16 Fighting Falcon, the hot-shit fighter plane that, along with F-15 Eagles and Navy F-14s and F-18s, had helped badly beat the Russians over the battlefields of Europe during World War III.

Yet the XL was different from all of them.

While it had a typical F-16's fuselage—mostly—its wings were of the cranked-arrow design. Arrowhead would have been a better description, because that's exactly what the superplane looked like going through the air—that is, if you were quick enough to catch it. This was difficult to do because with its killer engine pumping out an astounding sixty-five thousand pounds of thrust on afterburner, seeing the F-16XL in flight over head would usually be via the briefest of glimpses, less than the blink of an eye.

It was also heavily armed. In addition to having eighteen under-wing hard points on which to carry as much as twenty-five thousand pounds of bombs, Hunter's XL also had six M61 cannons sticking out of its nose. Not machine guns, these were cannons, so powerful that one round, or certainly two, could take out a tank. They were devastating against aerial targets.

It required a lot of extra power to bring a half dozen of these huge weapons into the air along with all their ammunition. But Hunter's designs, and his own sweat and elbow grease, had pulled off the engine's modification shortly after America was broken up.

Because the XL was such a rare airplane, Hunter knew he had to keep it hidden at all costs. He'd secreted it away at this tiny airfield, which he'd discovered two years after the end of the Big War. It had become his home away from home, a place he'd used when he was running secret ops or just wanted to lay low for a while.

Isolated, hard to see from the ground and the air, it was not unlike Dozer's camp in the Pine Barrens.

Except for the ghosts.

Hunter manipulated his parachute lines and began moving almost horizontally.

He'd jumped from the plane a half mile east of his secret base—he didn't want anyone to see exactly where it was. Only when he spotted an unusual circular arrangement of sugar maple trees among some slightly larger beech trees did he start to descend. It was literally an exercise in trying to find the forest for the trees. Like a lot of strange things Hunter had encountered in his strange life, the base was hidden in plain sight.

He glided for a few more moments over the forest, then, once in position, let the air out of his chute and down he went.

He hit the wet ground boots up and rolled a few times, getting momentarily entangled in the chute. Fighting his way out of the silk, he got to his feet.

His M-16 up and ready, he rotated 360 degrees, making sure everything was as it should be here. There was just a small hangar, a work shack, and a runway, all of it looking as if it had been abandoned long ago. The place hadn't changed in the week or so since he'd left.

So far, so good.

He walked over to the small camouflaged hangar, punched in the code, and the door slowly opened. His F-16XL was inside. It looked more like a race car than a fighter plane. A prewar Ferrari, maybe, and a far, far cry from his clown plane.

He walked around it, running his hand over its sleek lines, checking for anything out of the ordinary. But everything was A-OK.

He spent the next two hours fueling the superjet, loading in the ammo for the six-pack of cannons, and packing his high-altitude recon camera. He worked as quickly as he could while still doing the job right.

Because even though he seemed to be in a place where everything happened quickly—they'd firebombed the MMZ not even five hours ago—every second still counted.

The sun finally came up, ending his long night.

He started his steam generator to build up pressure in the base's catapult. This was the only way the XL could take off from the base—shot into the sky like a naval jet being catapulted off an aircraft carrier. His means of landing was similar to carrier operations as well—at the other end of the runway, he had four arrester hooks.

But now as he taxied the airplane out to hook it up to the catapult, he wondered if he'd ever return to this place again. He knew what awaited him, not just out over the Atlantic, but in New York City, where, even after the barrel-bomb raid, there were *still* sixty-five thousand Russian soldiers and nine thousand NKVD madmen. How were they going to handle that?

That's why he had a deep dark feeling that this would be the last time he'd ever see his private airbase. And that's why he'd left the rest of his fortune in silver inside the hangar with instructions that, on his demise, whoever should find it should spend it on a good time.

After hooking up the plane to the catapult and locking up the base again, he climbed back into the cockpit, strapped himself in, and, via remote control, hit the CATAPULT FIRE button. An instant later, he was rocketing down the short runway on full afterburner. A few seconds later, he yanked back on the controls, pulled the plane back on its tail, and went straight up for five miles.

Then he leveled off, pointed the nose of the plane toward the Atlantic, and hit the throttles.

He was gone in the blink of an eye.

CHAPTER TWENTY-TWO

SEARCHING FOR CONVOY 56 was Hunter's main objective—but he had a secondary mission before making his way to sea.

Climbing to a nose-bleed height of seventy-five thousand feet, he headed southeast after leaving Vermont. Within minutes, he was approaching Russkiy-NYC. Storm clouds blanketed the area and it was raining everywhere, but these were not factors at the moment. He activated his long-range, ground-imaging ALCN-6 recon camera, turned to a course that would put him right over Midtown, and started shooting video.

He was able to bring up a visual representation of Midtown on his control panel's main VRC screen. From this height, the MMZ looked like one deep, smoldering black hole with several twisting, tentacle-like paths of destruction leading to the East River.

He keyed in on 30 Rock. It was still standing, but looked hollowed out by fire and was still smoking heavily. Most pleasing, though, he could see streams of civilians leaving the city. The Triborough and the Fifty-Ninth Street Bridges were packed with them, all heading east. The same for the George Washington Bridge on the West Side; both levels were crowded with refugees heading into New Jersey. Many boats were in the Hudson and the East Rivers, as well, carrying people away from Manhattan. It was obvious the Russians were in such disarray there were no attempts to stop the exodus.

That was all he needed to see. No matter what happened in the next few hours, the 7CAV's attack on the MMZ had been a success. The epicenter of Moscow's military establishment in America was no more and thousands of New York's citizens had been freed.

Bull Dozer had wanted to make the occupiers hurt and to send a message to Moscow. Both missions had been accomplished.

Hunter was over the stormy Atlantic just a few moments later.

His F-16XL super plane was lugging two enormous under-wing gas tanks. Added to its full internal and reserve tanks, this gave him about six hours of fast, fueled flight.

Six hours sounded like a long time—but searching for a target at sea was one of the most time-consuming missions in aviation. Even in daylight, with clear visibility, and long-range forward-looking radar—and even when the pilot had a fair idea where the target was located—a lot of times, it was a matter of hit or miss, and many times, miss. Even from 75-Angels, the ocean looked huge, and the movement of its surface tended to hide things. Bad weather just made it worse.

Hunter knew he'd need every last drop of gas for this mission, which brought up a disturbing question. He was in contact with Dozer back in his spy tower in the Pine Barrens. Both of their radio sets had SCRAMBLER buttons, allowing them to talk without worrying that the Russians could hear them. Communication was not the problem.

The problem was that Hunter might reach his bingo point—that being the moment where he would have to turn around and return to land before he ran out of gas—without having found Convoy 56. He and Dozer had discussed it already, but Hunter knew, if the situation arose, he'd have few options. Locating the convoy was of the utmost importance now. If he had to keep flying and use up all of his gas to find the mystery ships and radio their location and type back to Dozer—and then go into the drink—then so be it.

At least if it happened that way, he would have died—for real this time—for a good cause.

For his country. His homeland in any universe.

America.

His plan was to fly out past Long Island Sound to a point about fifty miles off Nantucket and then start moving due east.

He'd calculated the date and time at which the secret document inside the red pouch had been transmitted and when Convoy 56 was expected in New York Harbor, and then he'd just counted backward. If the ships were traveling at twenty knots, and were due in New York at noon the following day, then they should be within seven hundred miles of New York Harbor and would show up somewhere within the search box he was planning. But if he was off by just a few minutes or a few miles, he'd miss the ships completely and possibly wind up crashing—and drowning—at sea for nothing.

This was the part of the hero business he never liked.

He reached his vector point five minutes after getting feet wet, and remaining at 75,000-Angels, pointed east. It was now 0600 hours, and while the day had brightened, the weather raged on, which only made his task more difficult. His FLIR imager—basically an infrared camera with a telescopic lens—could see through clouds, but the thicker the soup, the blurrier the reading. He'd have to pay very close attention to the imager's screen to avoid missing anything.

But this also gave him lots of time to think—another problem. It had all happened so freaking fast. One moment, he'd been in Dominique's suite atop 30 Rock, seconds away from catching up to her, then, suddenly, he'd been back at the Pine Barrens, then up in Vermont—and now he was out here, in his Ferrari jet, the minutes ticking away before he might have to give it all up and splash in. It was like this universe was stuck in fifth gear and still accelerating.

Where did Zmeya's helicopter go? That was the road not taken for him. Had he chased it, he would have been much closer to rescuing his girlfriend than he was now. Yet he might have shot it down—and it bothered him that the thought that she might be on the copter had never crossed his mind.

But every long conversation he'd had with himself about Dominique always came back to the same question: Was she a princess or a prisoner? It was more likely that she was a captive than a collaborator, at least the Dominique he remembered. But maybe he wasn't dealing with the woman he knew.

Round and round it went, each rumination hurting a little more than the one before. And he still didn't know. *And* the way this mission was looking, there was a good chance he'd never know.

Maybe I did fall into the wrong universe, he thought over and over. *Maybe I'm not supposed to be here. . . .*

He flew on for more than two hours and didn't see as much as a rowboat.

There was no commercial traffic on the North Atlantic these days; from Maine to Scandinavia, it was basically a Russian lake.

The Russians held sway in many other places around the world. Addendums in the Convoy 56 papers indicated places from which the *Okupatsi* could draw resources. If mountain soldiers were needed, a brigade or two from the Russian Alpine Corps, currently stationed in Switzerland, would be sent to the new world. Need someone to fight in the desert, the Corps Commander for the Middle East could spare a few thousand men. Need urban warfighters? A division from the Russian's Sixth Berlin Army would do a tour across the pond.

Moscow was on a roll and making things stick for a change. They'd conquered roughly two thirds of the landmass on the planet, including all of Europe, all of Africa, and all of the Middle East, in less than two years. They were quite literally in the middle of an Earth War; what was going on in America was just one example of how far Moscow had been able to spread its tentacles.

All that said, today, Ivan's Lake seemed maddeningly empty today.

And foggy. And very stormy.

Another long hour passed. He'd soon be near the point of no return. He'd flown straight over the ocean for three hours; it would take him three hours to get back. Simple as that.

Yet he'd seen nothing but storm clouds and fog and the green tint of the radar sweep of the empty seas below him.

Then . . . just as his bingo light began to glow, a buzzing saturated his ears. His eyes went wide. He flipped off his FLIR set. Suddenly, he didn't need it anymore.

The feeling. . . .

The original thing this time.

Something bad was coming. . . .

But . . . what was it?

He couldn't recall ever getting this sensation from an approaching warship. So what was going on?

Then it hit.

Airplanes . . .

Way out here . . .

Coming right at him.

His hands began moving in fast motion. He clicked on his FLIR again, booted the throttle, and pushed down on the stick, all at once. The XL went into a screaming dive.

He broke through a thick cloud layer at forty-five thousand feet—and that's when he saw them.

Two jet fighters, heading west at thirty thousand feet, both wearing red star insignias. But they weren't the elderly mid-level Soviet-type warplanes that were seen flying above America these days. And they certainly weren't Yak-38 jump-jet shitkickers. These planes were sleek, swept back, and modern—and Hunter knew what they were right away: Su-34 Fullback fighters, a plane that could blow most opponents out of the sky in an instant.

Now he knew what kind of warship the VLV was. . . .

They turned back to the east shortly after he spotted them. Although his bingo light had popped on, Hunter kept on going. Using his FLIR allowed him to stay high enough and far enough away from the two Russians that they couldn't pick him up on radar.

He was able to study them with his fairly primitive zoom function. It got him close enough to see that these two fighters were not exactly the same. They were not typical Su-34s, but rather some highly advanced naval variation of the fearsome Fullback fighter.

One was carrying two buddy tanks under its wings where its ordnance points would usually be. The fuel in these massive extra tanks could be used to gas up the second plane while still in flight, the air-to-air refueling extending its combat range by hours.

"Fucking Commies," Hunter said with grim admiration. "Dangerous when they put their minds to it."

The two Russian fighters started to descend. Hunter watched them go down through the dark clouds, expertly heading toward a vessel that, while hidden by a fog bank, was obviously going full speed west, toward New York City.

Hunter hadn't spoken to anyone at Dozer's base since he'd begun his search, and now he had something to tell them. Just as he was about to switch on his radio, the mystery ship broke out of the fog—and finally he saw it.

It was a Very Large Vessel indeed; there was no doubt about that.

Not a battleship or a heavy cruiser.

It was an aircraft carrier. . . .

An enormous one.

He even knew its name. Everyone did.

The *Admiral Isakov.*

Hunter watched the two fighters land, both screeching in through the fog and sea spray that covered the massive flight deck. Behind it was the rest of the convoy.

Hunter turned on his wing, climbed back up to seventy-five thousand feet, and began taking long-range video of the fleet. Then he turned on his radio to call back to Dozer, his eyes fixated on the huge aircraft carrier and the ships beyond.

"How *the hell* are we going to stop these guys?" he wondered aloud.

PART TWO

CHAPTER TWENTY-THREE

May 7

IT WAS NO myth that the *Admiral Isakov* was the world's most powerful warship. In fact, it might have been the most powerful warship ever.

Not only did it carry fleets of fighters and attack copters on board, it was also outfitted with long-range offensive weapons more typically seen on battleships. Four massive batteries, two fore and two aft of the carrier's immense, ten-story superstructure, each packing three gigantic eighteen-inch guns. Cruise missile launchers dominated both sides of the ship's wide deck, along with a line of antiship missiles, weapons that could be quickly adapted to carry nuclear warheads.

For its own protection, dozens of SAM launchers, rotary cannons, and CADS Gatling-type weapons could be found in place all over the exterior, threatening anyone who dared come in close.

But the *Isakov*'s supremacy lay in its air group. The ship carried three dozen Su-34 JLR Mach 2 fighters, extremely advanced and extremely dangerous airplanes. In air-to-air mode, a Su-34 JLR could destroy enemy airplanes up to a hundred miles away. It could also shred anything in near visual distance with its pair of massive nose-mounted cannons.

But the Su-34 JLR was also a bomber—a real bomber, not just some fighter plane with bombs attached. It carried a crew of two and a cockpit big enough to have a galley, a toilet, and a bunk bed. Its fuel capacity, bumped up to huge numbers in the JLR model, gave the plane the capability to fly fifteen hundred miles, drop its bombs, and fly back again—a three-thousand-mile combat radius, incredible for a midsize warplane. A Su-34 JLR taking off from New York City could fly to Kansas, drop ten thousand pounds of conventional bombs, and return with fuel to spare. But . . . if this bomber went with a buddy plane, they could fly the same mission all the way to the West Coast and back, again with leftover fuel. And their weapons systems could just as easily drop poison-gas containers or biological weapons or even nukes.

The carrier was also home to three-dozen Mi-24N helicopters plus just as many cargo lifters, guaranteeing the Russian helicopter shortage in New York City was about to end. The huge Mi-24s featured enough firepower to bust up anything from tanks to entire city blocks, all while carrying up to ten fully armed combat troops. They were so big, the *Isakov*'s gigantic main flight-deck elevator, used to bring aircraft up and down from the ship's hangar decks, was built to service its Mi-24s as well as other oversize Russian copters.

Most of the *Isakov*'s sea operations were run by computers— lots of them on the second deck. There were even some primitive robots—moving arms mostly—that chipped in on things like loading shells or remotely operating the main deck elevator. The carrier carried a crew of just four hundred, instead of the more typical four thousand. This left space for more weapons, fuel, and airplanes.

But the *most* unusual thing about the *Isakov* was who it belonged to.

The Russian Navy had been kept in the dark while the carrier was being built. This was not their boat. Constructed in the deepest secrecy per the wishes of the most shadowy group of characters inside the Kremlin, the *Isakov* belonged to the NKVD, the only secret police force in history to have its own aircraft carrier.

Its crew had been handpicked by the highest echelons of the NKVD and was much better trained than ordinary Russian sailors. All members had been indoctrinated to believe being insanely loyal to the Kremlin was the path to glory and that theirs was the greatest collection of ocean voyagers on the planet. The massive ship did little to dispel that notion.

This was also true for the carrier's fighter pilots. They were members of the NKVD's Special Naval Air Squadrons. The much-feared secret police had an air force, too. Their tactics were so merciless the NKVD pilots even frightened their counterparts in the Russian air corps.

The *Isakov* had seen action along Europe's Mediterranean and North Sea coasts. Sometimes, its planes would even carry out surprise attacks on civilians living deep *within* Russian-controlled territory, just to remind them who was boss.

Now the NKVD was steering its great ship toward America. With New York firmly in the hands of the Russian military, more or less, the massive secret police organization would indeed have a jumping-off point from which to terrorize the continent. This was why the carrier was packed with tons of biological, conventional, and nuclear weapons. It was the arsenal for just such a campaign.

But that was not all.

At the very bottom of the ship, there was a large container, twelve feet by twelve feet, locked inside a bright yellow, lead-lined storage compartment, which was on wheels. Someone had nicknamed it the Magilla. Located in an area of the ship that only the vessel's top officers could access, the item was never directly mentioned in any communiqués regarding the *Isakov*'s new deployment orders. In fact, no one but the highest echelons of the NKVD knew it even existed.

Its newly updated destination was the World Trade Center's Tower Two.

The *Isakov* did not have a captain. It was run by a committee of seven NKVD political officers, all of equal rank but with varying experience in naval warfare. No matter, because in true Soviet fashion, one of the committee members was actually more powerful than the rest. This person had attained this position because he had a direct line to the very top of the secret police organization. His name was Yuri Zmeya Mikhailovich. He was Commissar Zmeya's younger brother.

Just as handsome as Vladimir, and four years his junior, Senior Vessel Chairman Zmeya—or Commander Z (or just plain Z)—also bore a resemblance to the superspy Viktor Robotov, especially around the eyes. But however the DNA had been distributed, Yuri was as adept and as ruthless at his job as big brother Vladimir was at his. They'd both risen in the ranks very quickly and were plainly cut from the same cloth. And both were on the same mission: to make the NKVD the most feared police organization on the planet.

To this end, Z ran an extremely tight ship, rarely leaving the bridge. His pocket-size crew performed mostly as overseers of the *Isakov*'s vast computer systems—80 percent were IT guys. Still, they swabbed the decks, endlessly painted the ship, worked long duty shifts, and were fed the minimum.

Like his brother, Yuri Zmeya preferred to dress in black. On board the *Isakov*, he wore a nondescript black naval uniform, a massive naval cap, and large dark sunglasses, which he reportedly didn't take off even when he slept, which wasn't very often.

The convoy had left Murmansk ten days ago and had sailed in foul weather the entire trip—rain, high winds, very turbulent seas. This day promised more of the same. Torrential rain and the booming Atlantic had forced Z to clear the flight deck after just one abbreviated buddy patrol by a two-pack of its Su-34 JLR fighters.

By 0800 hours, the storm had grown even worse, forcing Z to reduce speed to eighteen knots.

The rain grew more intense, and the surface gale coming over the bow grew to fifty knots, blowing suds of salt and brine all the way down to the stern.

At 0830 hours, Z called off all air launches and ordered that once a transit air group from Murmansk landed later in the day, all air ops would be shut down entirely until the weather improved. While this canceled his surprise flyover of New York City by the carrier's entire complement of Su-34s, not launching aircraft saved wear and tear on the knightly Su-34 JLRs. Plus, with the flight deck empty, the surging waves would wash away the last of the oil and grease that had accumulated over the long voyage. Yuri wanted his ship to look as good as possible when it arrived off Battery Park around noon the following day.

After all, big brother Vlad would be waiting at the dock.

By 1430 hours, when the second-call meal was delivered to the bridge from the officers' mess, everyone but Z declined, all of their faces having turned some shade of green due to the heavy seas.

Z found this amusing. Going through major gales at sea was just another part of the job, he thought now, looking out on the nasty hurricane-like conditions. After all, he was commander of the greatest ship in the world, maybe in all of history, and he—

Suddenly, something crashed onto the carrier's storm-tossed deck. It made a horrendous noise coming in, a sort of screeching that went right to the bone. It was black, had propellers and wings, and was belching tremendous streams of fire and smoke. It skidded right past the superstructure, creating a giant spray of sparks and traveling so fast it was certain to drop off the side of the ship. But at the very last moment, its landing gear collapsed, twisting its wings and demolishing its two engines. All this wreckage served to slow it down. It stopped just inches from toppling over the bow.

Z was simply stunned, as was everyone on the bridge. They all jumped to their feet and were crowded up against the control bridge windows, trying to make sense of what had just happened ten stories down. One NKVD committee member voiced the only likely explanation: Had some random plane in distress just crash-landed on their ship?

But before anyone could reply, a second plane came out of the storm, and it, too, slammed onto the deck. It looked exactly like the first, black and stubby. It quickly caught fire as well. Z froze in place. This was too much like something from a dream, something that just should not be happening. This second plane also went screeching past the superstructure at high speed, snapping all three of the ship's arresting cables before crashing into the first plane. The collision resulted in so much jagged metal and steel, it served to keep both planes adhered to the viciously rolling flight deck.

Even before it stopped moving, armed men were jumping out of the second plane via its open cargo bay. Joining up with dark figures exiting the first smoking wreck, they tried mightily to push the two planes over the side, obviously to make room for a third plane, which hit the deck an instant later. Slamming into the far aft gun deck and cleanly severing its starboard wing, it scattered the armed invaders, spiraled into the first two planes, and finally knocked both wrecks into the sea.

Armed troops began pouring out of this third plane, too. Joining their comrades from the first two mangled aircraft, they took up positions among the automated weaponry in place along the forward starboard gunwale. Then, on someone's command, the invaders started firing their weapons directly up at the control tower. Suddenly, a giant fan of bright red tracer rounds lit up the blowing morning rain. Sustained and merciless, the barrage was intended to kill the ship's commanders and anyone else on the bridge.

But by this point, everyone inside the bridge had literally hit the deck as a storm of broken glass and machine gun rounds rained down on them—everyone except Commander Z. He remained absolutely still at the windows, awash in denial. That's how he saw the fourth plane bang in, skid down the flight deck, collide with the island, and then screech to a long, painful halt up at the bow, covering the entire flight deck with a flood of sparks. Even more soldiers began jumping out of it.

Only then did Z's security detail arrive and force him down to the deck.

"Sir—we are being attacked," the lead security officer shouted. "We are going to remove you to the secure point behind the bridge."

This knocked Z out of his trance.

He resisted the security team's efforts to carry him away. "Who would possibly be attacking us? No one knows we're out here."

The lead security man looked at his colleagues and then grudgingly nodded. They let Z up slowly, still protecting him from all sides with handheld body-length bulletproof shields. Most of the bridge's windows had been shattered by gunfire by this point, though the amount of incoming ordnance had not decreased.

Lifting Z only enough so he could see out one of these broken windows, the security man directed his attention to the wreckage of the fourth crashed plane. The flames around it were bright enough to cut through the smoke and spray and let Z see something had been painted on its fuselage right behind the wing.

It was a flag.

Stars and stripes. Red, white, and blue. . . .

Z began sputtering. "Americans? No way—they've been reduced to cavemen. There's no way they've gotten aboard my ship. No one knew we were coming. . . ."

The security team finally lifted Z off the deck and started moving him aft. While leaving the giant control room in this awkward deportment, Z ordered his fellow committee members to remain on the bridge and monitor the battle. They nervously acknowledged his command with a round of halfhearted salutes.

The security detail got Z into his large, fully equipped, steel-reinforced safe room located just behind the bridge. They locked themselves in with him. The mandated withdrawal had little impact on him, though. He immediately turned on the ship's intercom and began barking orders. His first was to call the crew to battle stations.

But this brought a moment of confusion. The *Isakov* might have been the greatest warship in the world, but it was crewed by only four hundred men, most of whom were technicians. Battle stations to them meant manning the screens at their Vector-06Cs and Mera-7209 computers and looking for some target out over the horizon. They were just barely sailors, never mind soldiers, and they'd never drilled for a physical attack on the ship because no one had ever dreamed something like this would happen.

Still, there were plenty of combat weapons on the carrier, thousands of AK-47s along with tons of ammunition. Some bigger, even more destructive combat weapons, like RPG launchers, were on board as well.

Z screamed for his NKVD security forces, real soldiers, about eighty men in all, to join with the three dozen Su-34 pilots and immediately confront the attackers on deck. Then he ordered the regular crewmembers to arm themselves with AK-47s and do the same thing inside the ship. Finally, he told his antiaircraft crews to activate their bow-mounted CAD Gatling-type weapons, turn their outward-facing barrels to point inward, and blast the aerial intruders off the deck.

But then, some of the CAD guns along the outer edge of the ship began blowing up on their own. Five in a row along the starboard gunwales were suddenly gone in five puffs of smoke, the debris quickly blown away by the high winds. By this time, more than half of the mystery soldiers had gained entry inside the ship anyway, most by swarming through a hatch at the bottom of the giant under-attack superstructure. Now, running past the mysteriously burning weapons, another dozen of the invaders made it through the hatch and joined their comrades in the first-deck passageway. Another half dozen were right on their heels.

By then, the automated CAD guns on the port side had spun around to point inward. These weapons could fire a hundred depleted uranium rounds *a second* and there were five of them. Aimed by TV cameras controlled from belowdecks, and unbeknownst to them, their aiming sights were turned on those gunmen still using the wreckage of the last two aircraft as cover while they continued to pummel the carrier's bridge with tracer fire.

The five Gatling-like barrels actually started rotating, a two-second exercise to get them properly lined up with their firing chambers. In one more second, they would have started firing, and those on the receiving end of the horrific barrage would be reduced to a bloody mist.

But at that last instant, the five weapons also blew up, one right after another. A moment after that, the carrier's main radio mast was severed in a mighty blast, killing all communications aboard the ship and spraying the deck with a rain of shrapnel. A moment after that, the ship's huge K4FN satellite dish antenna was blown to bits.

That's when a jet airplane suddenly appeared out of the storm, only to disappear an instant later.

Z was watching it all as a live TV broadcast being displayed on the phalanx of black-and-white monitors that dominated one wall of his safe room. He was the first to spot the jet. It had come right down the starboard side, not fifteen feet off the deck, strafing the area where the five antiaircraft guns had just blown up. Though it was being battered mightily by the winds and rain, its aim had been perfect. One, two seconds out in the open at the most, and then it disappeared back into the tempest, leaving Z to wonder, *What kind of plane was that?*

Though the TV reception was not good, it was enough for Z to see the jet's bright exhaust inside the low rain clouds. A moment later, huge streams of tracer fire came out of those same clouds, now hitting targets all over the carrier's superstructure. Antennas. Radar dishes. More antiaircraft gear. More deck guns. Z's safe room shuddered with the impacts; the whole ship was shaking. Every shot fired by the plane seemed to hit its target, leaving just smoky flashes behind.

Another sharp turn inside the storm, and suddenly the jet was coming directly at the control bridge. The multiple cannons in its nose were clearly evident. When they started firing, the flare they caused was so bright, it blacked out some of Z's TV screens. But on others, he saw the fusillade demolish what was left of the bridge's windows, killing everyone left inside. Some of these shells hit the exterior of Z's safe room itself, rocking it violently.

But before the airplane flashed over the ferociously burning bridge and back into the storm, it was caught by a TV camera mounted in the low radar mast, down one level, aft of the main bridge.

Z was able to freeze the frame and finally get a good look at the aerial attacker. His blood suddenly turned cold. Unlike his brother, Z had been spared having to look at a ghostly flying toy and wonder what the hell it was. Once he saw this plane up close, he recognized it immediately—and he knew who was flying it.

The legendary F-16XL.

Hawk Hunter.

The Wingman.

"I *despise* that guy," Z growled angrily to his security men. "And everyone thought he was dead."

The stark realization quickly sank in. Not only had Z heard all the tales about Hawk Hunter, he believed them. He hit his shortwave radio's ALL-SEND button and broadcast an emergency message to the rest of Convoy 56, something he wouldn't have dreamed he'd be doing just a few minutes ago.

It was just two lines:

ISAKOV UNDER ATTACK BY AMERICANS, POSSIBLY H HUNTER.
RENDER ALL ASSISTANCE POSSIBLE.

CHAPTER TWENTY-FOUR

HUNTER HAD CIRCLED the embattled carrier thirty-three times, fighting the storm, looking for targets and trying to provide cover for the 7CAV air-assault team.

The ship's main mast, all of its radar dishes, and all of its remaining antiaircraft guns and missiles from the superstructure down to the bow were gone, blown away by his six-pack of nose cannons. The control tower was in flames. Smoke was pouring out of hundreds of vents located under the flight deck and fires could be seen sprouting up all over. Meanwhile, the storm had grown worse, the rain had started coming down in sheets, and the enormity of the waves crashing onto the deck had reached biblical proportions.

All this had happened in just five minutes.

The plan to attack the *Isakov* was as improvised as anything Hunter had ever done—in any universe. There'd been no time to do it any other way. Dozer's men had somehow patched the Sherpas together in record time. Then out came the new gun stations and in went a lot of padding—mattresses mostly—to soften the crash-landings they knew were needed to make it onto the carrier's deck. Four planes, about twenty troopers in each plus aircrew, they'd left the secret base in the hands of their twenty civilian techs and 7CAV sentries. They would keep an eye on things while the team was away.

The flight out from the Pine Barrens had been turbulent and terrifying, but the assault force found the *Isakov* exactly where Hunter
said it would be. Still, it was only by virtue of the storm's high winds
and his flying ability that the Wingman was even still alive.

He'd managed to use the high winds to glide his way back
home after his initial ocean recon mission. He went not to the
Pine Barrens or Vermont, but to his old temporary base on the
highway near Trenton, next to the tank full of gasoline. While
the stale petrol was not the best fuel for the XL, it was enough
to get him back up to Vermont, where he pumped in some real
AV-8 gas, loaded his wings down with weapons, and then headed
back out to sea.

The storm and the carrier's own defensive dispersement
allowed the 7CAV to come as a complete surprise, slamming aboard unmolested. Flying in low to avoid radar, they'd
exploited the direction of the carrier's AA guns, all of which
pointed outward and away from the deck, to land free of any
immediate fire.

Now, by monitoring 7CAV's general operations channel,
Hunter knew as many as sixty raiders were already inside the
ship. The rest were firing continuously at the superstructure,
hoping anything hit up there would result in another lost system
for the carrier.

Just as he started his thirty-fourth orbit of the ship, Hunter's
secondary 7CAV radio channel started beeping. It was Dozer,
down on the deck, leading the operation, calling him directly.

"We got this for the moment," he told Hunter over the static.
"If you're going to do part two, now's the time to go."

Sailing ten miles behind the huge carrier was the rest of Convoy 56.

From high up through a FLIR sight, it looked like a moving necklace. Five ships made up the outer ring, the destroyers
packed with Styx missiles and, from the looks of it, many antiaircraft guns. In the middle was the massive Chekski cruise liner
turned troopship, painted in gray sea camo. The secret convoy documents said there were thirty thousand ZBG Chekskis
crammed aboard this ship. Carrying tons of medieval horror

weapons with them, they were ready to terrorize America from one coast to the other.

The converted troop carrier was unarmed; it had no way to protect itself. But in theory, it shouldn't need to. With the *Isakov*'s big guns and air fleets just a few seconds away, with its ring of destroyers, and no less than two battle cruisers just five miles back, bringing up the rear, there was no reason to put any defensive weapons aboard the ship. This left more room to squeeze in their human chattel.

Only a crazy person would try to run this gauntlet of ships.

But Hunter had come prepared to do just that.

Four Exocet antiship missiles, long stored at his base in Vermont, were hanging off his wings. Two per side, they were powerful weapons. Each carried a massive 350-pound warhead and a homing system that rarely missed anything at sea. The warhead was designed not to simply blow up on the target ship, but to crack its hull in two, causing it to sink under its own weight. If the warhead detonated, it was pretty much a kill shot.

While it might have taken a flock of Exocets to sink a titan like the armor-plated *Isakov*, the Chekski cruise ship had never been meant for combat. An infrared readout on Hunter's control screen told him via temperature fluctuations that the vessel had no armor anywhere. Compared to a warship, its hull was paper thin.

He just had to get close enough to ensure a good hit.

While some Exocets could be fired as far as fifty miles away, the missile's homing systems weren't infallible. When presented with a cluster of vessels, such as the five Styx missile boats sailing tightly around the huge troop ship, they really couldn't distinguish one ship from another.

Hunter knew if he fired from true back-off range—several dozen miles or so—there was a good chance his missile would hit one of the escort vessels and not the Chekski boat from hell.

For this attack to succeed, he'd have to get very close to the huge ship.

Hunter had screamed to thirty thousand feet above the huge troop ship, using his FLIR set to map out his best attack profile.

This would have been hard to do under the best conditions; the worsening storm below made everything much more difficult.

Finally coming up with the best solution for his missile run, he put the XL into a screaming dive, dropping more than five miles in thirty seconds. Leveling off just forty feet above the roiling ocean, he was now five miles to the east of his target. Three of the five destroyers immediately popped up on his weapons screen. He could see their armament had already gone hot, so he had to make this quick.

He pushed his throttles to three quarters power; the three destroyers started shooting at him an instant later. It was a well-placed barrage, opening up on him with expert fury. Whether warned in advance by the *Isakov* or just really good at what they did, suddenly thousands of streaks of orange light were coming at him from the escorts, deadly tracer bullets seeking him out in the wind and spray.

Through a series of violent banks and turns he was able to avoid the fusillade. This was not shocking. He'd done these types of maneuvers so many times before, he didn't even think about it now. He let his hands move the stick whichever way they wanted; throttles up, throttles back, it really wasn't up to him. Something took over when he was in situations like this, a sort of internal automatic pilot. And he'd learned a long time ago that whenever it happened, he should just go with the flow.

Suddenly, the closest destroyer was only a mile away. With night-vision goggles snapped down, he could see dozens of individual heat sources moving about the ship—crewmen rushing to service the antiaircraft crews that were firing at him. It was mostly cannon and heavy machine-gun fire coming his way, but a few antiaircraft missiles were also evident in the mix.

His run-in to the target lasted just twenty seconds, an eternity when someone was trying to shoot you down. But after just missing a cluster of incendiary antiaircraft cannon shells blowing up right in front of him, he went full throttle and with one great dash of power, and a brutal sonic boom, rocketing right over the escort vessel. Suddenly, he found himself inside the protective ring. The cruise ship was right in front of him, two miles away.

The other ships in the circle quickly became aware of what was happening and started firing at him. This was an unusual tactic because the destroyers were arrayed in a rough circle, and shooting at something inside it meant some of their ordnance would inevitably wind up hitting their sister ships.

No matter. Hunter knew the escorts were under NKVD command, and taking a little friendly fire was of little concern to them if it meant destroying their bogey.

With the cruise ship now just a mile away, Hunter jammed his throttles back down to low. He hit the back of his seat hard, not unlike some of the jolts he'd taken in the clown plane. Anti-aircraft rounds were flying all around him, fired by at least four escort ships. And once again, he was letting pure instinct guide him through them. The XL was continuously moving, going up, down, sideways, and once almost banking right into the water. But, as always, someone somewhere seemed to be looking out for him, and he proceeded without a scratch.

One mile from the target, Hunter flipped the B1 switch on his control panel and saw an arming diagram pop onto his read-out screen. By touching the screen in the right place, he armed the outer Exocet on his starboard wing. It was juiced and ready to go in two seconds. Hunter looked up at his target, and for the first time, he realized the troop carrier's decks were lined with people—Chekskis—and they were shooting at him as well. He was not concerned though. They were firing at him with AK-47s, and he was still way out of their range.

At twenty-five hundred feet exactly, he lit off the Exocet. It flashed out from under his wing and flew a straight, ten-second course right into the side of the cruise ship, hitting the waterline about three hundred feet back from the bow. The warhead worked as advertised. There was an initial explosion that lifted the huge ship about three feet out of the water. Then came a tremendous second explosion, many more times powerful than the first, and the ship came back down on itself, splitting in two.

Hunter rocketed over the scene a moment later. Both ends of the giant vessel were already slipping beneath the stormy waves, with hundreds of Chekskis being sucked down into a huge whirl-pool created as a result. It was as if a plug had been pulled some-where deep below and the ocean was draining out. Others tried to swim away, but the vortex just got bigger and quickly caught up with them, pulling them down too to their watery graves in a horrifying scene.

For Hunter, war was about two opponents with opposite points of view battling it out like soldiers. May the best man win. Sinking unarmed ships at sea did not fall into that category. But neither did beheading innocent men, women, and children. Or importing thousands of thugs, along with their barbaric arma-ments that would be of no use in modern combat, just to terror-ize and kill even more innocents. Or blowing yourself up to take even *more* of the blameless with you to the grave.

The Chekskis were not soldiers; they weren't even police-men. They were psychotic killers who'd already caused massive misery and carnage in many parts of the postwar world. And if Moscow had its way, they would be unleashed on America.

And Hunter just couldn't let that happen.

The two halves of the ship quickly disappeared in one enor-mous gulp, leaving almost nothing left atop the turbulent sur-face. Hunter took a deep breath of oxygen. One push of the B1 button and more than thirty thousand people were gone? No wreckage, no lifeboats. Nothing.

Just . . . gone.

"Do we get gold stars in heaven for that?" he asked the cos-mos grimly.

It might have been the only time in his life that he jinxed him-self, because not a heartbeat later, the water below him became agitated in a way no ocean storm could ever cause. The whitecaps were literally catching on fire.

Someone was shooting at him—and not from the direction of the escort ships, but from behind.

His hands pulled back on the stick and the XL went straight up, one mile, two, three, spiraling for good measure. That he hadn't been hit by the well-aimed barrage of incendiary cannon shells was a miracle . . . or something.

"The feeling" had arrived almost simultaneously with the incoming fire. That sensation telling him trouble was near. His body began buzzing all over again. He checked his weapons suite—every light was solid green. He looped over at seventeen thousand feet and started back down to find who'd tried to kill him.

That's when he saw them.

Six Su-34 JLRs superjets coming right at him.

They were passing up through twelve thousand feet going at least Mach 1. He looked down at his targeting screen; he'd never seen a Su-34 JLR up *this* close before. It was a huge airplane. Wide wings, twin engines, twin tails, a flat nose. And a really big cockpit. They looked more like little bombers than big fighter planes.

But Hunter couldn't believe they were really here.

How the hell did they get off the carrier?

This was not a good situation. Not only was he outnumbered by six pretty incredible aircraft, he was still carrying the three valuable Exocets, two on the port wing and one starboard. They were creating enormous drag and presented him with an unbalanced flight profile, making it difficult to fly at top speed.

Still, he had to fight these guys.

CHAPTER TWENTY-FIVE

IT WAS A STRANGE battle right from the start.

Typically, once an aerial engagement was on, the participants scattered and it became a free for all. But the six Su-34s were flying in a line-abreast formation, almost like an aerobatics team, and they stayed that way. That's when Hunter realized these were three buddy flights he was looking at. Three full-fledged fighters along with three armed refueling planes.

That answered one question. The planes hadn't come off the *Isakov*. They were transiting to it from someplace else—Hunter's guess being somewhere in Russian-controlled Europe—and joining the air fleet already on the boat. They'd just happened to arrive in the middle of the chaos.

Wherever they'd come from, they were at the end of a long journey, in bad weather, and that told Hunter they were probably low on gas. In fact, he could see one buddy pair was still hooked up, hose-to-hose via underwing receptacles. For these two to start a brawl in that configuration could only mean the fighter-plane half of the buddy element must have been down to fumes.

He was dropping at nearly Mach 1.5, and they were climbing at almost the same speed. They opened fire on him at exactly twelve thousand feet, all at once, fighters and tankers. But no cannons this time. Instead, they launched a spread of Aphid-6 antiaircraft missiles—weapons designed to hit targets ten miles away. Using Aphids for in-close combat was like taking a guillotine to a knife fight. It was nasty, but there were easier ways to make your enemy bleed.

But no matter how they were used, Aphids were killers. They didn't have to hit you; they just had to blow up near you. The resulting storm of shrapnel would do the rest. If just one of the dozen missiles went off in Hunter's vicinity, he'd be toast.

He yanked his stick sideways and banked hard left. It was such an abrupt maneuver, the shower of Aphids went right by him and continued on to points unknown. At the same time, he'd fired his six-pack of Vulcan nose cannons at the two hooked-up planes. His combined stream of cannon rounds perforated the twin tails of the Su-34 buddy tanker. It instantly flew out of control, catching fire and rolling over to plummet to the sea, pulling the other Su-34 that was still attached down with it, its pilot unable to disconnect the fuel hose in time.

He did a complete horizontal loop, trying like hell to get in back of the two surviving buddy flights, which were still flying in formation. He got within twenty-five hundred feet of them, his finger poised over the six-pack TRIGGER button, when suddenly the four airplanes split apart in four different directions. A diamond burst they called it—and again, it was not unlike an aerobatics display. But in combat? And in the middle of a hurricane?

"Holy Christ!" Hunter heard himself exclaim. Only a Su-34 could have pulled off a crazy jig like that. Small bomber in looks, yes. But these planes were every bit as agile as his XL fighter.

And their pilots were clever. They had drawn him in close. Now, linking back up while doing similar, incredibly sharp turns, they leveled out and were in back of him.

He banked hard left again, pulling on the stick with all his strength. In doing so, his nose went right across the canopy of one of the separated buddy tankers. A quick burst from the six-pack literally cut the Su-34 in two. There was one huge explosion, definitely no parachutes.

Suddenly, the odds were a little better. But it was still three against one.

The trio of Su-34s began turning mightily, trying again to get on his tail. He turned over and headed down again, this time at Mach 2. It was so unbalanced, it was all he could do to keep the XL from slipping into a fatal stall. But he didn't want to just dump the rare Exocets if he didn't have to.

Three Aphids were shot at him as soon as he started his plunge. In response, his inner light started him spinning again. The missiles roared by his tail a moment later, his gyrations screwing with their electronic heads. They blew up just a few hundred feet away, one, two, three. He felt the trio of shocks in the air but, luckily, was far enough away not to catch any of the shrapnel from the combined explosions. It had been close, though. At such high speeds, everything was relative. A few inches either way and he would have been reduced to cinders.

He was closing in on the wet deck. Once again battling gravity, aerodynamics, and the physics of balance and momentum, he pulled back hard on the stick, trying to level off before he wound up crashing into the storm tossed water. Finally, at just a hundred feet, he got some air under him. The pursuing Su-34s had backed off much higher, preferring not to follow a madman down to Neptune's realm. Once they saw his recovery, though, they had to hastily remaneuver to get back to an advantageous position.

This gave him a few seconds to breathe. He was streaking along at seven hundred knots, just a tick above the raging ocean, when suddenly he found one of the convoy's two battle cruisers began filling up his GEW-40 infrared targeting screen. He looked up, and piercing through the storm clouds with his night-vision goggles, he could just make out the outline of the giant battle cruiser a half mile away.

The people on the ship were very surprised to see him—but their antiaircraft weapons started lighting up right away. It didn't matter. Even as one of the Su-34s made it down to a hundred feet and began to get a missile lock on him, Hunter pushed his B1 button again and juiced all three Exocets riding under his wings. That's what it would take to whack this monster. The power light blinked green on the GEW-40IF, and he pushed the live fire switch.

The trio of Exocets flashed away—one, two, three—and headed for the huge warship. Due to electronic jamming or the weather or something else, they did not fly in a straight line. Instead, the big missiles began corkscrewing soon after coming off the rails, bucking their way through the high winds, leaving three bizarre exhaust trails in their wake.

They hit the ship, though. Not at the waterline, as designed, but all three square on its bridge. Close to twelve hundred pounds of explosives blew up, vaporizing the control room, along with the weapons systems room one level below and the officers' wardroom, which was adjacent to the weapons center. In one stroke, nearly every senior NKVD officer on board was killed. But the ship did not stop or even slow down; it didn't seem to miss a beat at all. It just kept moving, fighting the storm, but now without any senior officers, steering, navigation, weapons, or a control bridge.

An instant later, Hunter felt his hands grip the stick very tightly and pull it back. The XL was suddenly going straight up again, just missing a barrage of cannon fire from the pursuing Su-34. The other two Russian fighters saw him coming up and each fired an Aphid at him. Luckily, his quick ascent confused the missiles' homing systems. He hit the throttles and was quickly out of range.

Once again, he found himself three miles above the Su-34s, just about where it all started. *Enough of this bullshit*, he thought. He wasn't carrying any more extra baggage, and it was time to really dance. He turned over and started straight down again. At ten thousand feet, he began spiraling madly, engaging his Vulcan cannons as he fell. Hundreds of M61 rounds began gushing out of the XL's nose, and by twisting as he dove, he created a carousal of continuous fire. Looking not unlike lightning bolts, they were all entwined, but heading in many different directions.

Two of the Su-34 pilots guessed wrong and banked directly into the cone of fire. The buddy tanker of the two caught the worst of it and disappeared in a fireball. His partner tried to fall away, but jagged pieces of the stricken fuel ship got sucked into its air intakes, and he blew up as well.

It almost hurt Hunter to see these beautiful airplanes being destroyed, but this was war. Plus, one enemy fighter still remained.

He stopped spiraling and leveled off at five thousand feet, watching his velocity fall to zero. The XL stopped in midair; a trick not too different from the clown plane. The last Su-34 roared right by his nose.

He engaged his cannons and watched six lines of giant phosphorous tracers slam into the remaining Su-34. Hitting square on the cockpit, both pilots were killed instantly. The big plane turned over one last time and started its final plunge to the sea, spiraling out of control.

That was it. Total time of the fight: one minute, thirty-three seconds.

But no sooner was it over than his radio crackled to life.

It was Dozer, and he was shouting, "You won't believe what's going on here!"

CHAPTER TWENTY-SIX

THE CHAOS ABOARD the *Isakov* had only grown in Hunter's absence.

Positioned on the far end of the deck, near the wreckage of the last two Sherpas, Bull Dozer and a dozen 7CAV troopers were in a brutal gun battle with the combined trained security details for the ship's committee members, by far the best fighters on the carrier, and the fanatical NKVD fighter pilots.

There were about eighty of them in all, and they had taken up positions along the carrier's starboard gunwales near the bottom of the forward superstructure. Armed with AK-47s and RPGs, they suddenly started pouring it on Dozer's location and hadn't let up.

Because Dozer and his dozen men were at the far end of the bow, on the same side as these security troops, it had become a deadlock. There were two clear shooting lanes, which meant no one on either side could move or maneuver. There was a lot of ordnance flying around, but no one was going anywhere.

A much larger portion of the 7CAV force, seventy-two troopers and four deep recon men, had indeed gained entry to the carrier through a hatch in the devastated superstructure. They were now on the first deck, which was an interior passageway one level down from the carrier deck. Their objective was the *Isakov*'s electronic control center. The ECC was the carrier's brain; everything that made the ship so dangerous emanated from here. If they could seize it, they might at least bring the carrier to a stop.

The troopers were still battling the ship's crew, untrained sailors firing AK-47s, many for the first time. But this fight, too, was at a stalemate for a very unusual reason. Just as the secret Convoy 56 documents indicated, the *Isakov* was jam-packed with cargo. But to the surprise of the American raiders, crates and boxes of all shapes and sizes had been stored right inside the carrier's main passageways themselves. Deck one was the ship's Main Street; everybody had to pass through it at least once a day. It was now stuffed with cargo pallets, providing the inexperienced crew members with hidden places to fire.

Literally box-to-box fighting, it was going very slow.

All this pandemonium had a soundtrack. Klaxons were going off all over the ship. Smoke alarms, fire alarms, water breech alarms. The bell calling the ship's company to battle stations was still ringing. The carrier's electronic foghorn had somehow gotten turned on and was moaning away. The noise of the gun battle one deck below was almost as loud as the one out on the deck. A blizzard of tracers going in both directions. The occasional bang of an MK19 grenade going off. And a raging fire had engulfed the top of the enormous superstructure now, making it look like a skyscraper aflame. All the while, the enormous storm continued to rage, with titanic waves sweeping the deck at the most unexpected times.

Dozer crouched behind the crumpled wing of Sherpa 3, trying to avoid the incoming fire, as well as being swept off the deck by the monstrous waves. He had been in some crazy spots before, but he'd never seen anything like this.

And then it got crazier.

Dozer could not believe that he could hear anything else above the din. But incredibly, about five minutes into the battle, he detected something else. He was changing the banana clip in his M-16 when he heard a mechanical sound, out there in the wind and rain, faint at first, but getting louder. Not a jet . . . but another kind of aircraft. Something larger maybe?

He told his troopers to stop firing for a moment. All of them heard it then and agreed it was getting closer.

Suddenly, they saw it. Bursting out of the storm not twenty-five feet over their heads, it went right over the top of them and straight down the carrier's deck. Black, whirling, whipping the rain around, it was a giant Mi-26 Halo helicopter with a large red luminescent stripe running down its side.

Dozer was stunned—they all were. This was no weather for choppers, no matter who was flying them. But even stranger, Dozer had actually seen this copter before. They'd picked it up on their balloon cam a number of times, flitting around Manhattan at night. The bright red stripe was hard to miss. By tracking its movements and listening to reports on Red Radio, Dozer's intel guys had quickly determined this was the personal air taxi of Commissar Vladimir Zmeya, head of the Russian secret police in New York.

And now, for some reason, it was here.

The copter went into a shaky hover above the deck way down past the burning superstructure. Even the NKVD guards stopped shooting for a moment, surprised their supreme commander's chopper had suddenly appeared.

But why is it here? Dozer wondered.

The copter didn't seem particularly weighed down, as it would be if it were carrying reinforcements. And if it was here to attack them somehow, what was it doing hovering over the deck so far away?

Dozer put his night-vision goggles down just as the pilot's window opened on the hovering copter. The pilot reached out of the window, exposing himself to the wind and rain whipped up by the downwash of his spinning rotor blades, grasping what looked like a handheld remote control device. He was pushing a button on it madly.

Suddenly, a great opening in the deck appeared below the Mi-26. It was the *Isakov's* huge remote-controlled flight-deck elevator. At nearly 120 feet across, it was built to handle even the biggest of Russia's combat helicopters.

As the elevator slowly started descending, the copter descended with it, disappearing inside the ship. Dozer and his men were incredulous.

A moment later, they received a call from one of the 7CAV officers fighting in the crowded passageway on deck one. He was stationed right next to the elevator on a catwalk looking into the ship's main hangar. He reported the copter had landed on the elevator by this time and had continued on right to the bottom of the ship, where the carrier's helicopter storage hangar was located.

He confirmed to Dozer that yes, the copter was the personal ride of a top NKVD.

But he'd also seen something else.

As the trooper put it: "It's something Hawk should know. . . ."

CHAPTER TWENTY-SEVEN

HUNTER HEADED BACK to the *Isakov* at full throttle.

The NKVD carrier was hard to miss, even in the storm. Huge columns of smoke were rising above the giant warship, explosions were going off all over, fires were sweeping the deck and engulfing the superstructure. The battle was still in progress.

He turned his radio back to the mission frequency; he heard a cacophony of sounds and voices. It was the 7CAV, in combat, calling back and forth, reporting progress, reporting problems, reporting casualties. Hunter heard his own name amid the static. Several people were trying to hail him at once.

Finally, one voice came through.

Bull Dozer. . . .

He was yelling, "Hawk, can you hear me?"

Hunter quickly responded. "Affirmative—now I can."

"Hey, it's fucking crazy down here," Dozer told him. "We've got two major gunfights going on, shit is flying in all directions, and I'm seasick as a bastard. But, in the middle of all this, our pal Commissar Zmeya's personal chopper just came aboard. Went right down the main elevator shaft. Some of my deep recon guys have gotten down there. They say this copter is now at the bottom of the boat."

Hunter couldn't believe it. Zmeya's copter? Aboard the *Isakov*? "Who would be crazy enough to fly way out here in this kind of weather?" he radioed back.

After a brief pause, Dozer replied, "Well, *we* did. . . ."

There was a burst of static.

"But there's more, Hawk," Dozer yelled through it. "She's here, too. . . ."

Hunter froze. "Who is?"

"Dominique," Dozer said. "She's on the ship. Came in on the chopper. I'm talking to one of my deep recon guys on the other channel. He's got eyes on her right now."

Hunter felt a jolt of electricity run right through him. Dozer crossed the channels and had his recon trooper speak directly to Hunter.

"She's right across the hangar deck from me, Hawk," he said from his hiding spot, his voice low. "Not twenty feet away. Russian police are getting off the copter, looking like they're trying to find something. It's confusing down here, but she's right in the middle of it."

"Are you sure it's her?" Hunter asked. "There are a lot of Dominique wannabes hanging with the Reds these days."

"This is ten by ten, Hawk," was his reply. "I know it's her. She's looking right at me. Gotta go."

Hunter went numb. No feeling in his hands or his feet. Only his mouth could move, and it was only halfway open. He'd only just missed her atop 30 Rock during the firestorm. He didn't want that to happen again.

That meant he had to get down to the carrier. . . . And *that* meant he had to land somehow on the rolling, wave-swept ship.

Dozer came back on the line.

"I'm coming aboard," Hunter told him, beginning another orbit of the ship.

"You're *what*?"

"I'm landing," Hunter told him. "I've just got to figure out how. . . ."

The radio kicked out at that point, but that was okay with Hunter. He had to concentrate.

The carrier's deck was pitching madly and it was strewn with wreckage from the crashed cargo planes and other debris caused by the fighting. The ship's gigantic main mast was in pieces where it had fallen, scattered up and down the deck, much of it still on fire. Because the flight-deck elevator had descended to the bottom of the boat, there was a huge gaping hole on the deck near the bow. Worst of all, even though the XL had an arrester hook, when the second Sherpa had come aboard the carrier, it had snapped the trio of arresting cables stretched across the *Isakov's* flight deck, rendering them useless.

The XL was not the clown plane. Its absolute lowest landing speed was 110 knots. Hunter could manipulate his flight controls right up to that point, but anything less, he'd go straight into the sea.

He had no choice but to hit the deck going that fast. But once on board, how could he slow down? He flew over the burning carrier and surveyed it again. Huge waves were coming out of the storm from all directions and crashing all over the ship. More fires around the superstructure had popped up. And the wind was growing even fiercer.

But that's what gave him an idea.

His radio popped back on a moment later.

"Tell the guys to keep their heads down," he yelled to Dozer. "And you might want to block your ears, too."

He turned the XL on its wing for four seconds and then leveled out. Now he was staring down at the carrier's deck again, but from the opposite direction: bow-first. The wind was blowing at least fifty knots up from stern. If he flew directly into the gale, he might be able to slow down enough to get aboard in one piece.

He came down to just fifty feet, pulled back on his throttles, and lowered his landing gear. All this slowed him down to the magic 110 knots. Then he tried to ease himself, but the XL dropped quickly. It hit the deck with a great crash just a few seconds later and began skidding. Hunter lifted his landing gear the moment he touched down, hoping the friction would slow him down. He just missed some pieces of debris but hit others, and even this helped to reduce his speed a bit.

Halfway down the deck, he pushed the XL's landing gear lever, again hoping that the doors, in trying to open, would create even *more* friction and slow him even further. It worked, but not by much. With everything happening in a matter of micro-seconds, he could see the far end of the deck approaching very quickly. The wide-open flight elevator shaft was now right in front of him. Still, he needed more drag.

Then came one last desperate idea. He yanked his canopy-open lever. The bubble-shaped top snapped up and instantly acted like a speed brake, catching the ferociously blowing fifty-knot wind. With one last flick of the control stick, he had just enough air and momentum to go up and over the open flight elevator door before crashing to the deck on the other side. That did it. The XL came to a grinding, smoky, painful halt just inches from toppling off the stern.

Unprotected from the elements, Hunter was immediately soaked by the rain and sea spray. But it didn't matter to him. He was down. That's all that counted.

His beloved XL was a mess, though. A mess definitely beyond repair.

He loved his airplane. He'd often felt that it was a part of him.

But if Dominique was on board the carrier, he *had* to find her.

Dozer and five of his men arrived a moment later. They'd run down the deserted port side of the carrier, staying below the gunwales. The battle for the *Isakov* was taking place on its starboard side, because that's where the superstructure was located. They didn't see a soul on the opposite side during their carrier-length dash.

Hunter crawled out of the jet's wreckage, M-16 in hand. The 7CAV troopers took in the remains of the famous F-16XL and were horrified. The fuselage was almost unrecognizable. The cranked arrow wings were broken and bent. The once-mighty engine was now a trail of pieces stretching all the way down the carrier deck. It was like seeing a racing car all battered to shit.

Dozer was almost in tears. "Hawk . . . your ride . . ."

But Hunter didn't want to talk about it. There was no time.

"She definitely came aboard on that helicopter, right?" he asked Dozer as the 7CAV medic gave him a quick look over. "You're sure?"

"That's a roger," Dozer told him. "And you heard my 'deep guy' who has eyes on them. It's definitely Commissar Zero's chopper, and she was definitely on it. But the big question is: Why? For someone to fly way out here and come aboard in the middle of a storm, it must be very fucking important."

They all ran over to the open flight-deck elevator. Leaning over its edge, they peered into the abyss below. The rain and seawater were being blown into the gaping maw, but they could clearly see the massive Russian helicopter at the bottom of the boat—its crew had turned on their extremely bright exterior trouble beacons, lighting the scene more than 250 feet below.

"What the hell are they doing?" Dozer wondered. "It looks like everyone's just walking around."

"I've got to get down there," Hunter said.

He jumped up and was suddenly moving faster than he thought possible. Running toward an open hatchway on the burning superstructure, his weapon was up, and the rain was in his face. Dozer and his guys were right on his heels, yelling for him to slow down.

But he couldn't. His body was buzzing. He was in a zone. He could not only see farther and clearer than he could ever remember, he began seeing things before they even happened.

Two NKVD sailors with AK-47s up on a crow's walk about to fire down at them. Hunter cut them down quickly, but his rounds seemed to land before he even squeezed his trigger. Another sailor, one deck up, grenade in hand. Hunter's barrage hit it square on, blowing the man in two.

Behind you. . . .

He looked around. Four more sailors near the wreckage of his crashed XL, aiming an RPG at him. A four-second burst over his shoulder was all it took. Each sailor, two pop shots to the head, all without breaking stride.

He reached the hatchway, jumped through it, never stopped running. "Follow me, guys!" he yelled to Dozer and his men. "We've got to hurry."

Down the smoky passageway they ran. This was not the same claustrophobic battleground the other 7CAV troopers were fighting in farther down the ship. These passageways were filled with cargo, but it was mostly small boxes neatly stacked against the starboard bulkhead and atop a temporary ceiling, leaving a sort of tunnel.

Hunter charged right through it. NKVD sailors appeared in front of him, in ones and twos, some with just dinner knives as weapons. He shot them all.

Down a ladder to the second subdeck level. More cargo in the halls, more enemy sailors shot. And more explosions all around them. But still Hunter kept going, the 7CAV guys in tow.

Around another corner and suddenly they were in an officers' mess. Five enemy sailors were there, using an overturned dining table as cover. They were cooks. One was holding a kitchen knife to the throat of one of Dozer's deep recon men, the rest were wielding meat cleavers. Three other 7CAV troopers lay wounded nearby.

"*Ostanovit ili on umirayet!*" one sailor cried. "Stop or he dies!"

But Hunter never broke stride. He fired off a single shot, hitting the man with the knife in the forehead, slamming him into the mess table and sending the other sailors sprawling. Hunter dispatched each of them with a swift crack to the head via the butt of his rifle. Then he resumed running, yelling to Dozer and his men, "Keep up with me! Don't get lost now!"

Down another passageway, down another ladder. Bullets were whizzing by him, more explosions were going off. Another passageway where some cabins were on fire. Thick smoke everywhere. Down another ladder. He could hear people crying out in the distance, but he just kept going.

One more passageway, one more ladder—and then, suddenly, he was at the bottom of the boat.

He found himself in a long, dank, dimly lit passageway, the helicopter hangar nowhere in sight. The deck was really moving under his feet though, the outer hull being continuously hit by monster waves. The overwhelming noise down here was of riveted steel groaning.

"Let's be careful here," he said to the 7CAV guys. "We can't get lost in the dark."

But then he looked over his shoulder and realized no one was behind him. In fact, Dozer and the 7CAV troopers had lost sight of him back in the officers' mess, when they'd stopped for a moment to assist their wounded comrades. He'd been charging through the carrier alone ever since.

He slapped the side of his helmet once, calling himself a dope. Then suddenly, everything around him got very quiet. All the noise, explosions, the storm raging outside, the waves against the hull. They all faded away. It was dead silence.

He began walking and came to a compartment, barely seeing its toggle wheel in the dark. He turned it open and looked inside. It was a large room, filled with AK-47 ammunition. Tons of it. Another compartment down, he opened the door to find boxes of RPG grenades stacked to the ceiling. Hundreds of them.

The third compartment down had a door with two toggle wheels. Both were difficult to open, but he finally prevailed. The large space within was packed with thousands of artillery shells and something else. He took a deep sniff and found the air had a sweet citrus scent to it. Damn. . . . He slammed the door quickly. Hal-lou gas, the powdery toxic agent the Russians had spread over the Badlands after nuking it, making it even more uninhabitable, smelled just like oranges. Anyone who'd ever come within a hundred miles of the Bads knew it well. It floated on the wind like powder. And that's what he smelled now.

He spit a few times and tried to clear his nose. He saw powder on his hands and chest. Fucking Russians, he grumbled, can't put up a warning sign?

But then he froze again, just completely stopped in place. Something was about to happen. He could sense it.

Three seconds later, he heard the sound of many boots, walking quickly on the metal deck. Then, the clinking of weapons. Then guttural conversation, definitely Russian.

Five people, maybe more. Carrying a flashlight and coming right at him.

But then, speaking above the others, a woman said, "We are going the wrong way. . . ."

Hunter didn't move, didn't breathe. Once again, ice water was running through his veins.

He knew that voice.

Twenty feet away now, the flashlight playing on the deck. By
its bare glow, Hunter could tell there were five soldiers carrying
AK-47s and pushing a large yellow box on wheels. A sixth person
was slightly behind them. No faces were visible, but he could
see a large brass key dangling from someone's fingers. The key
glinted in the green artificial light.

"We are going the wrong way," he heard those words again—
and he knew it was her.

Dominique.

Not ten feet away.

He raised his M-16. He would have to be both quick and
perfect here, one missed shot would mean disaster.

He waited until the flashlight beam found his boots and
worked its way up his body. When it reached his eyes, he squeezed
his trigger—and heard nothing but a *click*!

His M-16 was out of ammunition; had been for quite some
time. And he was looking at five Russian NKVD gunmen, two
almost face-to-face.

His massive .357 handgun was out of his belt in a flash. His
first bullet blew away the man with the flashlight.

Then, everything went dark . . . for about two seconds. Suddenly, orange tracers were flying everywhere. They lit up the
scene enough for him to squeeze off four more rounds.

Then everything went black again.

Silence, for five long seconds. Then . . .

"Is it really you?" she asked.

"Is it really *you*?" he asked in return.

He took out his penlight, turned it on, and there she was.

Dominique. Standing right in front of him. Smiling . . .
slightly. Despite the form-fitting NKVD uniform, she looked as
good as the last time he'd seen her—and that seemed like a million years ago.

She had a small flashlight as well and pointed it at him.

"So it *was* you flying around New York in that toy airplane,"
she said.

"I was looking for you," was all he could say at first, his voice
starting to crack. There was an aura of unreality in the damp,

dank air. "It seems like forever since I last saw you, and I was sure you were in trouble."

He could see tears forming in her eyes. "But what happened to you?" she asked him in a whisper. "You were gone so long—I was sure you were dead."

He wanted to touch her face, to hug her, to kiss her. But he just couldn't. He remained glued to the spot. "I don't know what happened to me," he finally replied. "I'm still trying to figure it out. But I'm here now—here to rescue you."

She looked him straight in the eyes, her beauty undiminished. "I don't think there's any way you'll ever understand this," she said.

"I'm willing to understand anything you've done," he told her sincerely, wiping his own eyes. "Just as long as we talk about it."

But she just shook her head. "Not that," she told him. "I mean *this*. . . ."

She'd wrapped the huge gold key she was carrying around her fingers, as if putting on a pair of brass knuckles.

She said, "I'm so sorry," and the next thing Hunter knew, her fist was coming right at him, hitting him square on the jaw.

He fell backward, cracking his helmet on the hard deck below.

Then everything went black.

CHAPTER TWENTY-EIGHT

TOTAL SILENCE.
Total darkness.
No feeling.
No thought.
Just nothingness.
And floating.
And spinning.
Endlessly.
But then . . .
A different kind of light—at the end of a long tunnel.
Getting brighter.
. . . and brighter.
. . . and brighter.
Flash!
Hunter opened his eyes.

It was hard to see, hard to move. Everything hurt, especially his jaw.

He was on a hospital bed of some sort; that much he could tell. Figures in neon yellow hazmat suits were standing over him. They had lights attached to their visors, so he couldn't see their faces. The room itself was dimly lit. Anytime one of the figures moved, bizarre shadows played on the walls.

"What happened?" he croaked. "Did I take a bullet?"

"He's back," a voice said in response. "And he's stopped whistling."

Hunter lifted his head. Odd gleaming equipment was all around him, as were dozens of multicolored tubes with bubbling liquids running through them.

But he could also see . . . clouds.

Cumulus clouds.

Up near the ceiling.

What's going on here?

He looked through an open window next to his bed and saw not one, but two enormous moons hanging in the night sky. One was green; the other was blue. Beyond them, stars burning brighter than he could ever imagine.

This wasn't the *Admiral Isakov.*

This wasn't even Earth.

Goddamn. . . .

Did he jump universes again?

A flash of blue light exploded in the room, washing out the shadows. The men in the yellow suits immediately fell to their knees. Someone else was among them.

"Princess," one man gasped, "forgive us—we had no way of knowing you were coming. . . ."

"Please," a heavenly voice said, filling the room like music. "There's no need to kneel."

Hunter looked up to see a young woman in a long, flowing white gown surrounded by the blue haze.

Curly golden hair falling around her shoulders, a gorgeous face, huge saucer-shaped eyes. A smile like no other.

She was stunning.

And he knew her.

Princess Xara.

His one true love . . . at least in this universe.

She glided over to his bed and leaned down to him. Her lips touched his ear.

"Do you remember me?" she whispered.

Hunter nodded eagerly. She looked like an angel, especially with all those clouds billowing above her head.

She ran her hand along his cheek. It felt electric.

"I'm so glad, Hawk," she said softly. "Now, you won't understand this, but please try to remember these two things when the time comes: Just because you love someone doesn't mean you can't love someone else, too. Okay? Got it?"

She looked down at him, smiling, her fingers still running along his cheek.

"We'll see each other soon, I promise," she said. Then she started to fade away, but he managed to touch her arm.

"You said there were two things," he was just able to gasp.

She thought a moment, then laughed a little.

"Oh yes," she finally said sweetly. "Take the subway. It's faster."

Flash!

Hunter opened his eyes, and the first person he saw was the 7CAV medic. He looked distorted; his eyes were bulging, his face thin and rippling. He was waving a penlight in front of Hunter's eyes. Other people were kneeling around him, five of them at least.

Bull Dozer was suddenly in his face, yelling. "Jesus, Hawk—wake up!"

"I'm awake, okay?" Hunter finally wheezed. "I'm wide freaking awake."

The 7CAV guys collapsed in relief. The Wingman was alive—again.

Bull stayed right in his face. "Christ, man," he said. "Don't scare us like that."

"Why? What happened?" Hunter asked. "Did I take bullet?"

But no one said anything.

"Jesus—did I take *more* than one bullet?"

"We don't know what happened to you," Dozer told him. "We found you down here, sprawled out, with these five dead guys."

"So, I'm not shot?"

"No, you're not," the medic assured him. "You took a blow to the head or something. You've got a dent in your helmet, and you've got this powder all over you. But other than that, I can't find anything wrong with you."

Hunter looked down at his hands and chest. They were covered with the white dust he'd picked up in the weapons' chamber earlier.

"Jessuz, I got this hal-lou crap all over me!" he cried.

Dozer pulled out a flask. "Here, take some medication and relax," he said, handing it to Hunter. It was whiskey, and it burned all the way down, but Hunter couldn't wait to take another gulp.

Then he started looking around him. "So . . . where is she?" he asked, handing the flask back to Dozer.

"Who?"

"Dominique," Hunter said anxiously. "Is she okay?"

The 7CAV guys all scratched their heads.

"You were alone when we found you, Hawk," Dozer told him definitively. "Why? Was she here?"

Hunter was nodding furiously. "*Right* here—these guys were her guards—or they were with her, or something. And they were pushing this yellow box and . . . But then she . . ."

He had to think a moment. Did she really lay him out with a single punch?

"And then . . . I went . . . somewhere else," he began sputtering. "A place with two moons and stars out in the daytime. And I saw Princess Xara again. And she said . . ."

Dozer slapped his medic's shoulder. "Will you please give him some oxygen? He's going freaking Dixieland on us."

The medic put a small mask over Hunter's nose and mouth and said, "Seven deep breaths. . . . No talking."

Hunter took five and then brushed it away. But the pure oxygen helped.

"Jesus, how long was I out?" he asked, cobwebs clearing.

The medic checked his eyes again. "Hard to say. . . . A few minutes at least."

"And no sign of her? No sign of a yellow box?"

The troopers all shook their heads no.

"And how about the copter," he asked Dozer. "Is it still on board?"

"That's what we're doing down here," the marine told him. "Looking for it and looking for you. It definitely hasn't taken off. We'd hear it no matter where we were on this tub."

The last three words had not yet left Dozer's cigar-clenched lips when a horrendous roar rocketed through the bottom passageway. It was so loud they all put their hands over their ears, but when Hunter put his hands over his helmet's ear holes, it broke in two. A crack ran right down the middle of it.

"Fuck, man," he swore loudly. "You know how long I've had this thing?"

Dozer finally pulled him to his feet. The noise got even louder, more distorted, but they knew it could only be one thing: the huge Mi-26 chopper, straight ahead, starboard side.

They all ran in that direction, but the medic held Dozer back for a moment.

"He might have gotten a snootfull of hal-lou residue," the medic told him. "You know . . . the powder? I can smell it down here myself. It doesn't last too long, but it would account for the ragtime chatter back there. . . ."

Dozer just shrugged. "Or maybe he really did go 'someplace else.'"

It was a longer run than they expected and took a good five minutes of snaking their way through the bottom of the ship. Still woozy, Hunter was in the lead for some reason, his night-vision goggles guiding them as they were drawn to the noise that grew more thunderous with each step they took.

Hunter turned a corner and suddenly found himself on the lip of the immense flight-deck elevator. Black-uniformed NKVD policemen were loading the bright yellow box onto the copter, which still had its external emergency lights burning. The box must have been heavy, because a dozen of them were just barely able to lift it on board. As for Dominique, she was nowhere in sight.

"See? I'm not crazy," Hunter yelled to Dozer. "There's the yellow box . . . and whatever the hell is inside it."

Dozer fired an instant later. He let go with a stream from his M-16J banana-clip model, intentionally keeping his fire low so as not to hit Dominique if she was inside the copter. The barrage cut the legs out from under three of the NKVD policemen. A few of the copter's lights were hit, too, and suddenly the hangar was thrown into near-darkness.

The Russians returned fire and though everyone was shooting semi-blind, a major gun battle erupted. There was a lot of shouting and noise and confusion. Then the copter's huge rotors began moving.

The copter pilots were doing an emergency procedure called burn and turn. Although throttling to full power right away wasn't great for the engines, it worked well for quick takeoffs.

Someone in the cockpit aimed the remote control device at an electric eye hanging on the hangar's bulkhead. It activated a robot arm, which bent down and hit a switch. The gigantic elevator began to move upward.

The last few Russians standing scrambled aboard the helicopter, quitting the gunfight and leaving their wounded comrades behind. The 7CAV troopers and Hunter leaped onto the moving elevator, pushing off the wounded Russians. At the same moment, the helicopter started lifting off from the elevator itself.

"What the fuck?" Dozer yelled above the noise. "They're going to fly it out of here?"

Before they could get to the hatch door, the huge copter ascended from the still-moving elevator. It went up about six feet in just a few seconds.

"We can't shoot it down if Dominique is aboard!" Dozer yelled to Hunter in the vicious artificial wind. "How are we going to stop it?"

Hunter didn't reply. Instead, he jumped up and caught the copter's front left skid. The copter began to stagger. Dozer joined Hunter, grabbing the right hand skid. All 7CAV troopers now joined in. In seconds, seven people were hanging on the Mi-26's skids and trying to pull the thing right back down.

But the pilots leaned on the throttles some more, and with the added power, the copter began to pull away. Everyone had to let go and drop back down to the elevator.

Hunter was enraged, but he had to also admire the cool of the Russian chopper pilots. They were flying straight up, ten feet above the moving elevator, true and steady, while the carrier was rocking wildly and smoke was obscuring the upper decks.

This was an amazing feat, and Hunter could tell the copter was seriously overloaded. The pilots were trying to ease it up out of the great pit, a bit at a time, all the while trying to keep it out of the grasp of the seven Americans trying to drag it back down again.

"They're good," Hunter said. "The bastards."

It went on like this for more than a minute, Hunter and the 7CAV guys trying a few more times to try to grab onto the huge copter's struts before it reached the outside world. Meanwhile, Dozer was on his radio, yelling at all of his men to pass the word *not* shoot at the ascending helicopter. There was a "friendly" aboard.

Finally, the Mi-26 and the elevator were both nearing the carrier's flight deck. Only the great expanse of sky lay beyond.

The copter was still staggering due to its weight, and Hunter and the 7CAV troopers tried one last time to grab it and pull it back down. Again, it was just out of their grasp.

But just as it reached the flight deck, a dark figure suddenly entered the scene. Making a running leap, he landed on the helicopter's right-side landing strut. From there, he was able to get his hands onto the bottom of the open hatch door and hang on.

The elevator arrived on the deck and stopped; the helicopter kept on going. The 7CAV guys and Hunter scrambled off the lift, noting that all gunfire had stopped. Everyone was watching this new drama.

This wasn't another 7CAV guy trying to drag the helicopter back down to the deck by himself. This person was dressed all in black . . . including his cape.

"Jeesuz," Dozer exclaimed. "Is that guy the captain or something?"

He was close. It was Yuri Zmeya, senior ship committee chairman of the *Isakov* and the commissar's younger brother. The *Isakov* was in ruins. Most of his crew was dead. He was abandoning his own ship.

The copter continued going straight up, and he hung on. None of the Americans shot at him for fear of disabling the copter, but no one inside the huge aircraft was helping him in. Yet it was clear his added weight was beginning to destabilize the Mi-26 in the high winds. As big as it was, if he climbed aboard, the copter might become unbalanced and come crashing down. But if he stayed where he was, the copter could spiral out of control.

Suddenly, they all saw a dark figure come to the copter's open doorway. He, too, was dressed all in black.

This person didn't bend down to assist the helpless man.

Instead, he stepped on his fingers.

The younger Zmeya hung on for a long time, but finally, he could take it no longer. When a boot came down hard on his left hand, he had to let it go. By this time, the copter had moved out over the sea.

He held on for a few moments longer, dangling with just his right hand. But then his killer stomped on those fingers, too—and that was it.

With an otherworldly scream, Yuri Zmeya fell into the stormy sea and was quickly swallowed up by the waves. With that, the huge copter flew away, disappearing into the storm clouds.

Suddenly, Dozer's radio came alive. It was the men who'd made it onto deck one. They'd reached the EEC room, and after a quick firefight, they had managed to take it over. They were in the process of shutting down the carrier's engines. The group of 7CAV troopers down near the wreckage of the two Sherpas had finally overcome the special security troops and the pilots they'd been fighting in the gunwales, thanks to troopers who'd made it onto deck one attacking the Russians from the rear.

The carrier was theirs.

Great relief washed over the Americans when they realized what they had done—but the euphoria lasted about three seconds. Because at that moment, there was a great boom and three enormous flashes of light went over the carrier and crashed into the sea close by. The explosions were so hot and powerful, the water they threw into the air immediately turned to steam.

Now everyone looked down toward the stern to see Convoy 56's second monstrous battle cruiser coming up on the carrier's starboard side.

"Oh, fuck," Dozer cursed. "These guys must have orders to sink this baby if it ever falls into enemy hands."

Another fusillade of giant shells went over their heads, fired by the battle cruiser's huge complement of fourteen-inch guns.

Dozer quickly called his command leader back inside the ship and explained what was happening. But there was nothing anyone inside or outside could do. True, they were in control of the burning carrier and just about all of the crewmembers were dead. But the gun battle inside the ECC had ruined the primary and secondary command systems for all of the carrier's weapons.

Basically, they were sitting ducks, defenseless against the oncoming warship.

Another barrage went over the Americans' heads and hit what was left of the carrier's superstructure. Each shell carrying two thousand pounds of explosive, the three resulting blasts were massive, further tearing the carrier apart. There weren't many ships in the world that could actually sink a titan like the *Isakov*, but this battle cruiser was one of them. And its task was made all the easier because the stricken carrier was not able to fire back.

The next volley would be right in the middle of the flight deck, and that might be enough to crack the carrier in half. The battle cruiser was so close, Hunter could see the gun crews adjusting their aim points.

"We've come too far for it to end like this!" Dozer yelled over everything.

Hunter couldn't disagree.

But suddenly, just as the killing shots were about to be fired at them, there was another great roar and a mighty splash of fire and water.

When the smoke was blown away by the brutal wind, the battle cruiser that had been firing at them was no longer there.

Dozer turned to Hunter. "What the hell just happened?!"

PART THREE

PART THREE

CHAPTER TWENTY-NINE

May 8

THE HUMMER WAS taking a real beating as it made its way down the narrow, unpaved trail in the Pine Barrens.

Between the boulders, the sand pits, and roots as thick as tree trunks, its shock absorbers were ready to give up the ghost, in more ways than one.

The two men in the Hummer had just driven from Free Tennessee to New Jersey, seventeen hours, nonstop. Buzzcut and ripped, with tat sleeves and earrings, they'd gone by many aliases over the years. Currently, they were Phil and Don. But most people knew them as the Cobra Brothers, the best helicopter gunship team in the world.

They'd gotten through to Bull Dozer just two days ago; he'd said he'd be in touch. A follow-up message had arrived twenty-four hours later: Start driving and leave your copters home. We'll have some for you when you get here.

Normally Phil and Don flew AH-1 Cobras, heavily armed, highly maneuverable gunships—hence their nickname—but Dozer said he just needed pilots.

The Cobra Brothers were hardened veterans of the many wars fought across the continent in the past few years. They'd been in battles against the Russians, the Asian Mercenary Cult, the Fourth Reich, the Circle, and others—all of these clashes involving heavy combat. But they'd never experienced anything as frightening as driving through the Pine Barrens at night.

Strange lights in the trees. Bloodcurdling shrieks around every turn. Bizarre creatures running in front of them just long enough to get caught in the headlights before disappearing again. Worst of all, that feeling, which they could not shake, that someone was following them.

By the time they reached the base's main gate at about 2100 hours, just past 9:00 p.m., they were nervous wrecks. The gate consisted of a recently cut white birch that lay across two stacks of boulders. That was it. Two folding chairs were nearby.

But no one was there to meet them as Dozer had promised. True, they were about an hour early, but still, where were the guards?

They could see into the hidden base, which wasn't so hidden at the moment. Dozer had told them what to expect—and this wasn't it. The camouflage roof was wide open; anyone flying overhead could easily spot the place. Vehicles and runway equipment were scattered all over; the place looked abandoned. There was no sign of life anywhere.

"Not the fun place I expected," Don said dryly.

"All's not right here," Phil replied.

They collected their M-16s and night-vision goggles and started across the runway. They were heading for the Quonset hut, but halfway across the landing strip, they came upon a large red drawing someone had smeared onto the tarmac.

Viewed through night vision, it looked like a grotesque smiley face, except the smile was depicted as a semicircle of garishly drawn surgical stitches. The crudeness of it made it even more disturbing.

Phil reached down and touched the reddened part of the tarmac.

"Bull said this place was kind of spooky, right?" he asked Don.

"The ride out here didn't give that away?" Don replied, his weapon up. He was feeling the really bad vibes now.

"Well, it gets worse," Phil said, looking at the red substance on his gloved hand. "Because this ain't paint. . . ."

CHAPTER THIRTY

May 8

DOMINIQUE WOKE UP hoping it was all a bad dream.

But as soon as she saw the unfinished, plaster-patched ceiling above her bed and the MOP painter's cans and brushes and tarps in the corner, she knew it wasn't so.

"When will they get this room done?" she thought out loud. She had to admit she liked 30 Rock much better than Tower Two of the World Trade Center.

What hadn't been a dream but seemed like one was still fresh in her mind; sleep could not erase a moment of it. Flying out to the carrier in the storm, the battle to get on and then off the ship. Grabbing the Magilla.

Seeing Hawk. . . .

Punching Hawk.

Her hand still hurt from hitting him.

She studied the splotches of white paint over her head again and thought, *How can I expect anyone to understand all this when I can barely understand it myself?*

That was her daily morning prayer.

She slipped out of the bed and showered, methodically scrubbing herself up and down.

Toweling off, she prepared herself mentally before walking

back out. Although she'd been asleep some of the time—and pretending to be asleep for a lot more—she and Zmeya hadn't talked much since returning from the hellish trip out to sea.

He was supremely pissed off about what had happened to Convoy 56. But his successful retrieval of the special box he referred to as the Magilla seemed a bit of a balm to him. She'd heard him on the radiophone several times, basically saying that as long as they had the Magilla, they could live without everything else.

He had not said one word to her about his brother or what he'd done to him. She could still hear the horrible screaming; it echoed in her ears. At the time, Zmeya had mumbled that one more person would have overloaded the copter and doomed them all. But that was it.

Of course, she didn't mention her encounter with Hunter at the bottom of the ship.

That she would have to take to the grave.

She walked into the living area to find Zmeya at his desk looking out on the city as usual.

His aide-de-camp was there, updating him on the NKVD's relocation to its new headquarters at the WTC.

"Per your orders, about eighty percent of our people are here and in place," the man reported. "That includes all our field officers, as you requested. They are now populating the midlevel floors here in Tower Two, the spaces MOP had been working on before . . . the trouble started."

"Building security is in place?" Zmeya asked. "Inside and out."

"Again, exactly per your orders," the aide said, adding, "It won't be like 30 Rock. We won't be trapped if anything goes wrong. We'll have a way out. A secure way out. On the other hand, it will be very hard for any interlopers to go anywhere in this building if they don't know how our security is wired up."

He hesitated a moment then asked Zmeya, "Do you want the latest dead and missing figures from the fire inside 30 Rock? One of the CRPP members is among the missing."

The aide was sure this would give Zmeya pause; the members of the Committee of the Revolution for the Protection of the People were the closest Zmeya had to friends. But the commissar just waved him off.

"Next. . . ." he said.

Dominique walked around the side of his desk and into his field of vision. Off in a side room was the bright yellow box containing the mysterious Magilla. Zmeya was wearing its activation key attached to a chain around his neck.

He looked up at her and realized she was wearing nothing but a short silk robe. The aide was smart enough to make a hasty exit. Zmeya leaned back in his chair and turned his attention to her.

"I passed your test, didn't I?" she asked him sweetly.

"Yes, at the expense of five of my best gunmen," he replied with bemusement.

"I told you they panicked," she explained. "They got spooked by something and started shooting in the dark. It was unavoidable that they all hit one another."

"Five perfect shots, one each to the forehead?" he said with a cruel laugh. "My kingdom for some truth serum!"

She sat on his desk, very close to him, and pulled up her robe so he could see all of her bare legs.

"But I did what you wanted me to do," she insisted softly. "Wasn't that the whole point? Others came and retrieved the box, but you entrusted me to get the key. And without that key, the Magilla is useless, right? I had a chance to get away with it—especially when I was left alone after those boobs all shot each other. But I came back to you with it. Doesn't that mean anything to you?"

Before he could reply, his radiophone rang. He shooed her off the desk.

He listened to the phone for a few seconds, and then his face went red. He immediately turned on the AM radio on his desk.

It came on in the middle of a Red Radio News broadcast, but not a typical one. Speaking in English, a person was saying that the firebombing of the MMZ was an NKVD plot so they could take over the *Okupatsi* from the military.

"Look at the facts, Comrades," the mysterious speaker said. "Thousands of our military brothers died in the fires. Thousands more were injured and burned. Our four military headquarters buildings were destroyed. A large part of the MMZ was wiped out. It will take us years to recover.

"Meanwhile, the NKVD has moved into the two tallest buildings in the world, as if nothing has happened. They had everything to gain by staging the firebombing and manufacturing this crisis. So listen up, all loyal soldiers and sailors of Mother Russia. Think about it for just a few minutes, Comrades, and you'll figure it out. The NKVD are the ones who firebombed the MMZ."

Zmeya was absolutely livid.

"Goddamn lies," he seethed, the volcano rumbling. "That's not how it is at all. . . ."

He was quickly on the radiophone again. "Bomb that radio station if you have to, but I want it off the air now! And then collect those three idiots with all the medals. I think they need a little reeducation when it comes to their communications skills."

Dominique watched his face turn crimson while his eyes went absolutely black and searing. In another instance, she might have urged him to take his meds.

But not now.

Instead, she went back to her unfinished bedroom and locked the door.

The black Cadillac pulled up to the temporary hospital on the corner of Park Avenue and East Fifty-Eigth Street, stopping with a screech.

Four men in black coats, dark glasses, and fedoras got out and barged through the front door, brushing aside two army guards.

There were close to a thousand patients in the hospital, all of them injured in the firestorm. The NKVD was looking for one of them.

All activity inside the building's lobby came to a stop when they walked in. One was carrying a red striped pouch.

The head nurse greeted them nervously. One man spoke for the four. "You know who we are?"

The trembling nurse nodded twice.

"We are looking for this man," he said, holding up a photo for her. "His name is Colonel Sergei Gagarin, Russian Army."

The nurse checked a haphazard box of files then dialed a number on the nursing station's radiophone. It was a short conversation.

"Room thirteen," she told the men. "Down the hall to your left. I just talked to him. He is awake and waiting for you."

Nurses, patients, and doctors cleared a path for the four men as they walked down the corridor. They got to Room 13 and without bothering to knock let themselves in.

But the room was empty.

Gagarin was not there; his belongings were gone as well.

The only movement came from the curtains, which rustled in the breeze coming through the open window.

The large green helicopter circled the secret base in the Pine Barrens twice before coming in for a landing.

It was a Mi-8 Hip, a cargo-carrier by design, and was still wearing its Russian red-star markings, camo, and tail number.

The people below melted into the pines at the first sight of it. The woods were haunted; they all knew that by now. But at this point, no precaution was a stupid one.

Completely spooked, the Cobra brothers waited in the trees about thirty feet from the runway. Others had arrived after them. The JAWS team was here. Jim Cook, Clancy Miller, Shawn Higgens, Mark Snyder, Warren Maas, and Neil Luck, specialists in combat explosives who had been called sappers in the old days. Also on hand was NJ104, Frank Geraci's crew. They were a special ops group that had evolved from the 104th Battalion, New Jersey National Guard, and after the Big War, they'd specialized in all aspects of urban warfare.

Captain Crunch of the famous Ace Wrecking Company fighter-bomber team; Louie St. Louis from Football City; JT "Socket" Toomey and Ben Wa, two of the country's top fighter pilots; Colonel Don Kurjan from the United American Army; and Catfish Johnson of the Righteous Brothers Special Ops group—they were *all* here. All the people Dozer had tried so hard to contact for so long. They were all answering the rallying cry to fight back against the Red occupiers of New York City.

But if this was going to be like other adventures they'd had in the past, it was already off to a disastrous start.

The Mi-8 Hip copter bounced in. The arrival of the Russian aircraft was surprising enough for the men hiding in the woods, but even more surprising was seeing Hawk Hunter climb out of it.

He was ragged-looking, unshaven, his uniform still wet from the adventure on the *Isakov* earlier. After what had happened on the carrier, especially being knocked out by Dominique at the bottom of the boat, and then the strange ending to the sea battle, he was running purely on adrenaline and nothing else. Everything still seemed surreal.

Only St. Louie, Ben, and JT had seen Hunter since his return, so there were a lot of bro-hugs all around. But they had to be quick, because Hunter knew something was wrong here.

The Cobra Brothers finally walked him over to the grisly drawing left in the middle of the runway. Before Hunter could even ask where the base's personnel were, they pointed to a drainage ditch nearby.

It was filled with bound and gagged bodies. All their throats had been cut.

"Five 7CAV guys," Phil Cobra told Hunter. "Twenty civilian techs. . . ."

Minutes passed with Hunter unable to speak. He'd flown here expecting the base to be business as usual, to see his friends and allies.

Instead, he found this. . . .

He returned to the morbid bloody drawing on the runway. He recalled the Trashman talking about an NKVD officer with a brutal facial scar executing homeless New Yorkers in the middle of the street. The bloody image on the tarmac reminded Hunter of what he thought that man looked like.

But he just didn't know what to say. He was still reeling from the hideous slaughter.

"The Reds know we're here," he said at last. "But we still have to bury our men. . . ."

Both Cobras nodded grimly.

"We've already found some shovels," Phil said.

The job was done in just ten awful minutes, everyone chipping in to dig a hole next to the ditch and then lay the dead in it with as much dignity as possible.

St. Louis led a quick prayer. The grimness of the moment was almost overwhelming, especially for Hunter. He was the one who would have to tell Dozer.

Two seconds after the last shovel full of dirt was thrown on the mass grave, there came an earsplitting roar. Three rockets trailing smoke and flame went right over their heads. They crashed about a mile away, causing an explosion that shook the ground beneath their feet. No sooner had that sound faded away than three more rockets screamed overhead.

"Those are BM-30 Rockets," St. Louis said, coolly lighting a cigarette. "Long range, usually very accurate."

These three rockets exploded only a half mile from the base. They were zeroing in on them. That was enough for Hunter.

"Time to go," he said.

No one needed any prompting. They all scrambled aboard the Russian-built copter as Hunter rushed to get the rotors spinning and the Cobra Brothers flicked on all the systems needed for flight. They'd all fought Russian choppers in the past, but none of them had ever been inside one. It was big and thick and heavily armored, more like a flying tank.

Following his instincts, Hunter pulled up on the collective even before all his control lights were green.

They lifted off and went straight up through the open camo cover.

A fifteen-rocket barrage landed on the base just a few seconds later. The combined explosions actually pushed the helicopter up faster than its own engines, spinning it crazily. Only with the Cobras' help did Hunter get the Mi-20 under control.

Those aboard looked down at the base and saw flames enveloping it, with more rockets landing every few seconds.

They all knew there was a plan afoot to attack the Reds in

New York City. But the Mi-8 Hip aside, they also knew such an attack was going to be a huge undertaking.

"Were you guys planning to run this mission from here, from the haunted forest?" Phil Cobra asked Hunter.

The Wingman shook his head no.

"We moved the HQ yesterday," he said sadly. "I just wish we'd been able to do it sooner."

He circled the base one more time, allowing those on board to give a final salute to their fallen brethren.

Then he turned the copter northeast and pushed the throttles to full power.

CHAPTER THIRTY-ONE

THEY FLEW OUT over the Atlantic for the next half hour. The full moon rising on the horizon guided their way.

It was a gloomy flight, but Hunter went ahead and filled everyone in on what had happened over the past two days—the firebombing of Manhattan and the recent assault on Convoy 56.

But even with these two fairly successful actions, they—the Allies—still had a huge problem on their hands: the sixty-five thousand Russian troops occupying New York City, plus the nine thousand horrific NKVD policemen.

"That's who cut up our boys back there," Hunter told them. "And the rocket barrage, too. Their way of telling us they're in reprisal mode."

They finally spotted their destination, the once quaint island of Nantucket, just south of Cape Cod. Though largely abandoned since the Big War, it hadn't changed much in appearance. It was still picturesque, with weathered shingle-style houses and high-steepled churches. All lit up, from above, it was like a photo in a New England travel brochure.

Except now, an enormous, listing, smoldering aircraft carrier was anchored in its harbor—and taking up every last inch of it.

"Holy crap," JT gasped on seeing the gargantuan ship. "You really *did* capture Moby Dick."

"Yes, we did," Hunter said. "We captured the hell out of it. If anyone has any ideas on where to hide the thing, now's the time to speak up."

Everyone involved was hoping the Russians would eventually come to believe their mighty *Isakov* had sunk during the sea battle, just like their two battle cruisers and the Chekski troop carrier.

But an eleven-hundred-foot ship would be hard to keep under wraps for very long. Someone would spot it eventually, and the jig would be up. Then there was the added problem of the five Russian destroyers still out there. As far as anyone on the American side could tell, all five had survived, despite their shooting at one another during Hunter's Exocet attack.

These destroyers were armed with Styx missiles, massive antiship weapons that were easily adapted to strike land targets. One ship's barrage would destroy Nantucket Harbor and kill everyone in it. A full barrage from all five ships would most likely sink the *Isakov* for good, condemning it to foul the historic seaport for the next few hundred years.

"You could always put a camouflaged roof over it," St. Louis said wryly. "Better be a big one, though."

They flew over the seaport village next to the harbor. It was buzzing with activity. Members of the 7CAV were hurrying everywhere. Weapons and munitions were being moved about. Things were being welded, both onshore and aboard the carrier. The combined arc lights bathed the harborside in a cool blue glow.

Hunter explained that they were doing everything possible to get the mammoth, heavily damaged *Isakov* back to some kind of operational status as quickly as possible. And he meant hours, not days.

"And what about your XL?" Ben Wa asked him, spotting the wreckage of Hunter's superplane still smoldering on the carrier's debris-strewn deck. "Can you put it back together?"

Hunter unexpectedly choked up. "Not this time," he replied quietly.

They touched down at a small field just outside the seaport. The group of allies climbed out of the Mi-8 Hip and stretched. A row of Russian-built Mi-28 Kamov attack helicopters was nearby. The Cobra Brothers went to them like moths to a flame.

Mi-28s were absolutely fierce aerial weapons. Loaded with wire-guided missiles, a nose cannon, and twin rocket launchers, they were also fast, highly maneuverable, and so ugly they were almost pretty. And, as these were naval variants, they were equipped to carry torpedoes.

Hunter explained to the Cobras the gunships had come from the *Isakov*.

Phil smiled. "I hope this is why you told us not to bring our own rigs."

Hunter nodded. "We just flew out here in a Russian tank. Now—can you guys fly a couple of Russian Ferraris?"

A quarter mile away, across the beach and near the harbor jetty, stood an old lighthouse.

It was sixty feet high, and on clear nights, its powerful hundred-year-old revolving beacon could be seen as far north as Boston and as far south as New York City.

Atop the lighthouse now, though, something was spinning that was not anywhere as old: a Zhanya-616 *kolectrya* satellite dish. Taken from a NKVD storage bin on the *Isakov*, its name said it all. This dish could collect virtually any kind of radio signal from around the world and record it clearly and static free. It was the ultimate eavesdropping device.

Finding the 616 aboard the carrier was a dream come true for Dozer. He was at the top of the lighthouse now with two of his 7CAV troopers. Once they had realized they'd won the naval battle and actually captured the gigantic carrier, he'd gotten the 616 loaded on the first chopper off their new prize and had it brought here.

They'd been up here ever since getting it to work. Even when the *Isakov* limped into the harbor, Dozer hardly noticed. He was concentrating on his newfound toys.

He was surrounded by gear at the top of the lighthouse. To his left, his old but reliable shortwave radio set. To his right, no less than a ton of other NKVD communications equipment taken from the *Isakov*. Not just radio transmitters, but also override modules, signal-intercept generators, even a remote-controlled radiophone-tapping option. Typical Russian spy equipment. But Dozer had been a communications officer in the marines long before the 7CAV ever existed, and he had a few novel ideas on what to do with it.

When, on a hunch, he jump-crossed circuits between the Zhanya-616's enormous computer hard drive—it alone weighed three hundred pounds—and the *Isakov*'s frequency modulators, he discovered he could *get into* the same weighty hard drives that the NKVD used to control their radiophone traffic—and do so without them knowing it.

"We can hack into their computers—and they have no idea we're in there," Dozer told his men once he'd proved what he'd done. "We can hear and read everything they're doing and saying, and they don't have a clue."

"Breaking *into* someone's computer?" one of his men said. "That's freaking amazing. Imagine if something like that catches on."

Among other things, the new unexpected power allowed Dozer to create false signals—radio messages and telex—and put them out as originating from the NKVD. They'd already done it once. They'd broken into the Red Radio station's computer earlier and forced their own recorded piece onto the air. The three of them couldn't stop laughing as they heard the anti-NKVD conspiracy message broadcast and then watched the secret police network light up like a Christmas tree with NKVD bigwigs wanting to know what the hell was going on. It was called disinformation—and Dozer loved throwing it back at the Reds.

They finished installing the last of the Russian equipment, backup generators to keep everything going should the primary power source fail, and suddenly Dozer had one of the most advanced spy stations ever created.

From his little, battered radio set in the old shaky Pine Barrens tower to all this in under a week?

Sometimes crazy does *work*, he thought, truly in his glory.

Then Hunter walked in.

CHAPTER THIRTY-TWO

May 9

IT WAS 1:00 a.m. on Sunday morning.

Commissar Zmeya looked out on Manhattan from the new 110th floor of Tower Two, and like every other time he took in the view, he let out a long sigh.

In Russia, it was called *Krakh*. When things go to shit pretty quickly. The false broadcast on Red Radio being the latest setback.

They'd had it all, including the greatest city in the world, but for such a short time. And it all started to go downhill when that accursed clown plane showed up.

His radiophone rang, breaking his train of thought. He hoped at long last it was a report on the fate of the *Isakov*. But it was Sublieutenant Borski instead.

"Two things to report, sir," he told Zmeya, who could barely stand talking to the disfigured man even on the phone. "We found the American guerilla air base in the Pine Barrens where you said it would be. We left them a message."

Zmeya brightened up. Finally. "How many were there?"

Borski hesitated a moment. "About two dozen, sir. Americans for sure. The base looked like it could support about a hundred people and a few medium-size aircraft."

Another piece of the puzzle suddenly fell in place for Zmeya. The planes that had attacked the *Isakov* were medium-size. Plus, there was a good chance the firebombing raid had been launched from the hidden New Jersey base as well.

"Where is the rest of their group?" he asked. "Are there eighty guerillas unaccounted for?"

"That's unknown at the moment," Borski replied. "My guess is they heard us coming and hid in the woods. As the army missile bombardment followed us in, they could all be dead by now."

Zmeya made a note to send a battalion of Chekskis into the Pine Barrens immediately. Their mission: to look for any survivors and execute them all.

Then he asked Borski, "What is your second report?"

"Per your request, sir," Borski said excitedly, "we are holding two thousand people at Yankee Stadium. I'm awaiting your final orders."

"Have any of them come forward with information on who these American guerillas are?"

"That's negative, sir."

"Or where they are getting their support?"

"Again, negative, sir."

"Have they dug their own graves?"

Borski nodded. "They have."

"And have you come up with a more economical way of processing them? Something better than one bullet per person?"

"I have, sir."

"You're sure? You have everything covered, correct?"

"Yes, sir," Borski replied. With his next words, Zmeya would, in effect, be telling him to use knives to kill the hostages. It was Borski's favorite means of dispatching human beings.

Zmeya was about to say, "Then make it so. . . ." when he noticed Dominique standing next to him. She had stolen up on him again, making no noise at all.

She was barefoot, wearing only a stunning short black negligee he'd given her when things were still good between them. Her hair was fixed and she was wearing makeup. If possible, she looked even more ravishing than usual.

"Let's do it," she said to him.

"Do what?"

She ran her fingers down his chest.

"Guess."

It dawned on him an instant later. But he was more mystified than excited at first.

"Why now?" he asked, his hand blocking the phone's mouthpiece so Borski couldn't hear.

"I just thought I could get your mind on something else," she said, looking him deeply in the eyes.

That also took a couple seconds to sink in. He pointed at the phone. "This? You want me to stop this thing at the stadium?"

She came very close to him and said, "I want to make a deal with you."

"Spare them, and you'll have sex with me?" he asked.

She nodded and moved in even closer; she was practically on his lap.

He just laughed. "My God, I've been living with a humanitarian all this time," he said, mocking her. "Sometimes you just can't tell."

"This is how you say yes?" she scolded him. "After all your begging?"

He pretended to yawn. "How do I know it would be worth it? Or exciting enough?"

She didn't say anything. Instead, he felt something touching his crotch—a familiar feeling. He looked down to see she had her huge hunter's knife out again and was using it to softly jab his manhood.

It had happened before, but this time, her eyes told him it would go a different way if he didn't play along.

"Do it my way," she whispered. "Do it exactly how I tell you, and I guarantee, you'll never want to do it any other way again."

She pushed the knife in just a little deeper. Zmeya was suddenly more excited than at any time in his life.

He removed his hand from the phone's mouthpiece and calmly said to Borski, "Postpone the executions—until you hear from me."

CHAPTER THIRTY-THREE

May 9

TWELVE PEOPLE WERE sitting around the conference table inside the *Isakov's* combat center.

The room was a mess, just like everything else on the carrier where there'd been heavy fighting. But it was spacious and its table was still intact and large enough for all of them to fit. And no one was fussy.

Old friends and allies all, Hunter was sitting next to Jim Cook of JAWS and Frank Geraci of NJ104. The Cobra Brothers were to Geraci's left. Next to them sat the famous Captain Crunch. Beside him, Hunter's close friends, JT and Ben Wa, then Catfish Johnson and Colonel Donnie Kurjan of the United American Army. Across from Hunter was his old friend Louie St. Louis, mayor of Football City and CO of the famous Football City Special Forces. Beside him was Bull Dozer. They were all drinking no-name whiskey.

The meeting started with a ceremony for the twenty civilians and five 7CAV guys murdered in the Pine Barrens. Making it worse, eight 7CAV guys had been killed during the carrier fight.

Dozer led the service, but he could barely speak. More than 10 percent of his men had been killed in the last forty-eight hours. For a group of only one hundred, it was a devastating blow. Just as bad were the twenty dead civilians executed at the hidden base. He felt responsible for the loss of those men's lives and how it was going to affect their families.

This was why, when the service was over and the meeting began, Dozer had the floor.

"I'll keep it short," he said, still struggling to keep his composure. "I'm glad we all finally got together, but now we must be reasonable. Even if we raise our numbers to two thousand fighters, we still won't have a chance against the sixty-five thousand Russian troops in the city.

"However, I think it would be a worthy objective to destroy those NKVD devils inside New York. As for me, I want every last one of them dead. The world would be a better place without them."

He took a moment and cleared his throat.

"I'm talking about some kind of raid on Tower Two inside the World Trade Center," he went on. "We know through the 616 that's where they are, and we have all this new weaponry now. We can take out a lot of these guys if we can hit that building by surprise. It won't win us back the city, but it will show all those freaks in the Kremlin that we're not going away—we burned your MMZ, we captured your boat, and now we're going to fuck up your secret cops.

"In other words, we can all get killed fighting thirty-five-to-one odds, or we can take on these monsters, wipe them off the face of the earth, and have our revenge. Or at least I will."

There was no vote. They didn't need one.

As St. Louis said, "It *is* a noble cause. They don't come along every day."

So it was agreed. They would attack the NKVD headquarters in Lower Manhattan and try to kill as many of the secret policemen as they could.

But it wouldn't be easy.

Tower Two had been built to accommodate about ten thousand people. From Dozer's snooping, they knew there were now at least two thousand Militsiya inside, along with many administrative NKVD people, including computer operators. Plus, nearly all of the Chekskis were now guarding a huge perimeter around the two towers. This meant they would be up against at least five thousand of the psycho enemy fighters before they even got to the front door.

Even if the Allies were somehow able to battle their way through these Chekskis and get inside the 110-story building, they'd still have to fight their way to the top. That would be a long, bloody haul.

Just getting a substantial fighting force into Lower Manhattan seemed impossible. NJ104's Frank Geraci was a wizard at logistics. Moving troops around and getting them where they had to be was one of his talents.

But this was a real stumper for him.

"We could go over to Lower Manhattan in boats from the New Jersey side," he explained, "but that would be highly dangerous. Or we can somehow get up in far *north* Manhattan, right after their barbed wire and checkpoints end and just rush the gate. Then we'd have to do a Mad Mile the whole length of the fucking island—which would actually be thirteen Mad Miles in a row. But either way, we'd need transport, and that would mean those resurrected buses and cabs of theirs. But just our luck, they keep them all down in the Staten Island Ferry parking lot . . . in *Lower* Manhattan. We can't assume we could take over enough of some other kind of transport, like random cars or whatever, to get us all into the fight at the same time. And, let's face it, we can't walk it."

"Plus we've got to get it done before the remainder of Convoy 56 arrives," Crunch pointed out. "Wherever they are."

The newly arrived Allies had a hard time believing the story about the convoy. Hunter and Dozer and the rest of the 7CAV couldn't believe it themselves. Hunter had KO'd the Chekski troop ship and one battle cruiser plus the flock of Su-34s. And they'd seized the *Isakov*, devastated as it was, and made it move the twenty-six miles to Nantucket, and here they were.

But they still couldn't explain why the second battle cruiser had sunk. Everyone who'd been on deck and seen it said the same thing: The second battle cruiser had been about to fire a killer barrage at the *Isakov* when it suddenly blew up and disappeared beneath the waves, all in the blink of an eye.

Later on, someone had suggested the huge ship might have been nuclear-powered, and the reactor had exploded just as the ship had been about to blast 7CAV off the deck.

"Most convenient timing in any universe," Dozer mused in response to that theory.

But that still left the five destroyers unaccounted for, and they were all equipped with Styx missiles, which could really fuck up your day. Did they run into really bad weather? Did they turn back? No one knew.

Hunter remained quiet during the meeting. He listened to the theories, the plans, the complications. The odds. But he noticed no one in the room uttered one word of complaint or gave any indication of shirking off a mission that would likely get them killed. That aspect just wasn't part of the conversation. This was their country. The United States of America.

Their motto: Get Mad—*then* Get Even.

Finally, though, they all looked to him. He was the Wingman, their leader. There had never been a ceremony making it official, but then again, there'd never been a need for one.

He was the recognized expert because every plan he'd come up with in the past had somehow worked. It was his turn to play superhero again.

He drained the last of his whiskey, then said, "Okay—we might be able to do it like this: We can cross the river way up in Harlem, but maybe we don't need buses or cabs. And maybe we won't have to do thirteen Hell miles in a row just to get down to the WTC."

He continued to speak for twenty minutes, off the cuff, but with lots of detail. When he finished, they were all in agreement. Considering the situation, and the hundreds of risks, especially since they'd be outnumbered more than thirty to one, the men pronounced the plan brilliant.

Now Hunter just had to make it work.

CHAPTER THIRTY-FOUR

May 10

IVAN SAMSONOV LOOKED out the only window in his new office at the Liberty Court building in Lower Manhattan. It was still raining.

The weather had been wet and gloomy for the past twenty-four hours. Downpours nonstop, giant raindrops, like a million tears, rolling down his windowpane. He wondered how things were back in Petrograd. Was it sunny there?

The rain clouds had a silver lining, though. The fires in Midtown and southern Manhattan were finally going out.

Samsonov had been a hero for exactly one day. He was the guy who shot down the ghost plane. Not entirely accurate, but what did details matter. Praised by the Sostva, idolized on Red Radio, promised the People's Medal of Courage by the NKVD, his name had been on everyone's lips.

Until . . . the little clown plane showed up again the next night, sank the Yak barge and its fuel ship, and was spotted in the sky during the firebombing of the MMZ. After that, Samsonov's celebrity status went up in smoke quicker than the drug pens on Chelsea Piers. Red Radio stopped talking about him, the Sostva stopped reading his reports, and he never did get that medal. He was still worried that the NKVD was going to knock on his door at any minute and take him for a ride to the Staten Island landfill.

In the middle of it all, the army had transferred what was left of its staff people to the new headquarters down near Battery Park. Samsonov's office was on the top floor, and it included a tiny studio apartment. But it was nowhere near as luxurious as his old office in the immolated Army Building. It was cramped, and that single window looked out not on panoramic Manhattan, but on the smoky, greasy, trash-strewn communal canteen next door and the dreary navy ships in the harbor beyond.

Just a few days ago, the Russian military in America had commanded four mighty skyscrapers.

Now they had this second-rate twenty-story high rise, while the NKVD was suddenly in the tallest building in the world.

Nothing about his job had changed.

Security was in place around the new headquarters, and Samsonov still made rounds and still had to read and sign mountains of paperwork. The famously glacial Russian bureaucracy hadn't sped up just because the MMZ was now a smoldering hole in the ground. With the whole system in disarray, if anything, it would probably get worse.

It was 5:00 a.m. and he'd been working in his apartment, which contained a foldout couch, a personal desk, a dresser, and not much more. He'd fallen asleep on his couch, surrounded by piles of things he had to sign, when there was a knock at his door.

His heart immediately went to his throat. He took his LPG-3 pistol from his desk and opened the door. Two unsmiling Militsiya walked in, wearing their signature black hats and coats and dark glasses.

"You are Colonel Ivan Samsonov Mikalovich?" one asked as the other took the pistol from him.

"I am," Samsonov replied, just about losing it.

The first man reached into his interior coat pocket and pulled out not a gun, but a red-striped pouch.

He handed it to Samsonov, and both men left without another word.

Samsonov's hands were shaking so badly he could barely hold the pouch, let alone open it. But inside there were no pictures of naked women, but a note from the new NKVD HQ at the World Trade Center, signed by Commissar Zmeya himself.

It read: "You have been promoted to Supreme Commander of all *Okupatsi* forces in Russkiy-NYC. Report to my office immediately."

Samsonov ran in the rain.

There was no army transport available for him, and it was impossible to find one of the yellow cabs that were supposed to be providing rides for military officers.

But he didn't care. His head was spinning, his body still trembling. What was this all about? For his own sanity, he had to find out. It was just eight blocks to the WTC, so he'd thrown a trash bag over his head and sprinted down the wet and dirty streets.

He literally ran into a Chekski checkpoint five blocks out from the Twin Towers, which were hard to see in the rain and fog. He hated the Chekskis, hated having anything to do with them. Though they wore policemen's uniforms, they were always unwashed and unshaven and many of them went barefoot. The guys manning this checkpoint were no different. Madmen with AK-47s who gave everyone a hard time and seemed ready to fly off the handle at any moment.

He showed them the note from Zmeya, basically a writ of free passage anywhere in the city. But still, they delayed letting him through until everyone at the checkpoint—seven gunmen in all—had read the missive, discussed it, checked his personal papers, and then read the note again, all while keeping him waiting in the rain.

Once through, he began running again, only to encounter another Chekski checkpoint not a half block away. Eventually let through, he was stopped at a third checkpoint just a half block away from that. Across from him was Greenwich Street. It went for quite a way in both directions and he saw dozens of Chekski checkpoints and clusters of men and equipment set up practically on top of one another. Thousands of Chekskis had been ordered to security duty in the area.

He had to pass through seven more security checkpoints before reaching the entryway to Tower Two, where it only got worse.

As soon as he walked through the main doors of Tower Two, Samsonov felt really disturbing vibes. Every NKVD person he saw—officers, guards, apparatchiks—was not only busy, but in panic mode, *desperately* busy.

He could tell something had gone terribly wrong for the NKVD. He'd been in the Russian military for almost fifteen years. He knew what the shit drill looked like. But he could only wonder what it was, beyond the firebombing of Midtown.

He got rid of the trash bag and tried to shake the water out of his uniform and hair. The first interior checkpoint was near the elevators. It was guarded by the Milashkis, Zmeya's sexy, all-female, inner-sanctum protection squad. The last time Samsonov had seen the Cuties, he'd been smuggling an RPG launcher into 30 Rock. Now he had a letter signed by the commissar himself.

"I am glad to see you and not the Chekskis in here," he said as they were letting him pass.

"The Chekskis are not allowed within a quarter-mile perimeter of the commissar's headquarters," a Cutie replied.

Samsonov was in the building security business; he knew how to guard a skyscraper. A quarter-mile perimeter would be considered very loose and ineffective. If it were up to him, he'd have at least half the Chekskis closer in, if not inside the building itself.

"On whose orders?" he asked.

"The commissar's," she replied dryly. "He doesn't want them any nearer to him than that."

The next three checkpoints were manned by uniformed male Militsiyas. They had rigged the elevators to stop at three random floors for a security check. Every time the doors opened and a guard read his note, Samsonov could see more and more armed NKVD cops roaming around. Even some apparatchiks were now carrying weapons.

He reached the 110th floor, the site of Zmeya's new gigantic apartment in the sky, to find a small army of extremely tough-looking gunmen hanging around, special plainclothes Militsiya he assumed. Each was holding an AK-47 and eyeing him suspiciously.

Finally, the NKVD guard at the last checkpoint looked at the letter and told him, "Down the hallway, second door on the right. If it's open, go in. If it's closed, knock."

Samsonov walked down the darkened corridor, suddenly feeling very uneasy. Who knew what really awaited him? After all, this was the NKVD. Plus, he was mess. His uniform was soaking wet, his hair plastered to his head.

He paused before the second door and tried to straighten himself out. Deep breath. Push back the hair. Put on the game face.

Knock twice.

The door opened—and suddenly he was face to face with Dominique.

She was wearing a very short negligee and was smiling sweetly.

"Oh my goodness, you're all wet," she said.

Samsonov nearly passed out. The angel herself, standing right in front of him, dressed like . . .

"I am Colonel Ivan Samsonov, reporting as requested," he said, having no idea how he got the words out.

She never lost her smile. "Come in," she said. "He's on the radiophone, and that usually takes a while. In fact, you would not believe some of the things he's been missing because of that damn phone."

She fetched a towel for him and then led him into the huge living area. Zmeya was in the other room, his back to them, viciously berating someone on the other end of the phone.

"It's a *fucking* aircraft carrier," he was saying through gritted teeth. "It's enormous. You've got more than a hundred satellites. Why can't you find the goddamn thing?"

"Your next meeting is here," she called to him with mock weariness.

"Sit him down," Zmeya yelled back over his shoulder. "Give him some mineral water or something."

She led Samsonov to an alcove off the main living area where a curved couch awaited. They sat down, her right next to him. The view was spectacular.

"Looking out on the world from the top of the world," she said with a sigh. "It's like you can see all of Earth from here."

Samsonov was still in shock that this was happening, his brain's reaction to the sudden overload of stimuli. But now with her sitting so close to him, he began praying that another part of his body wouldn't start reacting. It was going to be a tough job.

She was so natural in her short negligee, her legs and feet as perfect as the rest of her. She smelled beautiful. And she was smiling at him, and sitting very close and giving off the aura of someone who was ready to have sex at any moment.

"You know, I know who you are," she told him.

That was it; he could barely breathe.

"Because I was the army liaison officer to the commissar's office?" he managed to spit out.

She playfully slapped his leg. "No—silly. You're the hero. The person who shot the ghost plane."

Samsonov flashed back to that awful night when he was holding on for dear life at the top of 30 Rock. He was so scared then. But how strange is life? He'd only done it in the hope that Dominique would become aware of his courageous act—and him. Now he was here talking to her. His plan had worked beyond all expectations.

But old-fashioned honor led him to reply, in a whisper, "But the ghost plane came back, my lady. The next night . . ."

She just touched his hand for a moment and said, "I know."

Samsonov could no longer sit up properly. He silently began reciting prayers at twice the normal speed.

"How did you survive the firestorm?" she asked. "Wasn't it horrible?"

"It was the one night I decided to go home," he told her. "The first time I'd slept in my billet in almost two weeks. It is only by luck that I wasn't in my office when the bombing happened."

"I'm glad you were not hurt," she said.

"I am as well, my lady," he said with a smile.

They looked out at Manhattan again. It was dizzying at this height.

"Such a great city it is," she said with another sigh.

"I think that's why we are here, my lady."

She laughed at that. She was so easygoing, he felt as if he'd known her for years.

"It would really be a shame if the city were destroyed," she said wistfully. "We came close with the firebombing. What happens next time?"

"Talking as a security officer," he replied, "it's always good to have a contingency plan."

It was more of a joke than anything else, very dry Russian humor. And she laughed at it as well.

"The way things are going," she said, "I think the only contingency at this point would be a gigantic submarine. Avoid everything else. Just come up, get us, go back down, and sail away. Who would ever know?"

"It is the navy who has the submarines, my lady," he said, kidding her again. "I'm no expert, but they have at least a handful. Nuclear-powered, of course. They could go forever."

"Really?" she asked, leaning even closer to him. "Are they here you mean? Attached to the *Okupatsi*? Nearby . . . underwater?"

Samsonov started to answer, but suddenly became aware of someone standing behind them.

It was Commissar Zmeya, looming over him.

"This is . . . what's the word? *Cozy*," Zmeya sneered.

Samsonov could already see the muzzle flashes of the firing squad in his near future. He'd just been caught talking mush with the commissar's mistress, who just happened to be the girl of his dreams.

But Zmeya was on another mission entirely. He made Dominique get up so he could sit down with Samsonov.

"Don't forget what we were in the middle of doing," she told Zmeya coyly.

Then she wandered away.

Zmeya gave him a perfunctory handshake.

"Congratulations, Samsonov," he said, not even looking at him. "Please try to do your best for the Motherland, so on and so forth."

"So, it is true, Commissar? I am the new supreme commander?"

"Of course you are," Zmeya snapped. "That's why you're here."

"But what about the Sostva? People haven't seen them in the flesh since the firebombing. They were not hurt I hope."

Zmeya was already getting exasperated.

"The Sostva officers decided to take some time off to work on their radio-broadcasting skills," he said, adding ominously, "over on Staten Island. Now, is there anything else you're curious about, Samsonov?"

Samsonov put his hand to his mouth, indicating he would shut up. Zmeya took out the contents of an envelope he was holding. Plans for the massive bombardment of a section of New Jersey about forty miles south of New York City.

"This is the only ongoing operation that's important at the moment," Zmeya told him.

"The Pine Barrens?" Samsonov asked, looking at the map. "The haunted forest?"

"Yes," Zmeya said. "Under NKVD direction, the army hit it with a series of rocket artillery strikes just hours ago. We're sending in a battalion of Chekskis to clear it of the guerillas who firebombed us."

"You *found* them, sir?"

"Of course we did," Zmeya snapped again. "And we've taken care of the problem, as you can see. But I brought you up here to warn you, Samsonov. The NKVD cannot continue to do things the army should be doing. These are critical times for the *Okupatsi*. If there are enemies around us, then do your duty, and do something about them, so we can continue our important work. That's it. You can go."

Samsonov got to his feet and saluted.

When he didn't move right away, Zmeya looked up at him. "Is there something else?"

"Yes, sir," he began, "I am now head of all the military in Russkiy-NYC. Is it because I was a hero? Because I damaged the ghost plane?"

Zmeya just glowered up at him. "Of course not, you fool. That bastard clown was back the next night—and look what that led to."

"Then why, Commissar? Why me?"

Zmeya stood up and faced him almost nose to nose.

"If you're a hero," he said, "it's only because you got Cadillacs and hookers for my men. Now, we are done here."

Samsonov saluted again and finally turned to go. But Zmeya caught him by the sleeve and added coldly, "And by the way, Samsonov—you weren't the first choice for the job."

CHAPTER THIRTY-FIVE

SAMSONOV RAN BACK to his office in the rain, this time without a trash bag for protection.

He felt like a young colt. Running through the depressingly gray smoke and mist, the stale smell of something burning inside the sprawling canteen. The stink of the Midtown fires still in the air. None of it mattered.

Dominique . . .

He'd met her, he'd talked to her, she'd *touched* him. And sex had been in the air. It was crazy, yet it had just happened. Cerebral orgasms. It was the only way he could describe the joy he'd experienced by being so close to her.

He reached the Liberty Building headquarters and took the stairs to the top floor, still floating. He would do everything Zmeya wanted and more. Not out of loyalty to the murderous thug, but to endear himself to the head of the secret police, just so he could see Dominique again.

He'd do anything for her.

The top of the HQ was deserted when he arrived. All the third-shift duty people were working on the floor below. He cut through his office to his small apartment and closed the door. He flicked the light switch—but no lights came on.

He tried again, and that's when he felt something cold pressing against his temple.

In the dim light coming in the apartment's only window, he saw the shadow of an enormous .357 Magnum pistol pointing at him. It looked like a small cannon.

Deeper in the shadows, a man dressed in combat fatigues but wearing a fighter pilot's helmet was holding the weapon.

Damn. Could this be who he thought it was?

"We need to talk," the gunman said. "You speak English, right?"

Samsonov nodded.

"You're the new CO of all the military in town?"

Samsonov nodded again.

"Okay, I'll say this once," he began. "In a matter of hours, this city will come under attack. The target is strictly the NKVD—this time anyway. Now, you can avoid a lot of unpleasantness by giving your people one simple order."

"What—to surrender?" Samsonov asked, almost interrupting him. "Just because you threaten to shoot me in the head? They wouldn't follow that order. I'm not that important."

"I'm not saying surrender," the gunman told him, pressing the gun deeper. "Just keep them in their barracks when things get going."

But Samsonov laughed—he couldn't help it. "You want me to tell my soldiers and sailors to stand down while you . . . what? Fight the NKVD?"

The gunman nodded. "That's exactly right. They've fucked with the wrong people. And now, they need to pay."

"Then you must be insane, whoever you are," Samsonov told him. "If I did as you want, those NKVD monsters would cut me up and feed me to the fish—me and everyone in this building."

"Not if all of the monsters are dead," the gunman said coolly.

This gave Samsonov pause.

"You're that sure of victory, are you?" he finally asked. "Who do you represent? An army of angels?"

The gunman yanked Samsonov over to his only window to get some light. He handed him an envelope. It was bulging with Polaroid instant photographs.

"Look at them," the gunman ordered him.

Samsonov did as told, holding the first one up to the light.

It showed stacks of lead-lined canisters, all labeled in Russian as being nerve agents and extremely deadly. Other photos were close-ups of nuclear warheads. Still others of long-range artillery shells filled with poison gas.

Samsonov had seen WMD before, but just not so much in one place.

"Where did you get this nonsense?" Samsonov challenged him.

"Look at the last two pictures," he was told.

Samsonov picked up the two photos. One depicted a group of men gathered in front of yet another array of awesomely deadly weapons. They were holding up a large American flag. The second picture was an aerial view of the *Admiral Isakov*. Several dozen men were standing on the crooked, smoky deck in such a way that they spelled out "USA."

Samsonov was totally confused now. "What is this all about?"

"The NKVD's toy boat? The *Admiral Isakov*, the largest aircraft carrier in the world?" the gunman replied. "It was on its way here, to New York, carrying all that WMD, when we intercepted it and captured it. Plus, a troop transport carrying thirty thousand Chekskis was sunk with no survivors. And you're hearing about all this for the first time?"

Samsonov couldn't reply. Clearly, the NKVD did not consider him important enough to be told of this military disaster. But now he knew why the shit drill was going on inside Tower Two.

The gunman pressed him. "I'd say for you not to be informed of this means the Russian military's role in Russkiy-NYC is questionable at best."

Again, Samsonov could not reply.

"Getting the idea now?" the gunman went on. "We can drop some or all of this scary stuff on top of all of you, and it won't bother us a bit. There are hardly any civilians left in the city; they all left after the firestorm, right?"

Samsonov could only nod. It was true; the city had emptied out so quickly after that night, there hadn't been enough time to seal all the tunnels and bridges. More than a few deserters were reported among the swiftly moving masses.

"Okay then, you see?" the gunman said. "Collateral damage will not be a concern. So we can get most of you with just a few punches. The question is: Do you really want New York to be the graveyard for you and all your people? Thousands of them? Stalingrad in reverse?"

Samsonov pushed the photos back into the gunman's hands.

"But I can't do what you ask," he told him. "It's . . . illogical."

"Screw logic, my friend," the gunman cautioned him. "You let us take care of the NKVD, then you guys can get on your ships and sail out of here, and we'll forget this ever happened."

"You're *that* certain of victory?" Samsonov asked him again.

"Let's just say we're all betting men," the gunman replied. "And we're betting you're not going to be a fool and let sixty thousand of your guys get killed by WMD that have MADE IN RUSSIA stamped on them."

"You'd destroy your own city, just for that?"

"We took out thirty-five city blocks, didn't we?" the gunman replied. "If the question is if we'll destroy it before letting you have it, the answer is yes. A thousand times, yes."

A long pause.

Then the gunman lowered his weapon. "Look, pal, just give us an hour. Just stay out of the way."

Samsonov shook his head. "I can't," he said. "It's a matter of honor. The thought of betraying my country like that? It's not like betraying Moscow or the Kremlin. I would be betraying Mother Russia herself."

"You need further motivation then," the gunman said.

Samsonov just shook his head and waited. The lights in his tiny apartment suddenly came on. Much to his embarrassment the walls were covered with photographs—of Dominique.

Many had been shot from telephoto lenses, skyscraper to skyscraper. Others were just enlargements of the famous Circle War photo. But they were all of the blonde beauty.

"Okay, then," the gunman said. "Will you do it for her?"

With the new illumination, Samsonov saw the man for the first time. Not his eyes, as his helmet's visor was down—and, strangely, the helmet itself was being held together by duct tape.

But Samsonov knew for certain who the man was.

Hawk Hunter, the Wingman. Back from the dead.

"I see we have something in common," he told Samsonov, indicating all the photos.

"More than you know," Samsonov replied. "I wanted her to notice me, one way or another. And I accomplished that by shooting at that flying bug of yours."

"You're the guy who shot the RPG at me?"

"I am," Samsonov replied with almost a bow.

"Well, next time, Comrade, learn how to aim one of those things."

There was a long awkward silence.

Finally, Samsonov said, "And what will I get if I do this? An autographed picture of her? A peck on the cheek at some point?"

"You get to help keep her alive," his visitor told him plainly. "You know Zmeya's track record. How long do you think she's going to last once the Kremlin realizes its flagship and all those weapons are now in our hands?"

Samsonov thought a few more moments, looking at her pictures surrounding them.

Then he said, "You have one hour—and none of my men get hurt."

"One hour. And you'd better be a man of your word, or you *will be* fish food. I guarantee it."

Then he was through the door and gone.

CHAPTER THIRTY-SIX

AT MIDNIGHT, A sound was heard high above New York City.

It was so distinct that no matter what people were doing, they naturally looked up at the sky.

Those with extraordinary eyesight or night-vision goggles saw something all too familiar cruising over Manhattan.

A tiny aircraft with a noisy engine and very big wheels.

The ghost plane was back.

Pitch-black. Absolutely opaque. A night sky without any stars.

That was what it was like to fly in a tunnel. And that's what Hunter was doing at the moment.

A passenger was squeezed into the clown plane with him—Colonel Donnie Kurjan of the United American Army, the large, well-organized quasi-militia that came together in national emergencies. Kurjan had cheated death several times in the conflicts that had followed the Big War, earning the nickname Lazarus.

His specialty—or at least one of them—was an expert knowledge of electricity. And while he and Hunter had fought together more times than they could count and were old friends, Kurjan might have been the most important person in New York City at the moment.

They were both wearing gas masks, which helped as they flew along in the darkness. They were also wearing night-vision goggles—but they were practically useless. Their sensors were so devoid of light that the illuminating gear could only provide crackling, indistinct images.

This was such a dangerous mission that, at first, Hunter had been determined to do it himself. Journey into the deepest part of the tunnels and do what he needed to do without getting caught. How could he ask anyone to join him?

But he was not an expert on everything, and there could be no guesswork here. That's why Kurjan was with him. He knew a lot about certain things that could be found deep in this abyss.

No surprise, then, that before heading out from Nantucket, they'd had a few shots of Dozer's brutal whiskey.

They'd performed the noisy flyover of the city earlier for a reason. Hunter wanted to see if the Russian SAM batteries would paint him with their radars. If they did, the city's air-raid sirens would go off. As for making the already jumpy city a little more on edge? Another part of the plan.

They'd found the tunnel entrance up around 168th Street in North Harlem. It was a very isolated place and about a mile north of the Russians' twenty-foot high barbed-wire outer defense line.

Hunter had done this very same thing back during his adventure at Area 51 not two months ago. But that had been in a more stable jet fighter, and the tunnel had been huge—and well lit. There was not a hint of any light or even the dimmest glow down here, and the tunnel was much narrower. Nor was it all one straight shot. The tunnels were full of twists and turns, and Hunter had to rely on Kurjan to cry out a warning to get them safely around every corner. They were both pros, but this was stressful.

Deeper and deeper into the blackness they flew. They kept track of how far they were going by silently counting the seconds. Thirty seconds should equal a mile; a minute equaled two.

They had to go in at least three miles. Ninety seconds, the longest seconds either of them had experienced in their lives.

Landing was virtually blind and bumpy. The big tires allowed the plane to come down on the rails and not the rock bed, meaning they should be able to take off again, but it was a painful touchdown.

They got out of the plane and grabbed their M-16s. As they alked slowly to their left, their hands out in front of them, their night-vision goggles showed just about a blank screen. They were mostly walking over sharp gravel and broken bottles, but also the occasional skeleton. The dead had lain here in the pitch-darkness for fifteen years, maybe more.

Kurgan finally found a wall; this is what they wanted. They began feeling along its base and even below it, trying to find something other than bones.

But it was not to be. They gave their best, five minutes of looking around for something that just wasn't there. They had to move on.

Takeoff was rough. They almost slammed into the ceiling. There was no wind in the tunnels and that actually made for a hairier ride. Once they'd counted off another three miles, they landed again, crawled to the wall, and felt around. But once again, they found nothing.

Six miles in. Two crap-outs.

Near the junction of two tunnels, Hunter landed again in another extremely rough touchdown. Still wearing his duct-taped crash helmet, he hit the top of the canopy so hard he put another large crack in it.

They crawled and groped and tried to sweep the bones and dust away—and finally Kurjan found it: a thick cable running along the base of the wall. It led them to a large metal box affixed to a pole nearby. They studied its insides. Up very close with their night-vision goggles, struggling, Hunter saw a panel of industrial-size circuit breakers and one large switch.

The switch was what they came here for.

"You're sure this is the right one, right location, and so on?" Hunter asked, whispering for some reason in the absolute black-ness.

"I think so," Kurjan replied. "I was into trains big-time as a kid—then I got into what made them run. The NYC Tran-sit Authority put junction boxes every three to nine miles along their subway routes. It was a safety thing, in case the third rail had to be turned off in an emergency. At most, only nine miles of the line would go down. But if you switched just one of them back on, the entire line would be back up and running."

Hunter took a breath and put his hand on the switch—but Kurjan brushed it away.

"Do you have a license to handle electrical equipment in the City of New York, Major Hunter?" he asked.

"No—I don't."

"And I don't have a pilot's license," Kurjan said. "So this one is on me."

He put his hand on the switch, drew a deep breath, and pulled.

There was a huge flash, followed by a storm of electrical sparks. In the same instant, ten thousand volts went right up Kurjan's arm, throwing him high in the air.

He came down hard, at least thirty feet away from Hunter. The Wingman frantically ran over to him, tripping and stumbling in the dark. Yet, incredibly, when he arrived, Kurjan was already standing up, all in one piece, dusting himself off.

Judging by the jolt he'd been hit with, he should have been dead.

"Mission accomplished, no?" he asked Hunter. They could barely see each other in the faint emerald night-vision glow. "The juice still works way down here in the tunnels."

Hunter was still speechless.

Finally, he said, "I guess that's why they call you Lazarus."

Kurjan was the first to hear them coming.

He and Hunter were still in absolute darkness, sitting now, backs against a wall from which they'd cleared any human remains. It had been about an hour since they got the electricity running again.

It came as a rumble at first; Kurjan actually felt it before he heard it. Hunter was aware of it an instant later.

It was incredibly loud. The squealing alone was enough to bust eardrums, the awful roar of something big and fast coming that might not be able to slow down. The noise of something unstoppable.

They were up in an instant, flattening themselves against the wall. They saw the light a moment later. Cutting through the black to their right, far off but still seemingly as bright as the sun.

The noise got louder. Everything around them began to shake, including the post holding the electrical panel and all those bones.

Kurjan tried to yell something to Hunter, but it was lost immediately, buried in the absolute shrieking going on around them.

The train went by them a moment later.

It had a dozen cars and each one was packed with United American soldiers, all in classic UA dark green fatigues, heavily armed and heading south.

The train was visible for just a few seconds before it disappeared to their left, vanishing into the tunnel as if it was plunging into the blackness of space itself. But the awful noise remained.

Another train went roaring by. This one was twice as long and carrying members of the Football City Special Forces, unmistakable in their black-and-gold combat suits.

A third train sped by. It was filled with soldiers in unmarked uniforms, but by their maroon battle hats, it was obvious they were members of the Free Canadian Special Forces. Sometimes *not* wearing a flag was the best way to let your feelings be known.

A fourth train was carrying the 101st Airborne Regiment of the PAAF—the Pacific American Armed Forces. They'd parachuted into Yonkers less than an hour ago and walked down to Manhattan. After them, more trains came. Some were loaded with local militia companies, some with mercs from as far away as Mudtown, Free Pennsylvania. Some were even carrying battle-field weapons—anything that could fit on board a typical New York City subway car. Recoilless rifles, small rocket launchers, small artillery pieces—and lots of ammunition.

There were thirteen trains in all. When the last one came screaming down the track, it actually hit its brakes and came to an earsplitting stop, the last car ending up right in front of Hunter and Kurjan.

The rear door opened and Bull Dozer stepped out. "We have a passenger to pick up?" he yelled.

Kurjan turned to Hunter and said, "Don't stay down here any longer than you have to, Hawk. You never know what's living down here these days."

Hunter was mildly shocked. "Now you tell me?"

They shook hands.

"See you on the other side," Kurjan said.

CHAPTER THIRTY-SEVEN

ALL THE TRAINS were rushing to the same place.

Pre–Big War, its official name was Cortlandt Street 1 stop, Level 2, New York Transit Authority. But most people had called it the One and the Two. The subway station below the World Trade Center's Twin Towers.

As Hunter had told the Allies at the Nantucket war council: "Just because the New York City subway system hasn't run since the Big War doesn't mean it's broken. If we can turn the power back on, we can commute to the battle underground. Avoid all opposition topside." And that's exactly what was happening.

"Hawk is scary sometimes," Kurjan said to Dozer as their train rushed headlong down the tunnel. "He always hits a home run when it comes to stuff like this."

Dozer checked his watch as they sped through one of many dark, long-abandoned stations. Time was an important element here.

"I hear you, Lazz," he replied. "And he's done it enough times to prove it ain't no fluke."

They could see the final station coming up. Though the power was back on, the station's lightbulbs had burned out long ago, so the platform was lit by thousands of candles of all different shapes and sizes brought in by the first troop train to reach the station. They gave off an otherworldly glow.

There were eighty members of 7CAV on the train, plus Dozer. They were already up and waiting at the doors, ready for a fight. All that time awaiting word from their fellow warriors in the haunted forest, and they lose thirteen of their guys in just a few hours? There was no question who would lead the impending assault.

The train squealed to a halt and 7CAV piled out. The platform was already crowded with more than two thousand raiders. Gathered under the direction of Geraci's NJ104, they'd been brought by boat to North Harlem from New Jersey to take the long train ride downtown. Different uniforms, different weapons, different kinds of soldiers, everyone wending his way through the sea of candles, but they all had one thing in common: the small American-flag patches on their left shoulders. That was the reason they were here.

More trains would be coming later, carrying reinforcements and ammo and returning to North Harlem with the wounded and dead. But for now, this was it. Two thousand against almost ten thousand—and possibly sixty-five thousand more.

"Another war," Dozer said to Kurjan as they were disembarking. "Does it ever end?"

"I don't know," Kurjan replied. "But either way, history is going to be made here today."

Suddenly, a loud, mechanical roar filled the station. Not the squealing and screeching of a train. This was a big, high-speed motor with no noise suppression gear. Something moving very fast and without a muffler.

It exploded from the tunnel a moment later. It wasn't running on the tracks, it was flying above them. Lots of smoke, flames coming from its exhaust pipes, big wheels, covered with duct tape, it was the clown plane with Hunter at the controls.

He roared over the platform, banking the small plane slightly to fit above the idling trains. Without warning, he did an incredible roll right inside the station, a way of acknowledging the Allies' presence. The soldiers let out a cheer. He straightened out and was gone in a flash, down the other end of the tunnel.

Then all was quiet. The only noise was the flickering of thousands of candles. It became like a church. Many of the fighters went down on one knee to await the next command.

Hanging above them, on a billboard over the tracks, was a faded tourist ad encouraging the use of rapid transit, reminding people, "Take the subway. It's faster."

CHAPTER THIRTY-EIGHT

NEITHER JT NOR Ben had ever flown a Russian fighter before.

They'd fought them, they'd shot them down, but they'd never gotten closer than the range of a Vulcan cannon.

But there are commonalities between airplanes. With all of them, you take off, you add power, you fly. It's what you do once airborne that tells the tale.

At the moment, though, they were being used as test monkeys. They were scheduled to take off from the *Admiral Isakov* in two Su-34s just after 2100 hours. Thanks to the 7CAV guys, the carrier's deck was clear and the stationary ship had just a 10 percent list to starboard.

The jets were armed and ready to go, but would the ship's leaky, jimmy-rigged steam generators hold enough pressure to shoot them off the deck? If not, even a Su-34 couldn't survive what would happen next.

The minutes ticked down; hasty, last-moment tests were done; and at precisely 2104 hours, JT went off the deck. Ben followed him two seconds later. Both Su-34s dipped precipitously after leaving the carrier's bow, but recovered quickly. In seconds, they were climbing to five thousand feet, going nearly straight up.

Thirty seconds behind, another Su-34 took off, Captain Crunch at the stick. He flew a souped-up F-4 Phantom in his day job, a rugged but aged stallion. Never did he dream he'd be flying a Russian jet on a combat mission, never mind a Su-34.

They'd found a lot of really nasty ordnance aboard the *Isakov*, both conventional and otherwise. The three purloined fighters were now lugging some of the worst: RBK-250 cargo munitions, better known as cluster bombs. Once dropped, each bomb, a large container with hundreds of little bomblets inside it, would split open, and the diminutive bombs would explode a few feet off the ground, killing large numbers of personnel in a short amount of time. Each plane was carrying ten thousand pounds of them.

This would be a one-and-done air strike, though. The *Isakov*'s arresting cables were unfixable, so returning to the ship was out. There was a tiny airport on east Nantucket with a small runway, but a vast parking lot beyond it.

Before the mission, some 7CAV guys removed the fence separating the landing strip from the parking lot, hoping it was a way of stretching the runway so JT, Ben, and Captain Crunch could manage to land their Su-34s. It was the best they could do, because by the time the Su-34s even took off from Nantucket, most of the 7CAV planned to be otherwise engaged.

The three fighters formed up at five thousand feet over Nantucket Bay. Power plants checked and single-pilot configs entered and confirmed, they set their flight computers to mission-command and turned southwest.

New York City was just a twenty-minute flight from here.

CHAPTER THIRTY-NINE

THE STRANGEST THING about Hunter's plan was that he really wasn't involved in it.

At least not at the moment.

He had another mission that was just as vital, but far from the action. Another lonely search over the ocean.

After exiting the subway tunnel near Chelsea Piers, he'd headed east, out over the water again. The real kink in his plan was the five Russian destroyers unaccounted for since the battle for the *Isakov*. The conditions out to sea had not improved much, which might be why the five ships had yet to reach New York City. But the danger they posed to the Allies could not be over-emphasized. Everyone around the war-planning table had seen a Styx missile in action, and no one wanted any part of them. Especially while in the middle of trying to clean out Tower Two.

These ships had to be found. And because the clown plane could fly low and slow and had such a tiny radar signature, the job fell to Hunter.

Reaching the eastern shore of Long Island, Hunter turned northeast.

If the five destroyers were taking the shortest route to New York, then they'd be out here somewhere. It was puzzling, though, that nothing about the ships' whereabouts had been picked up on

Dozer's 616 eavesdropping gear. Maybe even the NKVD didn't know where they were. Or maybe they'd all just sunk.

But going radio silent was usually a preamble to an attack. And considering the circumstances, that attack would probably come somewhere in Lower Manhattan.

This was not like looking for Convoy 56 in his now-departed F-16XL. This meant flying at nearly wave-top level and hoping you saw them before they saw you. As he was passing by East Hampton, three contrails went overhead, cutting through the stars. The three Su-34s streaking in the opposite direction, toward New York City. Hunter felt odd flying away from the action, but that's just how it was.

All this got him thinking again about the situation back in New York, which of course made him think of Dominique. His jaw still hurt where she'd slugged him.

She said he would never understand, and she was right. He was convinced that she was no longer the person he remembered. But now, as he passed Montauk Point, still dwelling on everything that had happened in the past few days, he couldn't help but wonder what she was doing at that very moment.

CHAPTER FORTY

THE SEX BETWEEN Zmeya and Dominique had lasted thirteen hours already.

Not thirteen *straight* hours—the sessions were interrupted by many radiophone calls and meetings Zmeya had to run. And no *real* sex. Not quite yet.

But that's how it worked. As she'd explained it to him, *sex* meant much more to her than the act itself. She called it tantric sex, where all aspects of one's lustful desires are discussed first and at length to heighten the pleasure that would eventually come.

It got off to a bizarre start. Dominique had turned Zmeya's cameras on him as if he were a common criminal and made him confess to all his fatal encounters with women over the past few years, including names and descriptions. One turned out to be the daughter of a Politburo member.

Then he took video of her as she dressed up, stripped down, and bathed. She obeyed all his commands but always stopped short of taking that one last step.

As promised, she'd used the tip of her hunting knife on his arousal. But these episodes were surprisingly short, because Zmeya would pass out whenever he spotted even the tiniest drop of blood on her blade. His reaction had been so odd that Dominique had asked him, "What did your parents do to you?" He'd replied, "Not my parents, just my father."

She'd let him watch her have sex with one of the Cuties, and then with two of them at once. And he'd filmed the encounters. Because of Dominique, he'd let all participants live.

But now, just before midnight, he declared the long mystical foreplay was over. It had to be—because he couldn't think of anything else to do but the act itself.

And neither could she.

Zmeya was sitting in his darkened bedroom, staring at the unpainted walls. Not moving, barely breathing, he was trying very hard to push the rest of the world out of his head for a little while.

This was it, finally. Dominique came into the room naked. No knives, no cameras, no other people. Just them, having sex. Making love.

He'd never wanted anything more.

She slipped under the sheets with him, smelling like a flower and wearing bright red lipstick. His favorite.

"Count to ten," he whispered to her.

She did as he said. Then she asked him why.

"This is your perfect opportunity to murder me," he told her. "Dark, secluded, a good escape route. No one would stop you from leaving. But I suppose if you were really an assassin, you would have killed me by now."

"That's not very romantic," she said dryly.

"What did you expect?" he asked, pulling her naked body closer. "That 'tantrum' thing was strung out over half the day. Are you sure that's the way it's supposed to go?"

"Some people do it over the course of *weeks*," she insisted. "And besides, you kept getting distracted by answering the phone and taking meetings."

He sighed deeply. "I'm sure this is how Nero felt."

She leaned even closer to him. His heart began racing.

"How about giving me credit for keeping my half of the bargain?" she said. "I've done all you've asked."

"Where's the credit you owe me for keeping mine?" he shot back.

She found and squeezed his manhood. "On the way," she said.

"I'll believe it when I see it," he replied, but he was beginning to pant.

Using her other hand, she put on another layer of red lipstick.

"Those people up in the stadium," she said, gyrating a bit. "You'll let them go, right?"

Zmeya was standing at attention to the point that small capillaries were bursting at different points throughout his body. The minor knife wounds from earlier were threatening to bleed again. He would have agreed to just about anything.

Except that.

"Not part of the bargain," he replied, his head back, eyes closed. "You'll have to earn it."

She tied her hair back to get it out of the way.

"Then I hope your constitution is strong enough to handle what's coming," she said, taking him in both hands.

"I'll die a happy man if it isn't," he whispered.

Dominique had just begun to adjust herself on the bed when the radiophone rang.

It wasn't the usual sequence of three rings. This was just a long constant bleating.

Zmeya was out of the bed in a shot. He ran to his desk in the next room, seeming almost desperate to answer the call.

Dominique stayed where she was, as she was. But she could hear every word he said and even had a partial view of him.

It was no ordinary conversation, not for the commissar. For one, Zmeya was hardly talking; mostly, he just listened. She saw him write a lot of things down on his desk calendar and even heard him say "yes, sir" a few times.

This wasn't anyone in Moscow he was talking to; he would have addressed his very few superiors there as *Comrade*, not *sir*.

He also usually ended each phone conversation by hanging up on the other person. But not this time. He hung up only after saying good-bye.

He came back to bed with his shoulders slumped, mumbling, unable to look at her.

"Who was that?" she asked.

He rolled away from her and hugged the pillow. "That was my father."

CHAPTER FORTY-ONE

THE THREE SU-34S arrived above New York Harbor in a tight, triangle formation.

JT, Ben, and Crunch had descended from five thousand feet off Coney Island and were now just two hundred feet above the deck. Once Lower Manhattan was within view, they centered their FLIR fire control pips on the throngs of Chekskis deployed around the World Trade Center.

Pre-strike intelligence from Dozer's 616 told them fifty-two hundred Chekskis were manning this gigantic perimeter around the Twin Towers. The semicircle of defense started in the south at the canteen near Battery Park and went up to the charred edges of Chelsea Piers. It looked impressive, but with manpower like that, it would have been more logical to put them much closer to the building itself, like troops around a castle, making it nearly impossible to take over.

But the human buffer of Chekskis wasn't really there to guard Tower Two; they were in position to fight a small war in the streets of Lower Manhattan—against their brothers of the military. This rapidly spreading paranoia was further stoked by a second phony message that had been broadcast that afternoon. Breaking in on all military and NKVD frequencies, the same voice that had accused the NKVD of firebombing Midtown claimed that the Russian Navy had just received orders from

Moscow to either shell or bomb the Chekskis sometime before daybreak.

"The Kremlin is not happy," the voice had said. "The performance of our secret police this last week has not been upstanding. The firebombing of Midtown and a mysterious 'failure at sea'? Wake up, Comrades. The NKVD is ruining the *Okupatsi*. Don't let them. The time for revolution is now."

The Su-34s' FLIR screens confirmed that at least eight hundred Chekskis were gathered at the south end of Battery Place. It was a staging area where numerous Brozi gun trucks were positioned. This would be the Americans' first target.

Down to a hundred feet now and passing under the Verrazano-Narrows Bridge, each pilot signaled one last A-OK by clicking his radio call button twice. Six clicks. They were all on the same page.

They swooped in off the river, over the docks, and over the canteen. On JT's call, they dropped their ordnance a hundred feet above the end of Battery Place.

None of the Chekskis below sought cover; there wasn't time. When the shower of bomblets hit, the NKVD fighters suddenly looked like they were dancing. So many bomblets were going off amid the fire and smoke, and so many Chekskis were being hit from so many different directions, they didn't even have a chance to fall down dead. It looked like a horrible fiery ballet.

The three Su-34s climbed out quickly, did a sharp bank over the harbor, and came back again, just as low. This time, they were aiming for the Chekski concentration near Brookfield Place. Ten old MTA buses were parked here surrounded by at least several hundred Chekskis.

Once again, each of the three planes dropped two cluster bombs. The explosions walked right down the street, tearing into the NKVD positions before many of the gunmen could move away. Because the site was more closed in than Battery Place, the thousands of bomblets tore into humans and concrete alike. Blood and glass were soon mixed together on the street.

Another turn out over the water, then six more canisters were dropped on the extremely large NKVD checkpoint off Vesey

Street. Though some of the Chekskis were now firing their AK-47s at the Su-34s, the jets were going too fast for it to have any effect. Some of the Chekskis found cover; many could not. There were only so many places to hide down here on a few seconds' notice. It resulted in another surreal display of Chekski gunmen flailing away like puppets in the flames.

The fourth and last strike came against the only rear area the Chekskis could claim, this on the northern part of the WTC plaza itself. This time, the cloud of bomblets and shrapnel went out over a wide area, taking down fleeing Chekskis like a scythe and hitting the front entrance to Tower Two itself.

But that was it. Total time of the strike, one minute, seven seconds. The three jets circled the area once for a quick post-strike eval, then took off to the northeast at full throttle.

During the strike, no SAMs were fired at them, and none of the navy ships in the harbor turned on the antiaircraft batteries.

CHAPTER FORTY-TWO

FOR THE SECOND time in four days, Dominique was hastily packing a bag.

Zmeya hadn't let her take her things when they'd evacuated 30 Rock, and she was not going to let that happen again. She needed her T-shirts, her lipstick, and her soap. Most of all her soap.

They'd seen the air strikes. Trying to comfort Zmeya as he stood by his favorite window, which looked out on Greenwich Street, Dominique probably had the best view of the brutal cluster bombing, because she was looking down on it.

They saw the three Su-34s approach, their sea-blue camo schemes clearly recognizable, as was the Russian naval insignia on each one.

"It's not true," Zmeya gasped as he watched the bombs fall from the trio of warplanes. "The navy *can't* be doing this. It has to be someone else."

Dominique had to turn her head—and so did Zmeya—when the bomblets started exploding. Even from 110 stories up, the resulting carnage was something nightmares were made of.

By the time the fourth target was hit, Dominique had already gathered her few meager belongings, including her knife.

Then she heard Zmeya crank up his suitcase phone and order someone to scramble his helicopter. Once again, it was time to go.

"You see what is happening here?" he was yelling to her from the other room where he was getting dressed. "No SAMs fired, and the ships in the harbor remained motionless. The army and navy and probably that fucking MOP, as well. They're all against me."

From his position on the subway platform, Dozer counted the four explosions up above.

The last was the loudest. That came when the Su-34s dropped almost four tons of cluster bombs on the big Chekski position at the WTC's northern plaza, unloading practically on top of the subway station itself.

That was their cue.

Dozer blew his whistle twice. The two thousand Allied soldiers waiting on the platform jumped to their feet. They checked their weapons one last time.

One more long whistle, and they were up a staircase six aisles wide, 130 steps in length.

Dozer and his guys were in the lead. Yet when they reached the top of the stairs, Jim Cook and the JAWS team were already there. Crouched atop the first step, the WTC loomed before them.

Dozer called the assault team to a halt.

"Any opposition anywhere?" he asked Cook.

The JAWS commanding officer shook his head. "Not yet." He pointed to Tower Two and added, "They're either otherwise indisposed, or they're waiting for us somewhere way up there."

Dozer contemplated the pair of 110-story buildings in front of him. He'd never been this close to them before. It hurt his neck just looking up at them.

"Jesus Eff Christ," he swore. "This is going to be that fucking aircraft carrier all over again—except this time, it will be all up and down."

The entire plaza was covered with the remains of the fourth cluster-bomb strike. The bombs had created a blizzard of shrapnel, and everything inside the impact zone—vehicles, buildings, Chekskis—had been perforated. The carnage was indescribable.

Dozer blew his whistle again.

"For the stars and stripes, boys!" he yelled. "Time to clean house."

Hundreds of Allied soldiers began pouring out of the subway exit, moving as quickly and quietly as possible. With Dozer and Cook in the lead, they scurried across the concourse, heading for the ground-level entrance of Tower Two. But the Militsiya gunmen stationed inside the lobby saw them coming and began firing at them right away, forgetting, or not knowing, that the lobby glass was bulletproof. None of the raiders was hit.

They reached the main entrance of the massive building, but three sets of revolving doors separated them from Tower Two's lower lobby. Going through the slowly moving doors would be suicidal. Cook solved the problem: He set up a handful of plastic explosive against the entranceway and took out a battery-operated plunger.

"Fire in the hole!" he yelled, pushing the plunger. The three revolving doors blew up in one great flash, killing some of the Militsiya inside and causing the others to flee.

The way to Tower Two was open.

Two more whistle blows from Dozer, and the American fighters charged into the building.

CHAPTER FORTY-THREE

ON THE 110TH floor of Tower Two, Zmeya was shouting into his radio phone, ranting about his helicopter, when his aide-de-camp ran into the room.

No knocking, no asking for permission to enter.

"They're here, sir," he yelled at Zmeya. "They're here."

Others had won a bullet in the ear for bursting in on Zmeya like this, but the man was obviously terrified.

"Who is here?" Zmeya demanded. "The army? And they're collaborating with the navy, right?"

"No, sir," the man said. "It's the Americans. They're attacking us."

Zmeya stopped for a moment. "The Americans are attacking *us*? What do you mean? In Queens? The Bronx or someplace? A diversion? They're in league with—"

The man shook his head vigorously. "No—I'm saying they're *here*, sir. The Americans are attacking *this* building. They're on the ground floor."

Zmeya froze for a moment, then fell into his office chair. He couldn't believe it.

"How many?" he asked. "Is it a band of terrorists? An assassination squad?"

The aide could only shrug. "It's not a small group," he said fearfully. "There are at least several hundred soldiers, maybe even a thousand or more."

"But . . . how?" Zmeya asked the officer, incredulous. "How did so many get this close? The bridges can't be crossed. The tunnels are blocked. Someone would have seen them coming from miles away."

The aide turned pale. "They used the subway, sir," he said. "Right underneath us. They came in on old commuter trains."

Zmeya's face turned a deep shade of red.

"But I was told the subways here didn't work," he said through gritted teeth. "And I think you're the one who told me. . . ."

"But that's what we all thought, sir," the officer pleaded.

Zmeya was beginning to perspire. He needed his meds.

"But wait a minute," he said. "Who just bombed the Chekskis? Unless . . ."

Suddenly, he was fighting to keep his composure. He was the head of the NKVD in America, and he'd just been double-crossed.

"Get the army on the phone," he ordered. "Tell them to move every unit down here right now, starting with the tanks."

"We already tried," the officer said, his voice still trembling. "They are not answering."

"Call that new CO—what's his name?—Samsonov."

"He's not answering, either, sir."

More sweat on his brow. A bit of a loss of balance. Zmeya held his head in his hands for a moment. While planning the America operation back in Moscow, he'd attended meetings in which senior officers gushed about how great it would be to claim Manhattan's forest of skyscrapers for the Motherland.

Fools! They were the worst possible objectives to defend.

But he took a breath and changed gears. A fight lay ahead. But he'd been in fights before.

"You instituted my Plan B under defensive actions, correct?" he asked the aide.

"The personnel are getting into position now," the man replied.

"And the stairways?"

"Everything is armed that needs to be armed," the aide confirmed.

"What's the number of our building security force?"

"There are two companies of our special police on the ground floor," the officer replied hastily. "Four more companies in reserve per Plan B. Two more on the floor below us. Each company is four hundred men. That's more than three thousand men, sir—all of them Militsiya."

"That gives us time," Zmeya said to himself. "But we've still got to get that copter up here."

The Allied assault force had advanced a hundred feet inside Tower Two when they were stopped in their tracks.

The Militsiya had set up four 50-caliber machine guns at the top of the pair of escalators that connected the foyer to the first level of the building.

Just out of range for a grenade toss, the NKVD gunners had the entire sweep of the lobby, plus a thick granite railing to use as cover from return fire below.

Dozer and many of the raiders were pinned down directly across from the blown-away front entrance. While Allied soldiers, mostly the Free Canadians, had taken up positions outside the building and were exchanging gunfire with the last of the Chekskis, those assigned to the assault force were getting increasingly jammed up near the still-smoldering entranceway. The lower lobby was already dangerously crowded, and the Militsiya gunners were regularly shooting down into it with their quartet of big 50-calibers. Good cover was hard to find.

Five minutes into this, Dozer got a message from the lighthouse back on Nantucket. Two 7CAV men had been left behind to monitor the 616, and they had two intercepted messages for him. First, they'd learned from the chatter that, as part of their security plans, the NKVD had wired up every fire escape, elevator, and stairway inside Tower Two with plastic explosives—with one exception. The emergency staircase on the southeast corner of the building was still clear. This was how the NKVD would fight its way out, if it came to that. But as far as the lighthouse techs could tell, the stairway was open for both attacker and defender alike.

Dozer passed the news to Jim Cook. The JAWS commanding officer signaled to his men in the lobby, just out of the fire zone. Not a half minute later, they all signaled back. His guys had scanned the air with their electronic sniffers and confirmed the 616 intel. The entire building reeked of explosive materials. Cook's men also added that all of the building's elevators had been disabled.

The JAWS guys were experts in explosives and would start clearing an alternate stairway immediately, but it was impossible to say how long that would take.

Dozer grimly acknowledged Cook's report. At least now they knew where this fight was going to take place. In the stairwell on the southeast corner of the building and in confined lobbies and hallways beyond. The Allies would still have to fight floor by floor, for 110 floors. Even Hunter's plan said there would be no other way to do it. But there would be no spreading out into the building itself; it would be a narrow battlefield, and that usually meant lots of casualties.

Dozer returned to the radiophone and asked the lighthouse for the second message. It was just as bleak. Radio intercepts from the 616 confirmed the five missing Russian destroyers had been spotted off Long Island.

They were heading for New York City at full speed.

CHAPTER FORTY-FOUR

THE COBRA BROTHERS were in the pilots' ready room aboard the *Isakov* when the call finally came.

They'd been waiting for the red radiophone to ring for the past hour. Now Don had a short conversation with the carrier's battered communications room. Not much of the equipment was working there, but it was enough for the techs to get an emergency call from Hawk Hunter.

"He gave coordinates for five surface vessels headed south and the message: 'Assistance appreciated,'" the tech told Don.

Scrambling their new Kamov gunships, the Cobras were airborne forty-five seconds later.

They immediately headed southwest at top speed and began long-range radar sweeps of the area where Hunter reported encountering the five ships. It took a couple of wipes, but on the third, the five blips suddenly appeared.

They were not sailing in a necklace formation; instead they were line ahead, like a spear pointed at New York City.

Yet they were all bunched together for some reason. The lead destroyer was only about a quarter mile ahead of the last ship in the group, extremely close when sailing at night. Plus, the Kamovs' defensive weapons suites said the destroyers' antiaircraft radars were hot and interacting.

Something else was going on here.

The Cobras' FLIR screens suddenly picked up a small blip zipping between the ships. Flashes of antiaircraft fire were following it in the dark. Don was the first to figure it out.

"Freaking Hawk," he said into his helmet mic. "He's nuts. . . ."

"He sniffed some of the hal-lou, brother," Phil explained. "Sometimes it takes a while for the powder to wear off."

By that time, the Cobra Brothers were close enough to see the action through their night-vision goggles. The light show was being caused by Hunter's clown plane flying madly between the Russian ships, taunting them to fire at him. But more than that, he was actually buzzing the bridges of the ships, doing the stop and hover, firing his M-16 into their control rooms, and then zooming off again.

He'd forced the destroyers to bunch up so they could establish patterns of cooperative fire—and they had to slow down considerably to do this. Every second they could be delayed from reaching New York would be a huge help—Hunter's thinking all along. Plus, they would make good targets for someone with some ammo.

Both Cobras streaked over the little drama and, interpreting all its elements, fired off three bursts from their cannons at about a thousand feet. Combined, they lit up the ocean for miles.

It was their signal to Hunter.

We got this.

The Wingman understood right away. They saw him do a complete flip and then an extreme wing wag.

And then he was off, heading back to the battle in New York City.

The next ten minutes were so surreal, the Cobra Brothers thought maybe they'd somehow gotten a whiff of the powder, too.

They'd spent the scramble time taping English translations over their Kamovs' panel lights. They'd gotten about a third of them done when the call arrived. The rest were still in Russian.

The Kamov was not unlike the AH-1 Cobra. Since it had dual controls, they could each fly one alone, without needing a copilot to ready and aim the gun. Unlike a lot of Russian helicopters that drove like trucks, the Kamov was made of composite materials and had that interesting Ugly Sister aerodynamic look. As Hunter had said, they flew like Ferraris.

They also packed a wallop. Each was carrying four *Stutsia* antiship missiles, plus two 30-millimeter cannons in a movable nose turret. And because this was a naval version of the Kamov, each was carrying a single 9ZN homing torpedo.

But there was a problem. The Cobras might sink two of these ships—and the first one might be a complete surprise since the destroyers were probably painting the Kamovs and assuming they were friendly aircraft that had just chased the bug away—but copters were slower than attack jets, and even if they got the first two, by that time, the gunners on the other three would have them locked in, and that would be the end of it.

But still, it had to be done.

They came out of the nearly full moon and attacked the last ship in line. Squeezing their FIRE buttons at the same moment, the Cobras sent two antiship missiles each rocketing off their rails. Designed to home in on electronic signals, all four slammed into an area right below the destroyer's bridge, most likely its combat room.

The combined explosion was tremendous. The ship broke in two, this time from the top down. It was soon dead in the water and sinking—at least the Cobra Brothers knew what the green FIRE button on the far left of their weapons panel meant.

But the trouble was, one missile would have been enough to easily sink the ship, two for sure. Four had been overkill and instantly depleted their supply of antiship missiles.

Now they had four ships and just one torpedo apiece, though, luckily, they'd translated its switch before liftoff. But the Russian ships were now tracking them with radar-controlled guns. And those guns were going hot.

Phil and Don Cobra had been working together for years. Each knew what to do. Phil swooped in on the next destroyer in line, firing his nose cannons but drawing fire from the rest of the ships. Meanwhile, Don snuck in from the opposite side and laid a 9NZ torpedo right on the stern of the ship third in line. The explosion created a strange blue flame, and the destroyer split in two. One half sank immediately, the other just kept on going, but with a lot of fire and smoke.

Before the surviving ships could react, Don played the part of moving target and Phil launched his torpedo. It clipped the bow of the second destroyer, blowing it off in one huge piece, definitely a mortal wound.

It had been lucky shooting. But two destroyers remained, and all the Cobras had left were their nose cannons, with only a couple dozen shells between them. Not good odds.

They knew that all of their efforts would add up to nothing if even one of the destroyers made it to New York, so they decided to disable, if not sink, both remaining ships. It would be an extremely perilous mission, though, as it meant coming right in on a ship's weapons-packed broadside and trying to hit its rudder or props.

They wished each other good luck, both knowing this would probably be the end.

But just as they were beginning their attack, both destroyers suddenly blew up and sank.

A little smoke, a little fire, a huge explosion of water, and then they were gone.

Just like that.

CHAPTER FORTY-FIVE

TWENTY MINUTES.

That's how long the Allied assault force had been pinned down in the lower lobby of Tower Two.

They didn't have the luxury of time. They had to seize this gigantic building and kill everyone inside it in just one hour. Before the army made its move. Or before the ghost destroyers of Convoy 56 showed up.

The JAWS team had begun the hairy assignment of clearing the building's northeast stairway of booby traps, but it was going to be time-intensive. The only way the present assault force was going up was by way of the southeast stairway, which they imagined was thick with NKVD defenders by now.

But before they could do anything, they had to get out of the lower lobby.

Suddenly, someone hit the floor on Dozer's right. The man was wearing all-black camos and had dreadlocks falling out from under his Fritz helmet.

It was Catfish Johnson, CO of the Righteous Brothers, an all-black SF unit. They specialized in highly mobile special-ops artillery, a rarity, and they were damn good. They used the 75-millimeter M-6 field gun exclusively and were providing high-caliber defensive fire against the surviving Chekskis around Tower Two. But now they were needed by those inside.

"How can we help, Bull?" Johnson asked.

The 7CAV's commanding officer pointed out the enemy machine-gun emplacements holding up everything. Then he indicated a large exterior stained-glass window located to the left of the NKVD positions.

"I'm sure that's a work of art," he said of the stained-glass window, "but can you guys put a couple of rounds through it?"

"We can," Johnson replied. "But you've got to know we're loaded with highly explosive shells. Lighter to carry than that deep-penetrating stuff. So, if we put two in the hole, we're going to start a fire. Do we want a fire in here?"

Dozer just laughed at him.

"Believe me, Cat," he said. "If we could have figured out a way to burn this fucking building down, we wouldn't be here right now."

Two minutes later, Dozer saw multicolored lights streaming through the stained glass.

He yelled for everyone to hug the floor. Two violent explosions followed in quick succession, raining pieces of tinted glass down on the American fighters below.

When Dozer looked up again, there was nothing left of the machine guns or the gunners—or the stained-glass window or the escalators.

Just as Catfish had promised, though they'd also started a fire in the upper part of the foyer.

"That could be a problem," someone called out.

But then Dozer calmly reached up and pulled the fire alarm directly over his head, saying, "If this is pressure-fed, this could be our lucky day."

No sooner were the words said than the sprinklers in the ceiling above them exploded in carousels of water. It quickly turned into a deluge, enough to put out the fire in just a few seconds.

There was some applause, some cheers, but then the indoor rainstorm did not stop. Dozer pulled the fire alarm again, hoping to turn it off, but to no effect. In seconds, the entire assault force in the lobby was soaking wet.

Dozer blinked the water from his eyes and blew his whistle again. Mostly air bubbles came out, but the sound was loud enough to be heard.

Stuck for so long, the Allies charged through the smoky, flooded lobby, heading for the southeast stairway.

The attack was moving again.

CHAPTER FORTY-SIX

CATFISH JOHNSON HAD originally positioned his M-6 mobile artillery pieces out on the WTC plaza to defend the assault force against attacks from outside Tower Two.

The cluster bomb strikes had been astonishingly effective. More than two thirds of the Chekskis, along their extensive defense crescent, had been killed. Their bodies were everywhere. And those few who'd been wounded weren't going anywhere.

But hundreds of Chekskis were still in the area. Many of them had taken up positions inside surrounding buildings and were firing at the Allied positions around the base of Tower Two. They'd become an army of snipers.

Johnson had given the use of half his guns to the Free Canadian ground commanders to help eliminate these threats. It was a simple strategy. If someone saw a gun flash from an open window, he put an artillery shell into it.

But with the successful assist they'd given the assault team to get out of the lower lobby, at Dozer's request, Johnson repositioned the rest of his guns facing in toward Tower Two, to help the assault force move up the southeast corner stairways, one floor at a time.

The M-6 was one of the few field artillery pieces that could be hand-transported. The secret was in its modular design. It broke down into ten primary pieces, each one light enough for one man to carry. Johnson's men could put one together and be firing in less than two minutes.

Johnson had been on the radiophone with Dozer the entire way; he heard how the stairwells were indeed full of NKVD fighters and they weren't giving up easily. So, they'd started an odd routine once Dozer reached the eighth floor.

Johnson had ten M-6s arrayed in front of Tower Two. Instead of battling it out with the Russian police in the eighth-floor stairwell—vertical close-in fighting *was* the worst—Dozer marked the contested floor with a flare shot out the nearest window. He yelled for his guys to duck, Johnson's men put two shells through the window, and that's all it took. The few NKVD gunmen who survived the mini-barrage escaped to the next floor, where Dozer started the whole process over again.

This wasn't how it was planned at all—literally clearing the building one entire floor at a time had been anticipated, before they realized there was really only one way up—but this approach worked amazingly well. Going up one or even two floors at a time, they reached the thirtieth floor in just ten minutes. They were on the thirty-fifth floor just a few minutes later, and they had no reason to slow down.

But that's when Johnson started doing some calculations.

His M-6s could elevate to seventy-three degrees—and that was just enough to hit a target on the forty-fourth floor—but no higher.

After that, the boots would be on their own.

Sixty-six floors up, Zmeya was on his radiophone directing the building's defense and constantly referring to his Plan B.

Though dreamed up to stop an army assault on his headquarters, it was working just fine against the Americans. For Zmeya, there was nothing like drawing prey into a trap.

His plan was simple. There was only one way up or down— that was the southeast stairway. Many of the offices on individual floors had been booby trapped as well, making a large part of the skyscraper a vertical minefield.

The Americans were using M-6 light artillery guns, great weapons, but Zmeya knew its firing angle limitations. Give or take a few feet, after the forty-fourth floor, the invaders would lose all artillery support.

His plan was to draw them farther upward than that. Past the forty-fifth, forty-sixth, and forty-seventh floors and beyond. Zero opposition, nothing but the clanging of retreating boots overhead. *Make them think we're giving up the fight.*

Then, when the assault force reached the fiftieth floor, they would come up against a wall of Militsiya—dozens of fighters firing into the stairwell with hundreds more waiting in the wings. All they had to do was keep firing down the staircase and replace any dead or wounded with new bodies. There was no way the Americans would get past them.

This is exactly what happened—but there was more to Plan B. The Americans did a quick strategic retreat back to forty-eight, only to find NKVD gunmen had infiltrated through the northwest booby-trapped stairway and were on the forty-seventh floor below.

In a matter of minutes, the NKVD had trapped two thirds of the Allied assault force—more than thirteen hundred fighters—in the southeast stairwell between the forty-eighth and fiftieth floors.

Down on the plaza, Catfish Johnson was putting together a rescue party comprised of his own men plus some Free Canadians.

The assault team was trapped, sucked in by the clever Russians. He'd taken one last grim message from Dozer: "We're going to try to work ourselves back down."

Then there was gunfire, and then his radio went dead.

The book said sending more men into the building was not the solution, but Johnson had to do something. He couldn't stand by and let his friends be killed off at the NKVD's leisure.

He got a hundred Canadian volunteers, added to fifty of his guys. They were about to enter the building when they heard a loud, screeching noise over their heads.

It was Hunter's clown plane returning from the waters off Long Island. Before anyone could move, it slammed down onto the plaza right next to Johnson's CP.

Hunter jumped out, still wearing his duct-taped crash helmet and carrying his M-16. He and Cat did a soul shake.

Johnson couldn't help but ask, "What's with all the rubber, brother?"

"Came like that from the factory," Hunter told him with a shrug.

Johnson updated him on the situation. More than thirteen hundred of the good guys were trapped about halfway up the skyscraper, lured there after his artillery had reached its elevation limit.

"Like when the B-17s used to lose their fighter protection halfway to Germany," Johnson said. "Those guys are on their own now. They've got Reds above them and below them. We were getting ready to go in."

He let his voice trail off.

Hunter bit his lip hard. This was certainly *not* in the plan.

But then a bolt from the blue. The funny thing was, it hit Hunter and Johnson at the same moment.

"Tower One," was all that Hunter had to say to him.

"Read my mind," Johnson replied.

In minutes, Hunter, Johnson, fifty of his men, and fifty Free Canadians were carrying component parts and ammo for ten M-6s across the plaza to Tower One. The remaining Canadians took over Johnson's CP and covered the hastily assembled team.

Compared to Tower Two, which was lit up with fire, smoke, and gun flashes, its twin looked dark and sinister. MOP hadn't gotten around much to Number One. There were no lights on anywhere, no signs of life. It looked like a huge black monolith stretching to the stars.

Airstrikes against Tower Two were out of the question. They'd agreed on that back in Nantucket. Even if they could somehow get more Su-34s down from the *Isakov*, if one of the powerful fighter-bombers unloaded all its ordnance on the tower's midsection, combined with the entire building being wired with explosives, it might send it crashing to the ground. The same for the Kamov gunships, if they attacked it repeatedly.

The M-6 was a much more precise weapon. Its HE shells went where you wanted them to go and caused a fire, but not an overload of structural damage. Or so they hoped. Nothing was ever certain in war. But the situation was getting desperate and they would have to chance it.

So they were going to bring the artillery pieces up to the same floors in Tower One that corresponded with those where their friends were trapped inside Tower Two, put the guns back together, and fire across at the enemy. Artillery support from the fiftieth floor.

But then they hit a roadblock of the strangest kind.

All the entryways for Tower One were not only locked tight, they were covered with plastic explosives. Warning signs, hanging everywhere, declared that any tampering with the locks would result in the detonation of *all* the explosives ringing the huge building. The notices were simply signed "MOP."

Half the artillery team dispersed, trying to find another way of entry or maybe a break in the line of interconnected plastic explosives. But when they all returned to the starting point, the universal report was the same: They could find no Achilles' heel.

"Fucking Russians," Hunter spat. It would take days for the JAWS guys to deactivate all the plastique around the bottom of Tower One. There was literally tons of it.

"What they do is never pretty," Johnson said, "but it always seems to work."

Then one of Johnson's men found a computer circuit box next to the building's main entrance. It seemed designed to take a four-digit code, which would turn off the miles-long string of explosives and open the doors.

"That sounds easy," Johnson said. "Got any ideas for the code?"

"N-K-V-D?" Hunter suggested—he was no good at these things.

Johnson shrugged and began to enter it. But before he could punch ENTER, a figure came out of the darkness and grabbed him.

Johnson's guys were on top of the assailant in a flash. Hunter and Johnson added their M-16s to the dozens of weapons pointed at the man on the ground.

He was wearing a hooded overcoat and was tensed up as if ready to take them all on in a fight.

They got him to his feet and patted him down for weapons. Only then did Hunter flip back the hood.

They found themselves looking at a man about fifty, thin face, almost regal-looking. Under the cloak, he was wearing a battered and burned Russian Army uniform with colonel's leaves.

He was also wearing a patch over his right eye.

"The code is $U \ldots S \ldots S \ldots R$," he told them in heavily accented English. "Had you punched in anything else, it would have detonated everything."

Before any of the Americans could say a word, the man punched in the code and then ran back into the night. He called over his shoulder to them, "And the elevators still work."

They did not pursue him. The doors opened, and they rushed the M-6 components into the lobby of Tower One. They pressed every elevator button they could find.

"How the hell did you arrange that?" Johnson asked Hunter, still incredulous over the encounter outside.

Hunter shook his head. "I have no idea," he said. "I'm just glad you saw him, too."

The fifty Free Canadians stayed on the bottom floor, covering their six.

Hunter and the Righteous Brothers took a total of twenty-five elevators up to the forty-eighth floor, bodies jammed in with jigsaw pieces of M-6s. It all seemed so surreal to Hunter, just like everything else that had happened in the last twenty-four hours. He still had the taste of oranges in his mouth and he hadn't been to sleep in almost five days. A lot of weird things were happening—more than usual.

But the man with the eye patch was the weirdest.

Hunter was astonished by how quickly Johnson's men could put the M-6s together. They were loaded and ready to go in under two minutes, and that included equipping each with a pair of mini-tires to help mobility.

Johnson's men pushed each of the ten guns up to windows looking right across at Tower Two, where the assault team was trapped. They looked like cannons on an old-time sea galleon, getting ready to deliver a broadside.

Now Hunter and Johnson talked strategy. If something like this was going to work, then they first wanted to clear out the NKVD troops on the floors below their trapped friends and hopefully open up an escape route down.

But then two problems instantly popped up. The first was they didn't know exactly where their friends were at that moment.

"The last time I talked to Bull, he was trying to make his way back down from forty-eight," Johnson said. "And then his radio went dead."

"So did they go down a floor?" Hunter wondered out loud. "Or are they still trapped on forty-eight?"

It made a big difference in where they would aim their guns.

Problem two: The way the exterior facade of the Twin Towers had been designed, it was difficult to tell one floor from the other when looking directly across the divide between the two mammoth buildings.

"In theory, we should be parallel to each other," Johnson said. "But these buildings are so damn big, we'd have to consider the curvature of the Earth if we decided to guesstimate where to put the ordnance. That would be very dangerous for Bull and the guys."

Even through night-vision goggles they couldn't see clearly into the next building; they just weren't close enough. Making it worse, the NKVD had shut off just about all the lights in Tower Two by now, including those in the stairways and in the office spaces adjacent to them. All this was totally unexpected, but the unexpected had to be expected in combat.

Johnson took off his battle hat and wiped his face with his hands. "How the hell do we do this, Hawk?"

Suddenly, Hunter jumped to his feet and started running for the elevators.

"Stand by," he told Catfish. "I'll try to fix this."

Johnson heard the buzzing about five minutes later.

He and his men knew what it was right away. Pressed up against the windows, they watched as the clown plane streaked by them in a flash of light.

It did a hard bank and was suddenly circling the midsection of Tower Two, going in the opposite direction. It went around the building three times. On the fourth orbit, the clown plane's engine gave out a mighty screech and suddenly it was standing up on its tail, hovering in flight.

Johnson's men were astonished by the maneuver. Their CO just laughed.

"He's done this before," he told them.

They watched as Hunter stuck his hand out the plane's open glass panel and fired a flare into a window right on the corner of the building.

At the same moment, Johnson's radiophone came alive.

It was Hunter.

"Bad guys on forty-seven, ten ball in the corner pocket," was all he said. Then the nose of the little plane came down, and it was gone in a flash.

Johnson clicked the radio twice then yelled to his men, "Go to the light, brothers!"

Hunter had veered away from the building just seconds before the M-6s fired. He had the best view of anyone of what happened next.

It really did look like a broadside coming from one old warship to another. This was no two-shot mini-barrage. It was a ten-cannon fusillade. The multiple streaks of fire crashed into the windows of the forty-seventh floor's southeast corner—but then blew out the other side, carrying a wave of flame and debris that was so powerful it disrupted the air flow around the circus plane. Some of the booby traps in the inner offices must have detonated, Hunter guessed, because Tower Two suddenly began to shake. He could see it plainly with his night-vision goggles.

"Stay together, baby," he whispered, desperately battling his controls to stay level. "You're made of good old US concrete and steel. You can take more than that."

For several long moments, though, he was sure the building was going to topple right over.

But then it stopped shaking. There was still a lot of fire and smoke, but everything seemed to settle down a little.

Hunter let out a long whistle of relief. Tower Two remained standing.

It had been a case of bend not break.

CHAPTER FORTY-SEVEN

BULL DOZER HAD lost his cigar.

Somewhere between getting trapped on the forty-eighth floor and the M-6–assisted breakout, he'd misplaced his box containing his one and only unlit stogie. Strangely, he still had the empty box, but the last cigar was gone.

"What am I going to smoke when I get to the top?" he grumbled.

The 7CAV was flying up the stairways now. All NKVD opposition was being crushed, thanks to Hunter's clown plane and Johnson's expert gunners. The unlikely tactic was winning the day, even though, at times, it felt like the building was coming down on top of them. Every floor from the fiftieth up to sixty-eight had been blown out in the advance. In some cases, if the floor was heavily booby-trapped, it caused the building to sway violently. But it did not fall.

The unusual bombardment killed dozens, then hundreds, of NKVD gunmen with each barrage. There was nowhere to run, and they had no weapons comparable to the M-6. By the seventy-second floor, the assault team was moving so fast, they were taking over floors before Johnson's guys could even fire into them.

Then they reached the 105th floor. As always, Dozer went to open the fire door, expecting to see, as in the floors below, an empty shell with lots of broken and burned office furniture lying around.

But 105 was different.

Dozer peeked in to see as many as five hundred NKVD cops looking back at him. They all appeared haggard, many were wounded, many were without combat weapons. *The last-ditch guys*, Dozer thought quickly. *Get by them, and we've got this thing dicked.*

But the Russians came right at them, and suddenly Dozer was fighting for his life. Sheer numbers allowed the assault team to push their way into the lobby, but it was quickly packed with so many struggling bodies, Dozer couldn't even raise his M-16 to fire. He was using his fists and the rifle's butt instead. One Russian came at him with an AK-47 with no ammo clip but an extra-long bayonet. He lunged at Dozer's chest, but when the tip of the blade hit his empty cigar box, the man pulled back and tried again. This gave Dozer enough time to push his M-16 into his attacker's stomach and squeeze the trigger.

The result was a bloody mess, but Dozer didn't care. He took the man's bayonet and started slicing his way through the Russians. It felt like he was in a dream. The battle turned into a rugby scrum stretched out for the entire length of the 105th floor. Brutal hand-to-hand combat, falling over old desks and office chairs, flattening cubicle walls, using massive copying machines for temporary cover. It was madness. The floor was soon slippery with blood.

Still anyone's game, the Americans kept pouring onto the floor from the stairwell, but they were coming in a very thin stream. And while many of the Russians had run out of ammunition, they were swinging their bayonet-tipped AK-47s like medieval swords—one swipe in the right place and you were KIA. Plus, as these guys were the cream of Zmeya's crop, they all seemed to be tall, hulking Slavic giants. On brute strength alone, they were beginning to win the battle.

Then a miracle for the Allies. At that moment, Jim Cook and the JAWS team broke through the booby-trapped stairwell on the northeast side, and a second wave of Allied fighters streamed onto the 105th floor from the opposite direction. Mercs mostly, they threw themselves onto the gang of Militsiya gunmen from their rear.

With two groups of Americans pushing the Russians from front and back, the NKVD line finally began to break. The Militsiya policemen began stumbling back over themselves as they were stabbed or shot by the stampeding Americans. Hacking with the bayonet with one hand and firing his M-16 with the other, Dozer was leading the charge. Blood, guts, and computer paper were everywhere. As everyone tripped over old telephone wires, huge sections of the suspended ceiling fell on top of the combatants. It was the most unlikely battle any of them had ever fought.

It went on like this for five more brutal minutes, but the Russian resistance finally ended. The wide-open office where the battle had been fought was devastated. Dead and dying NKVD policemen were everywhere.

Finally, Dozer blew his whistle and it was over.

As his men greeted the JAWS team and the mercs, Dozer just threw down his weapons, exhausted beyond words, covered in water and sweat and blood.

Then he spit on the nearest NKVD policeman's body and said, "Smile about that, you assholes."

But there was one more grisly sight awaiting him.

Once the 105th floor was secure and their dead and wounded brought back down, Dozer sent his deep recon guys to check out the next four floors.

If another assault was going to be needed for the top floor penthouse, he wanted to launch it as close as possible to their goal.

The recon team that went up to the 106th floor quickly declared it empty and free of booby traps. The same for 107 and 108. But the guys who went up to 109 called back to Dozer within two minutes.

"You might want to come see this," one told him.

Dozer quickly went up to the 109th floor. The recon team was spread out in the lobby in defensive positions. The squad leader led Dozer to an executive-style suite. The door had been blown off.

Dozer looked in to find another scene from a nightmare. Even in this building of horrors, it gave him a start.

Inside were a dozen young women. They were all blonde, all lovely, all spitting images of Dominique. These were the girl-friends procured for the NKVD's despised CRPP, the Committee of the Revolution for the Protection of the People.

But all the girls were covered, nearly head to toe, in blood. One practically fell into Dozer's arms, begging him to rescue her. Behind them was a sex-and-torture chamber filled with toys and restraining devices. But scattered about were the bodies of the four remaining committee members.

They'd all been mutilated by knives, broken glass, and even teeth. As battle-hardened as he was, the gruesome sight was almost too much for Dozer to take.

He immediately sent the girls down along with a medic. Then he looked back into the blood-soaked room.

"Jesus, who could be responsible for that?" the recon man asked him.

Dozer just shrugged and said, "Well, I don't think any of those guys killed themselves."

CHAPTER FORTY-EIGHT

ZMEYA'S SUITCASE COMMUNICATOR was dying.

Fifteen minutes ago, it had been flashing and beeping furiously with so many people on the lower floors of Tower Two trying to talk to him, get his orders, and find out what was happening with the battle.

But the higher the Allies had climbed, and the more floors they managed to blow out with their artillery, the fewer the calls coming in. Finally, the communicator fell silent, none of its lights were flashing. That had never happened before.

But Zmeya knew what it meant.

Hitler in the bunker. The end of the adventure. Time for the next one.

But where was his helicopter?

Suddenly, one light on his suitcase popped on. Zmeya answered it, wondering who could be left.

It was Sublieutenant Borski.

"Still standing by, sir," the hideous officer reported.

Zmeya had to think a moment about what he was talking about.

"The prisoners at Yankee Stadium," Borski reminded him. "We're awaiting your execution order."

"Oh yes," Zmeya said. "Moot point really. But, you know, all these fucking New Yorkers have caused me more trouble than they're worth."

"So we should proceed, then? Process the entire lot?"

"Yes, do it," Zmeya said coldly. "Rome is burning, but it's important to carry a message over to whatever's next."

Borski never heard him. He was so excited that once again there was no parting salutation, no acknowledgment. Nothing. He was simply off the phone.

"Idiot," Zmeya said.

Hunter had continued circling Tower Two, climbing as Dozer's troops climbed floor by floor, firing the flare gun he'd borrowed from the Canadians and acting as an artillery spotter. And Johnson's guys were always right on the money, now more than a hundred floors up. That *was* special forces.

Hunter had heard the radio chatter coming from inside the building the whole time. When the Allies broke through on two fronts on the 105th floor, he knew the vertical war was almost over.

But suddenly, his radio came alive with a message not from Dozer or Johnson, but from the lighthouse listening post back on Nantucket.

The 7CAV comm tech asked him one question: "Do you know how to get to Yankee Stadium from there?"

The lighthouse had been tracking fewer and fewer calls on Zmeya's communications board as the battle raged, but one caller was persistent in trying to get through. They went back into the taped archives, listened to previous conversations between the caller and Zmeya, and this led them to the mass execution plot unfolding at Yankee Stadium.

The battle for Tower Two was all but over, yet the NKVD was still going to kill two thousand helpless Americans?

Hunter pushed the throttles past full power and headed north.

The Wingman was needed elsewhere.

✪   ✪   ✪

Two long trenches had been dug in the weedy outfield of Yankee Stadium.

Each was 180 feet long and 6 feet deep. The two thousand hostages—men, women, and children—having dug their own graves, had been kneeling next to them for hours, blindfolded and waiting for death, while Sublieutenant Boris Borski anxiously awaited Zmeya's call to finally start the executions.

Borski had one hundred Chekskis with him, members of the Chekski First Police Battalion that had stayed behind while the rest of the unit—nine hundred policemen—had deployed to the Pine Barrens for the guerrilla-clearing operation.

But Borski was confident one hundred men would be enough to slit the throats of two thousand hostages. A little less than twenty hostages per man, as Borski intended to add his knife to the proceedings. In fact, he planned to kill all the children himself.

Now that Zmeya had given him the go-ahead, he was immensely excited to proceed.

Per the commissar's orders, the executions were going to be filmed. This meant cameras, microphones, cables, electrical generators, and lights. Lots of lights.

Borski ordered it all turned on.

That's how Hunter was able to find Yankee Stadium so quickly.

There was a problem, though. Hunter was unarmed.

His M-16 was empty, same for his .357 Magnum. He was the only friendly force to get to the Bronx with any speed, but all he had was his funny little plane and the flare gun he'd borrowed from the Canadians, one cartridge remaining.

This was going to take some ingenuity.

Just as the ballpark came into sight, the lighthouse radioed him to say they'd intercepted the live conversation in which Zmeya gave his okay for the executions at the stadium to begin.

So, there could be no circling, no time for screwing around now. Hunter put the plane into a steep dive, got right down on the field like a crop duster, and headed for the first group of Chekski guards he saw. They began shooting at him, but it was too late to worry about that now.

He unfastened his side window and then pulled up on his controls. The plane went into a stop and hovered not ten feet above the field. He stuck the flare gun out the window, fired it at the nearest guard, then slammed his plane back down and was gone in a flash. The fiery projectile caught the man square in the face, horribly imbedding itself in his cheek. When he fell over screaming, head aflame, some of the hostages used the ghastly distraction to attack the other guards.

That's all it took. There was a domino effect, and within seconds, a major brawl was under way on the baseball field. The hostages quickly got the upper hand.

Hunter flew low one more time to see if there was anything else he could do, but it wasn't necessary.

By that time, the hostages were tearing the Chekski guards apart.

Something strange was happening inside Tower Two's penthouse.

Still on the 109th floor, Dozer and his deep recon men could hear a lot of commotion above them. People shouting and breaking things. They all agreed it sounded like a fistfight.

The Allies would have to take over the penthouse to complete the victory—and 7CAV was the unanimous selection to lead the final assault. But before charging up there, Dozer had to be sure of what awaited him and his troops.

As the recon men set up some remote viewing gear, he was on his radiophone, checking the situation in the rest of the building. All resistance had ceased. Most of the NKVD fighters had been killed by Johnson's artillery strikes, though many fell to the bullets and bare fists of the Allied assault team.

The policemen who'd been shot and wounded during the Allies' dash to the top were being dispatched by second wave merc groups. The goal had been to kill as many of the NKVD cops as possible, and no one said it was going to be pretty. Still, it was a grisly job.

Suddenly, Dozer heard more noise overhead. It was the sound of a helicopter approaching.

The recon men reported they were ready.

"One more floor to go, boys," Dozer told them.

Zmeya's suitcase communicator was really dead now.

All incoming calls had ceased. Even Sublieutenant Borski had stopped calling him. That's how dire the situation had become.

The battle now lost, Zmeya had to get out, so he could go on to the next one. Or at least that was the plan.

So where was his goddamn helicopter?

"Are you ready to go?" he called over his shoulder to Dominique. "Just one small bag. We're going to be overloaded as it is."

His tongue stumbled over those last few words. His last helicopter ride—out to the *Isakov* and back—had not been a pleasant experience.

"Leave the lingerie," he went on. "Cheap domestic crap. We'll buy you the real stuff when we get to Paris."

He tried calling his helicopter team again. They should have been here at least ten minutes ago.

"Here's what's going to happen," he continued. "The helicopter will land, the crew comes down and wheels out the big yellow box, we put it on board, and off we go. But I want you to get on the copter first, before we put the Magilla on, okay?" He was interrupted by the unmistakable sound of a helicopter approaching. "Finally!"

The racket of the copter was getting closer. Maybe thirty seconds away.

"Okay—the aircraft is here," he yelled to her again. "Stop packing and let's—"

He turned around just in time to see Dominique coming at him with a plastic bag. Before he could react, she jammed it over his head, pulled it down to his neck, yanked it tight, and held it there. Zmeya began flailing his arms, trying to grab her, but he was already gasping for air. She picked up the radiophone and hit him hard on the right temple, knocking him out of his chair. When he was sprawled on the floor, she kicked him twice in the stomach and then on his nose, shattering it.

He tried curling up, at the same time desperate to get the bag off his head, but she would not relent. Another boot to the stomach, then a vodka bottle caught him on the left ear. The bag was starting to fill with blood; he couldn't help but breathe it in only to spit it out again. One last kick to the groin and he began to lose consciousness.

In his last vision of her, she was looking down at him, holding his desk calendar.

Despite everything, he couldn't help but wonder what the hell she wanted that for?

Dozer and the four-deep recon men quietly made their way up the staircase to the fire door leading into the 110th floor penthouse.

The recon guys had special fiber-optic camera equipment that allowed them to put a thin wire through a doorway and see what was happening in the next room via a small TV monitor.

Dozer nudged the fire door open with his toe just enough for one of the recon guys to insert the clear plastic wire. They looked inside.

The place was a mess. Furniture kicked over, liquor bottles smashed, blood on the carpet. A fistfight seemed like a good guess.

The second thing they realized was that the doorway and the hallway leading into the penthouse were heavily booby-trapped. Had Dozer opened the door an inch or two more, the whole stairway would have blown up.

This prevented them from doing a hot entry. Dozer called below for the JAWS guys to come up with their defusing equipment. Then he went back to watching the fiber-optic screen.

That's when he spotted Dominique. A helicopter had landed on the roof, and she was walking through the penthouse, carrying what looked like a desk calendar. A body was lying next to a business desk; it might have been Commissar Zmeya, and it looked like he'd gotten the worst of the fisticuffs.

Dominique opened an access door to the roof, and the people from the helicopter came in. But they didn't look like NKVD or Russians of any sort.

They were US Army soldiers. Not militiamen or team fighters like 7CAV, but regular American combat troops that looked like they were still serving back in the Vietnam era. The jungle-green battle uniforms, the camo helmets, the high-tie combat boots. Everything screamed 1960s.

"What the heck is going on here?" Dozer whispered.

The soldiers wheeled a huge yellow container across the penthouse and carried it up to the roof. It was the same box Dozer, Hunter, and the others had seen the Russians take off the *Isakov* in the monstrous Mi-26 Halo helicopter. It would have been hard to mistake its bright yellow paint job.

Lifting it out was not an easy job, but the soldiers somehow managed to get it up to the windy top of Tower Two, where their helicopter was waiting.

The recon guys manipulated their fiber-optic cable so they could see the helicopter taking off through the penthouse window. The copter looked like it was from a different era, too. It was an old CH-21 "Flying Banana," an early 1960s chopper with very few bells and whistles.

It flew away as the sun came up.

The last Dozer saw of it, Dominique was kneeling in the open hatchway, leaning on the yellow box, surrounded by soldiers from another time.

Dozer was quickly on the radio to Hunter. He was just a mile away and heading back to Lower Manhattan.

"I'm on the top floor, looking into the penthouse," he explained to the pilot. "And you're not going to believe what we just saw."

He filled him in on what had just happened inside Tower Two. And he was right; Hunter *couldn't* believe it. The strangely dressed soldiers were puzzling enough. But Dozer had spotted the mysterious yellow box.

"What *the hell* is inside that thing that everyone wants it so badly?" Hunter cried over the radio.

"No idea," Dozer replied. "But in just the last few moments, the commissar has come back to life and has climbed up to the roof. I think he's screaming for Dominique to come back. It's a little too late for that, though."

At that moment, a bright red light began blinking on Hunter's control panel. This wasn't a bingo light, saying he still had a half tank left. It was his fuel zero warning light. He was out of gas.

There was only one place he could land. Tower Two was looming before him, and unlike the still-dark Tower One, it was lit up, allowing him to see that the way was mostly clear.

"I can't believe I'm doing this," Hunter said aloud—and then he hung on.

He hit the top of the building a second later, coming down at an almost perpendicular angle. The propeller took it the worst, grinding itself into the rubber rooftop.

He was thrown violently forward, his battered helmet coming apart again, this time in at least a dozen pieces. He knew there'd be no more taping it back together.

The cockpit quickly filled with smoke. He opened the canopy and fell out to see that his poor little plane was just a hair's breadth away from being a total wreck.

But it had gotten him down safely—again.

He looked at the southwest corner of the roof—and that was when he saw Zmeya.

A bloody plastic bag hung around his neck. His eyes were bruised, his nose was broken, and there was a long cut on his face. He was sitting precariously close to the edge of the roof, trying to stem his nose bleed. Hunched over like a gargoyle in his long black leather coat, he was looking out on the city.

Hunter had but one weapon left: his Bowie knife. He took it from his boot and approached the man in black.

"Dear God, is there no way I can get rid of you?" Zmeya yelled at Hunter, turning his back to him. "You're a real pain in the ass."

Hunter said nothing; he simply took a few steps closer to Zmeya.

"You must know that America isn't the only place we're intent on conquering," the Russian went on wistfully. "We are on the offensive everywhere, all around the world—and winning, too. Until . . . well, now it's like someone flipped a switch, and you people appeared and fucked up the whole thing. The MMZ, our aircraft carrier, and now this? You dirt soldiers? We got beat by you?"

Hunter remained silent. Zmeya continued glaring out at the smoldering city.

"You know what I think, Mr. Superhero?" he went on, "I think you're more unbalanced than I am, if that's possible. You *firebombed* New York City, for heaven's sake. There's no place like this anywhere on the planet, and you wanted to burn it down. I see a lot of anger under that rock-star haircut of yours. A lot of animosity. I'm just surprised, I guess, that you hate us *so* much."

Hunter took a few more steps closer to him.

"What is it that you want, Mr. Wingman?" Zmeya asked wearily. "You've nearly destroyed the best city in history. You've ruined its ability to make money. You've driven everyone down here crazy with that goddamn clown plane of yours. You've got everything. You've won. Why not just kill me now and get it over with?"

Hunter hesitated for a moment, but then said, "I do want something from you. I want to know what happened to her. Where is she?"

Zmeya laughed so loud, it seemed to echo off nearby Tower One.

"I'm the wrong person to ask," he roared back. "As you can probably surmise, she tried to kill me before she left. Her way of saying good-bye, I guess. Some old American copter took her away, along with the most dangerous weapon on Earth—what more can I tell you? It doesn't make any more sense to me than it does to you, I'm sure."

Hunter took two more steps closer, holding the knife tightly in his right hand.

"The yellow box?" he asked Zmeya. "It's a weapon?"

"Good guess," Zmeya said, wiping more blood from his nose. "And I don't believe even she knows how powerful it is."

"Tell me, then," Hunter urged him. "Someone besides you should know."

Zmeya just laughed again. "I might have a crack in my head, but it didn't turn me stupid. But I must say, sitting here, thinking about it all, other pieces of the puzzle have fallen in place. The way she reacted when she saw you that first time when we were in the navy penthouse. You and that toy plane. She was, shall I say, just as 'concerned' as I was when she realized it was you, but for a different reason. Let's call it love. And you? You obviously had the firepower to attack 30 Rock directly a few nights later, but you thought she might still be there. So you didn't. Shall we call that love, too? You're a superhero, true. But so very sentimental."

Hunter took one more step, which brought him within an arm's reach of Zmeya.

"Well, good luck with her if you ever find her again," Zmeya went on. "She really is something else, though I'm still not sure what. But she changed me. No doubt about it."

He got to his feet. He was standing just inches from the edge of the roof. The wind was howling madly.

"Are you going somewhere?" Hunter asked.

"You know, I'm bored," Zmeya said. "Maybe the afterlife has something more to offer, who knows?"

Now Hunter laughed. "You know you're not going to bounce when you hit the bottom."

Zmeya's long leather coat was whipping fiercely behind him.

"And my alternative is what?" he asked Hunter. "To go with you? Be tried by a bunch of American hooligans and then lynched? I don't think so. I've already disappointed my father enough without being captured by the likes of you. Besides, people like me enjoy being the bad guy just as much as people like you enjoy being the hero. Or should I say *super*hero? Either way, people also love to punish bad guys in all sorts of malevolent ways. . . . I know. I'm an expert at that. So, I'll pass."

"Believe what you want," Hunter said, lowering the knife. "But I'm no hero. I killed thirty thousand human beings yesterday with the push of a button. You think I'll ever forget that?"

Zmeya turned to face him for the first time. Tears were running down his face.

"Probably not," he said. "But at least you didn't kill your own brother."

With that, Zmeya simply leaned back and fell off the side of the building.

Hunter ran to the edge, nearly getting blown off the roof himself. He looked down to see Zmeya falling, falling . . . falling until he disappeared into the smoke below.

PART FOUR

CHAPTER FORTY-NINE

May 16

HUNTER SPENT THE next five days sleeping.

He'd discovered Dominique had maintained a separate place at the Ritz during her month with Zmeya, so he just went there, pulled the curtains tight, and crashed. Many disjointed dreams followed.

When he finally let daylight in again, he discovered the majority of Russian troops had left New York City two days before. Moscow had declared their peacekeeping mission a success, with no reason to stay any longer. The *Okupatsi* forces loaded themselves onto their three gigantic troopships, and the entire fleet just sailed away as if nothing had ever happened.

Hunter walked the streets of Manhattan for the next few hours. It was raining again. With his collar up and his scally cap low over his eyes, no one recognized him, which was good. His spirits were still low.

He surveyed the damage to the city along the way. The devastation was incredible in some places, especially around the old MMZ. Yet other parts of Manhattan were untouched. The overall cleanup had already started; he even saw a few commuter buses making their way up Madison Avenue. Droves of people were returning to the city, many using the subway.

He walked up to North Harlem, past the tunnels they'd used

to get into the underground transit system. The boats Geraci and
NJ104 had secured to get the assault team across the Hudson
were still there, tied up along the shore.

He walked around Yankee Stadium, saw the trenches, saw the
blood on the field.

There was a dead Chekski hanging upside down, Mussolini-
style, from one of the sports monuments out front. He'd been
beaten to death, possibly with baseball bats. A sign tied around
his neck said he'd been executed by THE NEW DIRT ARMY FOR
CRIMES AGAINST AMERICA. On a closer look, Hunter realized
he knew who the dead man was. The Chekski executioner with
the scarred face. The guy who'd slaughtered the 7CAV people
at the Pine Barrens base along with many, many more during a
monthlong rampage in New York City. The guy who always left
behind a smiling, twisted caricature of himself, painted with the
blood of his victims.

Hunter had to laugh at the corpse, because the man's famously
hideous smile was now turned upside down—and looked like a
bizarre frown.

He ended his walking trip at an unlikely destination: a side
entrance to the practically untouched Empire State Building.

He took the elevator to the ninetieth floor. A hand-drawn
sign greeted him. It read MAYOR'S OFFICE, SECOND LEFT.

Hunter walked in to find Bull Dozer sitting behind an embarrassingly ornate desk in an embarrassingly ornate office.

"Holy Christ, what do I call you?" he said looking around at
the dark oak pageantry. "Is it 'Your Honor'? or 'Mister Mayor'?
Or 'Your Majesty'? What?"

"It's only a temporary position," Dozer replied, nodding
toward the mountain of paperwork taking up one end of the
desk. "But 'His Craziness' might be a good place to start."

"You'll get used to it," Hunter said, taking a seat next to Dozer's old radio, the one he'd had with him during the dark days
in the Pine Barrens. "Plus, now you have enough weapons to
outfit a pretty sizable army. Even more than the old days at ZAP.
Except it's all Russian."

Dozer poured each of them a whiskey, and then began ticking off a list from memory.

"One monster aircraft carrier, slightly damaged," he said. "Forty-three Su-34 JLR kick-ass fighter planes complete with buddy craft. Thirty-six copters, including eighteen of the attack variety. Two thousand and thirty *tons* of ammunition. Plus nukes, bio weapons. Poison gas. . . ."

"What are you going to do with it all?" Hunter asked him.

"Despite the Reds' missile attack, the refrigerated bunkers back in the Pine Barrens are still intact," Dozer reported. "So, we're putting all the really scary stuff in them for the time being. At least now those ice boxes will be good for something."

"And then?"

"Then we've got to put the city back together again," Dozer told him. "I'm guessing a lot of people will want to come back here, now that the Reds are gone and the situation has stabilized. Donnie Kurjan has arranged for a division from the United American Army to stay for at least a year, and Louie is sending five battalions of the Football City Special Forces to do the same thing. That will be an enormous help. Plus, JAWS and NJ104 will been around, and there are my guys, of course. It won't be easy, but it beats the alternative.

"As far as the big picture, with all the military gear we've got now, anyone who screws around this side of the Mississippi will most likely get a visit from us. Eventually, maybe we'll kick those Asian merc assholes out of the West Coast. It would be nice to get L.A. and Vegas back from them. Who knows? Maybe I'll meet wife number six in Hollywood. Anything is possible."

They both drank to that.

Then they fell silent for a moment, Hunter staring into his empty glass. "Nothing on Dominique, I guess?" he finally asked.

Dozer shook his head. "Nothing on where she is, or who those weirdo copter guys were. But I do have this. . . ."

He passed Hunter a black-and-white photograph that had been taken off a videotape. It showed two helicopters flying side-by-side over the East River. One was the same CH-21 "Flying Banana" Dozer saw carrying Dominique and the yellow box off the top of Tower Two. The second helicopter was a Russian-made Mi-26, the gigantic rotary craft Zmeya used as his taxicab, the same aircraft he'd been expecting that morning atop Tower Two.

"That was taken by an old security camera hanging off the UN Building about five minutes after you crashed on top of Tower Two," Dozer told him. "Don't ask me to explain it. I've got no freaking idea what's going on there, other than it appears that whoever was flying that Russian chopper never intended to pick up Zmeya that last time. He was waiting in vain."

Hunter didn't say anything; he just drained his drink and poured himself another. The mystery army copter flying alongside the NKVD's Mi-26 behemoth? What the hell was that about?

"Should I update you on other things that happened while you were taking your nap?" Dozer asked him.

"I'm all ears," Hunter replied. "Unless it's going to make me want to go back to bed."

"You never know," Dozer said. "So, did you hear about the First Chekski Police Battalion? The guys Zmeya sent down to the Pine Barrens to look for us?"

Hunter shook his head. "What happened to them?"

Dozer shrugged. "That's just it. No one knows. They disappeared. We found their clothes and their weapons when we went down there to check the ice boxes, but no sign of the Chekskis themselves. Vanished—*poof!*"

Hunter almost laughed again. It was a weird reaction, but he couldn't help it. "Hey, their own military guys told them not to go down there. Should have listened. . . ."

"Your pal, Samsonov, visited me the other day," Dozer went on. "You know he and a group of them jumped ship and stayed behind. They're asking for asylum, about a thousand in all, including lots of MOP guys. Sammy says he'll supervise them and help us get the mess cleaned up."

Hunter took another swig of his drink. "He might make a good mayor someday," he said with a straight face.

"All he needs is a girlfriend," Dozer replied. "And, by the way, I got a call from another old friend of yours, Roy from Troy."

" 'Selling weapons at discount prices since the end of the Big War,'" Hunter said, repeating the arms dealer's sales motto.

"Very good," Dozer said. "Anyway, he told me that by now, everyone across the country knows what went on here. So, he congratulated us. Then he said, next time you want two huge buildings knocked down, call him, because he has old remote-controlled airliners wired up with explosives for just that kind of job."

"Available to destroy tall buildings?" Hunter replied. "He's a marketing genius."

Dozer filled their glasses again. "Maybe so," he said. "But personally, I think this country is better off with those two towers still standing."

They toasted to that.

"Too bad Fitz wasn't here for all this," Hunter said. Of all the people he'd fought with after the Big War, Mike Fitzgerald might have been his closest friend. The little fireplug of an Irishman had run the Syracuse Aerodrome—a highly successful air mercenary business that sprang up in the early post–Big War years. He was a patriot, and absolutely fearless when it came to trying to save America, and he'd been killed during the battle of Indianapolis.

Dozer raised his glass in toast to their mutual friend. "I'll tell him all about it the next time I see him."

Hunter stopped in mid-gulp. "What are you talking about?" he asked. "Mike's dead . . . isn't he?"

Dozer just shook his head. "Will you please sit down with someone who can tell you who the fuck is dead and who's alive in this universe? Make a list; carry it around with you."

"Wow—Fitz is alive?" Hunter exclaimed. "Where the hell was he for this dance?"

"I saw him a couple months ago," Dozer said. "He told me he was starting to work on something extremely top secret—very scary stuff. He couldn't tell me what it was. But believe me, he's alive and breathing, and I expect him to come walking through that door any day now, bottle in hand."

Dozer looked at his old friend for a long moment. "But seriously, how are you doing, Hawk? You had it pretty rough—with the bang on the head down in the carrier, the powder, the XL getting DOA, and you know, Dominique being . . ."

He couldn't finish the sentence, so Hunter took him off the hook.

"Time heals," he said. "Plus, the guys told me they'll give me my own Su-34 fighter if I want it. JT, Ben, and Crunchie already got theirs. I might start working out in it if I come back this way again."

"You're going somewhere?"

Hunter nodded. "Got to get away for at least a while. Going back up to the Cape. To my old place on Nauset Heights. The hay farm."

"Skyfire?" Dozer asked.

"If it's still there," Hunter said.

"So, you're retiring?"

Hunter shrugged. "Call it a vacation," he said. "But you'll know where to find me. . . ."

Dozer poured two more glasses. "The Cape will be nice this time of year," he said. "But how are you getting there? You going to walk? Drive?"

Hunter drained his drink. "Take another guess," he said.

Dozer finished his drink as well, then asked Hunter, "Well, are you ready for this?"

Hunter nodded reluctantly. "You know I'm not good at these things," he said. "But let's get it over with."

They took the elevator down to the fifth floor, where Dozer led Hunter through a large function room and onto the building's outdoor concourse overlooking Fifth Avenue and East Thirty-Third Street.

The street below was mobbed with people. For blocks in all directions, tens of thousands of happy New Yorkers were holding patriotic signs and waving American flags. They let out a tremendous roar when Hunter and Dozer joined the group already standing on the concrete balcony, which included Ben Wa and JT Toomey, Captain Crunch, Louie St. Louis, the Cobra Brothers, the JAWS team, Frank Geraci's NJ104, Catfish Johnson, and

Donnie "Lazarus" Kurjan. It was Hunter's arrival, though, that got the biggest cheer. It also signaled the kick-off of New York City's own victory parade.

The participants had been congregating on Fifth Avenue all morning. On cue, a brass band started playing and the procession began. Troops marched past the balcony, heading down Thirty-Third Street. The United Americans, Football City Special Forces, the Free Canadians. Some of the surviving members of the 7CAV pulled a float bearing a ragged, humorously slapped-together Sherpa cargo plane made from the wreckage of planes three and four left on board the *Isakov*; others were carrying blown-up photos and memorial wreathes, honoring their comrades who had been murdered by the NKVD back in the Pine Barrens and those who had died in the Tower Two assault.

Following them were the most unusual participants of all. They were a ragged but proud group of about a thousand armed men, marching under a flag identifying them as the New Dirt Army. They were some of the former hostages that had been taken to Yankee Stadium and marked for execution by Commissar Zmeya.

Dozer leaned over to Hunter and said: "Meet the new NYPD. . . ."

Once the Dirt Army passed, civilians spontaneously took to the street and began marching as well. Almost all of them were waving American flags. Leftover Russian vodka and homemade American whiskey were plentiful. At some point, the parade took a series of lefts and marched back down Thirty-Third Street passing the Empire State Building again, much to the delight of everyone involved.

At the tail end was the pièce de resistance. Someone had found and inflated a huge, prewar parade balloon of a huge doghouse with a beagle on top. The dozens of marchers handling it, pulling on long ropes, let it go when they reached the front of the Empire State Building. It floated nearly straight up until it disappeared from sight.

After that, the parade turned into an enormous street party, which quickly spread throughout Midtown and then north and south, up and down Manhattan, during the rest of the day. Fireworks were lit off and people sang and danced in the streets.

Cheers of "USA! USA! USA!" were heard well into the night.

CHAPTER FIFTY

AT NOON THE next day, Hunter was circling Nauset Heights on the southern tip of Cape Cod.

He was flying the clown plane one more time. It was so beat up, it was almost foolish to do so, but the little aircraft was his only transportation.

He put down on Nauset Beach and walked the long path that led up to the heights. Years ago, he and Dominique had lived in a small house near the top of these bluffs; she'd named it Sky-fire because it was right on the Atlantic Ocean, with beautiful views day and night. That had been the longest time they'd spent together. Then the world had intervened and separated them again.

When he finally reached the top, he was surprised and relieved to see their house was still there. Four rooms, four acres, a barn—and that was it. That's all they'd ever wanted.

The back door was unlocked. He walked in expecting the place to be cold and drab and in need of cleaning, but it looked as if they'd never left. Everything was spotless; nothing looked out of place.

Then he heard voices.

He went into the next room, and to his astonishment, he found seven people sitting around the dinner table, watching a videotape.

The one who saw him first was Mike Fitzgerald—back from the dead.

"Hunter, me boy!" he yelled. "I knew you'd find us!"

But if that wasn't bewildering enough, sitting next to Fitz was the flying numbers runner, the guy they called the Worm. And beside him was the Trashman, the guy who drove the garbage truck up to the Pine Barrens. And beside him, the guy with the eye patch who'd helped them get into Tower One during the battle for Tower Two. Next to him were two guys in Russian copter-pilot uniforms. Paused on the TV screen was the smiling girl with the huge brown eyes, the blonde he'd rescued from 30 Rock.

And at the far end of the table . . . was Dominique.

This is the powder, Hunter thought. It had to be.

Dominique came to him immediately and gave him a long, tender hug.

"How's your jaw?" she asked. "I'm really sorry about that. I just didn't want to hit you in the nose and ruin that dreamy face."

Hunter was still in shock. He couldn't have spoken if he'd wanted to. His expression said it all: *What the hell was going on here?*

Fitz got up and gave him a bear hug, too. Then he studied him for a moment and asked, "So you really don't know, Hawk? You haven't been following along?"

The Worm said, "Give him some time, he'll figure it out."

But the Trashman protested. "God no, that will take all day. Just explain it to him now and bring him up to speed. We've got work to do."

Dominique led him out to the bluff. She was carrying a red-striped pouch.

She was dressed in a long white gown and looked gorgeous as always. But he didn't think she was real. He pinched himself hard—but she was still there. She didn't disappear.

"Are you okay?" she asked, holding his hand.

"I don't know," he replied honestly.

They sat on the old bench at the edge of the cliff, as they had done so many times before.

"Okay," she said. "Highlights first, details later?"

"Absolutely," he replied.

She took a deep breath and began.

"Mike and I and everyone else in that room have been working an extremely top-secret operation," she said. "We're up against something that has never happened in history—and I'm not exaggerating. Mike recruited the others; they're all intelligence pros. And he asked me to go *very* deep undercover. In fact, all of us were working covertly somewhere in New York City during the *Oku-patsi*. We all had to maintain our identities, me until the very end, because Commissar Zmeya had something we desperately needed.

"We figured out what you were trying to do flying that plane around the MMZ. And we knew it was just a matter of time before all the compadres got back together and tried to kick the Russians out. So we realized we had to help you, but at the same time, we couldn't blow our covers, because that could have cost us our mission.

"That's why we had the Worm land in the Pine Barrens, just to make sure what we thought was happening out there was true. Then, after we received his message, we sent the Trashman there to give you the clues you needed on how to attack the Reds. You just missed me when we evacuated 30 Rock, but luckily you found the doppelgänger I'd recruited from the inside. Thank God, that led you to finding out about the *Isakov*.

"And, by the way, I hate to burst your bubble, but that kiss she gave you on the airplane? It was to get a sample of your DNA—just to make sure it was really you, not some fake. And her name really *is* classified. You know how things are these days."

"I guess I'm learning," Hunter half muttered.

"We had to feed you information without your knowing it," she went on, "because what we are working on is even bigger than the Russians invading New York City. And I mean real, live, take-over-the world stuff. Enslave the planet or we'll destroy it. That's the level of crisis."

"But who could do something on that scale?" he asked.

She opened the red-striped pouch, pulled out a single photograph, and showed it to him.

It was a middle-aged man with a thin face, sharp features, a mustache and goatee, and a scar on his left cheek.

"Viktor Robotov," he said, not surprised. "The devil himself."

"That's going easy on him," Dominique confirmed. "Well, he's come upon a nuclear submarine that was built at the same secret base and at the same time as the *Isakov*. This sub is also highly automated and can launch nuclear missiles, but not just ordinary ones. It can fire a secret SBM called *solntse raketa*, loose Russian for 'sun bomb.' You've actually seen them. The warheads come in bright yellow boxes."

Hunter nodded. "Hard to forget that color."

"Sun bomb is a good name for it," she continued. "They detonate very high in the atmosphere with a flash so bright, it will permanently blind anyone within a two-hundred-mile radius. That could mean millions of people at once. It's a terrorist weapon. A weapon of control."

Hunter shook his head in disbelief. "Where the hell did that kind of weapon come from?"

"A place called the Kapustin Yar," she replied. "It's like a combination of Area 51 and Cape Canaveral in the Urals. The home of Russia's top mad scientists. They built the sun bombs there years ago, but even they realized how nasty the weapons were, so they just hid them away. Viktor found out about them and secretly arranged to have them included in the shipment of WMD heading for New York City.

"We're sure that his strategy is to hit a few random cities with the sun bombs, just to show the rest of the world what he can do. Any country the Russian military has conquered in the past two years would be on his target list, as well as a few that remain independent of Russia. After a few cities experience that kind of horror, who would want to go up against him?"

"And how does Zmeya tie into all this?" Hunter asked.

"You didn't see the family resemblance, I guess," she replied. "But those rumors are true. Zmeya was Viktor's son—so was the commander of the *Isakov*, Yuri.

"Brother Yuri was transporting the box of sun bombs, or the Magilla, as everyone called it. Again, it was hidden among the tons of other WMD aboard the carrier, and even the NKVD higher-ups in Moscow didn't know about it. The plan was to unload all that other stuff in New York and then secretly deliver the Magilla to dear old dad's submarine at a spot in the ocean somewhere off New York City.

"But when the commissar heard something was going wrong on the *Isakov*, he flew out there, not to save his brother, but to get the Magilla, just so Dad wouldn't go nuts on him. It was important for him to succeed in the eyes of his father, especially because his little brother had failed. I mean, number one son was virtually running the NKVD, and little brother was captain of the world's most powerful warship. Basically, the family had the Russian military doing their dirty work for them, conquering countries they planned to terrorize in the near future.

"But believe me, these people are right out of a bad Shakespeare play. Neither son dared disappoint his father, yet now they're both dead, one killed by the other."

She showed him a photograph of a desk calendar processed in reverse negative so the impressions of what had been written on it were easy to read.

In the box for May 11, four days after the MMZ firebombing, six rows of numbers had been neatly written in. The first row was seven-seven seven-seven. The last was four-zero seven-four. These had been circled.

"All we really wanted was that first row of numbers," Dominique told him. "I spent hours looking for them, so did Gagarin, the Halo copter crew, everyone. Trashman literally went through 30 Rock's rubbish looking for them. So did the Worm; he was working inside the rackets for the Reds as a real numbers dealer, but he was also on a mission for us.

"Anyway, Viktor actually called Zmeya that night, and in that conversation, he revealed the location of his sub's home base with these numbers."

Hunter was impressed. "How did you ever figure it out from just a bunch of numbers?"

"It's the old Ottoman Naval Purple Code," she explained. "Simple really, if you have the right numbers. Seven-seven seven-seven are the longitude and latitude coordinates for the secret shipyard where the sub and the *Isakov* were built. The rest of the numbers make up a nonverbal communications schedule. 'I'm going to start at seven-seven seven-seven. Leave your radio on, and when you hear three clicks, you know I'm at the next lat and long number, maybe off Norway somewhere. When you hear three clicks at the third number, you know I'm off Iceland, and so on.

"The numbers seven-seven seven-seven are for the Kara Sea off Siberia near the Arctic Circle. Four-zero seven-four is New York City. Viktor was telling his son that his sub was leaving the Kara Sea and would contact him at points along the way until they got to New York to make the Magilla switch. Zmeya wrote the numbers down because he wrote everything down, and when I took the desk calendar, we finally got the break we needed. We finally knew where Viktor's secret base was.

"Now, once he realizes what's happened here, I doubt he'll be sailing this way anytime soon. But because we know the location of the secret shipyard—and that it probably doubles as his base of operations—we're going to launch a strike on the place. Once we take it out, he'll be a man without a home base. The Russians certainly won't want him back, not after the debacle engineered by his two kids. And he won't have this load of sun bombs. But . . . we know he has at least a half dozen experimental warheads with almost the same capacity, so the threat has not diminished. That's why we have to track him down asap."

"But how did Fitz find out about the sun bombs in the first place?" Hunter asked. "Their existence must have been highly top secret."

She laughed. "Well, you know Fitz," she said. "He has people *inside* the Kremlin. No one sympathetic to our cause, they're all just paid informants. But they're deeply imbedded and high on the food chain. They tipped off Fitz about the missing sun bombs and almost simultaneously told him about Viktor's submarine. That's when Fitz knew he had to do something, but something very secret.

"Truthfully, things were happening so fast, we didn't know if we were going to make it. We had to find out Viktor's plans and come up with a way to stop him, all while a war was going on in New York City."

"But once you had my DNA," Hunter said, "why didn't you let me in on it then? I could have helped."

She laughed again. "Do you have any idea what your DNA looks like?" she replied. "All this jumping around that you do has altered it, to say the least. We talked about it, but in the end, we decided what we were doing was just too important to take the chance—and we knew you'd understand."

They were quiet for a while, just looking out on the ocean and feeling its cooling breeze. Hunter was trying to process it all.

"You've still got a tough job ahead of you," he finally said. "Finding Viktor's sub and stopping him? He could be anywhere. How are you going to do it?"

"By fighting fire with fire," she said, adding, "Let me show you."

They walked to the cliff and she asked him, "What do you see?"

"The ocean," he replied. "The cliff. The beach. The sand . . ."

"Look closer, at the bottom of the cliff," she said.

Hunter did as she requested. It took a while, but he eventually realized a lot of the shrubbery and beach flora was actually artificial and stuck into a huge net, at least as big as the one that covered the Pine Barrens base.

Underneath all that camo was a submarine. A very large, very powerful-looking one tied up in a deep trench next to the cliff.

"Jesus, is that a Trident sub?" Hunter gasped.

"The USS *Ohio*," she replied. "One of the first Tridents to go to sea, and also one of the first to be adapted for both an attack role and special ops."

Hunter just shook his head again. The engineering to dock the sub here and keep it hidden was enormous. "And let me guess, it now belongs to Fitz."

"He bought it because he knows it's probably the only way we can catch Viktor, sub versus sub," she replied. "But once we realized what you guys were doing in New York, he also knew we had to use it to help you out, but only from a distance."

"You mean the second battle cruiser?" he asked her. "And two of the destroyers? That was you?"

She nodded. "I was told the sub's crew—all Irish mercs by the way—had perfected their underwater attack skills by that time. They were out there watching for Viktor and following what you guys were doing as well. When you needed an assist, they're the ones who came through."

"And this ship the *Bruynyzi*? The one with all the firefighting equipment on board? How did you ever know that was something that would work so well into our plans? I mean of all the ships to hit . . ."

She smiled again. "Well, Fitz told me he can't take credit for that. Frankly, that was target practice after our sub crew spotted the original Russian fleet heading somewhere—and that somewhere turned out to be New York City, something that was confirmed by Fitz's Kremlin moles. As for hitting just the right ship? That was divine intervention. Or something."

Then she turned his attention to the southern end of the bluffs, the hayfield he used to work when they lived here.

"Once again, take a closer look," she said.

It took another few moments, but at last, Hunter realized he was looking at two helicopters parked under a hay-covered camo net. Again, more excellent camouflage.

One helicopter was the mammoth Mi-26 Russian Halo. The other was a CH-21 "Flying Banana" used by US troops early in the Vietnam War. This was the copter that had landed on top of Tower Two and spirited Dominique and the Magilla away.

"If you take an even closer look," she said. "You will see we have security in place around here as well."

Again Hunter squinted as he looked into the nearby woods and gradually saw there were at least a dozen armed men in green camouflage jungle uniforms watching over them from about a hundred feet away.

"They're all part of Fitz's new gang," she explained. "More Irish mercs. He got the old uniforms for a bargain—that's why everyone's dressed that way. The copter, too. So he has a little air force of his own, too."

"Figures Fitz would bring Vietnam unis back into style," Hunter said. "And save a buck doing it."

"Well, after buying an enormous Trident sub," Dominique said, "he had to be somewhat frugal."

Hunter looked around the property, realizing now that it was a very elaborately hidden military base.

"Well, I hope he's paying rent for all this," he said, only half kidding. At that moment, someone walked up behind them. It was Sergei Gagarin, the man with the eye patch.

"They're expecting the callback from Canada," he told Dominique, his accent now thoroughly Irish. "Mike needs you to be there."

Dominique walked over and hugged the man.

"Thanks, darling," she said. Gagarin kissed her cheek and then walked back up to the farmhouse.

Hunter was thrown for another loop, but only for a few seconds. There was something about the two of them standing together. They *both* looked regal. And they were obviously a couple. Did this mean he'd been right all along? He was in a different universe where he and Dominique were just . . . friends?

But she was shaking her head. She knew what he was thinking.

"No, Hawk, " she said. "I thought you were dead. Everyone did. Then I heard the rumors of the shuttle crashing out near Football City, and I began to wonder. But when I saw that little plane and the way it was flying, I was sure it was you. But I also knew what was at stake. And I knew I had to carry on with what I was doing. To tell you the truth, I just shut it all out and forced myself not to think about it until things were resolved."

She reached out and touched his face.

"It was ten long years," she said, her eyes welling up again. "And when Fitz brought Sergei in to help, well, we just clicked, and . . ."

She choked up for a moment and then said, "It's the same universe, Hawk. . . . It's just that people change. You certainly have. And so have I."

CHAPTER FIFTY-ONE

Otis Air Force Base, Cape Cod
May 24

THE FOUR SU-34 JLRs were lined up on the runway, engines turning furiously. Behind them, four more Su-34s—these were the buddy tankers. All the jet fighters were painted in naval gray and bearing American flag emblems on their sides and wings. Hunter was in the fourth Su-34 at the end of the first line.

The new American Naval Air Force had joined the plan to strike Viktor's secret shipyard—and the fact that the aerial portion of the mission would originate from Otis was drenched in irony. This was where Hunter and other American pilots had run ZAP—the Zone Air Patrol—soon after the Big War. In many ways, Otis was where it had all started. Hunter had a lot of history with this place. They all did.

The four fighters and their tankers were about to take off for one final training mission before the actual strike against the arctic shipyard was launched. Other elements of the newly combined air and sea assault were moving into place. Operation Skyfire was just seventy-two hours away.

Bull Dozer had been brought into the Fitz Group. At first, he'd been as incredulous as Hunter had been when he'd learned what Fitz's people had been doing in New York during the *Oku-*

patsi. But when he recalled Fitz's telling him earlier that he was on to something very hot, the pieces had fallen into place, and the old marine had become a quick convert. When he offered the Su-34s to be part of the strike package, Fitz quickly accepted.

Dozer had come up to Otis to help with the last-minute details of the mission. Fitz's people knew exactly where the secret shipyard was—the southern tip of the Novaya Zemlya archipelago in the Kara Sea, just off the coast of western Siberia—and the new expanded plan was simple. Hit the place with a massive air strike and then, with USS *Fitz* submerged nearby, sink anything that tried to escape. With the flight being four thousand miles one way, the mission would put the ultra-long range Su-34 JLR to the test. But that's exactly what the airplane had been built for.

Meanwhile, most of Fitz's intelligence operatives were undercover again, traveling to other locations around the world in hopes of determining Viktor's whereabouts in case they didn't catch him during the shipyard strike. Dominique was among those forward deployed.

Dozer appeared on the tarmac just as Hunter was doing his last preflight checks. He'd helped the Wingman strap in, handing him yet another borrowed crash helmet.

Cigar going as always, the marine told his friend, "I see they gave you the extra-large fuel tanks. I'm guessing they'll get you to Canada no problem once the training mission is over."

"I know what they're for, Bull," Hunter said, trying to ignore him.

Hunter had a classified radiophone number in his pocket, right next to Saul Wackerman's flag. He'd used it once, leaving a short message. But that's where it ended with him right now, he had more immediate things to think about. "Lots of stuff has changed in the past few weeks," Dozer went on. "Just look at yourself. In a new airplane. In a new American air force. These things usually come in threes, you know."

"I thought your lucky number was *five*?" Hunter joked.

Dozer laughed and patted him on the shoulder. "Touché, brother."

Then he was gone. Hunter punched his mission codes into the flight computer and then watched the control panel light up green. All the instrument translations had been done already, but he knew pretty much how everything worked anyway. It came naturally.

The special Su-34 JLR felt good underneath him. He fiercely disliked the Russians, but he loved this airplane. He'd been doing little else but flying it for the past few days. The Fitz Group was very excited to have him on board.

They started taxiing. JT in the lead, then Ben, Crunch, and himself. Their buddy tankers would take off right after them. Every plane in the training package had a two-man crew except for Hunter's. He just wanted to ride this one alone.

Besides, once it was over, his return destination would be different from theirs.

They got the final go-code for takeoff. Ironically, it came from Gagarin, who also passed on a coded message telling them Fitz's Boomer sub was closing in on the target and would be in position in less than forty-eight hours. So, a two-prong attack was assured.

Then Dominique's new gentleman friend wished them good luck and signed off. From that moment on, they were in radio silence.

Hunter took off in sequence and climbed to twenty-five thousand feet, where the entire package formed up. Then he turned with the others and headed due north.

It was a two-hour mission. They rehearsed both low- and high-altitude over-water strike approaches and then dropped practice bombs on an isolated island off the coast of uppermost northern Maine. Called Steels Harbor, it was almost an exact duplicate of the Novaya Zemlya archipelago in the Kara Sea.

The training mission was a success, with all of the practice ordnance hitting their targets. At that point, all the pilots agreed they were ready to do the real thing.

When it was time to head for home, though, all but Hunter turned south. Instead, he steered his plane northwest. He'd requested a twenty-four-hour leave, promising to be back at Otis in time for any last-minute preparations before they took off to attack the Siberian shipyard.

There was something else he had to do first.

As he flew over the coast and crossed the Canadian border, the events of the past few weeks ran through his mind. Trying to remember it all was like recalling an encyclopedia. Mudtown. The Pine Barrens. New York City. Nantucket. Yankee Stadium. Nauset Heights. Bombing the MMZ. The battle for Tower Two. . . .

But while he'd replayed all the strange things that had happened in just the past few weeks over and over, one stood out in his mind.

It was the night he'd crashed through the windows of the top floor of 30 Rock, retrieved the NKVD's master plans for Convoy 56, and found the blonde girl with the big smile. As he'd been flying around the seventy-story building, he'd felt his internal vibrations going off like never before.

But it had slowly dawned on him, and had later been confirmed, that these intense vibes hadn't been caused by Dominique. She hadn't even been in the building at the time. She'd already left aboard the helicopter he'd almost shot down.

And during some of his earlier flights, before he'd been spotted, she'd been at her room at the Ritz while he'd been feeling the feeling buzzing around the MMZ.

No, for the entire adventure, the cosmic, heart-pounding sensations—part of that instinct that never led him wrong—hadn't been caused by Dominique.

They'd been caused by that girl he'd rescued, the girl with the big smile and the big brown eyes.

The girl whose name he didn't even know.

It was dark by the time he spotted the enormous abandoned air base.

It was located south of the Canadian city of Sherbrook, not far from the Vermont border. It had been a secret joint US-Canadian facility, but had gone unused since the Big War. There wasn't even any electricity at the place anymore. But as he came within five miles of it, he realized electric lights would not be needed for what he was about to do.

The base featured an enormous five-mile long runway, and he could see it clearly now through his night-vision goggles because someone had lit both sides of it with hundreds, if not thousands, of candles.

He circled the base once and then came in for a bumpy but successful landing. Rolling the Su-34 all the way to the end of the runway, he shut down his engines and climbed out, shaking with anticipation. Waiting for him below, dressed in an old-fashioned US Army combat uniform, was the blonde girl with the enormous smile.

He didn't even have a chance to say a word to her. She ran to him and kissed him immediately.

There's that smooch again, he thought.

The kiss was followed by a deep, sensual hug and then another long kiss. Finally, he was able to croak, "You know, I don't even know your name."

"Well, you must have top-secret clearance by now," she replied, kidding him. "But I can only tell you once. It's Sara."

Then she handed him a box.

"I heard that you needed one of these," she said with a smile.

He opened it to find a new crash helmet inside. It looked like his old one, white with lightning bolts on either side, but its finish was almost translucent, and it was embedded with multicolored flecks that reflected the light from all the candles at every angle.

In a word, it was beautiful.

And so was she.

ABOUT THE AUTHOR

Mack Maloney is the author of numerous fiction series, including Wingman, Chopper Ops, Starhawk, and Pirate Hunters, as well as *UFOs in Wartime: What They Didn't Want You to Know*. A native Bostonian, Maloney received a bachelor of science degree in journalism at Suffolk University and a master of arts degree in film at Emerson College. He is the host of a national radio show, *Mack Maloney's Military X-Files*.

THE WINGMAN SERIES

FROM OPEN ROAD MEDIA

OPEN ROAD

INTEGRATED MEDIA

OPEN ROAD

INTEGRATED MEDIA

Find a full list of our authors and
titles at www.openroadmedia.com

FOLLOW US
@OpenRoadMedia

CPSIA information can be obtained
at www.ICGtesting.com
Printed in the USA
BVOW08s0753070417
480625BV00001B/1/P